By the same author from The Friday Project

# BRIAN ALDISS

# Comfort Zone

A novel of Present Day Discontents

The Friday Project
An imprint of HarperCollins*Publishers*
77–85 Fulham Palace Road
Hammersmith, London W6 8JB

www.harpercollins.co.uk

First published in Great Britain by The Friday Project in 2013

A catalogue record for this book
is available from the British Library

ISBN: 978-0-00-748248-1

Typeset in Minion by
Palimpsest Book Production Ltd, Falkirk, Stirlingshire

Printed and bound in Great Britain by
Clays Ltd, St Ives plc

All hands shall be feeble and all knees
shall be weak as water.
They shall also gird themselves with sackcloth,
and horror shall cover them;
and shame shall be on all faces,
and baldness upon all their heads.

– Ezekiel, vii

Phantom Intelligences open Thomas Hardy's drama *The Dynasts*. The Shade of the Earth interrogates the Spirit of the Years. This is their first exchange.

Shade of the Earth
  'What of the Immanent Will and Its designs?'

Spirit of the Years
  'It works unconsciously, as heretofore,
  Eternal artistries in Circumstance,
  Whose patterns, wrought by wrapt aesthetic rote,
  Seem in themselves Its single listless aim,
  And not their consequence.'

# 1

## *The Anchor*

A crouching figure was illuminated by the stub of a candle burning on a saucer. The figure was that of a full-skirted woman, kneeling before the candle on the floor of a little dark room in a hired house. Scalli – she now called herself Scalli, for none of the English for whom she worked could pronounce her real name – Scalli in her little dark room abased herself before the figure of her god. She addressed that imaginary figure, which she saw clearly, asking him to preserve her daughter, who was so far away. Her dog lay beside her in what it considered a reverential position: begging. Scalli also begged.

'Oh, mighty Baal,' Scalli said, 'I know I am nothing in your sight. I know I am mere filth on the ground over which you walk. Yet I beg you hear my despicable voice. I cry out to you for my daughter Skrita in Aleppo. In Aleppo she lies sick. As you rose again from the dead, so I beg you, raise up Skrita. I cannot be by my daughter's side. I beg you to be there in my stead and raise her back to health, oh mighty Baal!' She rose slowly from her crouching position and went to sit on the side of her unmade bed. There was nothing else she could do, trapped in this alien land of England.

At this hour of a summer evening, the road running through Old Headington was quiet. Two young people, both female, one black, one white, strolled along the pavement and turned down Logic Lane. Sorrow is a constant; fortunately, we take a while to learn that. Out of friendliness, Ken Milsome walked with Justin Haddock to the crossroads. They had been drinking tea with Ken's wife, Marie. It was no more than three hundred yards from this point to Justin's house. Justin's legs, a permanent trouble, were not troubling him too badly this evening. The two men stood together, watching the desultory traffic. Both morning and evening rush hour choked the road with cars driving to or from Oxford's ring road; but at this time of day the automobile might not have been invented. Justin was wearing a panama hat, to protect his head from the sun: that head from which a generous proportion of hair had retreated. On the corner, opposite where the men stood, was the Anchor, one of the two village pubs – this the bigger and sterner of the two. It had been bought by a married couple but had recently been put up for sale. Rumour had it that this couple, unlikely as it might seem to most of the villagers, had been born in the chilly reaches of Siberia.

'I was sympathetic at first,' said Ken.

'She's Russian, the wife,' said Justin.

'Latvian,' said Ken. 'They're both Latvian. She should have played to her strengths and served borscht and blinis or whatever Latvians eat. All she served was cod and parsley sauce.'

'With chips?'

'No doubt. She complained that she has no customers. "And I have so clean floor," she told Marie. But she wouldn't allow swearing in her pub, if you can believe it.'

'What? One goes to a pub in order to swear,' said Justin. 'Not just to drink. A sentence without a swear-word in it is a jigsaw with one piece missing . . . For some of us at least.'

'Some students from Ruskin College were in there, and one of them swore. This Latvian lass turned them all out.'

'Not exactly a gesture towards financial success . . . She should be running a church, not a pub.'

'She told Marie about it. Marie said she was crying, that all she could say was, "And I have so clean floor." Marie was sympathetic, being no enemy of clean floors herself, but in the end she got sick of it and told the woman straight that for anyone entering a pub, the cleanliness of the floor was hardly the thing uppermost on their minds. She told the woman to get her finger out.'

'I don't suppose that did much good.'

'It didn't. You know what Latvian fingers are like.'

Ken, an American, spent much of his time with the various computers in his study. He was a leading protagonist in WUFA, the World United Financial Association, as yet just a winged phantom designed to manage more equably the obscure workings of the World Bank. He had explained the workings of WUFA more than once to Justin, without great effect. Every so often, Ken disappeared to conferences in Stockholm, Orlando, or Istanbul. Justin, an older man, considered his days of wandering were done. The recession proved a godsend as an excuse. Justin lingered, hands in pockets, wondering about the present moment in English life. No one seemed to think it odd that the village had acquired its ration of Latvians, Muslims and Chinese. Yet it was hardly a rational process that brought them here. Some came by reason of wealth, some by reason of poverty. It was just – well, just Chance. Someone ought to do something about it.

The two friends lingered on the corner in silence,

contemplating the Latvian woman's sorrows. The sun was low, dusting the quiet street with nine-carat gold. The atmosphere was heavy and becoming thunderous, to celebrate the summer solstice. The Anchor was a large building, built of brick, tall and unwelcoming, whereas most of Old Headington was built from venerable stone; with their low roofs they showed no particular wish to dominate. This modesty included the Anchor's better situated rival, the White Hart, just down the road, opposite the church and almost as ancient as the church itself, both in its stonework and its aspirations. After a while, the friends parted by mutual consent. Ken turned back to rejoin his wife at home, a short way down Logic Lane. The crown of the great green oak growing in their garden could be glimpsed from the main road. Justin trudged slowly towards his house, careful of the uneven pavement. The birds sang under the street lamps. His way lay past the White Hart, across the road from the church whose origins dated from Saxon times. Justin was no great frequenter of the Hart. He had heard that the owners had engaged a new foreign waiter. He hoped that waiter might prove more effective than the foreigners who had closed the Anchor. At the church gate, the vicar, the Reverend Ted Hayse, was standing listening to an earnest young man, hanging on to his bike, as if in unconscious fear that the parson, forgetting his trade, might nick it. Gripping a handlebar, this youth was leaning towards Ted Hayse, and intensely pouring out his tale.

'Good evening,' said Justin as he passed the pair.

'Good evening, Justin,' said Ted in response.

'And even then, even then,' the young man was saying, emphatically, 'it was simply an accident—'

'Talking about Chance again,' said Justin to himself. 'But no good speaking of Chance to the Reverend Ted. He'd naturally ascribe whatever it was to the Will of God . . .' He shuffled onward, came to his gate and went into his little house. He hung his hat on a convenient peg. The house smelt comfortably of

4

burnt toast, coupled with the elusive fragrance of the clothes Justin had washed that morning, setting them to dry on various radiators.

'I'm home, Maude,' he called. 'Are you okay?' After a pause, reply came. 'Is Kate there? She could find it.'

'You know Kate's in Egypt.' He entered what had become known as Maude's room. Maude, his mother-in-law, was a small, stringy, bespectacled lady with a whiskery pale face and a hearing aid. She was surrounded by piles of books she had pulled off the bookshelves.

'What are you looking for, dear?' he asked.

She turned her dim gaze towards him, eyes grey and watery through her rectangular lenses, looking vexed. 'Dash it, I've forgotten. I know it was a book I wanted.'

He was used to Maude's fits of vagueness. 'I'm going to pour myself a glass of something. Would you like one?'

'Certainly not. I had one earlier when my friend from the pub popped in.'

'Oh, the Russian woman?'

'She's Latvian, so she says. They are selling up, you know. Such a pity.'

'I did know.'

'It was called *Best Behaviour in Baghdad*. Grey cloth, I think. About a conversion to Islam.'

'Not much good behaviour in Baghdad now.' He grinned at her and left her to it, amid the increasing piles of books.

In their shared kitchen, he found a bottle of Chardonnay standing open. It had lost its chill but he poured himself a glass, to retreat to his living room. A last beam of sun filtered into a corner behind the sofa. Here he kept his art books and a small hoard of DVDs. Justin, nursing the wine glass, sank into his favourite armchair. It was the armchair Janet, his late wife, had liked. After sipping the wine, he set his glass down on an occasional table and rested, closing his eyes. 'She have so clean floor,' he

5

murmured. Within a minute, he was asleep. He did not dream. These daytime sleeps, of increasing frequency he thought, more closely resembled unconsciousness. They were places, being empty, of some indefinable alarm. He heard Maude talking, or perhaps chanting, to herself. She had arrived to help look after her dying daughter and had stayed ever since. She was eighty-nine and, he considered, increasingly eccentric. He feared he must nurse her to the end, as he himself felt his faculties crumble. A genuine horror of human life gripped him.

He recalled that Gustave Flaubert, on whom he had once made a TV documentary, took a dislike to a female friend when it became evident that she put happiness above art. Perhaps Maude was sinking into a similar madness, putting religion above sanity. He stared down at his clasped hands; the freckles of old age were apparent. He was already in decay like an old tree, and had scarcely noticed the encroachment. He still relished life even if, like the Chardonnay, it had gone a trifle flat.

Maude and Justin supped together on pasta, followed by rice pudding with raspberry jam. Later, he tucked her into bed before returning downstairs and reading an old hardbound copy of Frankl's *Man's Search for Meaning*. Kate Standish, his lady friend, was away in Egypt, working on her good cause again. Justin was unhappy that Kate was away so frequently. He felt that the Aten Trust for poor Egyptian children was taking precedence over their love for each other. In the night, a short sharp thunderstorm broke out with a resounding crash. Maude cried out, but he did not go to her; he thought instead of his son Dave, who might have been frightened, with no one interested in comforting him. He found in the morning that his BT answerphone no longer worked. Fortunately, he also possessed a digital phone which was functioning. Kate had given it to him as a Christmas present. But it was a bugger about the answerphone. He would have to do something about it. Some time. Everything was an effort. Maude had found the book she wanted. He would be the one who would put the piles of books back on the shelves.

At twelve noon as usual, he boiled water in his kettle and made two cups of instant coffee. He called Scalli to join him. When he had first employed Scalli, he had tried to avoid the woman, and had left her to drink her coffee alone. But gradually he realized it might be pleasant to get to know her, particularly when he was missing Kate. They sat facing one another at the kitchen table as usual. He liked talking to Scalli. Although her main topic of conversation was her dog, on which she doted, she was an intelligent woman, and he imagined there was little intelligent conversation in her life.

'I read in *The Times* that Syria has held a general election. What do you think about that?' he asked her. Scalli said that one of her cousins had written from Damascus to say all was peaceful.

'He tells that they suffer many fears and shut up their shop with boards, but nobody did not riot. He has an Iraqi young man to work for him which came across the border in fear of the war which you wicked Britishers make. My daughter is sick in Aleppo – made worse by the election.'

'I'm sorry to hear it.' Her hair was pale and cut short. She wore a faded blue dress with a high neckline. Her chin receded while her nose compensated by being rather long. Her skin was slightly withered. For all that, Justin was pleased by her blue eyes and dark eyebrows, and a general alertness. She gave him a doleful smile, accompanied by an inclination of the head.

'To make the phone call to Syria, it's so much expense.'

Maude looked round the kitchen door. She was wearing her old brown hat. 'I'm just going out. I shall be back in time for lunch.'

Justin said with a touch of sarcasm, 'So, another lesson on being Islamic?'

'Whatever you may think, my decision is between me and my soul.' She nodded towards Scalli, as if for confirmation.

'Are you going to be a little Sunni or a little Shi'ite?' Justin asked. He was disturbed by his mother-in-law's espousal of Muslim faith, and occasionally – as now – his annoyance leaked out.

'Goodbye,' she said.

He was anxious. Excusing himself to Scalli, he hurried to one of the front windows, in time to see Maude closing the gate behind her. She set off down the street, moving slowly with the aid of a stick, and turned, as he had anticipated, left down Ivy Lane.

Maude walked at a steady falter, entering the drive of the Fitzgerald house. She waved to Deirdre Fitzgerald, who was gazing from an upper window. Deirdre returned the merest of nods.

'Grapefruit face!' said Maude to herself. The Fitzgerald home, named Righteous House, as wrought-iron lettering in the tall gate announced, had been built in 1919, in a style dating some two centuries earlier. It was faced with white marble; its windows with their pouting sills were shaded by blinds pulled half down, giving the façade a look of world-weariness, as Deirdre herself looked weary and as if designed some centuries earlier.

Maude proceeded to the rear of the house, crossing a lawn where no daisy had ever trod. The back of the big house was of brick; evidently the costly stone fronting the house served only as a mask. She came to a summerhouse, sheltered by two silver birch trees. This summerhouse, all of wood, had a small balcony at the front, facing south, towards Righteous House. Mounting the balcony, Maude tapped at the door.

A young woman opened immediately, welcomed Maude in, and then locked the door from the inside. She was of the lightest coffee colour, with beautiful deep-set dark eyes and a neat fleshy nose. Her intense long black hair was coiled over one shoulder, her head covered by a light shawl, the ends of which were tied beneath her chin. She clasped prayerful hands together. 'Salaam Aleikum.'

Maude had learnt to respond in kind. In the summerhouse was

the scent of sandalwood. A joss stick was burning. Om Haldar was the name of this young woman who, with grave courtesy, settled Maude in a cushioned wicker chair. She brought her visitor a plastic bottle of mineral water, which she opened for the old lady, pouring some of the water into a glass.

'Are you well, Om Haldar?' Maude asked. She could hardly bear to take her gaze from the girl, so graceful were Om Haldar's movements, and her every gesture, some of which rattled the bracelets on her arms.

'I am perfectly well, thanks to Allah.' With these words Om Haldar flashed a sad smile, showing even white teeth. She was also perfectly remote, despite her closeness. She gave a quick glance through the window to see that no one was approaching across the lawn.

'This morning, we will speak of the Hadith, the deeds and sayings of the prophet Muhammad. Are you prepared, please, Mrs Maude?'

'Yes, I brought my notebook.' She produced the notebook from a capacious side pocket and then looked up expectantly at her instructress. Om Haldar had never questioned Maude about the reason she was turning to Islam rather late in life. Maude's impulse was obscure even to herself. She knew only that she had been offended by her daughter Janet's funeral service, by the perfunctory way the parson had read the prayers and, in particular, the manner in which the coffin was almost dropped into its grave.

From that moment, inconsolable, she had sworn to have nothing more to do with the C of E. Yet, lonely woman that she was, she felt the need for a faith. And one day she had happened upon Om Haldar. She had never asked the young woman what she was doing, or why she was living in the Fitzgerald summerhouse. Although she was curious by nature, she liked the mystery; it reinforced the sense of adventure in turning to a new faith. To turn to this young woman was to turn to her faith. She thought – or liked to think – that behind the courtesy of this young woman lurked a terrible story. She revered, even loved, this strange girl with her isolating courtesy. Perhaps she could ask the withdrawn Deirdre Fitzgerald about it one day?

'Unfortunately, terrorists and obsolete traditions have given the name of violence to we Muslims,' the girl had said by way of introduction. 'Although I have my reasons to regret some of the laws of my country and my religion, I wish to stress to you, kind Mrs Maude, that for many centuries we have been peaceable. The West has in the past benefited from our learning. You may have heard of the Taliban, who banned women from education, but that was not the case everywhere.

'So now,' she said. And again there was this distance which Maude found intriguing. 'We speak of the Five Pillars. These are the basic religious duties, gladly entered upon. Firstly there is Shahada, where the formula we use is the declaration of faith expressed in the phrase, "There is no god but God."'

As she continued, Maude scribbled industriously in her note-book. There is no god but God. Yes, she thought, that must be true – but what did it mean? It meant nothing as yet, but first she had to believe and then meaning would dawn. That meaning could bring some happiness into the void.

When her session was over, Maude struggled to her feet, formally paid her teacher and said goodbye. She always wanted to kiss Om Haldar, but did not know if it would be acceptable. The session was closed, and Om Haldar turned her gentle back on her pupil. The way to the gate and the road wound close to the rear of Righteous House. As Maude was approaching the house she heard a shrill voice within calling to her maid: 'Vera, Vera, go and see who that is walking about my garden!' A minute later and a young woman whom Maude knew as Vera looked out of the back door.

'You all right, ma'am?'

Maude said gently, 'Please tell your missus it's Maude. I visit Om Haldar every day at this time – and with her permission.'

'Mrs Fitzgerald is a touch short-sighted.'

'Thank you, Vera. I'm sorry if you were upset.'

The maid grinned. 'I'm not upset. I'm used to it.'


Once she was alone again, Om Haldar's manner changed. She moved more briskly. She snatched a stout stick of a type known to the Irish as a shillelagh from its hiding place beneath a rug and laid it under the sofa on which she slept, so that she could more easily grab it if she was attacked.

A coloured curtain hung over the rear wall of the bungalow, concealing a wooden door. She checked that the bolt was secure. Going about these protective measures, Om Haldar sang to herself in a low voice.

> Grasses glitter with the dews of morning
> For the little birds to suck.
> Where I come from no birds or dews
> Came to greet the dusty pinks
> That herald one more starving dawning
> Where the wild dog comes and drinks –
> The Great alone feed, while for us to pluck
> No mangoes, schooling, justice, luck
>
> I drown in all my thoughts, my sorrows.
> How can my pa be so unkind
> Who once held me on his knee?
> How can I ever purge from mind
> The death, the dagger? I can see
> But pa is blind. From vengeance, death, I flee.
> My yesterdays and worse tomorrows
> Surely are not writ and signed?
>
> Here amid this land of strangers
> Much I see is clean and neat

Much I see is calm and sweet
And yet they have no god to praise
And those I know breed dangers, dangers.
Allah, let me see your face –
I must be ever on my ways
Or I will die for my disgrace –
My little fault, my love, my days –
To some other foreign place . . .

She took her duster to clean the windows and to watch, singing to herself, hoping Allah would understand her plight and be merciful.

Justin's house, Clemenceau, was solid. He had grown fond of it. Clemenceau aspired to none of the grandeur of Righteous House. It stood with its sturdy façade towards the street; it was the house in which Janet Haddock had died. It marked the end of the street, beyond Ivy Lane. The street was one-sided. On the other side of the road opposite Clemenceau was a wilderness of trees and bushes, behind which lurked a small special school. Sometimes, standing on his front doorstep, Justin could hear the cries and calls of a different species of being: schoolchildren. Since his wife's death, or – as he sometimes liked to describe it – the divorce, this old grey house of his had become the necessary shell of the crustacean within. Clemenceau was one of the old modest stone-built houses standing not exactly close, not exactly apart. It had originally consisted of two rooms at ground level and two upper rooms. Later, two more rooms, an upper and a lower, had been tacked on. Then a room serving now as a living room had been built to the rear. When Justin bought the house, he had greatly extended it, lengthening it with a generous hall and study, above which was a room Janet had liked to call her own, together with a spare bedroom and toilet en suite. This simulation of organic growth in the building presumably marked an increase in British fortunes across the years.

When he lay in bed of a night, he listened to the many noises the house made to itself, a succession of creaks, bumps and groans, as if the old place were talking to itself, muttering about its early past before central heating was invented. In the back garden, Justin had turned up the remains of a well, with an old mattress stuffed down it. Also, as he dug himself a vegetable bed, the yellowed bones of an aged dray horse had been uncovered. These were further indications of an earlier, less comfortable, age. Justin crept about his familiar rooms. A certain dread lurked that he might, through infirmity or impoverishment, have to forsake the house in exchange for a single room. He had a relationship with the house. Not quite a love affair, more a kinship: a place where he might cling to his humanity as long as possible. He had filled the place with etchings and paintings and some of his own abstract oils. The walls of several rooms were choked by books; books on or epistles by Byron or Mary Shelley and her group, histories of World War Two, catalogues of Kandinsky exhibitions, learned works on G.B. Tiepolo's etchings, biographies of John Osborne and the letters of Kingsley Amis, works on Sumatra and other countries, and of the solar system. It was not so much that he feared death: he hated to think of his library being broken up. That was the final dissolution of personality, of his personality and of Janet's. Sometimes he chose to forget Janet was dead and imagined her living in Carlisle. Surely she would return, wanting to see their son again?

He heard Maude enter the house, but did not go to greet her. She went quietly to her part of the ground floor they shared. He had recently redecorated the downstairs lavatory with a soothing green emulsion paint. A pretty green summer dress of Janet's hung on the back of the door. He had yet to make up his mind to part with it. Like the rest of the house, this lavatory was fairly shipshape. It was only the outside drains and gutters that still required the attention of the elusive builders.

He was comfortable enough in his house, even sharing it with Maude. No one had ever broken into it. Nevertheless he was uneasy, not understanding what trouble Maude seemed to be involved in. He had spoken to Guy Fitzgerald, with whom he was on fairly formal terms. Guy owned Righteous House; he was an anaesthetist at the JR, the local hospital, the John Radcliffe. He had shed no light on the matter of Maude's conversion, or of who was living in his summerhouse, beyond the fact that he thought their lodger held no immigration papers.

Justin's living room was unremarkable, somewhat dated. Janet had furnished it; he had never changed it, except to add a large TV screen to one corner. The windows looked out on the garden and his courtyard. Morning sun flooded into this room. The sun tried to tempt a big unkempt succulent standing on the window sill to flower. This tousled plant had not flowered for three years. He forgave it, liking its grand disorder. When and if it ever flowered again, it would give forth the most brilliant blossoms, opening mouths of unimaginable colour.

At the front of the house was a smaller and smarter room. He had taken some trouble with its furnishings. The basic colour was a sober deep blue, markedly enlivened by a large rug fashioned from many multi-coloured squares and rectangles of a durable wool. He had installed a small settee of a plump nature, on which he often sprawled to read the *TLS*. There had been a time when the afternoon sun had filtered into this room, making it glow with an amiable beauty. Over the years, trees such as leylandii and a magnificent horse chestnut had grown up on the perimeters of the school on the opposite side of the road, absorbing the sun's rays; so that only little trembling points of gold now broke through into this evening room. Justin's kitchen was old-fashioned, his pantry sparse. He rarely went into the dining room. Only when Kate came to spend the night with him did they have breakfast there. Eggs and bacon always featured on those happy occasions. In these various rooms he maintained himself and Maude. He had even learnt to tolerate the incantations Maude was learning from Om Haldar.

# 2

## A Note from the Summerhouse

Marie Milsome called on Justin, to see that he was not starving himself while Kate was away. 'How goes WUFA?' he asked.

'Don't ask,' Marie said. She brought him a package of home-made tongue sandwiches. Justin was immensely fond of Marie. He brewed some coffee and they went into the garden with it, to sit ensconced on wicker chairs under the sun umbrella. Marie was a handsome, well-set-up woman in her sixties. Her generous head of hair was dyed somewhere between ginger and gold; she flew once a month to her hairdresser in Paris to have her hair attended to. Not only was she adroit at swearing: the world, or many of its aspects, troubled her. There she and her husband were much in agreement. 'Was the world always in its present muddle or were we just too young to notice?'

'At least the world was not so over-populated,' Justin said.

'Shagging took one's mind off worse things,' she said with a smile. 'Probably better things too . . .'

'Such as?'

Justin had advertised for a gardener. A man called at the side door, dragging a dog with him. He announced himself as Hughes. Justin did not immediately take to the fellow, but he showed him into the courtyard, where Marie was sitting, in order that he might gain some idea of the garden. The new arrival was a big hollow-chested man in his fifties, wearing a mustard-coloured jacket at least two sizes too large for him: evidently bought from the Oxfam shop. His well-worn face might have come from the same source. The jacket stood away from him at the neck, hunching back at the shoulders, as if, of all the people who had worn the garment previously, this customer was its least favourite. Justin introduced himself and Marie and asked the man's name.

'Jack Hughes,' he said.

'Oh, how delightful,' said Marie, piping up. 'We are reading Zola's *J'accuse* in our French class. Was your mother reading *J'accuse* when she was pregnant?'

Hughes was completely baffled. In a short while he said he did not want the job and left, scowling and muttering to himself, dragging the dog after him.

'I could have killed you!' Justin exclaimed, and both he and Marie burst into laughter. Little did they anticipate the note, written in pencil, pushed through Justin's door, saying *You was rude. I did not have no mother, see.*

Marie left. Justin was alone again, thinking as he always thought, worrying about Maude. He could not understand how she had been moved to espouse a religion where women were so subject to male domination. In the house, a sickly smell assailed him. His cleaner, Scalli, had been over-liberal with the disinfectant again. He wandered about the house, feeling vaguely uncomfortable. In one of his rooms, facing south, stood a glass-fronted cabinet.

Although Justin was far from being a rich man, he had made a small collection of bodhisattvas, each about twelve inches high. He had four of them. These strikingly elaborate figures wore crowns and in general looked forbidding. Justin had no great interest in Tibetan Buddhism; he simply admired the alien nature of the figures. He had become so accustomed to them that he hardly glanced at them from one month to the next. But now he realized that one of the figures was missing. It was the bodhisattva which clutched a fish in its left hand. He began to look round the house to see if anything else was missing. That seemed not to be the case. He went to sleep in his armchair. He woke with the lost figure still in mind. He was philosophical. He had bought the bodhisattva fairly cheaply in Chengdu, China. He suspected that a Chinese merchant had stolen it from a Tibetan monastery. There was something like justice in the fact that it had now been stolen again – from him. He liked not thieves, but justice. If Maude had needed money to pay whoever she was paying for instruction into the Muslim faith, she would have asked him directly. He must tackle Scalli about it. 'Tackle tactfully,' he thought.

He was suffering from a headache, doing nothing. A woman called Hester phoned Justin. She said they had gone out together forty or more years ago. Did he remember? He pretended that he did. It was absurd of her to ask such a question. Hester? Hester who? She was having an exhibition of her abstract paintings at the Greystoke Gallery in Oxford. She hoped he would come along. 'Are you all right, Justin?' she asked. 'You sound a bit down.'

'I'm okay. Are you all right?' He had already forgotten what she had said her name was.

'I've been having a terrible time. I caught a bad dose of flu at the beginning of last year. Of course, I'm middle-aged now. Well, a bit more than that, really. I mean to say, my Maggie is coming up for thirty-one. It's sad to see your children grow old, and I know she doesn't get on too well with that daft husband of hers.

17

Anyhow, it took me ages to recover from the flu – and then I went blind in one eye.'

'That was bad luck, Hester.' Her name had come back to him. He thought he had better pronounce it before it was gone again.

'Well, for an artist, you know . . . I thought it was the flu but the doctor said it was the acrylics. I've just gone through the laser treatment and, thank God, my sight's restored.'

'Was it painful, the treatment?'

'So here we are, talking about our illnesses . . .'

'It's an occupational hazard when you are eighty.'

'Really! I'm only sixty-nine, you know. My friend Terry – I tell friends it's short for Terylene – she says the reason why no one likes old people is because all they can talk about is their illnesses.'

Justin chuckled. 'She could be right. Add a smell of wee . . .'

'I hope you will make it to the Greystoke Gallery. It would be nice to see you again. Or at least interesting. Oh, and I forgot to tell you, my father has died.'

Hester? He tried to conjure up a face. No luck.


Justin Haddock (or, as he prefers, Haydock) is eighty years old, and there are many faces he can no longer conjure up. For him, life is rich in small events, even phone calls. He values its every-dayness, knowing he will not live for ever. To survive for a goodly number of years is all very well, thinks Justin. The vital thing is to maintain something of a social life; it is there that enjoyment lives. This is not so easy when one's wife – as in Justin's case – has died. Or did Janet go to Carlisle? Surely Carlisle had just been a silly joke. It had become stuck in his throat like one of his warfarin pills. And again, he wondered about the world in which he lived: and about the lives of those about him. There might be someone hiding in his house of whom he was unaware. Supposing Maude unwittingly brought in a villain, a thief . . . He stood gazing out of the window. He was fine. Must not fall over . . . He seeks for an understanding of why we live our lives as we do – an ample enough theme for any novel. One thing in particular he likes about his mother-in-law Maude is her rejection of what he termed 'the Christian rigmarole' – the idea that bodies locked into a coffin would be resurrected and face judgement somewhere, perhaps in a celestial version of the Old Bailey. How could anyone believe that in the twenty-first century? Yet because of his religious upbringing, his rejection of the 'rigmarole' produced in him a certain feeling of unease: an unease justified by events, and by an alien religion.

A long while ago, back in the 1960s, Justin made a name for himself with a televised two-parter play entitled, *The Worm Forgives the Plough*. Justin wrote the screenplay from a book of that title, and took over as its producer at the last moment when the original producer fell ill. It was a lucky opportunity which lifted his career. *The Worm Forgives* was the story of a man who had served in World War Two and afterwards deliberately chooses the harsh life of a small farmer, to be close to the natural things he thinks most important. Carthorses and all that. And a beautiful woman who had been a Land Army Girl. This production marked the beginning of Justin's comparative fame. That fame is long behind him. Now he is adjusting to obscurity as well as decrepitude. Old Headington is a real place. It is a stony suburb of some antiquity within the embrace of the city of Oxford, where forgotten things belong. Most of the characters in this story are fictitious. They are not real. Nor am I Justin Haydock; but Justin's pains and uncertainties are real enough – all a part of experience. If you are fortunate enough to live that long. Only in your eighties do you realize how beautiful the world is. Or parts of it.

Justin was proceeding slowly along the Croft, an ancient walkway situated beside a high and venerable wall which runs from one side of Old Headington to the other. He encountered a thin man with a lined tanned face. It was Jack Hughes, unmistakable in that yellow jacket, the fellow who had applied for the job of gardener and then decided against it. He was leading his small black dog on a length of string. He put out an arm and stopped Justin. The sleeves of the jacket shot up almost to the elbow, revealing a tattooed arm and a red fist. He asked how old Justin was. Justin told him. 'Nice dog you have there.'

'You and that woman with you made fun of me,' Hughes said. 'Don't you have no sense of feeling?'

'I'm sorry, it was just a joke. We were not making fun of you.'

Hughes lowered his arm. 'Talkin' French at me . . .'

'Speaking a word or two of French is not in itself an indication of a lack of feeling.'

Hughes still looked threatening. Nor did the dog look particularly friendly. 'Yes, you was makin' fun. I don't like being made fun of. I would beat you up if you wasn't so old. You made fun of me just because I'm poor and down on me luck. I've had a rotten life. It's all I can do to keep myself together. I got no friends I can trust, apart from this here dog.'

In an attempt to mollify, Justin said, 'I like your dog.'

'It don't like you.'

'I'm sorry to hear that.'

Hughes shot Justin a glare of hatred, hunching up his shoulders to deliver the glare. 'I don't s'pose you are. Why should you be? My mother died the day I was born. Cold and waxen. Cold and waxen she was. I can never get it out of my mind. I go to church. I pray. But always there's that death of my ma in my mind. It was so unfair. An aunt looked after me. Kind enough, religious. It's like something lodged in my mind.'

Justin bit his bottom lip. 'Look, I'm sorry, Mr Hughes. Please accept my apologies if we offended you, but I must get on.'

'Do you read your Bible, may I enquire?'

'Of course not. I have no religion.'

'That's Oxford for yuh! You could learn som'ing. Take Ezekiel.' Hughes reined in his dog and struck a pose to declaim, '"Also out of the mist thereof came the likeness of four living creatures. And this was their appearance; they had the likeness of a man—"'

'Fine, thanks, great stuff, but I must be off. I have to go to the bank.'

Hughes seemed not to have heard. He continued his quotation, with gestures. '"And every one had four faces, and every one had four wings." It's going to be like that and I'll be glad of it!'

'It's nonsense, man. Ezekiel must have been raving mad, face up to the fact.'

Hughes stuck his face close to Justin's. The dog sniffed his trouser leg. 'I served my country. I was in the Falklands War. What does this rotten country care about me? It's like I got a plum stone stuck in the back of my throat.'

'Sorry, I must get on.' He saw to his relief that a man and a woman had entered the Croft and were approaching. He knew them.

'I'm uneducated.' Hughes was shouting now. 'I know that. Dirt poor. I can twig you despise me. P'raps you're right. But you can't help being what you are, can you, now?'

'Well, that's debatable.'

'How do you mean, debatable? I'm telling you—'

Maurice and his wife Judith were close now. 'You'll have to excuse me, Mr Hughes. I need to speak to—' Justin turned swiftly and, calling to Maurice, said, 'Oh, the very man, I need to have a word with you . . .' Thus he escaped from a fellow he was beginning to think was probably mad and dangerous. But Hughes still had something else he wanted to say. 'Oi, Reg!' he called. 'I hear as you wrote a book once.'

Justin looked back, exasperated. 'No, never, you are thinking of my friend, Tony Kenny. He has written many books.'

Hughes lapsed from an aggressive stance into something more abject. 'I thought about writing a book once. My life would make a good novel.'

'Come on,' said Maurice to Justin. He ventured to take Justin's arm. They hurried on.

'You look a bit shaken,' said Judith, 'I don't wonder. What a horrid man. How on earth did you get to know him?'

'I've just had to listen to a quotation from Ezekiel.'

'Yes, come and have a sit down, Justin. A cup of coffee,' said Maurice. 'Ezekiel is a real visionary, isn't he?'

Rowlandson, that was their name. Pillars of the church, he remembered. And, like Hughes, dotty about Ezekiel! He took a quick look back down the Croft before they turned the corner. Hughes was still standing there in his ill-fitting jacket, looking at the backs of Justin and his friends. One hand remained raised, as if he had forgotten it. The Rowlandsons lived nearby, in The Court, a grand house towards the end of the Croft. Justin was glad to sink on to their sofa. Maurice assumed his friend had been about to be attacked. Justin said that Hughes was unbalanced. But he had told Justin that he was too old to be hit, or words to that effect; Justin laughed as he admitted it, though indeed he did not find it particularly amusing. 'I can't help feeling sorry for the fellow. Well, not exactly sorry ... He said he was a regular churchgoer.'

Judith entered with a coffee tray in time to catch this last remark. 'You're not religious, are you, Justin? At least, we never see you in church.'

He said that as a boy he had prayed silently and constantly throughout the day. He then regarded himself as almost a saint, and certainly praying afforded some comfort. Only when he was older and looked back on an unhappy boyhood, did he see he had not been religious but neurotic. He smiled at Judith apologetically. 'Nowadays, I'm neither religious nor neurotic.'

'You would find a great deal of strength in Jesus,' said Maurice, kindly.

'He died for our sins, I understand,' said Justin. 'Rather presumptuous, I always thought.' Silence fell as they drank their coffee.

As Justin was leaving, Judith thrust a small book into his hand. 'It's the Book of Ezekiel, with charming pictures done by a Mr Heath Robertson. I think it may be a comfort for you, dear Mr Justin.'


One of Justin's lady friends, Mrs Wendy Townsend, drove him to the Manor Hospital for an appointment with his cardiologist. 'It's not so warm today, Justin, sweetie. You should have worn your scarf.' He had a feeling Wendy was slightly moving in on him since Kate was away so much.

'No, I'm fine, thanks.'

'And you are still taking your furosemide like a good boy?'

'Of course. I love it. And the other stuff Dr Reid put me on.'

'The spironolactone.'

'Yes. Exactly. Spironolactone. Pretty name, isn't it?' Professor Kenneth Fellows, the cardiologist, did not keep them waiting for long. He ushered them into his consulting room and made sure they were comfortable.

'You're looking better than when we last met, Mr Haydock. I want you to have an ultrasound scan, just so that we can check your kidneys. Nothing to worry about. We want to see that all's well below, and that the prostate is not too enlarged. Are you sleeping any better now?'

'Fine, thanks.'

'Good. And do I see you are losing a bit of weight?'

'I'm losing bodhisattvas.'

Wendy Townsend said, 'We have suppers with plenty of vegetables. No pork pies these days! We're doing very well. I tell Justin that he should be eating sensibly but he mustn't starve.'

'That's excellent. And asparagus is just coming in.'

'I love asparagus.' She told the consultant how she had been up early the previous Sunday and driven to Gray's Farm. She got there just after nine, when there were no more than five people picking the asparagus; but by the time she left before ten the field was crowded with people. So she invited Justin to supper, she said, and they enjoyed fresh asparagus served with a fried egg on top.

Justin liked it that way. When she was a little girl, the family had grown asparagus in their back garden. Her father had been a well-known accountant. Cocking her ear on one side, she enquired, 'Mr John Townsend? No? . . . Well, never mind.'

Justin knew Wendy was talking too much. Part of the moving-in-on-him business. He showed his embarrassment by staring fixedly at the floor, hands clasped. The professor nodded. 'Well, good to see you both, and keep taking the warfarin regularly, Mr Haydock. The secretary will give you a date for your next blood test.' He filled in the requisite form and handed it to Justin.

In the car on the way home, Justin said, 'I can't believe how much blood they have extracted from me over the last month.'

'They only take a tiny amount, love,' Wendy said, patting his knee. He reflected that his knee was among his most valuable possessions.

Wendy stopped the car by Justin's front door. He turned his face to hers and they kissed before he climbed out. He would have been embarrassed not to do so, knowing she expected it. Leaving and entering cars were major difficulties. He had little control over his legs, particularly with regard to lifting them. The birds sang under the street lamps. He found the front door unlocked. Either his mind must be going or Maude had returned. He was glad to be back in No. 29. The builders were not there. The house was quiet but oddly unwelcoming.

'Anyone there?' he asked. He thought there was someone in the front room. He went to look. No one was present, but he remained disturbed.

'You're there, are you?' came Maude's voice.

'Maude? Hello? Like a cup of tea or a coffee?' A prolonged silence. Then came her voice. 'Tea, please.'

In the kitchen, Justin brewed two cups of tea. The tea bag was one of Marks & Spencer's extra-strong teas. He carried the tea into the living room, placing his Carlisle mug on a mat before sitting down in his favourite armchair and calling Maude. But had someone just looked through the doorway and then swiftly withdrawn his head? He got up and went to look in the hall. No one was there. He could hear nothing. 'Old age,' he told himself. 'Going bloody daft.' He scanned the printout Professor Fellows had given him in the consulting room. His INR was 1.4. He was to take 3 mg of warfarin every evening at six. He immediately fell into sleep; it was indeed a steep fall. He became asleep without warning. When he roused, his tea was barely lukewarm. He had the impression that someone or something had been standing over him. He dismissed the idea. Justin sat where he was, leaning back, relishing his lethargy, missing Kate.

'You're awake at last!' He was startled. Maude was sitting by the door.

'How long was I asleep?' he asked.

'Justin, I must tell you something.' She spoke in a low grave voice. 'I resolved to tell no one, but someone ought to know, in case a crime has been committed.'

He stared at her. She was certainly pale and worried. When he asked her what the matter was, again she paused. 'Let me get you another cup of tea – that one's stone cold.'

'No thanks, Maude. What's up?'

Then she spoke. She had gone round to the summerhouse for her lesson in Muslim ethics as usual. She admitted for the first time that these sessions were held in the Fitzgeralds' summerhouse, where the Fitzgeralds had given shelter to a refugee. 'She was not there. Of course I was surprised. There was a note on her side table.' Maude fiddled in her jacket pocket, to produce a sheet of lined paper, possibly torn from a notebook. Without speaking, she handed it over to Justin. The note simply read:

*I must leave here. Thank you. Blessings.*

# 3

## Flying Iran Airways

Justin scowled at the message in puzzlement. 'She's gone? Left the village? Why so sudden? Is it a question of rent?'

Maude shook her head. 'Has she just run off? Or was she abducted and forced to write this note? The more I think about it, the more worried I become.'

The phone rang. Justin picked it up.

'Can I speak to Mr Haddock, please?'

'Justin Haydock speaking, but I'm not in a buying mood. What do you want?' He preferred the name Haydock, which was what he always used on his TV scripts. And not only there. Since his boyhood days, he had hated being called after a fish.

'So sorry, Mr Haydock. We are not trying to sell you anything.

We just happen to be in your area. We wondered if we could offer you a free modern-design kitchen. It comes—'

'Sorry, no, I do not want a free kitchen. Bugger off!' He put the phone down.

Maude looked enquiringly at him. 'Should we call the police?' she asked.

'It's probably perfectly innocent. Maybe she quarrelled with Deirdre Fitzgerald – she wouldn't be the first to do so. Should we go and see the Fitzgeralds? They must know something about this. The girl didn't even sign her name.'

'I still think we should phone the police. She was not the sort of girl simply to disappear.'

'You say that, but she has simply disappeared. Let's go and see the Fitzgeralds first, then if there's no joy we'll phone the police. If they haven't done so themselves.'

So they went together down Ivy Lane and used the formidable iron knocker on the front door of Righteous House. After a long pause, Guy Fitzgerald opened the door a little way. He nodded, with no change of facial expression. 'Might we come in and have a word with you, Guy?' said Justin.

'What about?'

'About the young woman who was staying in your summerhouse.'

'She's taken off – done a flit.' He had a wheeze in his throat.

'Precisely. That's what we need to talk about.'

Seemingly with reluctance, Guy opened the door wider, and with a gesture invited them in. He was wearing some kind of green knitted waistcoat under an old jacket with brass buttons. Maude and Justin came into a house of gloom, where heavily framed engravings hung on walls covered with a heavy green wallpaper selected for its funereal qualities. They followed Guy's bent back into a sitting room at the rear of the house, where most of the space was taken up by a table and a number of chairs upholstered with a material of a green similar both to the wallpaper and Guy's waistcoat.

28

In one of these chairs sat Deirdre, close to an empty fireplace. Deirdre Fitzgerald appeared to be dressed in a number of garments, among which a beige wool shawl predominated. There was also a harsh-looking skirt, possibly woven by a long-dead Fitzgerald, which hung down to meet Deirdre's button-up black shoes. They underwent the routines of greeting, at the end of which Deirdre said brightly, 'I expect you would like some sherry.' She had a small plump face with a sharp down-pointing nose which made her thin mouth almost invisible. Whereas her husband had clearly descended from a rather sturdy ape, Deirdre's ancestry appeared to be more on the flightless bird line.

'No, thanks,' said Justin. He never drank sherry.

'Yes, thank you,' said Maude. She sat down on the nearest chair to look about her, smiling vaguely, in the manner of one who enjoyed green. Neither of the Fitzgeralds made any move towards a distant sherry bottle, let alone considering uncorking it. Guy was leaning against the wall by the door, his arms folded, mainly staring at the floor.

'I see you have noticed the portrait of my mother,' said Deirdre, nodding and smiling towards the oil hanging prominently above the fireplace, as if the woman it depicted was still alive. 'You will notice she bears a strong resemblance to Lily Langtry, the Edwardian beauty. Everyone remarked on the resemblance. She went on a cruise to the Norwegian fjords once and was applauded all the way.'

'The Haddocks have come about Om What's-Her-Name, dear,' said Guy, prompting her.

'It's a shame they never met my mother,' said Deirdre, smiling forgivingly at Justin. 'At one time she was notorious for her affair with Solly Joel, the South African millionaire. He gave her an invaluable diamond which I could show you. We Hawkes were of aristocratic descent, a little haughty, I'll give you that, but fine people.' She repeated the phrase for reassurance. 'Fine people. Numbering among us an admiral and not a few poets. Colly

Cibber? You probably have never heard of him but he remains a famous name. I have to say that Guy's folk were of much humbler stock.'

'We won't go into that just now, dear, since it is not germane to the subject,' said Guy heavily, 'although my father's father was a friend of the architect who designed the *Titanic* and its sister ship. These good people have come to enquire about the black girl.'

'Well, she's gone and that's about it,' said Deirdre. 'I permitted her to stay in our summerhouse out of the charity of my heart, and she left without a word of thanks. She was probably an illegal immigrant. You know what these people are like.'

'I know what Om Haldar was like,' said Maude with spirit. 'She was like a well-bred young woman, sweet-natured and considerate.'

'But you cannot deny she has left without a word of gratitude,' said Deirdre.

'Yes, "done a runner", in fact,' said Guy, chuckling as he backed up his wife.

'I do wish you would not use these slang terms, dear,' said Deirdre. 'They don't suit you.'

'Might we look in your summerhouse?' Justin asked, turning to Guy. 'Just in case she has left a clue behind.'

'Er, I have had a look myself. Nothing. Nothing at all.'

Maude was already making for the door. 'Still, if we could just have a peep . . .'

'Of course. I'll come with you.' He slowly unfolded his arms, as if to demonstrate a lack of eagerness.

'I too have had a search,' said Deirdre, with some severity, twisting in her chair. 'I wanted to see if anything had been stolen. I remember my mother telling me that an aunt of hers, who lived in Cheyne Row, quite close to the Carlyles, had her house broken into and all her silver stolen.'

'You kept your silver in the summerhouse?' asked Justin,

deliberately misunderstanding her. They made their way across the immaculate lawn, Justin, Maude and Guy.

'She was rather a liar,' said Guy. 'Devious, you know.'

'That was not my impression. My impression was of a fine young character,' said Maude. 'Solitary, yes, and guarded. But there was a warmth about her somehow which I felt enhanced my life.'

Guy raised an eyebrow but gave no reply. Possibly the random enhancement of life was not his style. To Maude, the humble room seemed as it had always been when its gentle occupant was present. They looked about and found nothing. Everything was neat and clean. 'She must be in some sort of trouble,' said Maude, close to tears. 'We really should call the police.'

'I don't think Deirdre would like that,' said Guy. 'At all.'

'I'm sure she wouldn't,' said Justin.


They made their way slowly back up the hill towards home, passing the White Hart as they did so. A man on the other side of the street, walking on the cobbled stretch of pavement, was about to turn into the pub. He caught sight of Justin and Maude and made the drinking gesture of lifting his elbow with his hand near his mouth. 'Let's join George,' said Justin to Maude. 'I need a drink after all that.'

'I can't stand that man Guy. There's something wrong with him.'

'No, Guy's all right. He has a lot to put up with. That dreadful wife, for one item . . .'

'I am convinced they have separate bedrooms!' she replied distinctly. 'You go and have a drink, dear. I'm off. I need a rest.'

Justin followed George into the pub. George Ross was the local plumber. He also worked elsewhere, but the failures of ancient plumbing systems in Old Headington were sufficient to keep him in business for the rest of the century. He bought himself an Old Speckled Hen and Justin a glass of Australian Shiraz. They settled down comfortably behind one of the old wooden tables. The pub was almost empty. George had a round jovial face and a neat beard. Justin believed him to be amazingly clever, capable of thinking spacially in a way he could never manage himself. 'I saw you were coming out of Righteous House,' said George. 'You friends with them?'

'Far from it. George, you might know this. Do Guy and Deirdre sleep together? Maude would like to know.'

George grinned. 'Plumbers know everything. Separate rooms. Deirdre's room is thick with mementos of her family. At a guess it was last century when Guy last got his leg over.'

They started talking about women. While admitting how much they liked them and their company, complaint crept in like a hungry slug among lettuces. Justin complained about Kate's frequent visits to Egypt, while George complained about a divorce that he had not really wanted.

'I go into a house to fix their toilet. I see at once that the works are all this plastic stuff. It doesn't stand up to use. When I first went into the trade, it was all metal – copper mainly. Now this plastic stuff is perpetually having to be renewed. Marriage seems to have gone the same way!' They both chuckled at the analogy. Justin told George about the Iraqi girl who had suddenly disappeared.

'There must be a good reason for it,' said George. 'You don't suspect Guy of doing her in, do you? Don't go to the police, though, Justin, at least not yet. They're no good at these racial things. Ask someone who might know. There's a very nice Iraqi works here in the pub of an evening, calls himself Akhram. He worked with me for a spell. Akhram should know something about her. Maybe he met her. It wouldn't be surprising – this is supposed to be a village, isn't it?'

When it came to suppertime, Justin tried to assemble something edible to detain Maude, to whom he was determined to lecture. There was almost nothing worth eating in their pantry. He turned over a can of sardines, on the bottom of which was stamped the legend, *Best Before June 1999*. He replaced it on the shelf. A quiche with cheese and tomato needed only twenty minutes to warm up. The microwave had not been used since his wife died, as far as he knew. He popped the quiche into the gas oven at Mark 5. Two tomatoes looked edible. The last five inches of a cucumber had to be thrown into the swing bin. He spread two slices of a 'seeded batch' with a margarine named on the lid as Bertolli with the additional information that Bertolli was 'The New Name for Olivio, with pure Bertolli oil'. Accompanying it, he put a jar of Frank Cooper's Fine Cut Orange Marmalade on the table. He emptied the dusty contents of a sachet of Batchelors' Oxtail Soup into a mug, pouring over it boiled water from the electric kettle, adding a generous dash of the sherry he had recently claimed to hate. He switched off the television set, which sat on the top of the extinct microwave. A man and a woman were collecting items from a house to put into an auction sale. They hoped to raise nine hundred pounds, so that the couple could take their paralysed daughter to Disneyland in Paris. As Justin plunged them into darkness, they had just found a nineteenth-century horse whip in a back bedroom.

When Justin bought No. 29, Clemenceau, the house was in a poor way. He had had every inch of electric wiring and every inch of plumbing pulled out of the house and new wiring and new pipes installed. He had directed George Ross to run the water supply from the mains through a water meter, and was glad now that he had had the forethought to do so. Janet had not been feeling well even then. The bell on the timer pinged as Maude appeared. She had assumed a silken dressing-gown. Justin struggled to get up from his chair and went to collect the quiche from the oven. As he served Maude, Justin said, 'Now, dear mother-in-law, I fear I must put a case to you and ask you to be patient.'

'I'm always patient, dear son-in-law,' she replied, blinking at him, 'but let me just say that this tomato has passed its sell-by date.'

'Okay. That's not important.' He waved it away with a gesture. 'Maude, the world is in a terrible state. It always has been, but these days we are better informed of that state. Over-population and their – our – usages are causing a potentially calamitous global heating. However, I do see at least two hopeful elements at work. The European Union is one of them. For centuries, European nations soaked every kilometre of land with blood and corpses, for dynastic, territorial and particularly religious reasons. Now, instead, we settle arguments by sitting round a table and arguing. It is a magnificent social experiment. The second hopeful element I see is the way in which women, having won the right to vote and thus to be included in our political system, have to a great extent been able to make all kinds of remarkable contributions to our—'

Her eyes had lit upon the booklet Justin had just acquired. 'This looks interesting, Justin.'

'It contains paintings by Heath Robertson. Did you hear a word I said?'

'Oh, really, Justin, you would try the patience of a donkey. I know all this and on the whole I agree with what you say. Let's eat this quiche in peace. I'm still recovering from our visit to – what is it? – Righteous House . . .'

Admittedly, the quiche was not of the best. Or of the hottest.

'All right. To my main point. The progress I have mentioned applies to the West, not to the Middle East – or to much of the rest of the world, including Africa, but it is the Middle East I want to talk about. There, the religion prevailing is the Muslim religion. Do you doubt that? Do you doubt that women subjected to this religion suffer greatly?'

'I do think things are getting better there.'

Justin said, 'Let me tell you a personal tale. I was flying back from New York, where I'd been shooting some documentary

34

footage. Ayatollah Khomeini had just been installed in Iran. You remember they'd kicked out the pro-Western Shah? I flew back to Britain by Iran Airways, thinking I might find a subject on the flight, okay?'

Indulgently, she said, 'You've told me all this before.'

'I watched the passengers coming aboard. I was the only Westerner. The Iranian men all settled comfortably in the rear seats. Then there was a gap before the front seats, where all the women sat. There was no communication between the two groups. The kids were supposed to sit in the middle. Instead, they ran about in the aisle, shrieking. No one did a thing – no control.'

'Couldn't you have complained?' Maude asked.

'No. I was the one Englishman on board. Drink was forbidden. But it happened there was an English stewardess aboard, so there was a natural bond between us. She smuggled me a gin – a bottle which had somehow eluded capture when the rest of the booze was offloaded. This young woman was full of hatred and anger. Her Iranian husband had just divorced her. No apology. No explanation. He simply walked round her three times and that was it. Of course she was hurt and furious. She couldn't wait to get back to the UK, where she hoped never to see an Iranian again.'

Maude, looking down at her plate, sighed deeply. 'You condemn a whole nation on the strength of this one anecdote?'

'Maude, dear, perhaps you are getting old and losing your judgement, but scores – hundreds – of woman have now fled these male- and religion-dominated countries because of what they have suffered. Do some research, please. But forget this whole mad idea of becoming a Muslim.'

She dropped her fork and stood up, clutching the side of the table for stability. 'I have no plans to live in a Muslim country. I just admire their dignity, and I don't need your perpetual harrying me. You're as bad as the Muslim men you describe. I was benefiting from my relationship with that charming young Om Haldar, and I shall miss her.' She marched out of the room. He knew from

35

past experience that Maude would not speak to him for two days at least. Justin sighed and poured himself another cup of tea. He took a sip, replaced the cup in its saucer and was at once asleep.

He seemed to be halfway up a steep hill. A goat was following him. He knew the goat. He stopped. The goat stopped. It put its head to one side as if to enquire what was going to happen next. 'I am looking for a particular flower,' he said. The goat had a wise and doubtful look, as if it knew Justin was lying. 'It grows in Egypt,' he said. The goat shook its head. Not knowing what to say, Justin stood where he was. He woke. He had not had a proper sleep or a proper dream. It worried him. This could be how Alzheimer's began. He felt the cup. It was cold. He took the tea out to the kitchen and poured it down the sink. He poured himself a glass of wine instead.

On sudden inspiration, Justin dialled his builder's number. Only the answerphone responded. Justin cut it off and tried the builder's mobile. His call was not answered. He felt a sudden dread of being alone. If only Kate would come back, dear clear-sighted Kate. Fortunately, Ken rang. He and Marie were going over to Elden House to visit a remarkable elderly lady they thought Justin would like to meet. Would he care to come too? He recognized it was their way of looking after him while Kate was in Egypt. 'Ken, I'm worried about this young refugee girl. She's disappeared.'

'Yes, I heard she'd hopped it. Dodging the rent? . . . Did you hear that some yobs smashed most of the windows of the Anchor in the night? Anyhow, come on over and meet Lady Eleanor.'

Elden House stood at the end of St Andrews Court, a fine dull edifice which housed the elderly rich. Justin supposed he would have to enter there as a resident, if he could afford it, at some unspecified time in the future. Many of the occupants of Elden House rented one- or two-room flats. They could share a dining room. In effect, the institution was like a hotel for the over-nineties. Lady Eleanor Grimsdale was ninety-two. She sat in her room with a peignoir wrapped about her, reclining in an upholstered wicker chair. Her daughter, Enid, a mere seventy years old, was there, looking after her mother. Eleanor's withered facial skin was not disguised by powder or rouge. She used no lipstick to brighten her lips. She wore a wig of straight brown hair, with diamond earrings in the lobes of her ears. She was clad in a rich silk dressing-gown, which served her as a dress, thrown over the peignoir. It was difficult to know how to position oneself in the room, where comfort had taken second place to trophies of various kinds. One edged through the door past a bulky armoire. Small tables predominated, some with tops adorned with pietra dura. Sharp-edged birchwood dining chairs of a Chippendale-type constitution protruded; their primary function had been usurped by bric-a-brac, such as a canister containing a jigsaw puzzle of a Monet painting, a silver candlestick, a decorative china pomander, various baubles, including shepherdesses of Sèvres porcelain; while hanging from the backs of chairs were various kinds of necklace, silken scarves, and a chatelaine. Nothing of any great value or much interest. As a final deterrent to visitor comfort Regency furniture was aligned along one wall. The general effect was of an upper-middle-class shipwreck. Ken and Marie settled themselves on the edge of the bed, while Justin was given a kind of folding chair with arms. Daughter Enid served them all cups of coffee and a biscuit each from what appeared to be a cupboard. Eleanor kept a glass of gaseous mineral water by her side. She sipped from the glass occasionally.

'The vicar did his rounds this morning,' Eleanor said. She spoke slowly and clearly in a quiet, uninflected voice. 'While I do not dislike Ted Hayse, he does talk the most awful bilge. He attempted to console me with talk of the life to come. I really had to stop him. "Vicar," I said, "you are an intelligent man and I realize that religion is your trade or profession, but do you not understand that all you say is based on a false premise?"'

Marie laughed. 'How did he take it?'

'He is accustomed to this kind of talk in Elden House. We're all such intellectual snobs.' Eleanor sipped her glass of water. 'By false premise I meant the notion that one man dying on a cross could somehow absolve us all from sin, generations later, when new sins had come into fashion. Not to mention the notion of the – what? – yes, the Resurrection.' She gave a dry chuckle and drowned it in mineral water.

'So what do you figger happens after . . .' There Ken paused, although he knew Eleanor's opinion on the subject. His manner was almost deferential; perhaps, like Justin, he was awed by great age.

She turned her gaze upon him, cleared her throat in a surreptitious manner and said, 'You are from America, are you not?' Rather surprised, Ken admitted that that was so. 'You must find England terribly dull after the excitements of – where was it, now?'

He sighed. 'I was born in Utah, ma'am. Near a township a few miles west of Beaver. Not particularly exciting, I guess.'

The old lady appeared to be suppressing a smile. 'Beaver, eh? An odd name to bestow on a town . . .' Then, possibly to evade any elaboration from her visitor, she returned to the main drift of the conversation. 'Don't be afraid to say "death", dear boy. I'm looking forward to death in a way. I'm so bored. People bore me. Books bore me, these days.'

'This missing black girl is quite exciting,' said Marie. 'For a little place like Old Headington, I mean.'

'Oh, this girl from Afghanistan? How kind Deirdre Fitzgerald is . . . They come and they go, but England goes on for ever.' Dismissing the subject with a fragile wave of her hand, she returned to her previous line of discourse. 'The brain was never designed to work for so many years . . . I'm too fragile – well, too fragile to get up to anything. It's long ago that I fulfilled my biological function and reproduced my kind. Not that I can claim that was a great –' with a spiteful glance at Enid – 'success . . . There's something hideous about such industries as Elden, dedicated to protracting the lives of the useless, such as I.'

Enid butted in, saying, 'Domestic violence is the biggest single killer of women aged from nineteen to forty-four – precisely the most fertile years. After that, life becomes more peaceful. Old age is surely given to us as a time to find God.'

'I'm still waiting for God to find me, dear,' said Eleanor with a sob resembling mirth. 'I'm on his Gone Missing list, so it would seem . . . You see? With a daughter like Enid . . .'

Justin ventured to speak. 'So, Lady Eleanor, do you regard the sole purpose of life as to reproduce our kind?'

She gave him a severe look. 'So we once believed. So I once believed. Why should this whole notion of what one believes be so important to us?' She thought about it. 'I've long ago given up believing in anything.' They sat there waiting for Lady Eleanor to speak again. Marie fidgeted stealthily on her chair. 'Be that as it may, I now believe that we are – one must use the word programmed – programmed to protract, not ourselves, but our DNA.'

'I have heard you say that before,' Marie remarked. 'But it seems to me unlikely, if you don't mind my saying so.'

'I don't care what you say! Why should I?'

'Well, you make DNA sound like a kind of virus.'

'Perhaps it is a kind of virus, Marie. It seems to me it is a better – more functional – reason to continue to propagate than to have a God plotting our sins and circumstances. Speaking of sins, one of our youngest occupants here, an over-painted young hussy still in her sixties—'

'Oh, don't go into that, Mother!' Enid exclaimed. 'That's scandal. Tell Marie about the new story you are writing.'

Again the sob resembling mirth, again the glass lifted to the feature resembling lips. 'You are such a prude, Enid, dearest . . . But – as you wish. Anyhow, I am trying to write another story. Possibly in an attempt to justify my continued existence.' Eleanor had published a story for children long ago, when Enid was a child. 'All I have managed so far is the opening line. Er . . . Oh yes, it goes somewhat like this: "In the snowbound Far North on a throne of ice sat a great personage, King Chilianus . . ."'

After this meeting, Justin went round with Ken and Marie to Logic Lane for a drink. 'Old age in the Global Age,' said Ken, in admiration of Lady Eleanor. 'Can't beat it. Not by much . . .' Ken mixed the best gin-and-its in the world – or at least in Old Headington. They were all in a good mood, feeling they had done their bit for the day, although Marie often visited Eleanor.

'What did you think of her?' Marie asked Justin.

'Sensible of her to have rejected religion. I was sorry to hear she was bored. You might think her memories would entertain her.'

'Oh, she must have been over them dozens of times. She came from a wealthy family – Jewish. Did I tell you about her husbands? The first one was a manufacturer of Christmas cards and crackers, very prosperous – I forget his name. He was an atheist despite his trade. Somehow that marriage didn't work. She was caught in the wrong bed, and they were divorced. It was in all the papers.

'So then she married Ricky Grimsdale, whom we met once,' said Marie. 'He made a fortune from computers and a chain of retail shops selling everything electrical. Curry's bought him up. Seemed a really nice guy. He was an atheist too. Or an agnostic. And I think she was happier with him than with her other husbands. It turned out he was a philanderer, and when he tried to bring a mistress in, she moved out.'

'Who knows how many guys she had between times,' said Ken with relish. 'And she has had a whole clutch of offspring here or there, who have either been disowned or have disowned Eleanor. Only the brave if dull Enid has stayed with her till the end.'

Marie continued unabated. 'She then took a leap up the social scale and married Harry Stevens, the Earl of Pembroke. He was quite well known as a gifted amateur astronomer and scientist.'

'She seemed quite strong on science,' commented Justin.

'And against belief, although belief is very much a part of us.

40

Earl Harry also liked horse racing. Had a stable in Newmarket. Never won an important race.

'But she's still quite wealthy,' Marie added. 'And amusing in her way, don't you think? I mean, King Chilly Anus . . .'

Justin asked what happened to the Earl.

'Oh, he died ages ago. Had a stroke and fell over the side of their yacht. Bit of rotten luck, really.'

Ken noted with compassion the struggle Justin had to get out of a low chair. He had to swing his torso back and forth in the manner – as Justin himself said – of an ancestral ape, before achieving the momentum required to bring him to his feet. Ken said that he had received a furniture catalogue with his junk mail that morning. In it were offered some 'chair risers', as they were called. 'They might help a bit,' he suggested.

'How much do they cost?' asked Justin suspiciously.

'Oh, the usual thing. Buy four and get one free. Buy eight and save three pounds. Buy a dozen and they are delivered by a young female assistant of erotic propensity.'

'Mmm, sounds worth looking into.'

# 4

## Kate Standish Returns

A bright morning greets Justin as he lies in bed. He looks out on his garden and finds it brimming with blossom. The apple trees, plum trees, cherry trees, all blossoming. He is particularly fond of the cherry trees. He planted them as seeds and tended them, transplanting, then eventually planting out the saplings to form a short avenue. Something strikes him as odd about this spring and summer. Finally, while struggling to sit up, he realizes what it is: he has not heard a single cuckoo with its haunting call: once the very voice of early summer. He sits on the side of the bed, considering getting to his feet. He remembers that Eleanor yesterday had said something about Britain continuing. He could not remember what exactly she had said; indeed, he could scarcely remember yesterday. But after all, when you thought about it: To the East, President Putin turning Russia into a gangster state. To the West, at least thirty-two youngsters shot up on campus, victims of crazies and gun culture. Yes, with all its faults, there was much to be said for Britain. Then . . . that fatal madness of invading Iraq . . .

His thoughts drift as on a light breeze. Only rarely now does he conjure up the past. When his parents float into mental view, that view concentrates mainly on his plump little mother, with her good humour and generosity. Her kindness once had to centre on attempts to console Janet and him when their only child, David, was born with Down's syndrome. His mother had wept with them. They had looked after and loved David. He deflected his attention from Janet's illness and death as being still too painful. That deeper despair had lingered for years, remaining for ever as a quietly incurable regret. As counterpoint, his love for Kate Standish existed more as an atmosphere, an atmosphere embracing him, than as anything as individual as a thought. He gulped her love down without analysis. He thought of the pallor, the symmetry of her lovely buttocks. Dearest Kate Standish – the happiest chance ever to befall a man . . . Chance. The roll of the dice . . . His good fortune still enlivening him, he leans over and switches on the bedside radio.

Some mornings on, some mornings off, depending how he feels. This morning, the English cricket team is playing someone or other and losing – 'because of bad fielding', says the commentator. Putting on a pair of socks and a dressing-gown, Justin moves slowly downstairs to get himself a cup of tea. Legs are stiff. He goes down one step at a time. He tells himself he is not feeling lonely. He wonders what his old mother would say if she could see him, coping on his own. How long had she been dead now? He thinks again of Kate Standish, due to return from Egypt any day. He longs to see her again. Yet he is not desperate. They love – this is the miracle that continuously thrills him – they love each other so completely . . . but cannot verbalize it. He only knows that this love in old age is such a wondrous gift, beyond speech – yet he and Kate often talk about it, exclaiming how their lives have been changed, how each has changed the other's life for the better. Though they are not slaves to their delight, yet a sense of joy prevails. They greatly care for each other's looks, bodies, ways of speech . . . Their love, their particular love, makes them feel wonderful. They spend almost every day apart, alone. Both have work to do. Yet they meet together most evenings and sleep together most weekends. And he adores and admires his Kate Standish as much as he knows how – marvels, yet is certain – that she loves her Justin. Her early life had been one of difficulty. Kate had two brothers older than she was. A week before her third birthday, the three children and their mother had been turned out of their house. The father, Stan Standish, had sold the house over their heads in order to launch a hire-car business. They never saw him again, although Kate did think she glimpsed him once, helping an old woman out of the back of a cab. Kate's mother established them in one room in Stoke Newington. She went out to work, comforting herself with a bottle of beer every evening. Kate looked after her brothers. They were sad and self-pitying. Justin made Kate laugh by claiming that when young lovers first got together, the sweet nothings they whispered to each other were complaints about their parents. Even older lovers did it. No doubt it was Kate's hard-learned expertise with deprived children which had led her to set up the refuge in El Aiyat. Wonderful, wonderful Kate Standish! That this extraordinary woman should . . . Oh, every-thing . . . She had been rather formal, rather correct, rather spin-sterish, at first. And he had dared to grab her, to dance with her in her kitchen and sing to her – 'Oh, you beautiful doll, you great big beautiful doll . . .' And they had become delighted with each other – and consequently themselves – for all of three years now. And that delight grew. And she was coming home. The radio in the kitchen announces that some police officers needed to carry tasers. He is preoccupied with his thoughts of Kate, but the word

45

'taser' catches his attention. Or is it 'tazer'? You can't determine by just hearing it spoken. A rather nice word, though, as words go. Perhaps it is a corruption of 'blazer'. People don't wear blazers as they used to.

Moving at a snail's pace, commenting to himself, 'I'm moving at a sodding snail's pace,' Justin carries his mug of tea into the study. The mug says 'Carlisle' on it, printed in blue, above a picture of Carlisle Hall. It is his memento of that day, long past, when Janet and he had visited that northern city. He has owned it for many years and fears that, inevitably, he will break it one day. Shit happens. Today the venerable mug remains intact. He sits at the desk that catches the morning sun when there is sun, and switches on his iMac. With the tea, he washes down the two diuretic pills he has been clutching, the furosemide and the spironolactone, which latter is marketed under the patent name of Aldactone. It will be about an hour before their effects are felt. Few emails appear on the computer screen, most of them boring, either trying to sell Viagra or asking for money. The consolation is one from Eliza Blair. Eliza is no relation to the present Prime Minister Tony Blair. She is young, intelligent, beautiful, lively and a pupil at Swarthmore College in the USA. Justin met her on his travels. She has just had her first story published, and rejoices in the fact. Justin shares her rejoicing at a distance. He hopes her life will be a success.

He potters about, adjusting a few of the piles of paper in his study. He can hear Maude's radio upstairs. All today, but for Maude, he will be alone, as if on a desert island, unless the builders happen to turn up. This he does not greatly regret, because he will have time to prepare his lecture for the day after tomorrow, when he addresses a group of Christian ladies in a nearby church. He is not looking forward very much to this occasion. After he has showered and dressed, he walks round his garden. This always brings contentment, although Justin sees much that is neglected. He pulls up a strand of bindweed as he passes. A molehill has appeared on the upper lawn. The birds sing in the bushes. A pigeon cries monotonously 'Walpole stinks, Walpole stinks' – or so he imagines. But which Walpole is the bird criticizing? Horace Walpole, author of *The Castle of Otranto*, Robert Walpole, Prime Minister, or Hugh Walpole, author of *Jeremy at Crale*?

That sad creature, Hughes, had by chance directed him to the Book of Ezekiel. He rested on a bench in his courtyard and looked into the old Bible that had belonged to his mother. *I heard also the noise of the wings of the living creatures that touched one another, and the noise of the wheels over against them, and the noise of a great rushing. So the spirit lifted me up and took me away . . .* No doubt of it. Stark raving. But beautifully expressed. *The noise of the wings of the living creatures . . .* The living creatures. What if Om Haldar were no longer among the living . . . Not many weeks ago, Maude had suggested that the young woman should come and live with them in their house. She could have the spare room for her own and be more comfortable than in the Fitzgeralds' summerhouse. Justin rejected the idea indignantly, saying he refused to have his peace disturbed. His thought was that Kate would not like it, although he did not say so. Now a parallel case occurred to him. His aunt Phoebe, long dead, lived in a small house in St Clements. No garden. When World War Two broke out, there were many Jews trying to escape the cruelties of Nazi Germany. Two little sisters had been brought to Phoebe's door by a charity worker. Phoebe had taken them in. Phoebe had loved and cared for those troubled and displaced girls. In consequence, the girls had grown to make their way in the English world, successful, well regarded, one as a lawyer, the other as an academic historian. Justin clutched his cheeks. He felt the shame of it that he had turned Om Haldar away. She might well have proved a parallel case with the children from Czechoslovakia. 'Oh God, I am such a selfish bastard,' he reproached himself aloud – but quietly, in case the neighbours overheard.

He spent some while ripping ivy off a trellis before returning to his study. There, a woodlouse was crawling over the carpet. Justin liked woodlice and would never harm them, but he believed that each female woodlouse could lay a thousand eggs at a time. Since he could not tell the sex of this particular louse, he dropped it gently out of the window to the earth below, before settling down to compose his lecture. He banished the thought of Om Haldar from his mind.

Breakfast was a small bowl of one of the many kinds of Kellogg's cornflakes, with some canned raspberries added and milk poured on top. No cream nowadays. Kate had counselled against it to help control Justin's weight. He washed down his daily diuretic pills with a glass of Volvic water. He unlocked the side gate in case the builders arrived, and stood for a minute or two in the sun of the courtyard. The morning sun shone in the back of the house and the evening sun in the front. It circumnavigated No. 29 during the planet's daily duties. While he was standing there, Scalli arrived to do the cleaning and deal with his washing. They exchanged a few words. Justin apologized for taking the name of her god in vain. He felt too embarrassed to accuse her of the disappearance of the bodhisattva. It was a trivial matter compared with the disappearance of Om Haldar.

'How is your son David?' Scalli enquired. He said that Dave remained much as ever. Regarding her gravely, he enquired after Skrita.

'Oh, she is so bad. She needs her mother to be by her. She has messed her bed in the night and so they hate her. Were they never sick? That I ask myself, that they don't have pity?' She went more thoroughly into the events of the night, from which it could be inferred that her daughter had an anal fissure. Once in the safety of his study, Justin checked his emails. Again, not a word from his agent. Not a word from Kate. Going to the other desk, on which his older computer stood, he began to tap out a sentence or two for his talk to the Christian ladies on Thursday. This he had intended to do for weeks. He continually put it off. Procrastination was the very making of time. Today the task must be faced. One possible subject was the prevalence of chance in people's lives. It could be some kind of mischance which had overtaken Om Haldar. Her disappearance brought all that to mind again. He had used the theme of Chance in a TV documentary he once produced. But, according to his interpretation, chance ruled out religious belief. It was not the kind of theme to offer Christian ladies on a sunny afternoon. He decided instead to talk about ancient inventions which had reinforced civilized values – notably, the restaurant and the orchestra.

Justin recalled that Marie had once played violin in the Oxford Symphony Orchestra. He phoned her in order to check on a few details, and then they chatted for a while. Something Marie said reminded Justin that mention had been made of Ken's sister Catherine.

'Is Catherine married? Why doesn't she come and live in England, or have she and Ken quarrelled?'

There was a silence on the line, until Marie said, 'It wasn't quite like that, dear. Best to leave that subject behind a closed door, *comprendez*?' So Justin returned to his lecture notes.

Once he had decided upon a subject, the piece flowed easily. The doorbell rang. There stood his accountant, John Stephens. Justin had forgotten the appointment. He might once have been vexed by the interruption of his thought. But it was accountancy, in a way, which kept him afloat. He welcomed John in and got them both cups of coffee. Instant coffee. Douwe Egberts. 'I see the old Anchor has closed down,' John said. 'There's a For Sale board up.'

'It's not much of a loss. People living nearby were always complaining about the noise.'

John was a pleasant man. He wore a grey suit and tie, as became a respectable accountant, and made the collection of documents for VAT as painless as possible, despite Justin's awful muddle of papers on both his desks. John was also Justin's lady love's accountant. Justin's lady love – when not in Egypt administrating the Aten Trust in El Aiyat – lived nearby, in Scabbard Lane. Justin had lent Kate his Toyota while her car was being repaired; the Toyota was locked in her garage. He needed to take a suit to the cleaner and he wished to go into town to buy a particular book. When he asked John if he would mind giving him a lift, the accountant readily agreed. Justin suffered from getting into and out of cars, so John kindly carried his suit into the cleaner's for him. As they drove into Oxford, John talked of this and that; his character was on display. One focus for his interest was the sale of the site of the Anchor, currently awaiting demolition. He delivered Justin to the very door of Blackwell's bookshop. 'Tremendously good of you!' Justin exclaimed. He was amazed by John's kindness and the kindness of others.

The assistant in Blackwell's was agreeable. They did not stock the book Justin was after, but the assistant looked it up on the computer. '*The British Occupation of Indonesia, 1945–46*. By Richard Macmillan. Routledge/Curzon. Seventy-five pounds.'

'Heavens! Seventy-five pounds!' Justin exclaimed. 'I'm going to have to look at it in a library before I stump up seventy-five pounds for it. Keen though I am to read it.'

'It is a bit steep,' the assistant agreed. 'And no paperback available.'

But when the troops disembarked at Padang Docks, he said to himself, they had no idea that this was Indonesia. To them, it was just Bali. Sixty years ago, still vivid in mind . . . Bali! Had it been Bali and not Padang? He was unsure. And supposing Om Haldar had lost her memory and was wandering lost somewhere nearby? He ought to do something. Even though it was not exactly his business.

Making his way slowly to Queen Street, Justin stopped at the Gents in Market Street to relieve himself. In Queen Street, he went into Marks & Spencer to buy a packet of their Rich Tea Fingers. He invariably ate one Rich Tea Finger with his early morning mug of tea. He picked up one or two other things on the way. That was how stores made their profits – from human greed. He also bought a Lemon Loaf Cake. One of the things he disliked about capitalism was the way in which it encouraged greed. All commercial television was founded and funded on greed. With that profound thought, he crossed the road and climbed on a No. 8 bus for Headington. His left leg was painful today, both above and below the knee. It still hurt even when he was sitting down. He wondered how many other people on the bus were concealing aches and pains. Perhaps you keep quiet about it in the hope of arriving at an imagined Heaven after death, when aches and pains are swept away, along with the Oxford Bus Company and all.

When he entered his house, he found the phone was ringing. He rushed for it.

'Oh, you're there! Thank goodness! Justin, dear, I am back early and I've had a shock. Can you come round?'

'Kate! Are you okay, Kate?'

'Yes, yes, please come round.'

'I'm on my way.' As he dumped his plastic bag full of Marks & Sparks goodies, he caught sight, through the kitchen window, of Maude wandering about the lawn. Like a lost soul, he thought, with some distaste.

Kate's house was brick built, probably about 1875, in an imitation cottage style. It had a rustic porch, covered by honeysuckle, and a smart kitchen at the rear, recently added and installed by Kate. The house was approached by a shingled drive, fringed by pyrocantha and laurel. Before Justin had reached the door, Kate came out on the drive and flung her arms round him. She was a fair-haired woman in her early seventies, sturdily built, grey-eyed, her face showing a few wrinkles and browned by the Egyptian sun. She was wearing a light khaki suit, crumpled from her travels.

'I had a fright,' she said, when they had finished kissing. 'I'm really being silly about it.' She hugged him. 'Oh, good to see you again.'

'And you, darling. I have missed you so much.' As always there was an air about her as if something pleasant was about to happen, even as if there was something pleasant happening at that very moment. He marvelled at it; it was an air he never quite achieved. Kate explained that a taxi had brought her to her gate. As she was walking up the drive with her luggage, she saw a black dog lying sprawled by the porch. It wagged its tail in a lazy way. The shock came when she got up to the porch and found a man sitting on the bench there, in the shade. He gave every appearance of having settled in for good. 'He seemed apologetic, but did not move. He asked me if I wanted a gardener.'

'Oh! Don't tell me . . .' Justin enquired what the man looked like. Kate said he was nondescript, untidy and dirty, wearing a yellow jacket with torn jeans. Justin said his name was Hughes. He seemed to be a wanderer. A vagabond – and a nuisance.

'That would be he,' Kate said. 'He said he liked the look of my house, and had never had a house of his own. He said that hundreds of people were murdered for their houses every year. That did scare me, and the way he looked at me. I told him I needed to get indoors because I had an appointment with a police inspector. He did then get up and move out of the porch. As I was picking up my luggage, he said that his dog – who was tied on a length of rope – needed a drink of water. Could he bring it in?'

'I hope you didn't let him in!' said Justin.

'I certainly didn't!' Kate said she had bundled in with her luggage and hastily locked the door behind her. Hughes stared in the window. She got a cereal bowl, filled it with water for the dog, and offered it through the window. He took the bowl with one hand and tried to grab her wrist with the other. She remembered him saying, 'Let me in – I won't hurt you. I never hurt no one.' But she managed to bang his wrist against the edge of the window and then slam it shut.

'Very nasty for you, darling,' Justin commented. 'But he didn't threaten violence, did he? Did he clear off then?'

'He sort of hung about and then he disappeared.'

'Did you ring the police?'

'I rang you!'

They went inside. Kate sat on his knee and they kissed and cuddled each other.

'It's so good to have you back.'

'Oh, I missed you. But I was busy.' And so on.

'How's David?'

'As usual. It's time I went to see him again.'

'I've heard you say that before.'

He looked down at the ground. 'For once, things have been happening here,' he told her. 'A woman from Saudi or somewhere has disappeared. And they are beginning to demolish the Anchor.' He paused before saying with a laugh, 'And Ken and Marie took me to see a strange old lady in Elden House. It's been a full life, despite your absence.' He was determined not to tell her how much he missed her. That would seem wimpish.

'And how's Maude?'

'She's okay. Could become – well, Muslim.'

'Couldn't she go into Elden House?'

'Can't afford it.'

At length, Kate remarked that Justin was looking rather pale and unwell. He hated such observations coming from anyone, and in particular when the observations came from those on whom he depended; he needed them to see him looking as far as possible from either pale or unwell. 'A spot of eye trouble, that's all. In the hall, for instance. I thought I saw a headless being, confronting me in a rather headless way. It was just my raincoat hanging on a hook. Really ought to get to the optician. It's been three years since I last went . . . How's your hearing, by the way?'

\* \* \*

How curious life was, full of chances, coincidences, serendipity! The Fortuitous reigned. That evening the subject of Bali emerged again. No, not Bali. Sumatra. Of course, Sumatra. Kate had no sooner returned from El Aiyat than she was working again. She had much to say about the refuge she had founded, as she and Justin sat together on her blue sofa. The condition of some of the poor children they took in to the shelter was appalling. Many were orphans and needed a hug almost as much as they needed food. 'It breaks your heart,' she said. 'We need a million pounds to increase the work on hand.'

He could well believe it. He sorrowed for the poor. He sorrowed for Dave, his son – his son suffering from what he had been persuaded to call 'learning difficulties'. More like Learning Impossibilities, poor dear . . . He started to tell her about Dave, and his worries for the boy, but she cut him off. Although she admitted she was tired, Kate was now busy preparing supper for friends who were coming. 'So the Anchor's been sold off? Why's that?' she asked over her shoulder.

'It didn't pay. They sold it firstly to some Russians. It's being demolished.'

'It was a rowdy place. There's still the White Hart. Much nicer.' As they talked, he studied Kate's profile. To him, she was not old; her face bore the proud irreplaceable weather of experience. Seventy? It was nothing.

Friends were coming to dine, and of course Justin was invited. He regretted not being alone with her, but said nothing of that regret. The two guests who came to the meal were relations of Kate's ex-husband, Eve and Jannick. They were in Oxford to attend a wedding on the morrow. 'They're just flashing through,' said Kate. 'It will be lovely to see them again. I've known them for donkey's years.' Kate was well connected. She had known everyone for ages. Eve and Jannick were important members of Oxfam and had recently married. Jannick was Danish. He heard what she was saying. Both were people Justin respected, both had worked in some of the danger spots of the world. Both knew of and praised the refuge at El Aiyat. Eve had returned from Aceh a few weeks earlier. The news that Eve was to visit this secretive part of the world had stirred Justin. He had lent the young woman a book on the history of Java and Sumatra, which had included a chapter on Aceh. Of course it was Sumatra, not Bali. His mind was going. Now, almost a year later, here she was and returning his book! It smacked of the miraculous. No one else ever returned a borrowed book, particularly books that had been halfway round the world . . .

Aceh had always been reclusive and hostile territory. Situated in North Sumatra, Aceh had been opened up by the great tsunami which swept the lands bordering the Indian Ocean in the new year of 2005.

To Justin, Aceh was not history, more a kind of myth. He stared at the photographs on Eve's laptop, which she had brought with her, first at dark mountains fringing a new coastline, where a flooded road ran and not a single building was to be seen. Next he gazed upon a flattened, ruined land on which Oxfam personnel had built water tanks and green-painted toilets. An old man sat by the side of a track, holding his grizzled head in his hands. Here and there, tall palms, nature's flags, still waved in the ocean breeze. The grand mosque still survived. But mainly all was desolation. Eve had photographed some of the brave people she worked with. Many women appeared, smiling stoically for the camera, women who had lost children or husbands and all their possessions. Women who clutched small children to their breasts. Many were homeless and living in hastily erected 'barracks'. One woman was thanking Oxfam because they had given her new underclothes. All her old clothes had been lost to the great wave. Certainly reconstruction was in progress. But there was a difficulty. The Acehnese were Muslim and under strict Sharia law. One foreign aid worker, a French woman, had crossed a street from one Oxfam office to another without covering her head, and had been threatened with whipping by a local mullah. No ameliorating consideration that these Christians – or at least people from a nominally Christian country – had come freely to assist them through their catastrophe. Such was the kind of impediment which blocked their progress. 'The blind prejudice against the female', as Eve called it. Photographs of Nias were less depressing. High ground had formed a bastion for the mysterious island against the gigantic wave. Eve had found the people there gentler and more likeable than on the mainland. Justin gazed with reverence at these shots in particular. So unknown was Nias that he had once applied to work an Army wireless station – only to be turned down – there in that dot in the southern ocean, some fifty miles off the coast of Sumatra. Or was it Java? He was forgetting. Emotion – something grander than mere nostalgia – seized Justin at the sight of these photographs of distant lands, scarcely known in England.

'You should visit Nias before you are too old,' said Eve, on parting.

'I'm already too old,' he told himself. Perhaps he did not like Eve.

Wind was getting up as Justin made his way home. Maude was already in bed. As he went into his study to find a reference book, he saw, out of the corner of his eye, Janet running across the lawn. 'Janet!' he called, rushing to the back door, flinging it open, hurrying into the courtyard. 'Janet, darling!' Fitful gusts of wind played with his hair. No one was there, not Janet in her green summer dress. Only the wind blowing and a graceful syringa bending in the strengthening breeze. He stood there with arms spread, staring, tears in his eyes. Of course, she had left him. He was victim of an illusion. He returned to the study, to look out. To hope the illusion would return. Misery overtook him. Perhaps he had not made enough fuss of Kate. She seemed so preoccupied. He resolved that he would go and buy her a really nice chocolate cake the next day.

\* \* \*

No builders appeared the next day, a Wednesday. The business of getting up, showering and dressing, was always slow. Justin was looking forward to a visit from an old friend, Martin Sands, whom he had met in a television studio many years ago. Martin was coming down from London on the coach. The idea of the chocolate cake escaped Justin's mind. Martin had attended Justin's wife's funeral, some years previously. Martin arrived punctually at twelve thirty. The two men took coffee together in Justin's living room. Martin talked about the parlous state of publishing, and how the cult of 'celebs' and television told against regular authors, or even irregular ones such as he. 'Highly irregular,' he added. To cash in on TV and sport, publishers were now spending good money on flash-in-the-pan projects. 'Autobiographies of people who haven't been alive for ten minutes,' Martin said, laughingly. In a thoroughly good mood, they walked together up the road to Headington's finest feature, the Café Noir, where a table was booked in Justin's name.

Justin's legs were bad. He walked with the grand stick his friend David Wingrove had given him. 'I'm partly ashamed, partly proud, to be walking with a stick. At least I can drive off any sheep that get in my way.'

'They're an ever-present danger,' Martin agreed. The owner of the café and his wife were as always friendly and attentive. Both Martin and Justin chose the lamb dish, which they ate accompanied by a bottle of a good French Merlot. This was followed by crème brulée, after which they buttoned everything down with more wine. Justin paid the bill. The two men discussed many things, including past prime ministers. Both found a soft spot for Harold Wilson, who had withstood American pressure to send British troops to fight in Vietnam. If only, they said, Tony Blair had shown the same sagacity regarding Iraq. '"Iraq" will be the word on his tombstone,' said Martin. 'Preceded by the word "Bugger".'

The two men had to part at four o'clock, Martin heading for

the coach stop up the road, Justin hobbling home in the other direction, aided by his stick. His luck was in. He met no sheep on the way. It was then raining slightly. Birds sang under the street lamps. He had taken his furosemide tablets that morning, and the other diuretic, and had twice visited the toilet in the café. Now the urge, possibly prompted by the pain in his legs, came upon him again. He hobbled ever more slowly, whilst trying to get home as quickly as possible. When he reached the drive to the JR hospital, Invalid Walk, he had to give in to the demands of his bladder. Just inside the gateway was a short but steep slope on which chestnut trees grew. Beyond the trees, a little way off, stood offices in long huts. One had to gamble as to whether anyone would look out of a hut window, but Justin took refuge behind one of the stalwart chestnut trunks and there, to his great relief, let forth a stream of urine. He leant there for a moment, gasping. Turning, he started down the slope. Rain had made the grass slippery. He found himself rushing down the slope, out of control. He knew he would fall, crashing knees and possibly face against the inhospitable asphalt road surface. With quick thinking, he grasped an overhanging branch to stop his precipitate rush. It certainly saved him, but he swung round on the wet grass to find himself sitting, still clutching his stick in his right hand, on the edge of a muddy bank, close by the entrance to the side road. He was unable to get to his feet again, try as he might.

This inability to arise from a low sitting position was one Justin had found himself in before, though not in this outdoor situation with rain still falling. Ingenuity had previously seen him through. Sitting damp-bottomed, he summed up his prospects. Not more than a yard away from where he sat stood a large moss-covered stone. It might once have served as an old milestone. He shuffled towards it on his behind, hoping he might get enough leverage from the stone to raise himself to his feet. Shuffling quickly exhausted him. He was resting for a moment when a young man on a bike came from the direction of the hospital buildings. He stopped and got off his bike. 'You all right, mate?'

'I've just got a bit of a leg problem. I'm afraid I can't get up.'

'Let me give you a hand.' He did so, but the pain when the leg bent was too extreme. The left leg Justin decided was impossible. Luckily – just by chance – another cyclist entered from the direction of the road. He too stopped and dismounted.

'We can't leave you there, old chum.' Both men took his hands and pulled. Done quickly, with equal pressure on both legs, the pain being distributed was bearable, and Justin was vertical again. He poured out grateful thanks.

'No sweat, mate. We couldn't just leave you there, getting soaked to hell.'

'You could have done so very easily, so I'm profoundly grateful.'

'That's all right, mate. If you're okay, we'll crack on.' So then he hobbled home, heart full of gratitude for people's kindness. He felt proud of England, not for its economic success but for the way one stranger readily helped another. All the same, he had not helped Om Haldar.


Kate had pleaded she was so busy unpacking. He sat down. The house was silent; Maude had probably gone to see her friend two doors away. He glanced into the garden, hoping again to see Janet's ghost. Nothing was there. He rang the local Queen's Bakery, but they had sold out of chocolate cakes. They had some cheese-and-bacon puffs. He was asleep in his armchair when the vicar called. Ted Hayse's rubicund face looked smilingly at him. He said, 'Justin, my dear, I had to come and apologize for not greeting you properly the other day. I meant no offence.'

'And no offence was taken, Ted, thanks.'

'That young man was telling me all his troubles. Well, most of them, to be honest, and I could but listen. The young have much to bear.'

Justin nodded. 'Frankly, old age is to be preferred to adolescence, to my mind. Not that one has much choice between them.'

Ted looked contemplative, as if deciding what he might say. 'Yes, that young man . . . well, he has a bad father and much to struggle against. A great deal depends on one's father at a certain time in life. A good model is a great help. Our Heavenly Father of course is the best model of all.'

Justin agreed in part. 'My father was a brave man. He was awarded a DSO for his role in Bomb Disposal in World War One – the Great War. To me he was a hero, someone to look up to, but it always made me feel I was a coward.'

Ted said sympathetically that he was not a coward. A short laugh from Justin. 'I'm being brave about my age. Who was it said that old age is not for wimps? You know what Doris Lessing said about John Osborne?'

'No,' said the vicar, with vicarly honesty.

'She said he just wasn't very competent at life. I often feel like that too.'

'Jesus loves the incompetent, my dear Justin.'

'How about the incontinent?'

Ted managed to sigh and laugh at the same time. 'You know what He said in the Gospels? "The pee-ers are always with us".'

'What about those who aren't with us?' When he started talking about Om Haldar, the vicar chipped in, saying that of course she was not a Christian but nevertheless she was one of his parishioners for a while and he had visited her, taking some of his wife's buns with him.

'And did Mrs Fitzgerald mind?'

Ted Hayse looked searchingly at him. 'After all, Justin, Mrs Fitzgerald is a regular churchgoer. I cannot listen to any criticism of the lady. That would not be right.'

'Right!?' echoed Justin mockingly.

'That's what I said.'

Justin asked what they should do about the foreign girl. The vicar replied that he had phoned the Salvation Army. He told Justin that the Salvation Army was good at finding lost people and kinder than the police were when they found them.

# 5

## *The Antiquity of Restaurants*

On Thursday, Justin was due to see a doctor. Another doctor, the friendly Dr Reid. Justin woke early. His back hurt from the fall of the previous day. He rubbed some Deep Heat on his spine before going slowly downstairs, stair by stair. He took a bundle of dirty clothes with him and shoved them into the washing machine. Scalli would see to their drying and ironing, supposing she returned.

While the kettle boiled, he switched on the TV to BBC 1, curious to see what might be happening in the world, of which he was still trying to regard himself as one of its citizens, despite some evidence to the contrary. A news programme was talking about the A380, the gigantic aircraft now being assembled in Toulouse. Singapore Airlines had already ordered a number of A380s. Justin reckoned it would be worth flying in the plane, just out of curiosity. Maybe he could fly to Nias. And of course take a break in Singapore, where some of the most delectable food in the world was to be found. At one time he had worked on a documentary about the island and had been filled with admiration for the place, for its orderliness and its cuisine, as well as a sound judicial system. The weather was damp and thundery. The TV signal fluctuated. No doubt that would be eliminated when all television went digital in a year or two. He took his Carlisle mug of tea up to bed with him. According to the news, another mad suicide-bomber had been apprehended.

Dr Reid was prescribing warfarin as well as more diuretic pills. He asked, 'Do you want some anti-depressants?'

Justin was surprised. 'Why do you ask that?'

'Well, you are somewhat depressed, are you not?' 'Are you not?' – an interesting construction. He thought about it. 'Well, aren't you?' The doctor picked his right-hand nostril slightly as he rephrased his question.

'Whatever my problems, would an anti-depressant cure them?'

The doctor blinked at the silly question. 'They would cheer you up.'

'But there are genuine reasons to be depressed – I don't mean just my problems, but about the whole bloody world, the human race.'

The doctor tapped on his desk with the end of his pen. 'Very well. You prefer to remain depressed?'

'I prefer to remain as I am, thanks.' Then he found himself admitting – as if it were his fault – that one of his precious bodhisattvas had been stolen. The doctor asked what exactly a bodhisattva might be. 'Bodhisattvas are divine beings who could be in Nirvana but instead remain on Earth to help humanity to holiness.'

'I didn't know you were religious, Justin.'

64

'I'm not.'

'Maybe your missing bodhisattva got tired of your cabinet and escaped to Nirvana.'

Justin laughed. 'If only it were that easy . . .'

On his return home, he found a package on his doorstep. It contained four teak chair leg-risers. He was grateful and touched by this present from his friends in Logic Lane. There was no sign of a young female assistant with erotic propensities.

Kate Standish rang him. As ever, he was cheered to hear her voice. They would meet again at suppertime, when she would return his Toyota with many thanks. She was just off to work at the Aten Trust HQ – two rooms above a hairdresser's on the London Road in Headington. He was disappointed.

The hairdresser was called the Way Ahead.

He set the leg-risers aside and worked on polishing his talk to the Wives' Fellowship. He had decided that his topic should be on ancient inventions, some so ancient that inventions had become institutions. He would speak of orchestras and of writing, but more particularly of restaurants. After Justin had typed out a few sentences, he discovered he could not concentrate, and went out to his courtyard to admire the laburnum. The tree had grown to a considerable height and was now in full flower. He had grown it from a seed and twice transplanted it before moving it as a tender sapling to its present position by the wrought-iron garden gate. It was lovely to behold, light green leaf a perfect foil for the yellow-gold florets. 'My princess!' he addressed it, ironically adoring. Birds sang under the street lamps.

His mundane, humble, unique garden always calmed his spirit. He saw no need to invent God. Here was loveliness in growth, some trees and bushes planted by chance, by birds, by squirrels. Most things flourished here by chance. 'My secateurs are the guardian angels.' He persuaded himself to wander back to his desk. What he had written so far was,

In the years when the Han emperors ruled China, two centuries before the birth of Christ, the Chinese perfected the crossbow, with which to defeat the barbarians beyond their gates. The barbarians did not possess the skills necessary to cast the bronze locks which the crossbow required. And so, with the barbarians taken care of, an era of peace commenced within the newly united states of China.

It might have been like that. He could not be sure. His belief was fortified by his admiration for the Chinese people – despite their invasion of Tibet. They still quoted Confucius. Justin recalled an old school Confucius joke: 'Confucius he say panties not best thing on earth, but next to it.' He decided it was wiser not to quote that one to the ladies he was to address.

The West also was able to maintain its institutions. The Magna Carta of the thirteenth century still served as the basis of much law. NASA had sent off a probe to investigate Pluto. Not so countries of Africa and the Middle East, which had in the main still to advance to the water closet. Did they give a fig for Saturn or Pluto? They were not reliable, he thought. As Om Haldar had proved unreliable.

So he allowed his cogitations to wander.

Justin continued to tap sentences into his old computer, the Quadra – still working after fifteen years of constant use.

So from this Chinese crossbow developed one of the great culturing factors by which civilization itself is judged. I refer to the restaurant – and here admittedly I am guessing. But imagine the civility, the security, the confidence, the prevailing peace required for people firstly to come to a strange table – imagine a shady courtyard in Loyang – and to sit down with others whom they did not know, or perhaps only remotely knew, without fear of being attacked or stabbed to death.

Furthermore, an unknown chef then serves food which they eat without fear that it might be poisoned ... It's a revolution! One giant step forward au fond for mankind.

Nowadays we may eat at the Café Noir in Headington or the Quod in Oxford every evening, without a qualm. We take restaurants for granted. But that first one ... The restaurant opened a new phase in social discourse.

Furthermore, in restaurants one does more than eat. One converses. And from conversation, minds are changed and new ideas are born.

Justin was pleased with this. He was inclined to contrast restaurants favourably with churches and mosques. He went to sleep for half an hour in his armchair as a reward. He awoke as before, with an uneasy feeling that someone had been standing looking at him. Janet? Are you there, darling?

Later, he added to the list of ancient inventions the orchestra and writing itself. Of writing, he spoke of 'the long route from cuneiform to Jilly Cooper'. By lunchtime, he had produced a passable script. Since Kate still had his Toyota, the chair of the Wives' Fellowship came to drive him down to the church. She was a lady by the name of Christine Bower, very active and three years older than Justin. At the church, she left Justin and went about other duties. He was stranded alone in a large lecture hall. After a few uninteresting minutes, women began to flock in. All were delighted to see friends, and paid no attention to their guest speaker. Justin went to sit down and rest his leg. Then a woman came and talked to him out of courtesy. She remembered the time when Justin and Jan lived in Chalfont Road nearby; she proved an interesting person to talk to.

Eventually order was called. Justin was introduced. He launched into his talk, remembering the sound advice his friend Harry had given him long ago: 'Always start with a joke. Then they'll stay awake hoping you will tell another joke later.' Justin was cautious about that; after all, these ladies were or had been academics, or the wives of academics. They were accustomed to being talked at, with never a joke at all. All went well. Listening to talk of restaurants and their origins was not obnoxious to them. When Justin concluded, question time began. What most interested the assembled ladies was the question of how and where restaurants began and prospered. Justin defended his choice by saying that Chinese cuisine was generally considered the best in the world because the Chinese had had longer to practise. Furthermore, there had long been the puzzle of why, when the Chinese had begun so briskly in many arts (printing, landscape painting and pottery were named), they seemed at one point to have developed no further. That, Justin claimed, was because they were too busy sitting at, or serving at, table. He made this bit up on the spot and was proud of it. It seemed to prove his point.

All kinds of contradictions were offered up by his learned audience. The Arabs were noted for giving great feasts to visiting strangers. Queen Elizabeth I threw luxurious banquets. Hindus loved to bankrupt themselves on marriage feasts. And of course the French had been sound on restaurants for some centuries. Surely the ancient Egyptians had included grand banquets in their ceremonies. Such suggestions indicated how learned and well-travelled the Wives were. But one woman settled the question. She said that the prevailing characteristic of a restaurant was that you had to pay for your food; and unless the food was good, you would not return and so the chef would not prosper. At banquets you did not pay. Why had that point never occurred to Justin? Afterwards, all were friendly and came to have a personal word. Not only were the women nice to him, they brought him tea and biscuits and an envelope containing an unexpected cheque. They were friendly and equable – like an ideal family, Justin thought. And another lady drove him back to Old Headington and St Andrews Road. She was a local councillor, by name Annie Fanthorpe. She asked him what he was doing now he was retired.

'I'm working on a theory of Chance. On the whole, we don't think chance is a good thing.'

'The fortuitous . . .'

'No, that word has come to mean lucky, in a confusion with fortune. I don't use it. Its etymological meaning is "happening by chance". And what happens by chance is like breaking your leg – generally unpleasant.'

Annie Fanthorpe was a polite person; she did not tell Justin he was a pedant. 'On the whole, I must agree, chance is not pleasant. I suppose you have heard that the site of the old Anchor pub has been sold by chance to an international consortium.'

'I hadn't heard about the consortium, no.'

She cocked an eyebrow at him. 'But you live very near there. It's gone to the KIC.' He did not like to admit that he had not heard of the KIC, and they completed the drive in silence.

It happened that on the following morning, Ted Hayse came round collecting for Christian Aid. Justin told him about the talk, which Ted's wife had asked him to give in the first place. 'They were kind to you, were they?' said Rev. Ted. 'They have the reputation of being a pretty savage lot. They have eaten academics for breakfast and reduced strong soldierly types to tears . . .'

'Then I got off lightly. Maybe it was because I told them that the history of writing ran from cuneiform to Jilly Cooper.'

'That could very likely have saved your bacon,' said the vicar, gravely.

'Did you know that the Anchor site had been sold to a consortium?'

'It was in the local paper yesterday. You should read your local paper, my dear Justin! The Kuwaiti International Consortium.'

In Pen to Paper, Justin discovered a funny penguin postcard. A penguin was falling off a tall iceberg. Other penguins, watching from the top of the iceberg, were saying, *Monty was always one for fooling about.* Justin bought it. He knew his son Dave liked funny penguin cards. In no time, he posted this card to Eagles Rest, where Dave lived. He walked down Logic Lane to see Ken and Marie, where he found they had a visitor. They often had visitors; this was a particularly distinguished one – a cousin of Ken's, the Very Rev. Milton Milsome, just passing through Oxford on his way to the BBC in London, where he was to give the annual Emmanuel Graves-Janes Lecture. Milton Milsome was sitting in the shade in one corner of the garden, a large self-confident man in a panama hat, taking an occasional sip from a glass of Pinot Grigio which stood by his blazer-clad elbow. Ken and Marie were being attentive. Once Justin had been introduced, without much effect, he sat quietly to listen to the tail end of a lecture.

'Oh, *Religio Medici* still stands as a monument to whole-hearted faith,' said the grand visitor. 'Of course, Browne – Sir Thomas of that ilk – is an old duffer in many ways, but his prose style is exceptional. "Life is a pure flame, and we live by an invisible sun within us . . ." I couldn't have put it better myself.'

'Mmm, I must read *Religio Medici*,' said Ken, insincerely. 'Have you read it, Justin?'

Justin considered this was passing the buck. 'Religion is not my strong point – as you know, old bean.'

Milton Milsome's eyebrows rose to the occasion as he enquired, 'What is your strong point, may I ask – presuming you have one?'

'Oh, funny penguins, I'd say.' Turning to Ken he asked, 'Have you heard of the KIC?'

Turning his face away from his guest and, making a face which strove to imply that he hoped Justin would not be impolite to his pompous old fart of a religious relation, he said, 'Yes, why do you ask?'

'The KIC has bought the old Anchor site, so I'm told.'

Marie, handing round a plate of smoked salmon sandwiches, said, 'Well, that's good news, isn't it? They may put up something nice – a cinema, or a lido, or a hotel with a decent restaurant, or a Waitrose, let's say.'

Accepting one of the sandwiches, Milton Milsome said, 'There you are, you see, any form of indulgence. Never a thought of religion, of a new church.'

'We've just got a new Baptist church,' Marie retorted. 'It's Waitroses we're short of.'

'I suppose,' said the Very Reverend in a deep tone, 'it does not occur to you that the Kuwaitis are Muslim. I cannot but notice that folk like you are idlers. Here's a fine example of English self-indulgence which, by its laxity, lets in an alien creed.'

'But Kuwait is rather an okay place,' said Ken. 'International in outlook, prosperous, education free, women have considerable liberties not permitted in neighbouring states, although they don't as yet have the vote, and—'

'That may well be,' said the divine, interrupting, 'but they are still Muslims. No offence to Islam, but they should remain in their own hells they have created. Instead, they infiltrate our dear country and blow up buses. We need more religion, firmed belief. In Thomas Browne's day, religious institutions were adhered to, God was feared, and the Church universally respected. This is the subject on which I shall dilate this evening. More Christian religion required. A light to lighten our darkness.' He glared at them over his unbitten sandwich, as if he suspected they had suddenly turned into Druids. It was then, in the middle of this accidental encounter, that Justin realized, unbitten sandwich apart, that he had a destiny to fulfil.

'I don't wish to be impolite, sir,' he said, thus beginning with a little white lie. 'But to my mind we need less religion all round. Religion creates divisions, provokes antagonisms, schism, wars. Even more crucially, it forms a barrier against our acting rationally.'

A savage bite was taken from the sandwich. 'Who exactly is this atheist?' the Very Reverend asked through his mouthful.

'This is our friend Justin Haydock,' said Marie. 'And perhaps I can refill your glass, Milton?'

The denizens of Old Headington were dawdling towards a typical English summer, with sunny periods and showers alternating in a traditional way. Justin took an umbrella when he walked to the JR for a blood test. Unfortunately, he had not got a particular necessary pink form. They could have thrown him out, had not a kindly nurse written out a form for him. It was interesting in the little waiting room. By now, Justin was used to talking with old people in case he got to that stage himself. A couple of cheery women told him they had come in by bus from Woodstock.

'Men put up with old age better than us, don't you think?' one woman said.

'You mean we moan less and drink more?'

'I don't know about drink more,' said one of the two old girls, and they both shrieked with laughter.

'You don't seem to care so much what you look like.'

The needle did no serious hurt. He had resolved that it would not hurt, although the fold of his left elbow where the needle went in was looking rather bruised. Justin did a wee in a nearby toilet before leaving the hospital. He was thinking about *The British Occupation of Indonesia*, hoping he would not forget the title of the book. He remembered that in Medan, the capital city of Sumatra, the army had commandeered a local bakery and paid the native bakers to bake the troops' bread. The troops found the bread slightly crunchy. On close inspection, they saw that the loaves were peppered with tiny red weevils, baked in the dough. They complained, and the weevils were scoured from the bread ovens. The loaves then proved disappointingly tasteless, so the men had to request that the weevils were allowed back again. The things that they had put up with! For the first month in Medan they had been billeted in what until recently had been a brothel for Japanese troops. Scores were written up on the walls.

72

One day, the section's Dodge had drawn up by chance outside the house. The ground collapsed, the front of the buggy went down into a cesspit full of Japanese shit and French letters.

Justin slept the remainder of the afternoon following his encounter with Milton Milsome, and gardened slightly towards evening. Birds sang under the street lamps. A drystone wall at the bottom of his garden had collapsed. He met the genial Mrs Badger who lived on the other side of the wall and agreed they ought to do something about it, although neither of them really cared much. Justin said he would be happy to chip in with fifty per cent of the cost of repair. He liked to be obliging and wanted to oblige Mrs Badger, whom he wished he knew better. She had rather a sly look about her which amused him. He mentioned to her the fact that the old Anchor site had been bought by KIC. By the evening of the following day, the news had circulated all around the village.

Maude had returned from her art class and was resting with her feet up when the front doorbell rang. She went in her stockinged feet to open it. There stood the pale and waiflike figure of Polly Fitzgerald, the only daughter of the Fitzgeralds of Righteous House. Her hair, dyed blonde, hung down on either side of her face, framing it. A quiet and shy girl, currently working in the local Child Care offices while she thought about having a career. She had taken to looking in on Maude occasionally.

'Come in, dear. Would you like a coffee? The kettle has boiled.'

'No thanks, Mrs Winslowe. I just thought I'd drop in to see how you were. I'm sure you are still missing your daughter.' They sat in the living room, facing each other.

'Oh dear, I do miss the days when we enjoyed having a smoke. I always had a packet of Player's Navy Cut by me,' said Maude. 'It gave your hands something to do.'

Polly Fitzgerald nodded to a considerable extent. 'But ciggies were like bad for you. Same as drink. It's a bad habit.'

Maude sighed. She longed to put her feet back up on the sofa but considered it was bad form. 'They never did me any harm – or so I thought. Now that I am turning towards Islam, I see more clearly. For instance, I have learnt that the final suras of the Koran are good for various illnesses, which I consider includes smoking.'

Something in Polly's response indicated she had no idea what Maude was talking about. 'It's much the same as drink. It can become a bad habit.'

Maude was somewhat surprised to hear the girl repeating herself. 'I don't drink either. Perhaps an odd tipple with Justin some evenings.'

Polly exhibited signs of nervousness, rubbing the centre of her forehead with a hand in front of her face. 'My dad has taken to drinking himself out of his mind. It's bad for him – you know he works in the hospital? Of course –' she made an attempt to sound more adult – 'you know my parents don't get on particularly well together. It's got worse since Om Haldar left.'

This gave Maude a chance to talk about something that concerned her more closely than Polly's father's drink habits. 'People say such unkind things about the Muslims. Hand on heart, I can only say that Om Haldar was the sweetest, nicest young lady I've ever met. I really miss her.'

With a deep sigh, Polly said that she thought her father, Guy, had been in love with Om Haldar. He visited her so often in the summerhouse that her mother, Deirdre, got mad at him. 'Once he said to me, when he came home drunk, that Om had been mutilated. He wouldn't say any more. I took it to mean her – well, you know . . .' She hesitated before saying, 'You know, between her legs. It was about then that she vanished.'

Maude took a moment to wonder about this remark. She was thinking how much she enjoyed *Antiques Road Show* on BBC Sunday television. This consideration rather got in the way of current considerations. 'Polly, dear, are you trying to tell me that your father murdered Om Haldar?'

Polly threw up her hands in horror. 'Maude, are you going bonkers? Of course not. You really freak me out. I am just saying he drinks more heavily since she's done a bunk.'

The suggestion that she might be crackers greatly offended Maude. She said stiffly, 'We all miss that young lady. We don't however all get intoxicated as a result. It's disgusting. A real sign of our unhappy times.'

In her turn, Polly was annoyed. Her pale face coloured. 'Haven't you yet grasped the Eastern idea of honour killings? Om had to move on because she feared her family would kill her if they caught up with her.'

'Just because your parents don't get on so terribly well, you imagine Om Haldar's parents would do that to her? It's absurd!'

Polly stood up. In a monotone, she said, 'I have to go now, Mrs Winslowe. I am sorry you miss Om, as we all do. But you need to catch up with some of the facts which trouble us in this modern age.'

'I'll show you to the door.' Heaving herself up, Maude led the way on her stockinged feet. As she let Polly escape, she said, 'No one misses Om Haldar more than I do . . .'

'Goodbye, Mrs Winslowe. Thank you,' said Polly, with sufficient emphasis to ensure the words sounded false. She made her way reluctantly down Ivy Lane and back to Righteous House.

Maude stood at her open door. 'I'm getting to be a rude old bird. It's old age, that's what it is. "Between her legs", indeed . . . I so miss Janet. Janet had her faults but she was a good daughter, as daughters go nowadays. Still, I did hear that this flighty young Polly had had an abortion. Amy Holmes told me. Did she? Somehow, I can't think as clearly as I used to. It's since Janet died . . .'

Her daughter and Om Haldar became confused in Maude's mind. She closed the door and returned to her sofa. This is what it came to when you got old. You simply could not sort things out.

# 6

## Mrs Arrowsmith's Establishment

Justin was afraid of driving the car any great distance. It needed two buses, with a wait of twenty minutes between them, to get to Eagles Rest, where his son Dave was confined. Eagles Rest was in the quiet village of Compton Burnett. Kate sometimes came with him on these visits, but she was busy. On the trying journey, he found himself thinking of Milton Milsome calling him and the others 'idlers'. But he was not idle: he was beginning to think of a way of changing the world. If only he could change his poor son. If only Janet and he could have had just a normal little girl . . . Oh, Janet dear . . . The trouble with old age was that it left so much time for regret. It was a short walk from the village market square to the outskirts of Compton Burnett. Justin came to Eagles Rest, announced on a blue board amid the laurels of the narrow front garden: *EAGLES REST CARE HOME, Prop. Mrs Arrowsmith*. A narrow upright Edwardian house built of red brick, stiff, standing behind an array of spiked iron bars and a second board announcing *EVERY COMFORT, Prop., Mrs Pauline Arrowsmith*.

Justin rang the front doorbell and finally a woman of bustling corpulence opened up and showed him into the waiting room. She was Nurse Gillott. The waiting room seemed designed for sadness, with a great black yawn of an open fireplace dominating the place. A tall bush growing outside the window made the room dim. By the window sat an old shrunken lady in a wheelchair. Justin sat down near the door, away from the wheelchair, near a shelf of World Books featuring works by a man called Bryant. The shrunken lady stared fixedly at him for a while. Her face and her hair were of a similar dusty white. 'Do I know you?' she asked, hollow-voiced.

'I don't think so,' Justin replied, hoping he was correct.

'I do know you,' said the shrunken one, evidently with distaste. 'How've you been?'

'I've been nowhere.' Silence fell between them. A nurse looked round the door, whispered something and nodded her head backwards. Justin followed her along a brief corridor.

'Your son is not too well, I should warn you, Mr Haddock.' The smell of ancient carpets and fresh urine thickened. Dave Haydock was sunk in an armchair, wrapped in a towelling dressing-gown. He was wearing only one shoe; the other shoe had fallen off his right foot. He looked slightly fatter than Justin recalled. His eyes were closed in his heavy face and a purple bruise coloured his forehead. His mouth was open and he breathed laboriously. As usual, Justin felt a turbulent mixture of love, pity and disgust. Dave was confined to a small room. It contained two beds of an iron ex-army nature. One was Dave's bed; the other bed held a sleeping man in what looked like a grey shirt.

Justin hovered nervously over his son. Janet had been horrified to discover that her baby had Down's syndrome. On later diagnosis, it was found that Dave also suffered from congenital heart disease. His mother became depressed. She blamed herself. She blamed a hidden defect in her body. Did she drink too much? Did she smoke too much? Had she been on the wrong diet? Depression enfolded Janet like a cloak. An operation was performed to open up an artery from David's heart. It was not a great success. After that, David never fully recovered. Decline was hastened when, at the age of eight, he was hit by a cyclist pedalling madly along the pavement outside their house. David ran out of the gate – Justin had not been watching him for just a second – right into the bicycle. Dave's head hit the pavement. He was in a coma for two days. 'I can't cope any more,' Janet had said, amid weeping fits. Nor could Justin. He had been promoted to TV director/producer and could afford to put his son in care, despite the protests of Janet's mother, Maude. Dave was now fifty-one, still in care, still sitting out his patient days. Janet had once said to Justin, 'I wish I had never married you.' He had tried to comfort her, himself uncomforted.

Now Justin sat on a fold-up canvas-bottomed chair next to his son and gently took hold of his wrist. Without opening his eyes, Dave said in his slurred voice, 'Doctor, am I okay?'

'Hello, Dave, it's your dad here, come to see you.'

The eyes opened. 'The porridge they give you is nice.'

'What has happened to your forehead?'

'Something happened. I banged it.'

'Does it hurt?'

'Not really. Just my foot. It's too big. Where's Mum today?'

'She had to go to Carlisle, Dave. Let me put your shoe on, or your foot will get cold.'

Dave asked, 'Will Mum ever come back?'

'I'm afraid she's not on Earth any more.' Dave often asked where his mother was.

Resignedly, Dave said, 'She's being a long time away.'

'Yes, my dear boy, that's true. A long time.' Justin was feeling

Dave's pulse. It was steady but sluggish. He began to sing to his son. "'I'm leaning on a lamp post at the corner of the street, In case a certain little lady comes by . . .'"

Dave joined in. It was his favourite, his only, song. He sang in a clear, musical voice. They both used a George Formby accent. 'She wouldn't leave me flat, She's not a girl like that.' While they were singing, the manageress of the establishment looked round the door, smiled briefly, and withdrew her head.

After a desultory conversation, Justin said goodbye to his son and promised to come back in a month's time. 'Are you going to be all right, dear old boy?'

'The porridge is nice. I like the porridge. We eat breakfast . . .' He opened his eyes momentarily to smile at his father. His eyes were blue and clear. '. . . in the morning.'

Justin kissed the bruise on his son's forehead. Dave said, 'You won't forget to come back in a month, will you?'

Justin swallowed. 'Of course not, my dear old boy.'

Justin knocked on Mrs Arrowsmith's door, preparing to pay her bill.

'Enter,' Mrs Arrowsmith said sharply. Her room was small and curtained. A narrow window gave a view of some laurels. Beside the good lady herself, seated in her massive plastic chair, the room contained a side table, on top of which stood a laptop and a TV set; nearby was a large filing cabinet, and a shelf with some paperbacks standing aslant. Mrs Arrowsmith sat at a desk which held an answerphone, a pile of paper and a large tabby cat. Justin knew this cat was called Archimedes, without knowing why.

Archimedes looked at Justin with an unwinking gaze. It occurred to Justin there was something strange about the owner of Eagles Rest he had not observed previously. He had not noticed how protruding were Mrs Arrowsmith's eyes, how puffy her eyelids. Of course, she had never been a great beauty.

'Excuse me, Mrs Arrowsmith, but I was wondering why Dave had that large bruise on his forehead.'

Placing a plastic pen to one side of her mouth, she said, 'A perfectly fair question to ask, although the implications are that we – our little team – were culpable.' She removed the pen from her face and began to tap the edge of the desk with it. 'In fact, that is not the case. As you know, your son is – well, let's just say, to spare your feelings, a trifle troublesome. He tried to get out of his room during the rest hour. When Nurse Gillott went to intercept him, he turned suddenly and banged his head on the door.' Mrs Arrowsmith picked up a tissue lying on her desk and dabbed her eyes with it.

'I see.' Even as he spoke, he realized this woman would never tell him the truth. And in a defeated way he did not wish to know the truth. He remained standing. She did not invite him to sit down. 'So I'll just pay you—'

'Look here, Mr Haddock, I take good care of my cases.' She pointed an accusatory finger at him to reinforce her remarks. 'As you are aware, our local parson comes to see the patients every week – or most weeks. I worry about them, all of them. I've got so I can't sleep of a night, or relax, thinking about them.'

'I'm sorry to hear it, Mrs Arrowsmith. We all have our responsibilities, so I'll just settle up with you—'

Mrs Arrowsmith interrupted him. 'I think I should tell you, Mr Haddock, that you over-excite your son by making him sing that vulgar song. It is not really appropriate to the tone of Eagles Rest, now, is it?'

Annoyance stirred in him. 'And what sort of song would you think was appropriate to Eagles Rest, Mrs Arrowsmith?'

She seemed to fluff herself up, an old chicken before an adolescent fox. 'That is entirely for you to say, Mr Haddock, but I would suggest that "Jerusalem" would be far more appropriate.'

He clasped the back of his chair in case his anger should cause him to fall over or jump on her. 'And what do you imagine my

David has ever seen of England's green and pleasant land, Mrs Arrowsmith?'

Mrs Arrowsmith pursed her dry lips. 'Perhaps you would be good enough to send me your payment through the Royal Mail in future, Mr Haddock. Your visits only tend to upset your son. They have a subversive tendency which disturbs the tranquillity of Eagles Rest, of which we are justifiably proud.' Archimedes fixed Justin with an enigmatic look, awaiting his response.

'You cannot say that, Mrs Arrowsmith.'

She raised her chin and appeared to survey the ceiling. 'Do you wonder I'm getting palpitations? I am within my Human Rights to say what I please in my own establishment, thank you all the same.'

Justin tried to quell his anger. 'Please do not think of trying to stop me seeing my son. Dave would imagine I had abandoned him. I must have access to the dear chap. I come here infrequently enough as it is . . .'

'I will consider the matter. Now if you will excuse me . . .'

He travelled back on the buses, in part recalling how Janet had found Eagles Rest and placed Dave there. Janet had got on well with Mrs Arrowsmith, describing her as 'God-fearing' and 'self-denying'. Maude would never go near the place. He also reflected on Mrs Arrowsmith's threat to cancel their arrangement if he dared return to her establishment, and in predominant part reflecting on what a poor parent he had been. Sorrow for his son and guilt for his feeble ability as a father – for who else had let the boy run out from the open gate on to the pavement and under the bike, if not he? All of this, as the bus rumbled onwards, caused him quietly to shed a few tears into his cupped hands.

'Are you all right, dear?' asked the woman sitting next to him, a thin woman in jeans with a low-cut blouse, showing withered cleavage.

'I'm fine. Been to see my son . . .'

For some reason the answer seemed to annoy the woman. 'And how was your son? Cause for grief, is he? Ungrateful for everything, is he? Married, is he? They're all the bloody same.'

He hid his face in his hands, saying, with muffled effect, 'Oh, fuck off, dear, will you?'

# 7

## *Types of Rudeness*

A twenty-minute walk along hard paved streets took Justin from the bus stop to his home in St Andrews Road. Along the way, he passed Captain Derek Dalsher. The two men nodded a curt acknowledgement to each other, but did not speak. Justin at least was conscious of being very English about it. Back in the safety of No. 29, Justin sank with relief into his armchair. He had been away for over four hours. He felt exhausted. 'Idle,' he told himself. Visiting Dave was always a sad occasion. He switched on the TV to cheer himself up. A man was reading out the weather forecast. Justin was immediately unconscious. As always, the picture in his mind was as clear as a page of print. He was looking at a crane, its arm looming over a house.

Muzzily awakening, he recalled the moment when Dave had

opened his eyes. Just for a second or two, Dave was looking at him before the heavy lids fell once more. They were clear grey-blue eyes. They stared beyond his father at something unknown. Again Justin found himself close to tears. Such purity! Levering himself upright, he went and rinsed his face under the cold tap. That pure glance was of a man who had never encountered the adult world. 'What a misery life is! And the mental wear and tear of it,' he said to himself. His face was buried in the towel when Maude looked in and asked him if he was all right. 'I don't know. I know I feel bloody miserable.'

'Hear hear, my dear. So do I. Everyone going about their everyday lives as if nothing had happened.' She put her arms round him. 'No one giving a jot about poor Om Haldar . . .'

He stared helplessly at her. 'Face it, Maude, dear, that poor creature is probably dead by now!'

Her answer came swiftly. 'And you think Janet is in Carlisle and not dead? What's the matter with you, Justin?'

'I'm talking about Dave. What does he think about or imagine, every day? Not just all the physical effort required to get to him . . . I wonder how long I can go on seeing him.'

'You've done the best you can for the poor lad.' She was tired of his complaints on that subject.

Burying his face in the towel again, he said indistinctly, 'Mrs Arrowsmith is not a very pleasant woman. You can't help wondering if Mr Arrowsmith, whoever he was, ever enjoyed sex with her. Perhaps she was never married. The inmates of Eagles Rest are her substitute children . . .'

'I never liked the woman,' Maude agreed. 'Try not to worry. Come and take your pills.'

'I've taken my pills. You saw me.' So suppose I do what the Arrowsmith says, he thought. Send her a monthly cheque and don't go there ever again. It's not such a bad idea. Dave's all right, or as right as he can be. Does he even recognize me as his dad? Would he miss me if I didn't see him any more? I doubt it. As for that daft 'Leaning on a Lamp Post', he can always sing it to himself if he wants. I'd save money on the bus rides too . . .

He felt extremely uneasy. He made Maude and himself a cup of Marks & Sparks' tea. Why had he been thinking like that? He could not possibly dream of abandoning his poor son. No, no, he had thought of it. He could possibly . . . But he had really been thinking only of himself. His old vein of selfishness was still running strong. An immense surge of love for his son overwhelmed him. Oh, Janet, he's your son as well as mine . . . As he leaned against the oven, he said, close to tears, 'How patient Dave is! No one knows what he inwardly endures. Could he be secretly happy, communing with – well, not with God, but with a deep secret self, a pure inward light of which Ken's pompous old uncle Milton spoke?'

'Don't worry, dear,' said Maude. 'I'm sure he's happy in his way. When you think about it, he doesn't have to make any decisions like the rest of us. P'raps he'll get married one day. So cheer up!'

It was that pure inward light of which Justin stood in need. After the misery of Janet's death, of her dying, he had undergone – he felt – he knew – a spiritual revelation. It had inspired him, so that he was sure he had become a better man. Now perhaps the effect was wearing off. He must work on his theory of malign chance and not be idle . . . Maude sighed deeply. 'What a life! When I think of my life – I've never seen anything like it before.'

Kate appeared in the Toyota, which she parked in Justin's drive. While apologizing for being so busy, she said she had to be away again that evening. Barton needed her.

'You're so elusive, darling! Just when I need a bit of comforting, too.'

Kate held his hand across the table, smiling tenderly at him. 'You are a one for picking on yourself. What exactly are you worrying about now?' She wore a garment of beige and brown with a wide unlikely collar of red, which he admired.

'For instance, I take buses to Eagles Rest. I can't really afford to run the car any longer. Besides, I have lost my confidence for driving. And – well, I've rather quarrelled with the old hag who runs Eagles Rest.'

'That's rubbish, my love! You just don't like driving any more. You don't go anywhere, except to see David once a month.'

'But not going anywhere, isn't that itself rather an indication of encroaching feebleness?' He clicked his fingers. 'Blow! And I forgot to buy you a chocolate cake.'

She ignored this remark. 'We went to Sicily back in March, don't forget.' She sipped her tea, twinkling at him over the rim of her mug. 'That's not so long ago.'

'Kate, that was because you persuaded me.' Justin changed the subject. 'All right. Jewish jokes are world-renowned. Did you ever hear an Islamic joke?'

'Don't start that . . . that's just being racist!'

'Then I will tell you something else racist. A Kuwaiti company has bought up the old Anchor premises. How do you like that?'

She frowned with thought before saying, 'Perhaps they could be persuaded to build a refuge for Egyptian children and orphans.'

'I don't think the aged of the parish would relish the idea of Egyptian kids running about the place.'

She came round the table and kissed him. 'Why always look on the gloomy side? This could prove a good chance for some disadvantaged kids.'

'Yes, maybe. It's true that sometimes Chance works to human advantage.'

'There's a chance that if you came round to mine for supper, you might get some lovely smoked salmon.'

He pulled a face. 'Egyptian smoked salmon?'

'Tesco smoked salmon.' She gave him another kiss.

Then she was off again. He watched her neat figure going down the street. Justin rang Ken and they agreed to meet for a quick drink in the White Hart. They went through the low doorway.

Half-hearted attempts had been made now and again to modernize the place, but basically the interior was plain wood with tables and chairs jammed close together. The first room was almost empty, since most customers had gone through into the garden behind the pub. Ken and Justin sat in a corner, where Justin had sat to talk to George Ross. They talked of this and that, including the forthcoming London marathon, in which one of Ken's nieces was running.

One of the waiters was of Middle Eastern appearance. Justin got himself to his feet and went and asked the man if he would speak to them. Looking defensive, the waiter followed Justin to the corner where they had chosen to sit. Putting a hand out, Justin asked the man if his name was Akhram.

'Why do you want to know? Who are you?' Justin and Ken introduced themselves and said they were anxious about Om Haldar, and wondered if Akhram could help them. Did he know Om Haldar? Akhram remained guarded. Yes, he had spoken to the young lady.

'No more than that?' Ken asked. 'But would it not be natural for you two to be friendly, coming from the same part of the world?'

'We have not come from the same part of the world. She is from Pakistan, while I am from Saudi Arabia.'

'Well, I meant to say both of you being Muslim.'

The waiter said, with a grin that was possibly a grin of pain, 'I am no Muslim. I left all that behind. Don't go blaming me for any terrorist activity.'

'That was far from our minds,' said Justin. 'Sorry if we upset you. We just wanted to ask if you knew where Om Haldar was now, and why she left so suddenly.'

'I tell you I know not any things about it. Now I must work. Excuse me.'

Akhram left with a nod, to station himself behind the bar. Later, as the two men were leaving, Akhram came up to them again. 'I regret to appear unfriendly. It was rude. I have had so much difficulty in my life. I truly regret my rudeness. Truthfully, I believe the lady you enquire for had no legal right to be in UK. It is best if you did not seek her out.'

'We understand what you say. Thank you,' Ken responded. 'You believe Om Haldar is still alive at least?'

'Who can tell that?' Again he gave them the painful smile.

As they left the pub, Ken asked Justin what he made of the conversation. 'He was guarded. I think he may have something to hide.'

'We all have something to hide . . .'

In the street, cars were edging past each other, some going north, some south, on the whole their drivers showing each other courtesy.

'You know what I'm thinking?' said Ken. 'What I'm thinking is I sure hope he didn't murder the girl. He plainly knows more than he wants to say. I hear he's quite popular and does a conjuring trick of an evening, but the guy's not a happy bunny.'

Justin said, 'Okay, so he's hiding something, as you say. It occurred to me that he was not against the girl but for her. The question remains, why did she suddenly bugger off? Maybe she was afraid. Maybe the poor girl has to keep on the move. Maybe someone's after her. Suppose she's threatened by an honour killing?'

'So would she have told this guy, Akhram, where she was going?'

'I'd say she wouldn't dare tell anyone. I wonder what the police make of it.'

'Ah!' Ken exclaimed, raising a finger as revelation struck. 'The cops have already interrogated him. They got nothing on him. He didn't like us because we look like plain clothes men . . .'

'You're right. We're badly dressed. We look like plain clothes men.'

Kate's salmon was tender and delicious.

Hollandaise sauce served with it was accompanied by tenderstem and mashed potato. Justin cheered up considerably in Kate's company. He told her about Jack Hughes and Marie's unfortunate joke about *J'accuse*. They talked about the earthquake in Java. The Indonesians lived along a major fault line.

A few paragraphs in the next day's newspaper reported a coup d'état in a distant province of Central Asia. The ex-president had been hanged in public. A mullah had attended the hanging and had announced that from this day forth, under the new president, there would be no more oppression or corruption. The rioting in the capital had been suppressed. Justin read the brief report over twice. How clearly it demonstrated the miseries of the human race. Would anyone be naive enough to believe that life in that distant province would improve from this day forward? At least Western Europe had managed to erect barriers against the worst of barbarism. Although it had not stopped someone nicking his bodhisattva . . . He went to the supermarket to buy marmalade and canned raspberries, telling himself he was not gloomy. He selected a pack of fine-ground coffee and some marinated Greek olives with feta cheese. At least he had learnt to live on the fringes of the present, drink cappuccino, work a computer, have regular blood tests and pronounce without smirking the latest coinage of the Nanny State, Wheelie Bin. As he was sitting later in Kate's tiny garden, drinking coffee with her, he said, 'I saw Captain Derek Dogshit on my way home.'

'Don't call him that, Justin darling. He's a perfectly nice man.'

'Perfectly? You know he rents out property – ill-maintained property? My cleaner lives in one of his dumps.'

Kate shook her head, smiling. 'You know you were terribly rude to him.'

'Of course I was fucking rude!' He laughed. 'That bald git! That affected voice of his! Percy Shelley probably talked like that.'

He still felt sore. Dalsher was a churchgoer, and proud of his belief in God. He made the rounds every month, delivering the parish magazine – and a short sermon with it if he met an unlucky parishioner who lived in the house. Justin claimed the Lord Almighty was insufferably proud to have such a parishioner. Janet had been dying inch by inch. Justin was at his most distraught. Only that morning Dr Reid, with tactful indirection, had told him to prepare himself for what would inevitably befall. Furthermore, the doctor suggested that Janet would be happier if her remaining days were to be spent, not under Justin's devoted care, but in the local hospice, Sobell House, with its superior resources. Justin was rushing out to the chemist to buy some kind of cream to ease Janet's back pain. Not that Janet had been refused morphine, but that her sick fancy had turned to the idea of Justin gently rubbing an embrocation into her spine. 'Embrocation, embrocation, embrocation,' he said in a kind of mantra to himself as he hurried along. It was then he had encountered Captain Dalsher.

'You're in a terrible hurry, Mr Haydock,' said Dalsher, jovially. He spoke in his usual high strangulated voice, his bald head ashine.

'Can't stop, sorry. Shopping for my wife.'

Dalsher laid a detaining hand on Justin's sleeve. 'I want you to be reassured that, in this hour of sorrow, I am praying for you and of course for your good wife. I pray devoutly for her every morning.'

And Justin, instead of thanking the well-intentioned man, had retorted, 'All that claptrap may make you feel good. It's doing sod all for my wife.' That was now nine years ago. He still regretted that he had spoken as he did. And he knew that if the same thing happened again, he would say the same thing again . . .

Kate and Justin sat and watched a TV documentary about the caribou. Those beautiful animals were on the run throughout life, migrating or, if not migrating, then running to keep off the wolves. When an infant caribou was born, it was able to stand on its four feet within the hour. In five days, it could run with its mother. It had to recognize its mother and she it. If they were separated by mischance, there was no reprieve. Mother caribou looked after their own and would never adopt another little animal. It was left behind for the wolves. But the wolves were equally beautiful, and as deserving of compassion. One of the virtues of the documentary was that it did not take sides between herbivore and predator. Both had to play their predetermined roles. The mother wolf was as caring of her offspring as was the mother caribou, and those offspring were just as vulnerable, poised always on the brink of starvation. The wolves contributed to the fitness of the caribou herds. The caribou on their annual migration were forced to cross wide rivers. Stones and boulders lay on the riverbeds. Some caribou were lamed on the stones as they crossed. If they gained the farther bank, they would be unable to keep up with the fast-moving herd. So then the wolves would take them.

Kate and Justin found this interlocking of nature very moving. She slept with him that night. He took a Viagra and they made love, hugging each other together in the bed, flesh against flesh, in the cosy darkness. *How lucky I am,* he thought, a dozen times over. The birds sang under the street lamps.

# 8

## *Bumology*

It was Justin's custom to walk about his house in stockinged feet. He liked his life to be as event-free as possible. The great world was as full of events as if a great dice-shaker had been shaking his cup. In Java, the earthquake had caused five and a half thousand deaths and rendered thousands more homeless. Many nations were sending aid in various forms. That was the good side of the human race: the wish to help those in trouble – a large-scale version of the two cyclists in the hospital grounds who had helped Justin to his feet.

The cleaning lady came every morning for an hour. Scalli Daklun complained about the inconvenience of the small house she rented – from Captain Dalsher, as it happened. She had taken in a lodger in order to help pay the rent. Still Justin did not bring up the subject of the missing bodhisattva. He began to think he was afraid to do so in case she lost her temper and left. Then there would be that nuisance of advertising and interviewing all over again.

'Do you like Old Headington?' he asked her. 'To my mind it's a paradise of a kind.'

Scalli shook her head. 'Paradise, not.'

The laburnum in his back garden continued to flower, offering forth its yellow florets. It gave him great pleasure. He was alert for signs of his deterioration. He noted his sloth in getting up. He always woke early. In these summer months, he awoke to sunshine at five o'clock. He sat on the side of his bed, contemplating rising, awaiting the moment when his legs felt able to bear his weight. Sometimes he sat there for a full ten minutes, feeling quite pleasant, looking forward to his cup of tea, thinking of the caribou always running, running, beautiful beasts ever driven. Sexual thoughts often drifted through his mind. It did not disturb him that he was no longer very capable, or very inclined to be capable: not that he did not cherish the entire tactile enjoyment of Kate's body against his. And when he did get downstairs and into his kitchen, he would generally switch on the television to BBC 1, where there were several women announcers he enjoyed gazing at, imagining how pleasant it would be to undress them and kiss them here and there.

The lovely month of May was ending and chestnut trees were sending up their candles. At the stationers, he bought postcards depicting planes or the funny antics of penguins, to send one every week to Dave at Eagles Rest. He met up with Kate most evenings. They always found something to talk about, something to engage their wits and their humour. Only on the subject of religion were they more seriously at odds. Kate disputed all Justin's criticisms.

'Religion fertilizes our lives. It's valuable,' she said. 'Of course it can be perverted, but so can science and everything else.'

'And religion most easily. It so easily generates lies. Take the Devil! A dangerous myth generated by religion.'

She saw he was growing heated, and said consolingly, 'Perhaps the Devil is an exception. Besides, we don't hear much about him these days. Moral ambiguity often prevails.'

He would soon recall those words of Kate's. For the untroubled present, he let them soothe him. 'Be kind to me,' he said, 'I may have to go into the hospital for a colonoscopy next week.'

It was warm enough for them to eat their modest suppers at a little table outside Kate's garden door, where the evening sun slanted down on them, filtered through apple trees. This was the summit of Justin's happiness. He was always in a good humour. He suffered various aches and pains. But what luck it was that he was still alive and enjoying life at eighty. He would have liked a week's stay on a Greek island, in a hotel he knew, where the manager had become a friend, and his chief worker spoke some English and liked to talk to him. She was a young widow. When he left, the previous year, she kissed him goodbye. But at present, with the warfarin and the constant blood tests warfarin required, going abroad was an impossibility.

He quite enjoyed visiting the hospital. There he saw conscientious nurses and doctors and the whole complex machinery of care and cure in working order. This was something he admired about England. For all that politicians and papers said, the ordinary people went about their business and kept the wheels turning.

A strange choked cry, inhuman, more like an animal in pain. He was immediately anxious. Justin was heading for the hospital that afternoon when he heard the noise, a something not quite a scream, a yelp, a snuffle. Looking about, he saw something happening in a side lane. A black thing, struggling. He went frowning to look at it.

The black thing was a dog, seeming to be swimming in air. It hung by its neck from the branch of a sycamore tree, as it fought for life. He ran to rescue it, not stopping to wonder what a dog had been doing, trying to climb a tree. As he reached the animal, it ceased its kicking. He stood there, staring at it rather helplessly. The poor thing had been tied to the branch by a string knotted tightly round its neck. Its tongue lolled from its open jaws. Its eyes bulged at nothingness. He took out his pocket knife to cut it down, when a voice called, 'Let it be!'

Justin turned. Leaning against a nearby tree, one hand propping up his head, stood Jack Hughes, shrunken and dishevelled.

'He had to die,' Hughes said, before turning his face to the tree bark and bursting into loud cries of anguish. He beat the tree with his fists, as if it were responsible for the dog's death. At this, Justin lost his fear of the man. The shoulders, and with them the old mustard-coloured jacket, heaved. Justin patted the shoulders rather timorously, asking at the same time what had happened.

'He – he – he got the Devil in him.'

'The Devil? What do you mean, man? The Devil in a dog?'

'As I believe there is uh uh uh a God, so there must be a Devil. Stan's to reason.' He broke into renewed tears. They coursed down his worn cheeks. He cried uncontrollably, unashamedly, as if proud of his misery. Gradually his story came out. A kindly black preacher from Kinshasa who lived in Headley Way had allowed Hughes and his dog to sleep for a night in his house, in a small back room. He had fallen and could not make his way back to his place. 'He was a good man. He said his house was a temple. Real good. Kind, fierce, strict, mega-religious. Best black man as I ever knew.'

More sobbing. Hughes managed to tell Justin that on the previous night he had got drunk. He did not walk the dog. He came into the room and fell into a deep sleep. The dog had a shit by the door. In the morning, the preacher came in to see how he was, slipped on the dog shit, fell, broke a rib on the edge of the table and two fingers on the floor. As the paramedics came to take him off to hospital, the preacher proclaimed that the Devil had got into the dog. Hughes had to dispose of it immediately.

'So you believed him?' Justin exclaimed. 'So you hanged your own dog!?'

'What else could I do? My only friend . . .' He collapsed on the ground, putting his head between his knees, and cried brokenly. 'I found a woman what will rent me a room cheapish. But my dear old chum . . .' When he wiped his eyes with his fists, dirt ran down his cheeks. 'Winston, that's what I called him. He'd answer to Winston.'

Justin cut the dead dog from the tree and handed Hughes the corpse. Hughes hugged it as if it were a doll, pressing his face to the already cold body.

'I'm so sorry,' said Justin, lamely. 'I've got to go to the hospital now. Do you want to come with me? They'll look after you.'

He turned red-rimmed eyes up to Justin. 'I'll stay here. This bloody fucking world! I don't want no help. I just want to die.'

As Justin, sighing, began to go on his way, the other called in a choked voice, 'Thanks all the same, mate!'

Justin sat in the hospital awaiting the specialist, thinking about the idea of Nirvana. Perhaps love and sex were allowed in Nirvana, unlike in the Christian Heaven. He was still trying to puzzle out the idea of God. But God and the Devil . . . The yin and yang of human psychology . . . Although fewer people attended church nowadays, it seemed to Justin that the residue were on the whole the same sort of people they had always been, decent enough on the whole, but people of habit. But if some sick idea got hold of them . . . True, in Britain, rape and knifing and murder took place, but these cases were always seized upon by the media for sensationalism because of their comparative rarity. Most people went quietly about their business, always striving to keep their heads above water. Much like the caribou crossing icy rivers, come to think of it.

When Justin presented himself to an anti-coagulant nurse in the curtained booth, she asked him if he was unwell. He said he was fine.

'You don't look well, dear,' she said. 'I'm not sure if I should take a blood sample.'

'No, I'm okay. I've just had a shock. I saw a man hanging his dog.'

The nurse began to laugh and then realized it was no joke. 'Oh, how dreadful! I can't believe – oh, what a dreadful thing to do! The world is full of evil.'

'Terrifying,' he agreed. He rolled up his sleeve.

Justin suffered his little phobias, but he was more good-humoured than once he had been. The hammer blow of Janet's death had changed him. His disposition had shifted. Every few weeks, Justin got himself up to London. In the Leather Jug in Greek Street, he met up with six or seven old friends for drinks and lunch. They were less rowdy nowadays than in years gone by. Several of them were still working. Ramsay Cotterell was still serving in a marginal capacity on a BBC TV Advisory Council, and still laying down the law. A late arrival at the Jug was Sammy Batacharya. Sammy had gone from being a spare regional reporter to a lead announcer and then had become the presenter of a game show of his own invention, *Bizarre Bezique*. *Bizarre Bezique* was still being played on an obscure channel, long after the fashionable had ceased playing the card game after which it was named. And Sammy was still deriving a royalty from it. He raised his glass of Beck's and drank deep. 'Remember Gloria, my fiancée? She jilted me last Saturday.' They poured forth their condolences, although those who had met the lady regarded her as a pain in the neck.

'How come you are not madly downcast?' Dick Shackleton asked.

'Best thing that ever happened to me.'

Justin was returning to the table with a plate of sausage rolls for them. 'But you were crazy about her the last time we saw you.'

'Crazy is the word.' He went on to explain how he had been drunk and took on Gloria for a one-night stand. She had seized on it and got a real grip on him. Making the best of it, he told himself it was about time he married someone. 'I'm free, free, I tell you! What a bit of luck! I had gone off her anyway.'

'All right,' said Ramsay. 'Let's have a few jokes. How about the hospital that advertised itself with the slogan, "If you're at Death's Door, we'll pull you through"?'

Later, as they were parting, Ramsay asked Justin if he had any bright ideas for a TV series. He was due to come up with something shortly and could not think of anything at all viable.

Justin hated to appear sterile, and spoke off the cuff. 'How about a series on the fashions for various gods and goddesses – how they come and go – all round the world? You could work in lots of impressive scenery . . .'

'Mmm. What would be the carrier theme of all this?'

'Oh, I don't know. Perhaps that there's only Chance, and gods are believed necessary as protection against ill fortune.' Perhaps he listened to himself. Perhaps he thought about Jack Hughes' dog, dangling from the sycamore tree.

'Okay, I'll chew it over, Justin, thanks,' said Ramsay Cotterell, without great enthusiasm. 'Myself, I can't see it, but at least I can talk about it at the next committee meeting. Buddhism and all that?'

'All that, yes. Bodhisattvas and all.' A brilliant idea, he thought, travelling on the X90 back to Headington. So much happened, there was not proper time to take it all in. What about that poor devil Hughes? The very kind of person to believe in the Devil! Yet the summer days passed, and more peacefully than the summer days over many parts of the planet.


Telling Ramsay about his forthcoming colonoscopy had not seemed to be a good idea. Only the old, he thought, had colonoscopies. Justin subscribed to BUPA; he was thus able to enter the Manor Hospital for his inspection. Just as well, he thought, since the big NHS hospital was engaged in fighting more than

101

one super-bug. Kate drove him to the Manor, coming with him as he was shown into a neat one-patient ward. Justin undressed and put on a hospital gown which opened at the back.

'Oh, it makes you look so seductive,' said Kate, smiling. 'Well, they should be able to get to the bottom of things.' She kissed him tenderly. When she had gone, he was given an enema. In the operating theatre, he lay on his right side while an anaesthetic was about to be administered. A clock on the wall declared the time to be nine twenty. He thought of Dr Reid, who had sent him to the proctologist. He thought he had remarked to the doctor, with whom he was on friendly terms, that he was looking tired. He thought Reid had replied that his marriage was breaking up after nine years. He thought – absolute nothingness. Then he was surprised to see the clock said ten thirty-one.

The colonoscopist – referred to privately by Kate and Ken and friends as the bumologist – had pumped warm dry air into Justin's bowels in order to have the route clear for the inspection and the insertion of a rectal bougie. All had been well, said the bumologist, except for one over-large polyp, which he had snipped off. Consciousness, that tentative thing, faded again. Justin was vaguely aware he was being moved to a Relaxation Room, so called. He had reason to think of it as Farters' Corner. A nurse tucked him in snugly and then left him alone in the room. *Light the blue touch paper and retire immediately* – he recalled the instructions on the fireworks of his youth as he noisily expelled the warm air from his bowels. It was a positive pleasure to lie there, loudly, proudly, breaking wind. As once he must have done when a baby, although without the practised flair of an adult. The mellow noise gradually faded away. Once that was over, he was installed in his bed in his ward, and a light meal was served – a meal which included a glass of Chardonnay. He ate slowly, vaguely aware of an empty feeling in the stomach area. A nurse came to see how he was. He pushed his tray away and sipped the last of his wine.

'We'll give you a sleeping pill this evening,' she told him. 'You'll sleep well and feel perfectly okay in the morning.' She added, smiling prettily, 'You are looking pretty perky now, Mr Haydock.' He thought he would not mind having her in his bed.

To prolong their conversation, he asked about the super-bugs endemic in hospitals. Referring to the nearby large hospital, the JR, the nurse said that there they had big wards, always scrupulously cleaned every day, yet still they faced problems with super-bugs, MRSA in particular. 'That's Methicillin-Resistant Staphylococcus Aureus,' she added, helpfully. 'And they are very careful now about washing their hands. We're lucky, we don't suffer from MRSA in the Manor.'

When she had gone, he slept, waking to find that he was thinking about super-bugs. Another of mankind's enemies. Why was there no MRSA in the Manor? Was it just because the hospital was new? After dozing and puzzling, he thought of an answer. When a bed was made in one of the big JR wards, the removal of bedsheets would serve to distribute the super-bug, to be inhaled elsewhere. The Manor had single-bed wards. Super-bugs like MRSA could not travel from bed to bed, or mouth to mouth. The human tendency to gather in groups was partly a cause of the trouble. Congregations of people in churches or mosques or temples were ideal places for germs and bacteria to spread. The poor devils in the fourteenth century who gathered to pray for deliverance from the Black Death had merely served to propagate it. To pray for salvation was to get it in the neck sooner than expected.

Kate arrived and took Justin home. She was all solicitude. Maude greeted them in a curiously reserved way. Kate prepared a simple meal for Justin. He went and looked up plagues in an encyclopaedia and on Google. He was gratified to read that 'the aristocracy suffered less than the population at large'. Of course. The blighters could remain aloof from the crowded and contagious villages. However ghastly the plague, it proved a shot in the arm for the class system. Which continued to this day: you had to pay to get into the comparative safety of the Manor Hospital.

# 9

## Baal is Mentioned

He was strongly inclined to relax on the following day. The odd fart still escaped its captivity. Justin descended the stairs carefully. His legs were never fully working in the morning. He brought both feet on to one step before attempting the next. He held tightly to the banisters. His hands were growing skeletal. He felt neither worse nor better for the colonoscopy.

As Justin was sitting back, reading a book entitled *Great Lives*, Maude appeared and sat next to him on the sofa in rather a mummified way. 'We never use the spare bedroom, do we?'

He was wary of the question. 'Not at the moment, no.'

'Justin, my dear, we could put that room to good use.'

He raised an eyebrow enquiringly. She wanted him to know how uncomfortably Om Haldar lived. How restrictedly she lived.

Much worse, she felt her life was in danger. No, she had never actually said that, but Maude understood. Om was a quiet person, and private. But she, Maude, had had a brilliant idea. Their spare bedroom was empty, unused. It had a nice view of the back garden from the window. What was more, there were bars up at the window, left over from the lives of others with a child.

Although Justin was puzzled, he held his tongue. Maude said that she felt that she and Justin had a moral duty to help this poor isolated girl. There was no reason why Om should not come and live in their spare room. She was very quiet and would not be a trouble. This speech was made not without grunts and gestures of protest from Justin.

'Sorry, Maude, but no. You are forgetting something. Your friend has done a runner. She's not in Old Headington any more. She skipped it, remember?'

Maude's mouth fell open. Wide-eyed, she slowly shook her head. 'I am nine years older than you. You're just making an excuse.' She squeezed her lips together, making her face more puffy than usual. 'No? Has she left us? It's an excuse . . .'

'It's no excuse. She's vanished. In any case, we don't know what this girl would have been like. She'd not stay put in her room. She'll want to use the loo and the kitchen. She'll want to go in the garden. She'll most likely have been a hell of a nuisance.'

Maude gestured with one hand as if driving a fly away. 'She has vanished?! Oh, forgive me, Justin. My mind! How could I have forgotten? Of course. Vanished . . . Oh dearie me!' She banged her temple with the palm of her hand.

He was alarmed by her forgetfulness. Attempting to console her, he said, 'I would not have had her in my house in any case.'

Maude's face became an unattractive red. 'I can't help it if my mind is going. You're just being racist!'

He was furious. 'You are getting dotty in your old age. Why are you so mad about this girl? I couldn't bear to have had her yowling her prayers here five times a day. It's bad enough with you doing it. We're English, remember?'

Maude ignored the complaint. She stared down at the floor, squeezing her features as if by so doing she might extrude the truth. 'But she would not have left without saying goodbye to me . . .'

'She left without saying goodbye to anyone.'

Maude seized up a nearby vase and flung it against the wall. Fragments went flying across the room.

A hand-delivered note lay on the front doormat. Justin bent stiffly to pick it up. It contained a printed notice which announced a meeting to be held in the village hall to discuss the KIC's proposed purchase of the Anchor site. Justin stuffed it in his dressing-gown pocket. He was more preoccupied with the workings of chance. What had made Maude forget that Om Haldar had left the village? Was it part of the eccentricity that had made her decide to become a Muslim? Was this something lurking in her DNA, suddenly coming into play? Alzheimer's? He could not bear to think of it. In the kitchen, he brewed himself a cup of tea and dropped a slice of bread into the toaster. He tried to consider how greatly BBC TV had improved its pre-programme trails since his day. Often the trails were cunning mixes of real and computer work; sometimes you could hardly tell which was which. He looked out for them, often preferring them to the programmes they announced. They seemed to pop up by chance and then were gone. Perhaps Maude was also becoming unable to distinguish what was real, what not.

He could not be sure whether the day was Friday or Saturday. It was a toss-up. He told himself that little bout of anaesthesia had misplaced a day. He remembered that Scalli was coming. Scalli it was who picked his dirty shirts up from the floor of his bedroom, who did his washing-up. She was due at ten thirty. He locked the glass-fronted cabinet.

So there was time to shuffle up to the shops on the main road and get more prescribed diuretic pills from Boots. It always surprised him that, although he was shuffling pretty quickly, everyone else overtook him.

As he was leaving Boots with the prescribed diuretics and warfarin packets in his pocket, he met a friend. Of course he knew the man, knew his face, knew he liked him, but was unable to recall his name. He had drunk coffee with him, not so long ago. They were pleased to see each other and agreed to have a coffee at the patisserie on the corner of Old High Street. It was a fine warm day. They sat outside on the aluminium chairs. They chatted away happily over their cups; Justin kept quiet about the colonoscopy, thinking that it made him seem old. Yet all the time they chatted Justin worried about what his friend's name was. Maybe it began with a 'K'. It remained a blank. They were discussing the foibles of Vicar Ted. Blank was relating how, only the previous day, the vicar had passed him on his bike. (Was he Keith? Dickie? Castro?)

As Blank was speaking, Justin glimpsed a woman walking along the pavement towards them. She was a newcomer to the parish and he remembered her name. She was Brigette, a Canadian, and getting very close now. At any moment he would have to introduce them, and confess he could not remember his old friend's name – a clear sign of Alzheimer's. Agony! (Colin? Claude? Clive?) Blank's anecdote was unfolding. He chuckled. 'So the last time Ted had seen me – since church – I had been with Billy Carter. Ted waved as he passed me, calling out "Hello, Billy!" Old idiot! He knows jolly well my name is Maurice. Of course I called a greeting back at him—'

But Brigette was upon them, smiling. Justin heaved himself to his feet. 'Oh, hello, Brigette! Maurice, I'd like you to meet Brigette. Brigette, this is my old friend, Maurice . . .' What a narrow squeak! Dame Fortune had been on his side at this instant. In the very nick of time. Maurice: of course it was Maurice.

On his way home, Justin, reciting Maurice to himself, passed a ceanothus in full bloom. The blue of it was amazing. Justin could not think what you could call that particular blue. Approaching his house, going slightly downhill with the curve of the road, he saw that someone was sitting on his doorstep. Justin was immediately anxious. Not Hughes!? His eyesight was not what it had been. He could not determine whether the figure was male or female. Only when he was almost upon it did he realize it was Scalli. He had forgotten her in the pleasures of conversation with Brigette and What's-his-name (bugger it, the name had escaped him again). Scalli was always punctual and it was now ten minutes to eleven. She had been sitting on his doorstep for twenty minutes.

'Do forgive me, Scalli! I had to get some pills from Boots.' To add to the verisimilitude of his story, he produced the packet of warfarin from his pocket. 'They were maddeningly slow about the prescription. Perhaps they have to make the pills behind the scenes.'

'It don't matter, Mr Justin.' Scalli smiled her grim smile. 'It's so nice today to sit here just. I come from work with Wendy Townsend of down this road.'

He unlocked the door and they went in. Scalli was wearing sandals, chinos and a large faded blouse. Her hair was trimmed short. She wore a string of beads tight about her throat. Her skin was pale fawn in colour. She had, he recalled, two small daughters, one of whom lived in Aleppo.

Scalli went straight to the vacuum cleaner in the broom cupboard and began to vacuum the carpets downstairs. Justin disliked the noise of the vacuum cleaner but put up with it in the name of hygiene.

'What about the new government in Syria?' he asked Scalli over their regulation cups of coffee.

'New gov'ment don't likes England because they don't know it. Oh, what the president most worries is how many Iraqi men come across the border with their own kind of Islam. He tells that into the future this will cause a great trouble.'

Justin grunted. 'Always religion, religion! What a nuisance it is, even in this country.' He almost added, 'Where people can be persuaded to hang their dogs in the name of religion.'

She helped herself to a little more sugar. 'You should not say so. Religious is the good weather of the spirit. Is a part of life, Mr Haydock.'

'So is diarrhoea a part of life, Scalli. All religions provide pretexts for trouble. Gods go in and out of fashion, but religion remains like an old tattered coat. Half the world worships Jesus or the Virgin Mary, half the world worships Muhammad. Once they worshipped such weird creatures as Mithras, the soldier god, or Baal. Don't Hindus still worship Ganesh, the elephant god? Who nowadays would bother to worship Baal – or even to blaspheme against him? These old gods are dead as dodos.'

Scalli flung down the sugar spoon on the table. Furiously, she stabbed a finger at Justin. 'How you to dare say the great god Baal is like to a dodo! I am worship Baal! Baal is great! Baal died and rised again. Your Christ did not do no better! Baal holds the thunderbolts and will strike you with them! Baal is delight of the world!'

'World?' Justin shrank back in his chair under the force of this tirade. Scalli's face was alight with anger, as sun upon stony seashore. 'Hold on, Scalli! I really had no idea—'

She stood up, leaning across the table, her face close to his. Her breath smelt like an old tomb. 'I will never hear his great name mistaken! He looks after me – like what? Yes, like a person-ally! I am a Saphonist, the taken name from the mountain where great Baal lived when he was alive first time. There are many of us, always persecuted, worshipping in secret. I will not hear a Christian abuse his name. I shall leave from here now!' She straightened up, a woman transformed, one arm raised above her head as if clutching an invisible sword. Justin also stood.

110

'Scalli, please . . . I'm extremely sorry. Don't get ratty. Baal was just an example I chose at random. I don't believe in God Almighty either. All these gods are just myths, and it's only the superstitious—'

'Baal is no a myth! How you dare to say it! He will strike you. Great Baal guides my life. I feel his presence every moment.'

Justin clasped his hands before him, protesting his innocence, following her as she waded through the slurry of her anger towards the door. Scalli turned furiously upon him. 'Did Baal not fight the sea god Yamm? Did he not bring the rains? Did he not eat mud for our sake? Did he not mate with a calf for strength? It was Baal who told me to come to work here and be a slave for you, wash your dirty filthy clothes, and also Maude, her clothes. Now he tells me go, leave this place of the wicked who make fool his name!'

As she flung wide the front door, Justin tried another tack. 'That's all nonsense, can't you see that? Please, Scalli! You're an intelligent woman, Scalli, dear! Can't you understand that we as humans are free to do as we like, as conscience dictates? You want more money? I'll pay you more!'

'Money, pah! You damned Christian brutist! It's just money you think, all of time.'

'I'm not Christian! I'm an atheist. I keep telling you—'

But Scalli was through the door and slamming it hard behind her. Maude, upstairs, started screaming.

His fingers tapping lightly on the table top, Justin stood thinking. He could understand why Scalli was irritated by his unwitting scorn for Baal. But why the passion, the excitement? Why, for that matter, could the woman not see the absurdity of the feats she attributed to her god? Supposing he had said to a Christian, 'Jesus seems to have had some brilliant ideas for his time, and to have been immensely kind. Immensely kind but psychotic. There was a lot of it about – like leprosy. In the end it all came to nothing and they killed him. The pain on the cross must have brought him to his senses. Didn't he say something like "My God, why hast thou forsaken me?" So that at the moment of his death, the poor chap realized he had lived under a delusion . . .? The Christian might have been a touch peeved . . . But there he stood, going over it all again. Hasten after Scalli and apologize for his error! He had upset her. She could have little enough to cling to but her religion. All right, it might humiliate him slightly, but one had to fight one's own illusion of self-importance.

He moved hurriedly out of the house. A light rain was falling. Ignoring it, he hastened down the street. He saw no sign of Scalli. Of course, she might have turned down the Croft. Pausing, he tried to decide which route the woman might have taken. He opted for the Croft. As soon as he entered the Croft, the rain became a downpour. Justin dashed for the nearest shelter, a rustic porch built out over the door of a modest cottage, presumably with the intention of lending it a sense of style. Clumps of lavender, now bending to the force of the rain, adorned each side of the small structure under which he stood. *Well, this is a class of experience*, Justin told himself, thinking that no class of experience was to be despised. The thought led him to recall the years of his boyhood, then the youthful years, the hearty disregarding years, the exquisite or distasteful smells of women, the men he had consorted with without much liking, the boozers, the friends he had loved, their fun, his dislike of certain children, deeds done without thought . . . and what of them, what of all that? Had it all been what he was meant to do? His time had gone by like the rain that fell, soaking into the ground.

Then there was the question of whether he had been happy or not. Did regardlessness count as happiness? Of course, there had been the human pair, the crucial pair, the inspiration ever of novels and operas; he and Janet had been affectionate component parts of such a pair. What had come of it? Janet was dead, he was probably near death, their son was lying in care, forever incapable of normal existence. And then that post-mortem package from his wife which seemed to indicate she didn't like him much after all. He faced this adverse judgement, delivered without God's comfort. Perhaps he should be proud and happy that he had come at length to this – this repentance of a kind – standing beneath a leaky porch roof. At least there was Kate in his life. Yes, she loved him. And yes, he loved her and admired her honesty, and the good work she did in Egypt. Possibly it was simply that sadness was a natural condition of mankind. Nothing could dispel it – or not until gods, and the great god Baal himself, had been invented. The world's untrustworthy comforters . . . A man trudged past along the Croft, collar turned up, evidently soaked to the skin. Catching sight of Justin as he passed, he nodded, raising one hand stomach-high in greeting. 'Lovely weather we're having,' he said.

Justin remembered the traditional response. 'Good for the crops,' he said. This momentary exchange with a fellow sufferer served as some consolation.

# 10

## A Garden Party

When the rain stopped, Justin returned to his house. He towelled himself down and changed his clothes, expecting Kate to arrive at any time. He had given up on Scalli. After his lunch, which consisted only of a mug of packet soup, Justin settled in his favourite armchair for a nap. These little blackouts seldom if ever held any dream content. Yet suddenly he found himself in a dense forest. From the press of branches hung immense black leaves. Perhaps it was rural Romania. The place was remote, inaccessible. Snow fell in large flakes, straight down, undisturbed by wind. His carthorse was pulling a cart. He had a glimpse of himself unshaven. The horse had a large biscuit-coloured skull. It looked at him with affectionate understanding. He awoke as he was about to speak to the horse.

Looking round the humdrum room, he found it remained as usual. Television set, sofa, grate, television, sofa, grate . . . So he was not dead, as the dream fragment had led him to believe – not dead, unless there was a terrible kind of afterlife where everyday events had to continue remorselessly as a simulation of the world he had just left. But the horse . . . He grieved that that large gentle creature did not exist.

The phone rang. Someone at the police station in Cowley spoke. They asked Justin to come over and see them, if that was possible. No, there was no trouble. It was just a matter of identification, if he would not mind. Yes, if he could come this afternoon, that would be very satisfactory. Justin told Maude.

'Oh dear!' She put a finger to her lips. 'Perhaps I shouldn't have done that. I told the police – at least I think I did – that you were worried about the young lady who was missing from Restoration House.'

'You mean Righteous. Righteous House.'

'That's what I said. I said you were suspicious of the Fitzgeralds. So now they've gone and arrested them both.'

'Thanks so much, Maude. Very helpful.'

Justin told Kate. Kate was briskly sympathetic, and said she would come round immediately and drive them to the police station. She immediately did as she said.

She sighed. 'You should have told the cops you weren't well. Okay, hop in, darling.' The rain had ceased and the roads gleamed. Kate drove him over to the offices on the Oxford Road in Cowley.

'Why is it that just entering a police station makes one feel guilty?' he asked, as they entered the station. But the young officer they met with was pleasant and thanked Justin for coming so promptly. They talked for a while about the litter on the streets, before the officer produced a plastic box from the shelves behind the counter. He pulled out a bangle and set it in front of them.

'Ever seen this before, sir?'

'It's a bangle,' said Kate. 'A girl's bangle, foreign. More like tin than silver. So, very cheap. Well worn, I'd guess.'

'I've never seen it before,' Justin said, thinking, *But Maude probably has.* Thinking of Maude reminded him of something she had said. He asked the young officer if the Fitzgeralds had been arrested.

'Mr Fitzgerald is helping us with our enquiries, sir.'

'What enquiries?'

'The missing young lady from India, sir. This bracelet was found in Mr Fitzgerald's bedroom. It's almost certainly Indian. We had an anonymous phone call suggesting we should search the house.' He asked Kate if she knew the young Indian lady concerned.

Kate said she had only just returned from Egypt. The officer's eyebrows moved slightly upwards.

'Egypt is some distance from India,' said Kate, sweetly.

Ignoring the jibe, the officer addressed Justin. 'I'm afraid that is all I can say, sir. The station nurse will just take a swab of your DNA, if you have no objection.' So that was really what they had wanted. He thanked Justin and Kate for their cooperation. Clearly it was meant to be a dismissal, but at that moment an older man in uniform appeared from the rear of the premises, bearing a tape-recorder. He addressed himself to Justin, asking him if he was a friend.

'You mean with Guy Fitzgerald? No, I know him but I can't say he's a friend exactly.'

The swabs were taken. They were walking towards where Kate had parked her car, when she said, 'I've just remembered. Fitzgerald! I was at school. Our maths teacher was dismissed because he had stuck his hand up the knickers of one of the bigger girls, Amy someone. That was Guy Fitzgerald! We laughed because we said Amy liked it and probably asked him to do it.'

Justin chuckled. 'That can't have much to do with these days, though, can it? It's hard to imagine him sticking a hand up his wife's knickers.'

'You never know, do you? They have had a defenceless girl, hiding away in their garden hut, unprotected. He might have been tempted to have a go. That could be why she left in a hurry.'

'Oh, or he raped her, strangled her, and buried the body?'

She aimed her key zapper at her car. Its headlights flashed in recognition of its mistress. 'You never know, do you?' Kate repeated. He thought of the face of the carthorse in his dreaming vision. There was a model of reliability.


The Milsomes lived just round the corner in Logic Lane. Justin and Kate went to have tea with them, Kate wearing a new summer hat at a dashing angle. The rain clouds had moved on. It was cloudy but sufficiently warm to sit outside.

Their home had seen many lives come and go, lives good, lives bad, lives happy or glum. A thatched roof was retained, although the Milsomes had brought sundry amenities up to date, installing central heating, a washing machine, and electronic communication systems. Ken and his French wife, Marie, were sitting in their garden, sipping Pinot Grigio. Ken, now in his sixties, was reading a collection of short stories, written by an eccentric neighbour. He was a trifle deaf but did not let it spoil his enjoyment of life. Marie was a violinist who suffered from rheumatism in her arm – which did not stop her drawing or sculpting.

'Welcome to Retirement Temple,' said Ken, dropping his book and coming forward with a smile. Once compliments concerning the new hat had died away, Kate and Justin were introduced to Edgar Milsome, Ken's uncle, now in his nineties and reduced to being a withered old chap in a wheelchair. He offered Kate a yellow claw to be slightly shaken. Edgar's wife was in hospital; he was staying with his nephew for a few days.

Ken went into the house and collected two more glasses, which were rapidly filled with wine. Relaxing into a comfortable garden chair, Justin felt pleased to be with his friends. He was keen to tell them about Scalli and her worship of Baal, but Ken waved a sheet of A4 paper and said, 'This has just come through. It's an email from my brother, Rory. I have a feeling you will like it.'

'It shows the cunning of the Milsome family,' said Marie, beginning to chuckle. 'Rory – cheeky devil!'

'Rory was always a farmer,' said Edgar.

Ignoring his uncle, Ken continued. 'Rory has quite a large bit of farmland in South Carolina, just about half a mile outside Wilmington city limits,' said Ken. 'Marie and I stayed there with him two years ago. The property has gone to seed a bit since Rory's wife died, but it's still a very nice place. Lots of apple trees and a small lake beyond, where Rory has built a changing room and a diving platform. Anyhow, he says here that he picked up a five-gallon bucket to go out and collect a few potatoes for supper. As he got near the potato patch, he heard shrieking and splashing coming from the lake. He went to have a look and there in his lake were a group of girls skinny-dipping, pretty girls, evidently from the university. Directly they saw Rory, they all stopped swimming and splashing and only their heads were showing above the water.

'Although they were trespassing, they came over all moral. Several of them called to him to clear off and said they were not going to get out until he left. Rory was so crafty. He looked all innocent and said, "Sorry, ladies, I wasn't intending to catch you naked." He showed them the bucket. "I just came down here to feed the alligator." And out those pretty young ladies all jumped, to scamper about in the nude looking for their clothes!

'At the bottom of the page Rory says the moral is that youth and innocence can be beaten by old age and cunning every time!' All four of them were laughing – including Edgar.

Ken, before retirement, had worked for Rolls-Royce as a body designer. He was attached to a group collaborating with the Chinese in Chengdu, the capital of Shizuan Province. The group had been formed within a year of Chairman Mao's death in 1976.

In Chengdu, Ken the American had met Marie Duvic, then a secretary in the French Consulate in Chengdu. His fate was sealed, as he said.

Both Ken and Marie adored Chengdu. It was a thousand miles from Peking, and so fairly immune from the politics of the capital. They fell in love with each other, despite opposition from a fellow with the surname of Ladyman. 'He must have been teased at school,' said Ken, 'but he proved no lady's man.'

'A fellow near to our house was called Saligand,' said Marie. 'That is pretty near a disgusting word in French, and he was always teased.'

When leaving China and marrying Ken, Marie did not wish to live in the States. She had lost her religious beliefs and so felt ambivalent about returning to France; she had come from a religious clique. Since Ken had earned promotion within the Rolls-Royce organization, they decided to give England a try. After twenty years, they were still giving it a try. For their children, now adult, England was a permanent home. Ken's parents eventually joined them, together with Uncle Edgar, now in a wheelchair.

'I wouldn't go back to the States,' Ken said. 'There's too much born-again stuff. Marie and I, being atheists, feel comfortable with all you sinful unbelievers over here. It makes life less stressful.'

'Don't be too sure,' said Justin. He saw his moment. 'I was talking to a believer in the great god Baal only this morning!'

'Baal!' Marie exclaimed. 'Baa aal . . . god of sheep!'

He told them Scalli's story. They listened with interest. Finally, Ken said, 'You might as well pick a god at random, for all the good it will do you.'

'I agree, but Scalli certainly wouldn't. She's a true believer, believe it or not.'

From his wheelchair, Edgar said, 'And there was this chap on the wireless called Luke Walmsey. He must have been teased . . .' He gave up on the end of the sentence.

'There's a fashion in gods,' said Ken. 'They come and they go.'

'Except that now we are stuck with our God Almighty,' said Marie. 'And the Virgin Mary. How is it that God Almighty doesn't have a nice crazy name like Baal? And who's the Holy Ghost? Doesn't he or she have a name?'

Justin suggested that it might be worth enquiring into the proliferation of gods. Presumably as each one was seen to fail, they faded out before the next one. The way, he said, makes of car came and went. Kate said that was not necessarily the case. Jews still believed in Jehovah, despite the Holocaust.

'Yes, but not all Jews,' said Ken. 'It would be interesting to find out what percentage of Jews no longer believed in any god.'

Edgar stirred in his chair. 'Haydock is a funny name too.'

He launched into a rambling story of people he had known, such as a Miss Snatchett of Minnesota, who had married a Drabcock. Justin's gaze wandered to the façade of Ken's house. In Queen Victoria's time, the house had been owned by a Catholic family. The large room at the end of the house, on the right as Justin looked at it, had been converted into a private chapel. Later had come the Laurences, with a large family. One of the Laurence sons had hit a cricket ball through the stained-glass window, a prized relic of Victorian times. When Laura Broughton had married into the Laurence family, she had persuaded her husband to replace the damage with a stained-glass portrait of Benazir Bhutto, whom she admired and had known in the Pakistani lady's Oxford days. The idiosyncrasy, Justin thought, had its appeal.

At this point, Justin remembered the leaflet in his pocket. 'What's all this about the KIC buying the Anchor site?' he asked. 'Is it good news or bad?'

'And where is your sister Catherine, Kenneth? Have you seen her recently?' Edgar asked.

'We've all received these notes,' said Ken, ignoring Edgar and addressing Justin. 'The KIC are quite reputable. They had a share in the building of the new airport in Frankfurt. They're currently building oil pipelines all over the place.'

'Kuwait?' said Justin. 'So it's a Muslim company?'

'Invaded by Saddam Hussein, remember?' said Marie. 'First Gulf War, remember? You Brits ran the place for a couple of centuries, so it can't be all bad. How do I know so much about it? My pop was part of the Kuwait Port Authority until they kicked him out because of his booze problem.'

Edgar asked, in his rickety old voice, 'Booze? Where's the booze?'

'Anyhow, it is an international company. I think the Kuwaitis have only about a twenty per cent stake in it?'

When Justin, astonished, asked how Ken knew so much, the latter said with a grin that he had been reading about the KIC only that morning in the columns of the *Financial Times*. They agreed that they might attend the meeting, and then went on to other matters, discussing why Guy Fitzgerald was in custody. And if he might have had a finger in Om Haldar's little pie.

Kate remarked on how seriously the ancient Egyptians took their gods. 'One god in particular still deserves respect – the strange young man who became a pharaoh and took on the title of Akhenaten, the sun god. He has been called "the first individual in history". This remarkable man had a vision of universal and all-pervading love. He wrote a famous sun hymn—'

'It's the World Cup at the end of the week,' said Edgar. He wiped his chin.

'It's time you had your milk,' Marie told him, severely.

'Yes, how much pleasanter the world might have been, had Akhenaten prevailed. The dispossessed priests, and the darker side of humankind, overcame him.'

'How was Egypt this time, Kate?' This from Ken. 'Were you teaching in Cairo again?'

'Not so much teaching as being a general dogsbody,' she replied. 'It's a village outside Cairo. The Aten Trust, it's called. I go twice a year now, sometimes more. It's about enabling the underprivileged, teaching them skills. Pottery, for instance. I teach them about art and – oh, about society in general. Poverty makes for narrow horizons. Very poor kids and some adults too. I'm on a voluntary roster. I love the work.'

Justin gazed admiringly upon her. An oak tree slanted over a part of the garden, its outermost twigs, leaf covered, seeming to come to a point. It was a beautiful tree, grand, untiring, producing its fine leaf-cover year after year without fail. Justin almost wished they would all shut up and leave him simply to study the oak, to learn from it – what? That beauty was above all things. Perhaps that man's nature might be improved if he reverenced nature more. No more adverts for lipstick and new model Toyotas. Just this wonderful tree, living its ancient life. As the carthorse in his vision, his fragment of vision, uncomplainingly lived out its life of labour.

'You teach them about Akhenaten?' Ken asked Kate.

She gave a sad laugh. 'They don't want to know. Akhenaten's old, he's history. They want to know about Manchester United and the price of an iPod.'

'But that's an advance of a kind,' said Ken. He and Marie decided it was time for tea. They brought out from the house an array of cakes and biscuits, all home-made, together with a massive teapot.

'It's just an ordinary kind of tea,' said Marie. 'I'm afraid that I dislike your Earl Grey tea.'

They all leapt to the occasion, agreeing they loathed the flavour of Earl Grey, which was designed for snobs. Kate was not done with Akhenaten yet. She greatly admired this arrogant young Egyptian, long dead, who understood intuitively so much about earthly existence. 'He understood that the sun was distant. He spoke of its rays warming Earth, although it was far away. "Though you fill men's eyes, your footprints are unseen . . ."' Kate accompanied Marie and Ken into the house to organize some food.

Looking for something to say to Edgar, Justin remarked that he did not know much about Ken's sister Catherine. The old man said it was best not to talk about Catherine. He shook his head for a while before saying, as if with an involuntary impulse, 'But she was a real beauty, was Catherine.'

Marie and Ken reappeared with a sponge cake and a radio. Marie switched the radio on. A song from *My Fair Lady* was being played. She set down the cake and seized her husband.

'I'll never know what made it so romantic
But all at once my heart took flight . . .'

They danced on the lawn, she and Ken, in the dazzling light.

# 11

## Headington and Disappointment Street

After the visit to Ken and Marie, Justin and Kate were wandering back up Logic Lane. The grass that fringed the pavement was full of cow parsley with its lace of white blossom. A cat disturbed by the passing couple leapt up to the capped churchyard wall and disappeared behind an old gravestone. Unheeding, Justin asked Kate for more about Akhenaten. 'He sounds like one god I could believe in. Didn't Turner on his death bed cry, "The sun – the sun is god!"?'

'Together with Nefertiti, his beautiful wife, Akhenaten built a new city, Akhetaten, the city of the sun god. He was rather autocratic. But in his great hymn to the sun there is no fear of darkness. It was the darkness in human hearts that killed him. At least the sun still shines . . .'

'He seems rather a tragic figure. Ahead of his time.'

'You're more interested in Akhenaten than in my project.' They turned into St Andrews Road, negotiating a bicycle chained to a lamp post.

'He never came back from the dead, then, like Baal or Christ?'

'No. And worse things succeeded him, as it did when Jesus died on the cross. There's something morbid about the Christian obsession with the cross, don't you think?'

'Does Father Ted ever talk about the Devil, do you know?'

'Goodness, I would think the Devil's not quite PC these days.'

All was quiet along the road. The mad rush of cars that choked the road by morning and late afternoon died away. The road had turned into a village road again. The time was after nine o'clock and still light. Chuckling, Justin said, 'At this time of year especially, when shirts are open, you see endless people with crosses on chains round their necks. If Christ came back from the dead, the last thing he'd want to see would be a fucking cross! And he would find he had not redeemed us from sin as he intended.'

'Well, gods also die,' said Kate. 'Like politicians, thank heaven . . .'

Birds sang under the street lamps. A squirrel climbed swiftly up the trunk of a flowering chestnut. Said Justin, reciting, '"The drunkard homeward wends his weary way, And leaves the world to Guinness and to me . . ."' They paused at Kate's door, set back a little way in her drive. A spiraea, just finished flowering, was entangled with a yellow rose just coming into flower. They stood in the threshold, holding each other, stroking each other, embracing and kissing. 'Kate, I love you so!'

'Oh, darling Justin, I'm so lucky!'

'The good fortune is all mine, my sweet love.' When they had lingered and wished each other pleasant dreams, Justin retired down the road to his house. *It is my great good fortune. She's so admirable. A scrupulous woman . . . I was never scrupulous. But I'm so happy, I can't believe it, so deeply happy . . . It's simply astonishing. I'd say incredible, if it was not that I do believe it to be really true* . . . He had forgotten what he had recently thought of the misery of human existence. His joy was tempered when he remembered Hughes, driven by a priest's illusions to hang his dog.

And as he was getting into bed with a glass of milk on his bedside table, the stream of thought continued. *This happiness . . . I can't think I deserve it. Yet everyone deserves happiness – a quiet reserved happiness, I'd say . . . Even poor Hughes. Somehow he's excluded from happiness. It's just that no one expects to be happy in old age. That's why it is so miraculous. I've got all sorts of things wrong with me. I'll probably be dead this time next year. Still, there remains the wonderful here and now. I actually think I'm a nicer person than I used to be.* His stomach rumbled as if in agreement. He heard a scuffling downstairs. Grabbing the walking stick he kept by the bedside, he went cautiously downstairs, switching on the light as he went. A black triangular thing lay in the hall, below the letter box. He went more slowly. Something told him this was not good. He bent down to pick up the black triangle, but did not touch it. Bent, he stared at it, swallowing his spittle. It was a dog's ear. The dog. The dog with the Devil in him . . . He walked round it, and round again. Anubis – the funerary god with a jackal head: Anubis, the guardian of the old Egyptian underworld. Always smartly dressed. Pointed black ears . . . Posted here as a gesture of thanks or as a threat? He dared not open the door and look out in case Hughes was lurking there.

Justin was chilled. He wrapped himself in his dressing-gown and crawled back to bed. Leaving the dreaded ear where it lay, covering it with a folded copy of the day's newspaper, he had poured himself a glass of milk and a jigger of brandy. The brandy he drank on the spot. Back under his duvet, he picked up Tolstoy's magical novel and read as he sipped the milk, cold and fresh from the refrigerator. Prince Nekhlyudov has visited the wealthy Korchagins after a meeting with Maslova, the girl he had seduced, in her cell. He is gloomy, and Missy – the young woman he once thought to marry – tries to cheer him up. *'There is nothing worse than to confess to being in low spirits,' said Missy. 'I never do, and so I am always in good spirits. Well, shall we go to my room and try to dispel your mauvaise humeur?'* Tolstoy disapproves of this small hypocrisy, but Justin thinks there is something to be said for it. Directly after Janet's death, he was entirely wretched. But he would not show a long face to others. After all, they all had their sorrows – sorrows sometimes locked deep into their beings. Toying with such considerations, he fell to sleep and his paperback fell from the bed to the floor. Thanks to a nitrazepam tablet, together with a quinine sulphur tablet taken to ward off cramp, Justin slept well.

He woke at five thirty-five and sat on the edge of the bed to muster up the energy to begin a new day. Sunlight poured through the curtains. His senses were duller than he imagined. He was slow to perceive the gigantic creature standing nearby, watching him. 'Oh, oh, mercy!' he begged, flopping back against the pillows. The creature gave every appearance of being about to advance towards him. Then it faded from sight. Justin did not move. He lay staring at the space recently occupied by this august creature. Only slowly was he able to think that he had imagined the whole thing. There had been nothing, no one in his bedroom. It was merely a hallucination born of old age, prompted by the arrival of a dead dog's ear.

He got at last to his feet. Some slight dizziness. He weighed himself in his pyjamas as Kate advised. Still 14.4 stone. He could not get his weight down. Miserably, he went to the bathroom and rinsed his face and eyes. The garden looked beautiful, with rambler and climber roses round the south-facing walls of the house, either in flower or about to come into flower. It was warm enough for him not to bother with a dressing-gown. He went slowly downstairs, holding on to the banisters, telling himself that he was not sad, merely human. He bypassed the ear. In the kitchen, before switching on the kettle, he switched on the TV, and BBC *Breakfast* came to life. He had become rather detached from world news, although each day he worried in case mad extremists had blown up something. Rather, he watched because he liked the two presenters, who seemed to get on so well together. The woman's name was Sian Williams. Justin liked Sian, with her elegantly unruly hair and sharp features. She was pleasant-looking though not beautiful, and seemed always humorous and cheerful. Justin felt all the better for seeing her. He hoped Sian enjoyed a very happy life. He observed that she was pregnant.

Today was Thursday, 8 June. It seemed that American forces in Iraq had killed a murderous deputy of al-Qaeda. His name was al-Zarqawi. But the real interest of the day, both for TV and the nation's newspapers, was Wayne Rooney's metatarsals. Justin could not understand why this one footballer commanded so much interest. True, there were only two days to go before the first round of the World Cup, when an English team was due to play Paraguay in Germany. If you believed Sian and her friends, everyone in England worried about Wayne Rooney's injured metatarsals. It was true that Justin had seen cars driving by with England flags attached. He felt it was nothing to do with him. 'The flags of the Metatarsal Republic,' he told himself. Another news item was that retail sales of things like clothing and liquor had increased by £2,085 or something, because of the forthcoming match. Sian said it, so it must be true. She did not mention what was happening to Guy Fitzgerald. In all this news, on a Richter scale of one to ten, Justin rated minus five. What he liked about it was that England apparently had nothing more pressing to think about than a football match and some fellow's metatarsals. An event-free day was to be cherished. He himself was looking forward to an event-free day. Of course, there was always that ear to be disposed of. The washing had to be done. That had been Scalli's job.

He had filled the washing machine at about six o'clock that morning. Now the cycle was over. He pulled out the wet clothes and hung them on the line outside the kitchen, in the sun – pants, two shirts, handkerchiefs, pyjamas. Humdrum occupation for a failed man. Then he recollected his imprisoning the woodlouse. The little creature had been moving humbly across the expanse of carpet in his living room, the previous evening. It proved trickier and more resourceful to catch than most of its kind, swerving and dodging until finally he caught hold of it. Justin popped it into an ornamental bowl, meaning to release it outside when he had drunk his glass of milk. He watched as the determined insect climbed the slope of the bowl towards freedom, only to fall back where the slope steepened. Still it persevered, always falling back at the same spot on the slope. Then he forgot about it, the dog's ear having driven it from mind. Now, in the morning, he remembered the woodlouse with sorrow. It would surely be dead by now, without nourishment for so long. It lay curled up at the bottom of the bowl. When he touched it, its legs waggled. It was still alive! He unlocked the side door and strolled out to his courtyard, carrying the bowl. He tipped the woodlouse gently into a patch of weed and grass, to watch it creep slowly down into green shelter and sustenance. And presumably to live a happy marmoreal life.

The two rambling roses that covered his study wall had burst into bud and flower overnight. They were the first beneficiaries of dawn and the early sun. The sharp little buds were more beautiful than the blossoms to which they aspired, which all too quickly resembled used tissues. Much like human life, from Justin's perspective. Justin strolled round, pulling up the odd weed. Nothing serious. He thought, *Yes, I'm strolling . . . Still able to stroll. The legs are getting to be a bit of a problem, though . . .* He reflected on what a mobile species humanity was.

Mobility had served to foster human intelligence. Once humanity walked upright on two legs there was no stopping it. Useful evidence for this lay in the number of technical terms there were for walking, from toddling to staggering. *In the army we march, while only civilians take a stroll . . . I do better when I'm sitting and not on my feet at all. A case of devolution, no doubt. This bloody bindweed. Gets everywhere. Yeah, gets everywhere despite its absence of legs. God, imagine if bindweed had legs! It would be all over us. Lucky chance it developed no legs . . .* After hanging about, thinking over his theory but doing nothing in particular, he decided to go to the supermarket to buy a pork pie for lunch. He circumnavigated the newspaper covering the dog's ear.

Headington itself was a straggle of undistinguished streets. Yet many people loved it, even among the distinguished. People passed through Headington on their way to the great intellectual centre of Oxford. In Headington lived many who had never entered an Oxford college. They remained contented or discontented at random, as far as could be determined. Most of them were in trade or in medicine or in poky solicitors' offices. Yet Headington had its positive aspects. Its air was better than the air down the hill in Oxford. Headington was a great centre for hospitals, to which the sick of Oxford made pilgrimage when overcome by asphyxia. There were general hospitals, orthopaedic hospitals, a new children's hospital, smaller specialized hospitals for foot and leg complaints, a swagger new hospital, and a hospice. And, when medicine failed, a capacious cemetery to engulf the remains of the weary citizen. As for those weary citizens, in life at least they engaged even from early childhood in an attempt to make something of their lives, if it was only to marry or indulge in that famous drug, sex, or other lesser escapes, such as skunk, alcohol, morphine, crack cocaine, and so on: to work harder, or to avoid work entirely. Local schools worked dedicatedly to turn out more scholars than scallywags. Local people laughed at the number of charity shops abounding. And there were numerous estate agents displaying dismal dwellings for dismal prices – an indication that many families were hoping to improve their circumstances, or else had been forced to trade down as Justin had done, or else dreamed of getting out of town into a quiet nearby village.

Rarely in the windows of the estate agents was advertised any property in Disappointment Street. Disappointment Street, situated off Lime Walk, was established by an enlightened councillor in 1920, after the First World War. As more men and women applied to live in this admittedly dismal street, a questionnaire for entry was instituted. Those who filled in the form correctly were not allowed entry; the sheltered housing provided was reserved for the dysfunctional. It followed that the housing was more drab than usual. The uniformity of the houses was alleviated, if indeed that was the word, by a Starbucks coffee shop. On the Lime Walk corner just beyond Disappointment Street stood the house where Scalli had taken up her temporary abode.

Buses roared through Headington, carrying old people to relations or youths to Brookes. Brookes University, once a mere polytechnic, was a Headington success. Streets which had recently been populated by ancient persons pushing Zimmer frames had become dominated instead by youths eating fast food and casting their gaudy cartons into gutters. You could buy perfumes or detergents in Headington, but few toys or books, except for those paperbacks rotting on shelves in charity shops. On the other hand, you could seek mediation from charming young ladies or indulge in strange religions from sterner ladies; and there were noodle bars in which you need do neither of the above. You could catch convenient coaches to Heathrow and Gatwick, or quickly have a car exhaust fixed, or buy litres of petrol. You could have your hair cut a hundred times over. You could not find an art gallery or cinema; but you could wander in a pleasant park which had a library attached. In short, there were many compensations for the shortcomings of a suburb without marked character. Here lived many races, in tolerance if not in total harmony. It was not unusual to see a man and woman of different skin colours walking hand in hand, or a black child in a brown pram. All these families or single people had their own particular problems to work out or endure. They could strive for wealth or sanctity or at least stability. Or they could pass their entire lives enmeshed in personality problems of which they remained scarcely aware.

Justin cut a few familiar trails through this urban sprawl. His relationships were cordial with people in a computer dealership, a stationer, a hardware store, an expensive cleaner's, a furniture shop, and the owners of the best local restaurant – in fact, with the traders he used most. A travel service he particularly liked had been driven out of business by a combination of rate increases and the incursions of email. The people in a large supermarket and a small chemist were indifferent to their regular customers. If Justin's usual trail through Headington was marked in red on a map, it would be seen to be limited. He had not trodden half its streets. Now here he was, trudging once more through the car park to Somerfield's to buy a pork pie. And in so doing he encountered Jack Hughes again. Hughes was sitting slumped on a low wall, staring at the ground. He happened to look up and catch Justin's eye as the latter was about to pass him.

'See, I'm not just a layabout,' he said, as if continuing a conversation. 'I got a job as delivery man. That surprises you, don't it?'

Justin halted. 'I meant to ask you. This black priest who told you your dog was possessed by the Devil – what's his name?'

'You got a dog too, have you, squire?'

Ignoring the question, Justin asked, 'Where does this priest, so called, live?'

'What's it to you? He's moved on, any road.'

Justin stood in front of the man, contemplating him. 'I was thinking. He should be reported to someone – the police, for a start. He is spreading mental poison. Getting him returned to Africa might be a good idea.'

'He took money off of me and made me kill my dog. Still, for all that—'

'And what about the bloody dog's ear?'

'What about it?'

'Think of Britain as a system. Cash slots at Barclay's and elsewhere form part of a financial system. It works well on a modest scale. Most people avail themselves of a cash slot now and again – until some loony jams it up. Britain is a similar kind of system on a grander scale. It works well, or well enough. Most people are secure, most of them enjoy what passes for happiness. But people who believe in the Devil or in Sharia law – well, they could jam up the system by deliberately running counter to its values.' He was warming to his theme when Hughes interrupted, saying he did not know what Justin was on about.

'You standing there like you was addressing a public meeting. Clear off! Leave me in peace, will you . . .'

'You leave me in peace, Mr Hughes. I want no more dog's ears in my house.'

He blew his nose on a filthy handkerchief, saying indistinctly something about a souvenir. And, ''Ullo, what now?' This last question was provoked by a woman with an old-fashioned wicker shopping basket, approaching with a glad smile on her face. She was wearing a cape of some sort over a jumper and a blue denim skirt, the hem of which almost trailed on the ground.

Ignoring Justin, she addressed Hughes. 'Oh, there you are! How fortunate! How are you? I was so sorry to hear that your doggie was dead.'

'Yeah. Got run over by a lorry,' Hughes said.

She tut-tutted considerably. 'So sorry about it. I couldn't afford to buy you a new dog but I have brought you a little present instead.' Fishing in her basket, she brought out a teddy bear wearing

134

a tartan hat. 'There now!' She pressed it on him. 'He's so sweet! He's for you, Mr Hughes.'

'How kind of you, ma'am,' said Hughes, grabbing the bear. 'I much appreciate your kindness. You're so good to me. It's a real tonic to have kind hearts like you around.' He gave a grin.

She beamed, saying, 'Well, I must be on my way. God be with you!' Off she bustled.

'She's a Mrs Dasher,' said Hughes to Justin. 'Blinking nuisance she is – never divvies out any money.'

'Dalsher,' said Justin, correcting the name. 'I know her. I was rude to her husband once, so she ignores me now.'

'You and your lot are rude to everyone. What am I supposed to do with this ruddy teddy bear?' A man loaded with two shopping bags passed by, his small son following.

'Here, here's a teddy for you, kid!' As he spoke, Hughes held out the stuffed toy. The boy hurried on and caught hold of his father's shirt for security, without looking back.

Two Asian women came slowly past, talking to each other in a foreign tongue, followed by three daughters. 'Here, here's a teddy for you,' Hughes called. 'It entered the country illegally. Catch!' He threw it to the nearest little girl, who caught it and then ran after her mother, crying and looking back with tearful distress.

'No pleasing some people,' said Hughes, with a contemptuous laugh. 'What a fucking country this is!'

After lunch – which consisted of soup from a packet of Batchelors' Oxtail, and a slice of the pork pie recently bought – Justin greeted his cleaners. They came to clean the house every fortnight, to scour the rooms as Scalli never did. Two women, one his favourite, Louise, a small dapper woman with fair hair, very businesslike but chatty, and in command. Of the other woman, June, he had heard part of her story. She and her husband once ran a pub in Old Marston. Then they fell out. The man disappeared, and now June was living in a flat in Disappointment Street. With a cleaning job to make ends meet. Both women looked hot, as they entered with buckets and vacuum cleaners and other equipment. Justin poured them glasses of Evian water. They accepted the glasses with gratitude.

'I done me back in,' June told Justin.

'Lucky it's not your metatarsals. You'd better get fit for watching the match on Saturday.'

She laughed. 'You won't catch me watching that stuff. I hate football. It's only meant for men.'

'I'm sick of hearing about that chap's metatarsals,' Louise said.

*So much*, Justin thought, *for the popular misconception that it is the working classes that are mad about football.* 'Still, it will be fun to see the German police hosing down the hooligans after the match.' On that they agreed, laughing.

'What about this here dog's ear?'

'You'd better throw it away, Louise.'

The two women set to work with vigour. Justin was grateful for their industry. He found the roar of their industrial-strength vacuum cleaner reassuring. They worked under the banner of OXCHORE SOLUTIONS. The sort of name that would get them into *Private Eye* – of which Justin was a devoted reader.

The women slaved away, the hours leaked the afternoon away. At four o'clock, Justin stopped making notes to get both the women a mug of tea. He made a mug for himself. He found he was almost out of milk and would have to go up to the supermarket again for a container of semi-skimmed. Good excuse for a short walk. And he had a package to post. But that could wait for a while.

All the time, a part of his mind was working on a sort of slow whirlpool of subjects, luck and the gods, and how one race chose a god of the sun and another race a hard-working devil, and another the god of agony on the cross. Was it choice or was it

Chance? As an atheist, he suddenly found himself absorbed in the subject of gods. From a very early age, he had taken a scientific line – an assumption, really, that the entire complex story of the development of life on Earth, the abundant biomass, with all its accidents, was itself a sort of accident, a biochemical explosion, requiring no intervention by God, and no further dotty explanations – a world teeming with an enormous variety of life, in which only humans found any necessity to believe in religion. Just supposing a god had created the world, that does not resolve the riddle. It simply sets the mystery back one step, one unresolvable step. What was this god up to? Judging by the misery into which many people fell, the god-figure had been either careless about detail or else malign. But why? How? As such thoughts passed through Justin's head, he was absent-mindedly unpegging his washing from the washing line and bringing it indoors.

He had been five years old, he was standing in the family's living room. Sunlight was pouring into the room. The wireless was on. He heard the BBC announcer saying that a new planet had been discovered on the outer fringes of the solar system. It was to be called Pluto. Pluto was so far from the sun that it would be eternally cold and dark there. Plutonian darkness . . . A new planet! The boy was transfixed. How long had that amazing little planet been there, darkly serene, orbiting the sun? Had Jesus known about it? Nothing in the Gospels. Had God known about it? But now humanity knew about it!

It had been just as he remembered; never had he forgotten that moment. He remembered standing there on the sunlit carpet and the solemn voice of the BBC announcer. Why, he could almost recall the pattern on the carpet. That moment which so astonished him would be with him till his dying day. A whole new planet! And now . . . Just this year, NASA had launched a probe which would make a fly-by of Pluto in 2012. The probe would transmit its data back to Earth. If he was lucky, he might still be alive to see images of that strange world he had first heard of at the age of five. Only six years to go. He could be lucky!

Before going to the supermarket next day for his milk, Justin had a package to post. His legs weren't bad at present. He walked down Osler Road, crossed the main road, and entered Mail Boxes Etc. He preferred this shop, with its fitted carpet and friendly personnel, to the main post office. The men he usually dealt with were not present. Instead, behind the counter stood a small woman of pallid complexion with pale hair cut short neatly round her head. She was wearing jeans and a T-shirt. She charged Justin £1.18 for the package. He remarked on how cheap he thought it.

'You may pay more if you like.'

They both smiled at the suggestion. He said, 'If you don't mind my asking, are you from Poland?'

She said, 'Oh, it's my bad accent. It gives me away!'

'No, no, your English is very good. It's just that suddenly everyone is from Poland.' She was glad to speak. She said that Poland was so poor and everyone was so sad. They could not afford to go out for a meal. In Oxford there were many places to choose from and the price was not so dear. Where her parents lived, the houses were old and falling down. Poland was a very unhappy place. He asked about the millions of euros that had been poured into Poland for modernization and the improvement of the infrastructure.

'All the money has all gone through corruption. The rulers are the same as before. They steal the money. So the nation remains poor.'

'I'm sorry to hear it. I hope you are not too sad in Oxford.'

Her wry face brightened. 'Oh, I like Oxford much. People are polite and cheerful.'

'Yes, it's a good place to be. It's a long way from the sea. That's my only complaint. I was born by the sea.'

'I don't mind about the sea. I feel content here. Here we can say what we think.'

They would have conversed more, but another customer entered with a parcel to post. He bought Kate some flowers to give her in the evening, while he turned over what the young pale woman had said about Poland. It was indeed sad. How light-hearted the English were by comparison, with only Wayne Rooney's metatarsals to worry about . . . Global warming, fuel supplies, water shortages, counted for little beside those metatarsals.

# 12

## *The Secret Shooting*

Justin fell asleep that night thinking of what the Polish woman had said. He judged her to be an immigrant who wished to integrate with the community, who believed in that wise old adage, 'When in Rome, do as the Romans do.' Why had Om Haldar been unable to do that? He woke at four thirty, perching himself on the edge of the bed to have a good cough – that was new – and as usual went downstairs. The night was so mild that he needed no dressing-gown.

Whilst waiting for the kettle to boil, he switched on the television, to find himself in the middle of a documentary about the grand airport now open and functioning in Madrid. It was a thing of beauty and awe, its roof built like a series of rolling waves making for the shore. It had been conceived in the mind of a British architect, the materials had been tested, workers had been employed, and gradually the structure materialized from computer screen to reality. It would be used day-in, day-out, and maintained. He marvelled at Europe, so brilliantly diverse yet of a unity. Europe, where much was invented and much maintained. Things kept going. The countries of Europe attempted to ensure that law prevailed and justice was administered. There was at least some attempt to see that the poor were provided for. Humour, hard work, ease, were all hallmarks of Europe. In its glittering cities, an attempt at civilized life prevailed. There were universities and a diversity of institutions in which learning was preserved and increased. Many institutions had come into being which cared for those most likely to end in the Disappointment Streets of the nation – mainly those who could not or would not read. One index of civilization was how free women were to live their lives. A counterbalance was the proliferation of prisons, with their crowded inmates. An engaging variety of lifestyles flourished, with an amazing number of restaurants, cafés and bars to sustain much of the variety. If some politicians proved corrupt, they were eventually arrested or voted out. Yes, with all its blemishes, Europe was sans pareil. As was embodied in the new Madrid airport.

As he sipped his tea from his Carlisle mug, the news came on. A suicide-bomber had blown up himself and a London bus. Ten people were dead and sixteen injured. What hatred and envy could have been in that man's mind to do such a thing? Prompted, of course, by a warped version of his Muslim religion, but murder nevertheless. If his kind had their way, they would make of Europe a desert. Why not turn their minds to improving their own deserts? Sadly, he switched off the TV. It was five oh five. There was a rapping at his front door with a simultaneous vigorous ring at his doorbell. Justin was as one turned to stone with fear. Who would visit him with good intent at such an hour? He switched off the kitchen light and stood in the dark, clutching his mug with both hands, listening. He had lost the strength to repel attacks. The knocking was not repeated.

Mustering his courage, he crept into the hall, still holding the mug. He peeped round the corner to look at the front door. The door had two old-fashioned panels of frosted glass. He could make out a huge figure standing in the porch. It appeared to be staring into the darkness of the hall. Justin remained where he was, afraid to move. He felt freezingly cold. Of course, the man could break in. Perhaps it might be best to leave the house by the back door. That he was afraid to do: supposing the man got round into the garden . . . Scarcely daring to breathe, he remained mouselike, hidden but peering at the door, waiting for something to happen. He said to himself, 'You could cut this solid silence with a knife.' Nothing happened. Eventually, the dark figure outside faded and was gone. Had it been ill-intentioned? Or had it been seeking help? He fell prey to fantasies. Supposing it had been his son David, miraculously recovered and coming to seek out his father. Or, more likely, it was Jack Hughes. Or – and he hated himself for superstition – the god Baal himself, come to exact revenge for Justin's snub . . .

Baal or no Baal, he needed to buy some cough mixture from the chemist. At the corner of the road that morning, he saw that demolition of the old Anchor was already advanced. He stood on the pavement, staring. To get moving again required a decision; nothing was left of his previous spontaneity. His mind struggled to regulate his legs. Once across the road, he ventured to walk through the pub door. He came into an open space. Only the front of the pub had so far been left intact. Another day and it too would be demolished.

Justin stood staring at the new space. All that remained of the rest of the pub was a pile of masonry. Two young men in overalls stood by a bulldozer, chatting and talking. They nodded at Justin, otherwise taking no notice of him. Walking up to them, he asked, 'How's it going?'

The younger of the two made a gesture, including the space around him, for answer. 'Got to wait for safety fencing before we knock that lot down,' nodding his head towards the front of the building.

The more surly-looking man added, 'It should have been here Monday. Then we could be done by end of the week. Who are you, any road?'

'I live down the street,' Justin told them. There was no answering comment. 'What's going up here in place of the pub?' he asked.

The younger man answered. 'Nothing to do with us. We're Demolition. We heard they might put up one of them gambling casinos on the site.'

'I see.' The conversation seemed to be over. The men gave Justin a nod and headed towards the rear of the site. Justin sat down on a girder. He felt tired and sad. His stomach was paining him. He had never had a drink in the Anchor; now he regretted it.

There had been an unspoken agreement regarding the two village pubs. The White Hart opposite the church was for ordinary civilized people – nurses and medical students, for instance – the Anchor for rough and noisy people from nearby Barton. On this spot, a way of life had died. For centuries, working men had come to the Anchor for a pint and a bit of conversation. Nothing very elevated, but a place where, as the old expression had it, one 'drowned one's sorrows'. He sat looking down at his worn trainers. They were the most comfortable for his feet with their fallen arches. He listened to a car revving up as the demolition men drove away. He was left there in silence in the new open space.

The Anchor was no more. Though situated far from any coast, its name had celebrated the centuries when Britain was a seafaring nation. Those years had fled; now even the memory of them was disappearing. Justin sat where he was for a while, resting, looking at his old trainers. When he got home, he found his mother-in-law asleep on the sofa in the living room. He looked down with compassion at her worn face. Going into the kitchen, he warmed up a mug of her favourite Horlicks before rousing her.

'Oh, goodness me,' she said. 'I found myself in Wolvercote. I can't think how I got there. Then it grew dark and the shop shut.'

'What shop?'

'The shop. I went to sleep in the porch. Then who do you think woke me?'

'Oh, I don't know, Maude. The President of the University?'

'It was Mujeed, who owns the Café Noir. He owns the Wolvercote shop too.'

'You're slopping Horlicks down your front, Maude.'

'He was very kind. He looked after me and brought me back here. But I had lost my key.' She gave a short laugh. 'So I was locked out.'

Justin stared at her in hope. 'So at what time did he bring you back here?'

'I don't know. Anyhow, you were out. There was no answer. I went and slept on one of the folding chairs in the summerhouse. After all, it was how – what was her name?'

'Om Haldar, do you mean?'

'Oh yes, of course. Om Haldar. I was perfectly sober. But it was silly of me to go to Wolvercote. I wasn't likely to find anyone there.'

'You must be more careful.' His relief at discovering the identity of his night visitor faded before the realization that he was going to have to look after Maude for the rest of her life. 'You should cultivate more friends nearby,' he told her gently. 'Maude, dearest, how is it you never associate with Ken and Marie? They are really good friends of mine.' It appeared she huddled herself up as if protection were needed.

'I don't feel comfortable with your friend Ken. I suppose you know why.'

'No, I don't "know why". You surely can't mean that he's American!'

145

'Janet knew why. She told me. I wonder she didn't tell you.'

'Husbands and wives don't always tell their partners everything.'

Maude sniffed. 'She knew you were friends, you and Ken. That could be why she didn't tell you. Janet was always kind – too kind for her own good . . . Do you ever think of her? She was a good wife to you.'

Justin rose from his chair and began to pace the floor. 'So, come on then, tell! What is this great secret?'

'Don't get angry . . . Besides, he was only fourteen at the time.' And Maude then went on to explain that the Milsomes lived in Oregon, where they owned several hotels in Portland and along the coast. Ryan Milsome, Ken's father, enjoyed hunting and kept guns of various kinds, despite his wife's objections. There were three children in the family, the oldest being Catherine, followed by Kenneth and Rory, the youngest.

On one of their holiday properties, a handsome young stable lad worked. He got into the ranch one evening when the Milsome parents had driven down to the local store. The story always was that the lad had intended to rape Catherine. She had cried out. Ken was in the next room, playing with the guns his father had been cleaning. 'They all had guns.'

He snatched up a Colt revolver and ran to see what was happening. The stable lad had his arms round Catherine. She stood struggling, trying to fight him off. Ken fired the gun, almost without thought. He missed the stable lad. The bullet entered Catherine's head just under her left eye. The stable lad, yelling in terror, ran off. When the Milsome parents returned, it was to find Ken sprawling over his sister's dead body, crying.

'Terrible!' said Justin. 'How terrible! How appalling for Ken! What did they do?'

'Life was harsher then. They sent Ken away and he was adopted. Can't you see by his manner that he has killed someone?'

146

Justin held a hand over his face. 'Of course I can't. Poor kid! Poor little kid!'

'Marie told Janet about it. The younger brother, Rory, was traumatised for some time . . .'

# 13

## *Akhram's Tale*

It was Friday and a perfect summer's day, never to be repeated. This was to be Justin's event-free day. His garb for the day was a light sleeveless shirt and a pair of chinos. No socks. He boiled himself an egg and spread margarine thickly on his toast. His mother would never have allowed margarine in the house. Tastes and fashions changed. He could not determine whether his mother's preferences had infected his.

What effect would shooting one's sister have on one's later life? The death had been purely accidental. One might feel sorrow but not guilt. Presumably you would never forget what you had done. Justin had learnt of the existence of Pluto when he was five, and had never forgotten it, far less than a death though it was. What had changed, and by no means in Oregon alone, was the treatment

Ken had received after the shooting. Nowadays, he would be given counselling, and would not be separated from his family. Not unless the parents demanded it. He thought about the misery of Kate's early years, when she had looked after her two brothers, older than she. In adolescence, they had run away and she had never heard of them since.

He rang Marie and Ken. 'I heard that the old Anchor site might have a casino built on it.' He always regarded Ken as more intelligent than he was.

'Awful! More New Labour strangeness,' said Ken. 'We'll talk later. We've got Maurice here at present.'

'He'll sort it. He'll tell you God moves in a mysterious way, his blunders to perform.' He clicked off his mobile while Ken was chuckling. Eventually, Justin went into the garden, determined to put up his large French sun umbrella. He dragged the umbrella from the garden shed. Its fabric wings and creaky wooden arms were persuaded to open like the wings of an ancient pelican, until finally they assumed a shallow dome over his head. This was perhaps the umbrella's fifth season of use. He had planned a little meal for Kate. He had spring onion and lettuce grown in his garden to eat with a pork pie, followed by a trifle from Somerfield, and then coffee. This they could eat under the sun umbrella.

Kate arrived promptly at six, dressed in a pretty coloured dress. She had had her hair permed and looked beautiful. They sat and drank glasses of Pinot Grigio, accompanied by Greek olives. On Justin's wall was a Rambling Rector, petals of which were beginning to fall, drifting past them like snowflakes.

'Oh, these halcyon days!' he exclaimed, gazing up at the blue of the sky. 'You could imagine they would go on for ever.'

'As indeed they do in Egypt,' she said, smiling. 'I'll show you a short film this evening.'

He rested an elbow on the table. 'There was a time, back when we were filming in Pergamon, or what was left of it. The others – maybe they were having a swim or something. I was reminded of the occasion when I was in the empty space where the Anchor used to stand. I was sitting in what had once been a courtyard—'

'You've told me this tale before,' said Kate. 'You were thinking of old times.'

'In fact, I was wondering how greatly mankind had changed, if at all. I'll get our supper, shall I?' As he stood up, a figure came round the corner of the house and bowed. It spoke.

'My name, it's Akhram, sir, in case you remember me.'

'Yes. I remember you. You work in the White Hart. What exactly can I do for you?'

Akhram bowed to Kate. 'Forgive me, ma'am. I live here since five years, but still we don't really belong.'

'I'm pleased to meet you. Are you looking for a job?'

'Such an English question! As Mr Haydink has said you, I have a job.'

There the three were, Kate leaning back in her chair, Justin and Akhram facing one another. Justin remembered his manners.

'Can I give you a glass of wine, Akhram? Do take a seat.'

'Please do,' said Kate. 'My friend and I were just going to have supper.'

'I will not stay, ma'am. Nor will I drink your wine, thank you.' Seating himself, he said, 'I come merely to give some information. I apologize if I intrude.'

'No, you don't intrude,' said Justin. 'Please don't worry.'

Kate looked puzzled. 'What exactly is this information you have?'

Akhram gestured, throwing up his hands. 'I merely explain to our English friend. I have something to tell that I would not tell before.' Justin took a sip of wine. Kate sank back in her chair.

'I tell of that young Pakistani lady who has disappeared. Yes, she is from Pakistan, not anywhere else. I am from Saudi – very different place, but she recognized we had some things in

151

common. Her name once was Ayaan Ali, not Om Haldar. She lived in Rawalpindi, of rich father, although she claims that her father was beating her cruelly. You have probably heard of such treatments?'

He looked at them for approval and then continued.

'At fifteen she had to underwent marriage to a fat businessman who is a friend of her father. He also beat her and mutilated her private parts. They had been treated when a child as is the custom.' He stared piercingly at Justin, who merely nodded.

Kate said, 'It's a not unfamiliar tale.'

Frowning, he asked if she did not believe what he said.

'No, no, you misunderstand me. I have myself seen such things.'

Akhram nodded, not entirely satisfied. He continued. 'Ayaan Ali blooded so much. She decided to escape from the beastly husband. An Italy man smuggled her in the cargo hold of an airliner. She nearly died in the flight – from coldness and lack of air to breathe. She arrived in some British airport or another. You understand?'

They nodded.

'After illness and misfortunes, she came in Oxford. She met Mr Fitzgerald at the hospital. You know where he is living? In a big house? He said she could stay in the summerhouse for one month with no rent to be paid. He was kind to her, at first at least.' Akhram sighed deeply and stared down at the table top. Petals from the rose blew down on them. 'I tell this next thing with shame although I am no longer of that Islamic faith. I have no faith, an empty man.'

Although Justin listened with attention, he was aware of this century embedded in past centuries and centuries to come. And of them sitting at that particular table in the sunshine, on this particular day.

'Ayaan Ali knew that by escaping from her forced marriage,' Akhram was continuing, 'she sentenced herself to death. She could be hunted down anywhere. There is this matter called an honour killing. In England it has no honour, nor is there killing allowed, as in Pakistan. Nevertheless, she knows that paid killers of her father will hunt her out. They will find her. She can have no rest, no peace. She must always move on – and not to tell a single person when or where she goes.'

Akhram broke off, tears glistening in his eyes. 'You see? She is without relationship. Imagine a life without relationship! That's what the ancient Koran has done!' He breathed deep before continuing. 'Grieve for this poor person. Evil fortune is always against her. I fear that because I became in a little part her friend, so she becomes afraid of me, that I might be an enemy, preparing to kill her. So now she is somewhere else, and we can never hear of her again.'

Akhram reached out a hand across the table, without allowing it quite to touch Justin's. Justin looked first at him, then at Kate, then up at the sky. 'I'm so sorry,' he said in a whisper. 'Thank you for telling us. Poor darling! I wish we could have done more for her.'

'Why I tell this to you? Your mother loved Ayaan Ali. That's why.' Akhram covered his face with his hands and wept convulsively. Kate put her arm round his thin shoulders. 'We all weep for her.'

As Justin was bringing his amateur supper to the garden table, Kate asked why Akhram had come to tell Justin his tale.

'He knew I was sympathetic. And I suppose the Maude connection.'

She made no answer. After sitting in silence for a moment, she said, 'And you found his tale perfectly credible?'

'Yes. Why not?'

She gestured dismissively. 'He had it off pat.'

'Probably the police questioned him and—'

'Lives of immigrants are so difficult. Just think – supposing Akhram had murdered this young girl . . . An honour killing – which

153

he mentioned – or she had a secret cache of money . . . I only ask.'

'It never entered my head.'

She sighed. 'All I'll say is that such things happen.'

Another day passed. Another British soldier was blown up in Iraq. Justin and another friend were talking to Mujeed outside his café. Mujeed said he had a friend, Jacquetta, who wanted to interview Justin for a book she was writing. Justin said he could wait till six o'clock to see her. Meanwhile, a professional photographer, David, appeared, and sat down to talk to Justin. His studio was just round the corner.

Now David and Justin sat talking about Australia, where both had lived for some time. Mujeed joined them when he could, always being liberal with the wine, for which he would accept no payment. Customers were gathering for a drink and a chat, or for an early evening meal. Meanwhile, David was clicking away with his camera. Justin was slow to realize that people liked to regard him as the Grand Old Man of the Café Noir. Not very grand, he thought. At least he had shaved that morning. When Jacquetta arrived, it was possibly six twenty, but no one was taking account of time. This glorious afternoon might have gone on for ever. Jacquetta proved to be an attractive and lively woman in her early forties. Lively? She was certainly talkative. Something wild showed in her face, her dark eyes. Her book was to be about how she and others lived, how xenophobia was on its way out, at least in some places, and how one best should live. Ample scope for discussion there. She had spoken with the Home Secretary about Britain's overcrowded prisons and managed to make him angry. Justin strove to put in a word occasionally.

Akhram passed by, off for his evening's work at the White Hart. Mujeed plied them with more wine, at one point also producing a further bowl of olives. Justin was eager to introduce some matters Jacquetta had overlooked – for instance, the accidental properties

154

of life, the rigmaroles of diurnal existence, the role Chance played . . . Possibly those who enjoyed the good fortune of having caring parents became adults with a sense of being integrated personalities. Those less fortunate must assemble a personality, rather as one did a jigsaw. A bit here, a bit there. Jacquetta kept chipping in. She was intense and bright. They leant towards each other across the table. He was conscious of the working of her mouth, of her teeth. A vivid, restless character, he thought. Desirable certainly. David kept clicking away with his big portrait camera. *Why is he photographing me and not this attractive, erotic young woman?* Justin asked himself. Jacquetta kept referring to the death of her mother. So much so that Justin, following Dr Johnson, said that if a mother's daughter died, that was a tragedy; if a daughter's mother died, that was simply in the nature of things, and should not too greatly overwhelm with sorrow the more youthful survivor. It must be accepted and digested to allow the bereaved to move on – probably as the dead mother would have wished. He was thinking of someone he knew who was locked into a past bereavement and who could not or would not put it behind her – thus destabilizing her whole family. Deirdre Fitzgerald came to mind, for ever sitting under the portrait of her mother. But what he said to Jacquetta was, 'Think of Miss Haversham, for whom time has stopped.'

'Who's Miss Haversham?'

Oh dear, of course – the generation gap . . . 'I don't want to appear to stick up for grief,' he said, 'but it contains several components, remorse being one of them, and possibly relief another . . . It also contains a seed for future development, even happiness. If time is not deliberately stopped.'

'No, grief kills happiness by definition. Misery and happiness are opposites, like left and right.'

He said, 'If you are going anywhere, you may need both left and right. I wouldn't say the two were separable.'

She clutched his bare arm. 'Gosh, how you do argue!'

'Isn't it odd that we are well aware when we are miserable and yet unaware of happiness when we are happy? That is, unless attention is drawn to it.'

She asked, 'Would you say you are happy now?'

'Of course. I'm talking with you, aren't I? I'm enjoying your company, your good looks, your intelligence. If I were miserable, then I probably would not wish to talk. Even to you.' He saw she had no objection to flattery. 'But to go back to grief, wouldn't you agree that whereas happiness is an entirety, indivisible, grief – misery – has various components? We all know people who live with low-level misery all their lives. They qualify for a house in Disappointment Street. Yet they may be people of great fortitude. Always travelling in first gear, you might say. People, too, who are ever ready to pick a quarrel. People who grumble when it's cold and then grumble when it's hot.'

'Certainly we have customers like that,' Mujeed interposed, with a chuckle. He returned to the table briefly, to listen to their talk. 'I am patient with them. I consider such people are rewarded with bad luck, bad career moves, and so on.'

'Character is a bit of a mystery, like consciousness. Of course, luck plays its artful part.'

All this and more Jacquetta took aboard, although not without a certain argument in her own forceful way, enjoying the discussion. They sat on either side of their little round table, staring closely at each other, occasionally clutching one another in the vigour of argument. Mujeed was there at intervals, smiling, to intercede, although by now his clientele was increasing as shops and other institutions closed, and people came for a drink or a snack. Most of them seemed to be talking about the World Cup. Without arriving at any great agreement – let's say about religion – nevertheless Justin and Jacquetta became more fond of each other, because they lived real lives and because they argued with good humour and some wit. It seemed that both believed many people were too fearful to lead other than pallid lives from cradle to grave.

It was difficult afterwards to determine whether they had expressed this opinion or that, or whether it had merely been an unspoken assumption. Also, he found later, thinking over this long animated conversation, he occasionally romanticized, if not actually lied: for instance, in telling Jacquetta that as a boy he had lived by the sea – 'that great grey mysterious sea', he believed he had said – merely to emphasize a point. True he had, as a boy, visited the coast frequently. But it was not true to say he had lived by the sea. Of course, in conversation one spoke without premeditation. Often what emerged surprised one. If something was less than the truth, perhaps it was something one wished was true, even more than the truth itself.

Time faded by unnoticed under the cloudless sky, taking it easy outside the café. Abruptly, Justin remembered that he should have presented himself at Kate's house for an al fresco supper at seven. It was now almost eight. He could not understand how the time had slipped by so fast. Where had the time gone? Mujeed kindly phoned Kate on his mobile. He reported her to be vexed that Justin had not appeared.

'I'd better go,' Justin said, rising reluctantly. Jacquetta also got up and they kissed affectionately, more than once.

'Look, you better take Kate these flowers,' said Mujeed, offering up the very bunch of roses Justin had brought for Mujeed's wife earlier.

Justin made a grand gesture. 'No thanks, Mujeed, old pal. I'll fight it out – with bare fists if necessary!' Nevertheless, he left his friends rather reluctantly, to make his way slowly back up Osler Road. 'Walpole stinks, Walpole stinks,' the pigeons insisted. Not only had time passed unnoticed. He had been so involved in the conversation he had forgotten the need to pee.

# 14

## A Hint of Eternity

He washed his hands and combed his hair. As he stepped out of his front door, he was surprised to see Kate passing the house. It turned out she had been posting a letter in the nearby pillar box. She was furious with Justin. 'What do you mean, "you forgot"? How dare you forget? I had prepared a beautiful supper for us. It was all laid out on the patio – my surprise for you. Of course I have now eaten my supper – eaten it all, and all alone. And meanwhile I am planning never to see you ever again. I'll sell the bloody house and go and live in London.'

He poured out his apologies. He knew he was an awful chap. It was genetic, the bad blood of the Haydocks. He was constantly giving some of this blood to the hospitals, just to offload it. But he really loved her and always tried to do exactly what she wanted.

Besides, there was this woman who needed to interview him, very talkative, and so the time just overran. Really sorry, darling.

'Oh, so there was another woman, was there? That's what made you so late for your dinner date. I suppose this creature was pretty, was she?'

'Oh, Kate, it's true she excited my "amorous propensities" a bit, just a minuscule bit, but she means nothing to me. The whole affair was one of sentences, not sensuality.' By this time, they had entered Kate's drive and were at her front door, where roses fought spiraea for survival.

'I've a good mind not to let you in!'

'You've got a good mind and a good body too. Of course you'll let me in, because we love each other so much. I can see you have forgiven me already, haven't you, darling?'

Despite herself, Kate burst into laughter. 'Oh, I can't cope with you. You're awful!'

He put on a hangdog face. 'And not only awful. Also old and absent-minded.'

'And an absolute pain.'

'Yes, sorry, I forgot, and an absolute pain. But cute with it. I can't imagine why you are so nuts about me. Probably it's because I'm irresistible.'

'Unstable, you mean!'

Once they were in the house, he seized her and pressed her to him. He kissed her neck and her cheek and her hair. 'Oh, sweetheart, I'm crazy about you, bad temper and everything.'

'I'm mad about you, darling. Despite all your sly excuses. You're so handsome.' She squeezed his hand before backing away. 'I adore your misjudgements.'

So then they fell to kissing and feeling each other in the usual way and the usual places. She did not display her usual fervour. She had preserved a plate of food for Justin which included a slice of delicious salmon with horseradish sauce. He poured them both a glass of white wine. They toasted each other and drank.

'I don't know how I'd live without you, you lovely girl. You are the best thing that ever happened to me.'

'As you are to me. As I have told you before. I'm sorry I flew off the handle.'

'Oh, but you looked so captivating when you were doing it.' So peace was restored between them. They sat together on the garden seat. The way that days were now so long, so delectable, carried a hint of eternity with them; yet he could not but reflect on what Jacquetta had said: 'We all know people who live with low-level misery all their lives.' Justin and Kate were calm – becalmed. The beautiful neglected yellow rose at the bottom of the garden was flowering, simply to gratify itself.

'Thank heaven I don't suffer from hay fever any more. There's a high pollen count today. As an adolescent I would have been entirely incapacitated.'

'You're still an adolescent,' she said affectionately.

Saturday dawned. Kate had agreed to sleep in his bed with him. Her usual enthusiasm was muted – for which she pleaded jet lag. It was the day of the World Cup when the English team played Paraguay. Justin hoped England would win; it was an automatic response. But an imp within prompted him to wish that, after all the bullshit, Paraguay might get lucky. He saw much of the match, while dozing off in the second half. *The Times* got it about right the next day: ENGLAND STUTTERS TO VICTORY. Except that it was not 'England'. It was simply eleven well-trained, well-paid, young men who had never heard of Kafka or Kandinsky. While they had been playing and the crowds were roaring, Palestinian families were dying on a Mediterranean beach from Israeli shells. The triviality of Europe . . . He went down the garden with a pair of secateurs and cut one single bud from the neglected yellow rose. This he took indoors and put in a small vase.

*   *   *

161

Justin was depressed on Sunday. He woke to the sound of the church bells ringing. He wrote a postcard to Dave, making no mention of the visitor in the night; that might frighten the dear boy. As the days passed and the vividness of the incident faded, Justin began to believe that he had dreamed it. Maude was quiet; she had possibly relinquished her embrace of Islam. Kate had gone to London for a conference of the Aten Trust committee members. She hoped they might amalgamate with a larger and more prosperous charity. She said they were suffering from a cash crisis. As he made his way slowly downstairs, step by step, Justin thought, *I may not be able to do this much longer*. A thrill of fear and excitement ran through him at the thought of what would inevitably come to pass. His turds were almost black. Possibly an effect of the warfarin he was taking in increasing amounts.

One of the annoying things about death, he reflected, was that you would miss the absorbing serial story of what happened next to all the others, the people of Earth. A luckless lot, mainly, to be frank. England being on the whole more fortunate than most other nations, and hence inclined to indulge in frivolous pursuits, although its prisons were crammed to the eyeballs . . . He respected and loved Kate for her dedication to the encouragement and enabling of unwanted kids, the less fortunate – even if it was inconvenient for him. As he ate a bowl of cereal in his courtyard, under the sun umbrella, he listened to a bishop on the radio discussing the divisions remaining between the Church of England and the Roman Catholic Church. Clearly, these divisions were important to those involved, trivial though they might seem. It was something not unlike the divisions between Sunni and Shi'ite Muslims. Only much more polite. No grenades had actually been lobbed yet. Of course, it had once been different . . .

It was the roll of the dice. As congregations dwindled, there was pressure for the two sides, Protestant and Catholic, to stand shoulder to shoulder. Or knee to knee, as the case might be. Justin fought against his depression. But really, when you looked at the state of the world . . . A military chap was forecasting the decline of the West. China was rising grandly in the East. Immigrant groups would owe increasingly little allegiance to their host countries when mobile phones connected them to their families. Some Muslims had openly declared their wish to turn Britain into a Muslim country, with Sharia law and all. The sheer impertinence of it! Cheap flights and the Internet meant that these communities remained closely connected with their homelands, so that hope of assimilation was becoming ever more remote. More and more hooded women trailed behind their bearded men in Headington streets. At eight in the evening, Justin was mowing the lawn in the cool of the day. The phone rang. Kate was back from her committee. 'I'll come round,' he said.

Kate was wearing smart business clothes, which made her look all the more impressive. She kissed him at her door. 'I may have to go back to Cairo,' she said.

The shadows were lengthening. The birds sang under the street lamps. It was almost as hot as it had been at midday.

'What's the problem?' he asked as they went in.

'Would you like some coffee, Justin? And I've still got half a pineapple left.'

They sat on tall stools in her immaculate steel kitchen, looking out on Kate's chicken run. He was a little annoyed that she tucked a hand in his armpit just to help him on to the stool. He could have managed for himself. She said, 'The woman who runs the El Aiyat establishment has become ill and run off with all the funds – such funds as there were. I'll have to go and sort things out. It would be disastrous if the Centre was forced to close.'

'I'm sorry to hear this. Shall I come out with you? Maybe I could help. Or at least persuade someone to give you a slot on television.'

'No, it would be too hot for you.'

'A slot on telly would change the whole situation, moneywise.'

'It would be too hot for you. Honestly.' They looked at each other until Kate dropped her gaze. She sat with both elbows on the counter, sipping her coffee. She said, not looking at him, that she had a DVD she wanted to show him. He would see what the group did and the difficulties they faced.

'I'd like to see it,' Justin said, although he regarded it as rather a nuisance. They went to her snug living room, where carpets were white and furniture was mainly scarlet and a scarlet-and-white decor painting hung on one wall. A sweet slight aroma hung over the room, probably emanating from a white bowl of carnations. She had a wall TV screen. She posted the DVD into the slot of the machine and the screen lit.

'It's very amateur,' she warned him. A heavy bird took off from a corrugated-iron roof. Desert land spun, dissolving to a shot of a fan spinning in a building. There the artistic manner ceased and the camera fixed instead on the various participants of the El Aiyat Centre. Some of these dry-skinned young people exhibited what they were doing or making. Two boys were carving a wooden gun. Justin wondered if the shot reminded Kate of her two brothers, long grown and gone. A wizened boy held up a wooden panel on which he was painting in vivid colour a selection of fruits. An old lady in a sari balanced on a tremulous hand a delicate two-handled vase she had fashioned in the pottery class. Four women spread out an unfinished rug or counterpane they were weaving. A portly black woman with spectacles, wearing a blouse and a pair of khaki trousers, addressed the camera, speaking in perfect English.

'Here we are at peace with each other. We do not preach any religion. We forbid religion to be spoken of. What we worship here is collaboration. Also, the collaboration that work can bring. We are poor. At the El Aiyat Centre, this poverty brings us riches.'

A cheeky-faced girl said, 'Here we can learn to be a success. If I work hard I can be Queen of Egypt. Well, I mean, a politician at least, and get rich that way.'

A bent old man with a stick said, 'We have much sickness here.

164

Poverty brings much sickness. The waters of the Nile are more poisoned than formerly. Drink boiled water, I tell them, but do they listen? Then you can learn to mend a car here and that skill will help you to sustain a family.'

There followed a photographic tour of the main building and various outbuildings. 'You see – I don't wish to be prideful,' said Kate, 'but we are building a better, fairer world in our small way.'

Suddenly, the scene changed. Outside, on sparse land, an Arab rode a camel. 'Oh, this is where I sneaked a day's break,' Kate explained to Justin. 'Len Overton said I should see something of the wildlife of that part of the world.'

'Len Overton? Who's he?'

'Oh, you know Len Overton. He used to be a television chef. Then he took up travel and photography. He's very clever.'

'What age?'

'Oh, about my age. Watch this bit, Justin! This is our little trip.' A crescent moon shone. Day was about to descend abruptly into darkness, as the fire curtain falls in a theatre proscenium, with no twilight to linger in such latitudes. A brief glimpse of a tent. The woman sitting outside it wearing a bush hat was undoubtedly Kate. The shot was momentary, before focusing on movement beyond. Animals were jostling about. Sound came on abruptly, with noises of snorting and trampling. Now a bright light, a searchlight or something similar shone on the animals. The animals were zebra, a small herd. Eyes flashed green when they turned to look at the light source.

'They're about to go on their annual migration,' said Kate. 'Do you see what's disturbing them?' Now, more distantly, red eyes shone. The roving light revealed wild dogs, a pack of them, harassing the zebras. Occasionally, one of the zebra would perform a mock-charge, in an effort to chase the dogs away. The searchlight was attached to the roof of a Land Rover. The Land Rover drove nearer the zebra. Those animals snorted and kicked and finally galloped away. The wild dogs followed them. The DVD ended.

'That was so romantic,' said Kate. 'So close to raw nature. Next morning, we had to get back to the Centre.'

Justin tried to conceal how upset he felt. 'Did you share a tent with this Overton?'

She gave an artificial titter. 'There was only one tent available. If we had slept in the open, we would have been eaten alive by mosquitoes. This safari was some distance south of El Aiyat.'

He took refuge in pedantry, trying to escape suspicion of what had gone on in that tent. 'The shots of the zebras confirm what I was told about them. Did you notice that the animals on the outside of the pack were pure black, without white stripes?'

'What does that signify?' asked Kate, coldly.

'It's only recently – well, perhaps twenty years ago now – that an answer was found to a long-standing question, whether a zebra was a white animal with black stripes or a black animal with white stripes. The latter was found to be the case. The zebra is a black animal with white stripes.'

Kate showed signs of impatience but he pressed on with his exposition. 'Sometimes, the animals are born without white stripes. It's rotten luck for them. They are pushed to the outer ring of the herd. They are most likely to be attacked and least likely to find a mate. Owing to this colour prejudice, they lead very sad lives. You see the analogy with human life? The older you are, the less likely you are to find a mate.'

Kate said, 'It's not really an analogy, since you are supposed to have mated by the time you are old. Anyhow, what did you think of the work of the Aten Trust Centre?'

'Very good. It's a tribute to all your work through the years, Kate.'

'So it fucking well is!' she hissed in sudden spite, as if contradicting him.

Backing off, Justin said, 'There's a poem by Roy Campbell about zebras. How does it go? I've forgotten. I know it ends, "But round the herd the stallion wheels his flight, Mammal of beauty and delight, To roll his mare among the trampled lilies . . ." I always liked that last line.'

Her response was largely negative. 'Who's Roy Campbell, anyway?'

He sighed. 'A now-forgotten poet. Famous long ago.'

Kate made no answering comment. She rose and carried their cups over to the dishwasher. She spoke again in a while. 'You're feeling a bit sorry for yourself tonight, Justin, aren't you?'

# 15

## *Bangalore on the Line*

He made his way back up Scabbard Lane. Thoughts of the Pakistani girl came to him, silent as a night owl. He went out of his way to go down Ivy Lane and look at Righteous House and into the garden where Om Haldar – as he still thought of her – had spent some days of her fugitive life. The house itself was silent. A light burned behind curtains on the ground floor. A dimmer light burned behind blinds on the upper floor. Justin stood staring, waiting. Waiting for he knew not what. After a few minutes, he turned away and trudged back to No. 29. He unlocked his front door. He staggered into his house. He leant back against the inside of the door. The worst loss had been waiting for him in the hall. Maude's radio was playing softly in her bedroom upstairs.

He could not believe that his dearly beloved had made love with another man, had opened up her cosy little bolt hole to a virtual stranger. She had not said she had done that. She had, however, hinted at it. He could die. He wished he could die. Why had she shown him the DVD if she had wanted to keep the affair a secret? Of course, it was in the tropics . . . He leant where he was, back against the door, trying to think of the easiest way of killing himself. How could he blame her? He was not much catch. His legs were so bad, so prone to cramp, they could hardly make love in the usual way. And even with Viagra, he was not much of a man any more. Your penis shrinks when you are eighty, whether from overwork or whatever . . . Use it or lose it . . . Kate was still only in her sixties or early seventies. Why should she not have it off if the opportunity arose? Alone in the bush with those sodding animals buggering about outside, and this hearty young chap in the tent with her. After all, she worked with him. Besides, it was only a one-off. Why not take the chance if it arose? He should be glad for her. And in a way he was glad for her. She was an erotic woman. Yes, he was glad for her, but appallingly sorry for himself. Ah, and then all his stupid pedantry about whether those fucking animals were black or white. That was hardly likely to win her over . . . Perhaps he had made the same mistake with Janet, always too interested in abstracts. No wonder she had cleared off to Carlisle.

He really hated himself. Why on earth should any other person love him? He could kill that bloody TV chef, Overton . . . He went up to bed, swallowing two sleeping pills rather than one, hoping he might die painlessly in the night.

A light was flickering, shining on his face. Justin opened reluctant eyes. Last night, he had forgotten to draw the curtains. Now he was getting the full force of the early sun, shining through the apple trees, shining on his pillow. At least no horrible man had come banging at his door. He might have imagined it: a premonitory psycho-vision of Overton crashing into his life. Both nights and days were hot. People called them 'sticky'. Even Sian Williams on TV said it was 'sticky'. A big fan now operated from the top of Justin's chest of drawers. He liked its white noise throughout the night. The fan was one he had bought for his dear Janet, to ease her feverish last weeks of life.

He needed to relieve himself. He went barefoot downstairs in his pyjamas, holding his penis. Unlocking the back door, he stepped over to the choisya growing in a large china pot. It was five fifteen of a motionless morning. Birds sang under the street lamps. He pissed on the plant and into its soil. Choisya needed watering and there was a severe water shortage. 'Not much of a hose, I'm afraid,' he told the suffering plant. As the urine poured from his body, he thought how miserable he was. How could he face Kate again? Did she know that he knew? Did he know what he thought he knew? Why was he acting in this adolescent way?

How right that old blighter Thomas Hardy was in his poem about old age. How did it go? 'Mmm mmm . . . And shakes this fragile frame at eve, With throbbings of noontide.' Throbbings – yes, bang on, Hardy!

He went inside, where fallen rose petals had drifted in to strew themselves about the hall, creating a not unpleasant aspect of melancholy. This is what it would look like when he was gone. When the undertakers came in to collect the body. When neglect had already set up its stall. He absent-mindedly ate his usual bowl of cereal. He switched on TV but Sian Williams was evidently on holiday. He visualized her floating on a lilo, somewhere on a warm sea. Her substitute announced that in the World Cup, Italy had beaten Ghana by two goals to nil. Justin felt a vague regret that the Ghanaians had been unable to score at least one goal.

As he made his way back upstairs, step by slow step, he reminded himself that he was eighty. His father had died at the age of sixty-three. He himself should be long dead. He must not expect the joy of having a female companion to see him through his last years. Of course, he could take Kate some flowers. Or a bunch of condoms. Little good they would do. Or perhaps he should go

171

and see how Scalli was getting on. Silly woman. He lurked about the house in his socks. Old copies of the *TLS* could be gathered up and stuffed into a Somerfield's bag for the recycling people. His mail came through the front door. The usual junk mail, which followed the *TLSs* into the Somerfield bag without even being opened, and one letter in a blue envelope, addressed to him in what he thought was a woman's handwriting. It was a woman's handwriting. The letter came from an Amy Bresson, a name Justin did not at first recognize.

*Dear Jus,*

*You may or may not remember me but I certainly remember you and your good humour. I must tell you that I am now very old, and will be seventy-something next January. In the old days, women kept their ages secret. But when you get to seventy you start to boast about it. Anyhow, I write to tell you that my husband of many years, Edwin Colin Holderness, has died, aged eighty, or thereabouts. We had our good years and our bad. Recent years have been pretty chilly. But I feel sad now that the old devil has left this earthly sphere. His funeral is to be held at the local church here on Saturday next, 2.30. Could you come, please? It's short notice but you're about the only one of his old friends still alive. I would be grateful. I'll look after you and see you don't fall in the hole after him. Your dotty old friend, Amy (née Bresson, in case you have forgotten, as I expect you have)*

Slowly, a memory came back.

Not just of Amy but of the period in the eighties when they – his sort of people – seemed to shuttle between Berlin and Birmingham. A cheerful, carefree bunch, all involved in the media, mainly film or television. When the Beeb had lots of money to throw around . . . After a little mental work on the period, Justin remembered a time when he had been in bed with Amy in some hotel somewhere, possibly Geneva. She sported a lot of jet black hair. They were resting and drinking coffee when the phone rang by their bedside. Amy answered it. Edwin Holderness, a smart and rich young man, was on the line, stuttering somewhat, proposing marriage to Amy.

'Of course, darling, why not? Lovely!' she had said, hanging on to the first syllable of 'lovely'. 'How absolutely charming of you to think of it! We'll talk about it later. I'm busy just now' . . . Mumbling from the other end. 'I'm in the bath, dear. Speak to you later.'

Putting the phone down, she turned to Justin. 'I had to say yes, didn't I? Sorry to put you off your stroke, as it were . . . I bet you weren't ever going to propose!'

'I couldn't afford you, sweetie,' he had replied. He knew Edwin was something in the city: indeed in several cities, while his pa owned about half of Hereford. He could not help laughing at the memory. It cheered him greatly before his attention turned to the Kate situation. Kate and that sod Overton. Yes, that sod Overton. 'Oh well,' he told himself, 'the worm forgives the plough . . .' In fact, he had quite a few things he must do.

He let Scalli in and they drank tea together. She made a brief apology for her bad temper. 'Don't mention it, my dear Scalli. These things happen.' Actually, he could not remember for the moment what had happened, or for what she was apologizing. She wore a faded blouse, chinos and a pair of sandals, as usual. She complained about the heat. He remarked that it must be hotter than this in Syria.

Scalli ignored the remark. 'My family, they integrated to survive. How you think the new immigrants integrate? They can be always in touch with their families back home wherever it is because of the Internet and email and so forth. It's a big difference from before.'

'My apologies, Scalli, my dear. I was speaking loosely. And what you say about immigrants is entirely correct. Many don't bother to learn to speak English. But everything differs from what was . . .

Do any of the new wave of immigrants worship the great god Baal, do you think?'

She preferred to ignore that joke, if it was a joke. 'They are not individuals as we are. They are groups. They believe what others believe just because they believe it, because they believe in believing.'

'Will Baal punish them?' he asked, jokingly.

She shook her head and made a face. 'That is a Christian question. Punishment, always punishment. Baal simply looks after his own. He minds, like you say it, his own business.'

Justin put his mug down on the table. 'You know, Scalli, I am beginning to like your god Baal.'

She smiled and waved a hand in front of her face. 'Forget it! You don't condescend me. I go and I do the washings up.'

He could not let her get away with it. 'Oh and by the way, there are some dirty clothes for the wash, and some needing ironing.'

She turned in the doorway. 'You care only that I do the work, isn't it?'

Encouraged by what he regarded as a humorous remark, he said, 'You know, Scalli, I don't believe in any gods. I'm an intellectual of some kind or other. Your great god Baal is just a superstition really, isn't he?' The way her face changed astonished him. Suddenly she looked old and ugly. She took a step back towards him, bringing her hands out like claws before her.

'What you are telling of Baal?' She looked murderous.

'Well, no offence, but I was saying that Baal is like our God – just a – well, a superstition.'

She was spitting fury before he got to the end of his sentence. 'You say no defence? To say this about Baal and he can kill all don't-believers! Oh, such insults!'

Justin jumped up in alarm, as far as he was capable of jumping, and stood with his chair between him and the furious Scalli.

'I will no work for you more. Too much of insults! Bad things will now happen to you as a curse!'

'You may be right. They may have started. I'm due to go to a friend's funeral on Saturday.'

Scalli turned and rushed for the front door, ran through it and slammed the door behind her. The noise of it echoed through the house. 'Bloody loony!' he exclaimed. He was considerably shaken.

He determined to go down to the Greystoke Gallery to see this woman Hester's paintings. It would get Scalli's ridiculous curse out of his mind. And maybe thoughts of Kate in Overton's hairy little arms too. He liked abstract painting and had done so since the days of his youth, when he first encountered Kandinsky's late geometric compositions. He hated British topographical watercolours. All the same, it would be a bit of a sweat getting down to the bloody gallery. Oh go for it, man, don't fuss! And another thing he had been putting off was the question of the ruined answerphone. He could probably claim on that, on the insurance. He disliked ringing big companies. He was intimidated by long waits and the demands that he push button One, Two or Three. He generally disliked the type of music injected into his ear while waiting on such occasions. Once, his house had been insured by Royal. He could walk into their office in the Cornmarket, on the corner opposite Austin Reed, and pay with bank notes. But Royal had gone, taken over by another company, who had been taken over by a further company. Now he was insured by an organization called MORE TH<N. He disliked the introduction of something into a word masquerading as a letter, regarding it as a sign of deterioration in literacy. But they seemed nice enough. He nerved himself to dial Customer Services, whose address on the letterhead was Bristol.

Eventually, he got through to a human being who gave him a number he should ring to make a claim. The man spoke perfect English with a slight Indian accent and sounded so agreeable that Justin asked hesitantly if he could possibly have a discount on his house insurance because of his age. The other man asked him to wait a minute while he got someone to scrutinize the request. Justin hung on, feeling he might have to ring off because of a growing desire to pee. He was less than optimistic. There was the case of Barclay's Bank, who had suddenly ceased to allow him to buy travel insurance because he was over seventy-five. There were many similar examples of Ageism. He began to think he had been silly to ask his question. MORE TH<N were more than likely to put his insurance up. The smart English-Indian voice came back. Justin's present cover was £1,847.16 per year, or £153.93 per month by direct debit. MORE TH<N would reduce it to £1,308.49 per year, which was £109.04 per month.

Amazing! He was so delighted that this giant company would do something for him that he thanked the man effusively. So much for Scalli's curse! The man himself seemed pleased.

'Forgive my asking, but are you in Bangalore?'

'Yes, Mr Haydock, I am speaking to you from Bangalore.'

'A delightful city. I was there once.' They had been making a documentary series called *Wicked Cities*. 'How is your weather today?'

'It is actually very hot but our office is air-conditioned. How is your climate in England?'

'Today happens to be very hot, though it won't last. All my roses are in bloom.'

'Very beautiful. I also try to grow a rose against my house. This morning before I came to work I watched part of the World Cup.'

'Yes, I was sorry the Ghanaians did not win.'

'The Italians were the better team. Well, I must go, sir, and I wish you much happiness. I am glad to have talked with you.'

'Thank you, and many thanks for the Age Discount.' Seeing that not all conversation was unthought, he made his way towards a final remark. 'I wish you a long and happy life.' This humane concession made him feel radiant for a long while afterwards. What a nice bloke! To think the bloke's father had once been part of the British Empire . . .

\* \* \*

Once he was home, Justin rooted about in the drawers of his desk and dragged out a slender file. He really was getting old and doddery: he had forgotten his determination to write about the falsity of religion. He had made various notes, such as that there were forty million Americans with mental disorders. Ten million needed psychiatric help. In Britain, he had written that neurotic disorders abounded. Almost ten million people were mentally ill. Religion was involved, whether as cause or effect.

He had tried to link these figures with the Bible, without success. He had read the Bhagavad Gita, the Koran and the Old Testament. He preferred the Bhagavad Gita for its poetry and its wisdom, although much of it seemed crazy. He strongly disliked the Koran, with statements to which present-day Muslims still clung. 'Men have authority over women because God has made the one superior to the other.' The statement was doubly offensive to a country like Britain which, after all, had kept female slaves and in which the enfranchisement of women had taken place only a century previously. The Old Testament was a ragbag. Many of its stories concerned chaps like Jeremiah and Job having a bad time. God could be objectionable. On the whole the Old Testament seemed to suggest that life was tough: better toe the line. Jeremiah seems to have the right idea; when God has been a bit rough on him, he says, 'Pour out thy fury upon the heathen that know thee not!' The Koran relies on humourless repetition: 'God bears witness to all things.' Justin had then written in brackets *(We all know Jewish jokes, name a Muslim joke!)*.

Scanning these notes now, he wondered why the differences should matter – and to some, matter so much. These books were all three relics of a different and more primitive age. They had grown whiskers.

He wondered if he should take up the razor again.

# 16

## Real World Stuff

But before a new razor, a new answerphone, although he still had not visited the Greystoke Gallery; nor had his builders returned. Justin dealt with a small electronics firm in Harefields, just north of the Oxford ring road. He could never think why. He liked the small town atmosphere of Harefields. You never saw anyone about. He could remember when the area was just neglected orchard and wilderness. There had been a place where an old boy bred greyhounds. All gone. Swept away in the name of progress. The man in the electronics shop Justin dealt with previously was not there. Instead, Justin was served by an attractive young woman wearing a head scarf and spectacles. The spectacles were of a trendy oblong design. She wore an agreeably short denim skirt. How old was she? Twenty-one? Already getting on a bit. The shop had ordered the digital cordless phone Justin wanted. The girl gave a clear explanation of how easy it was to set up. As he paid with a credit card, he asked the girl casually what she did when she was not working in the shop.

'I'm not all that grabbed by working here,' she said, in an idle kind of voice. 'You don't see enough customers. Anyhow, mostly like you they're a tad ancient. Sorry, don't mean to be rude, but if I worked in a dress shop I'd have much more fun. People would be younger like.'

'So what do you do in your time off?'

'Oh, I got lots of friends. Us girls, we have lots of fun. We drink in some of the bars in Oxford, knock it back a bit . . . I can see you don't approve of that, eh?' She looked at him cheekily, head on one side. She had taken his money. She could afford to be cheeky.

He said, 'You must ask yourself that.' He was going to say, 'Every action has its consequences' but, for one thing, he disliked issuing preachments and for another – this suddenly struck him – it wasn't true. Many actions – many curses – were actually attended by no consequences. This occurred to him with the force of revelation. The girl was watching him, probably thinking him an old git who found difficulty in talking.

'I s'pose you are too old to have fun,' she said, not without a certain sympathy, touched by curiosity. 'No girl friends or nothing.'

He said with a half-smile, 'I don't get too drunk any more, if that's what you are implying. To me, the idea of "fun" seems dismally empty, but then – I grew up in wartime England. Life was pretty grim then.'

'Well it's not like that now. It's diff'rent.'

He sighed. 'I know, my dear. The pendulum swings. But the next generation may have to be more serious, with global warming – maybe with global freezing – and also a severe decline in the importance and prosperity of England. You know how India and China are rising in strength, don't you?'

180

'Whatever.' She smiled, showing good teeth, but looking blank. 'Oh well, better crack on . . .' She suddenly put a hand on his hand gripping the phone carton. 'Don't grudge us our happiness, grandad, just becoz we're young. You can't expect us to be miserable just becoz you had a crap time of it, can you?'

He laughed. 'Quite so. I just don't think your idea of having fun sounds much fun. But then – I'm old and grumpy.'

'Take care of yourself,' she shouted as he left the shop.

*Fuck*, he thought.

She was a pretty cool little chick, he told himself, striving for the demotic. But what when she gets beaten up in a drunken brawl? Or of course gets pregnant? It's all a matter of luck. Maybe she will meet a really nice Polish plumber . . . He read that things were so bad in Russia that there were more abortions than births. In 2004, at least 1.6 million women underwent abortions as against 1.5 million giving birth. You could bet there were not so many Polish plumbers going to Russia . . . At least this lady lived in a better country. Sighing, he thought how disgraceful it was that he, at his age, should have wanted to feel her breasts.

Justin felt oddly drained. Kate had deeply upset him. He drove back to the Headington car park. With an effort, making himself move, he extracted himself from the car. Going to the Queen's Bakery nearby, he bought a cheese-and-bacon pastry puff and a box of apple juice. He ate the puff in the car. It was delicious. The apple juice was as good as any he had ever tasted. When he had revived, he unpacked his purchase. It was a BT Freestyle 2500 Twin. It had an additional handset and charger. It looked splendid, he thought. He found it was made in China. After a light doze, he roused, without generating enough energy to leave the car park. He watched a tired but attractive blonde woman passing with a pushchair. He judged her to be just the sunny side of forty. She had bags of shopping with her, and was trying to control two young boys. The boys ran about madly. Their mother called to them and was patient. Her car was a Volkswagen. She stowed the shopping bags in the boot and then turned to order her two boys to climb into the back seats. They climbed in, still shouting and fooling about. The woman said something approving, which looked as if it might have been 'Well done'.

Her next move was to push the baby round to the passenger's seat in the front of the car. The child was smiling and complacent. She kissed its cheek before securing it to a baby seat. The empty pushchair was manoeuvred to the rear of the car, collapsed, and stowed away with the shopping. She brought the lid down with a slam, before climbing into the driving seat, backing the Volkswagen out of its parking spot and driving off.

Justin watched this manoeuvre with interest, admiring the good nature of the woman. He reflected that, with all her responsibilities, she had much that Om Haldar would envy. His thoughts drifted back to a shop full of women he had known in the East. Had it been in Singapore, or possibly Macao? It was so long ago; there were not enough months to calculate it. He had been drinking some exotic killer-liquid with a friend. Both had become extremely drunk. The friend had tottered off. Justin felt too exhausted to go far. He crossed a broad pedestrian walk to rest on a sea wall. There he lay, half-paralysed, staring down at the darkly glittering water. Out of the corner of his eye, he saw two men approaching him. One carried a knife. Although he realized they were probably coming to beat him up and rob him, he was unable to move. He thought in a dim way that he would jump up at the last moment, startling them and scaring them away.

A woman came running across the walkway, waving her arms and telling the men to clear off. She helped Justin to stand up, saying, 'Oh, what a state you are!' She was Chinese, large and strong. Supporting him, she guided him across the open space and into a building on the corner. She locked the door behind them.

'I'm all right,' said Justin.

'You not all ri'. You stay here. I shall put you into the bed.'

182

'Thanks for saving me. Gimme a kiss.'

'Stop it! Here, in this bed.' Her broad Chinese face was lit by her smile.

The bed was more like a cot, with bars. It stood in a room containing other beds. The woman made him climb into the cot. She was taking his shoes off when he fell into a heavy sleep.

A clatter of Cantonese roused him in the morning. Looking about, he saw several young Chinese women walking about in various stages of undress, some yawning, some scratching their hair. The room was dimly lit by bars of almost horizontal sunlight shining through slats in the blinds covering the windows. Two sleepy-looking young women met. Both wore only short vests and had flip-flops on their feet. They kissed and each poked a finger in the other's neat little vagina by way of additional greeting. An older woman, nursing a mug of tea, came and looked at Justin. She patted his shoulder. 'I give you tea in a minute,' she said. When the tea arrived it was brought by Justin's saviour of the previous night. Once she had handed him the mug, she climbed into the cot with him. She was wearing a shabby nightdress. She told him her name was Mai.

'You very bad boy,' Mai said, affectionately. 'How you feel now?'

He said he was fine and, as he sipped the sweet green tea, she started to play with his dormant organ. It immediately woke up. Her ingenuity was impressive. Justin groaned with pleasure and the two youngsters came to watch in a professional way. Mai heaved up her nightdress and lowered herself slowly, teasingly slowly, down on the stiff penis. She was a big comfortable woman. Her moon face smiled into his. He handed his mug to one of the onlookers and lay back to enjoy the action. When he was on the point of orgasm, Mai heaved herself off him and finished him off by hand. The young women tittered to see the semen fly.

'Is good for you, yes?' said Mai. She led him to a wash place and helped him wash under a tap. After he had towelled himself on a thin towel, leaving him damp, she made him dress and told him he would have to go. He thanked her again, as the two younger women waved him mischievously goodbye. Another older woman came from the rear quarters and shouted at them in a lazy fashion. Justin left and the door was closed behind him.

Many of Justin's working-class friends scorned prostitutes, although they used them. He recalled now, sitting in the car in the car park with the crumbs of the cheese-and-bacon puff still on his lap, how he had felt at the time, and still felt. He had been allowed into the secret lives of women, had understood something about them, and their tolerance. He had not offered to pay Mai, feeling that would have insulted her; maybe he should have paid her. But she had not exactly been behaving as that scorned thing, a Prostitute. The women were forced into their dubious trade. Their men had been killed somewhere during the war; they had to make a living through their resources – for which there was a steady demand from young men exiled far from home. Yet they had retained their human qualities. He had loved and respected women ever since. Even the girl in the electronics shop.

Ken saw that Justin was depressed and persuaded him to go to the cinema. They sat in the Phoenix and watched *United 93*.

Marie would not accompany them. Nor would Kate. Both women said the movie would be too brutal for them. Why had it been made, they asked? What was the purpose of such a film, where everyone got killed? But *United 93* was a kind of palimpsest of how the world was: not exactly the little world of Headington, but part of the violent death and vengeance overtaking the West: record of a tragic incident that one day had brought darkness at noon to thousands. The very act of entering the cinema, going from the bright world into the darkness became significant. The film was about just that. There had been a mock air operation in progress over New York, with 'the Bears' as imaginary enemy. So that when two planes were hijacked from Boston, the people in Air Traffic Control ask each other, 'Is this sim?'

'No. This is Real World,' is the reply. Indeed it is. United Flight 93 is delayed, so they actually see the Twin Towers of the Trade Center burning. The image, with its terrible science-fictional beauty, has been engraved in all minds. Even the capable personnel at Air Traffic Control cannot imagine the destruction could be the work of an enemy. But the passengers on the fatal flight are cool earlier. We see them in the airport at Newark, the usual calm jostle to check in goes on. The four terrorists who will commit the outrage mingle with the crowd. This is where the film has one striking advantage over all others. With a similar film – say with Jodie Foster's *Flight Path*, where a woman's small child is stolen aboard an airliner – you would not wish to know the end at the beginning. In *United 93*, you know the end at the beginning. You know these people are never going to make it to San Francisco. The casual prelude to flight acquires tension, even austerity. Then the passengers are boarding. One air hostess tells another, 'I want to get back to my babies.' It's just a casual remark. Everything is bland, banal, while outside New York starts burning in Real World time. There is no attempt, as in a customary disaster movie, to build up characters, to give them a back-story, no Shelley Winters, no Gene Hackman, to relate to. These are ordinary people playing ordinary people. As, in a different sense, the four hijackers are also playing ordinary people. Those of us sitting in the dark know what they don't: that they are all going to die. Of course we feel bad. To make us feel bad is one of the true objectives of art. So these followers of the Koran take over. The captain gets killed. It is a glimpse of his dead body that prompts some of the male passengers to do something. They are going to rush the hijackers, with courage born of desperation. But leading a rush down a narrow corridor between the aisles is almost doomed to failure. Passengers with mobiles whisper last words of love to their families far away on the ground. Two hijackers are killed in the fight. The plane goes down in the movie as in real life. All are killed. We do not see this. We already know this.

Justin and Ken came out of the cinema in silence. They went back to Ken's place and sat in the garden under the trees with a drink. Birds sang under the street lamps. Marie came and asked what the film was all about.

Justin once met Paul Greengrass at a benefit. It was wise to have an English director on such a film. He kept it all cool.

'He did a massive amount of research on this,' said Ken. 'But the scene of the final struggle had to be prompted by guesswork. You just believe it was that way, with the male passengers finally convinced they have to do something, despite the goon with a bomb strapped to him, guarding the cabin door. You ought to have seen it, Marie.'

'Why should I? What's the good of making such a film? And won't it make the Muslims even more vengeful?'

Justin said that the word 'Muslim' was never mentioned. Although the film did open with shots of the killers reading the Koran in their various hotel rooms.

'It sounds like a horrible film,' said Marie. 'I'm glad I didn't see it. What good can such a film do?'

At that moment, Kate arrived. The men arose and kissed her in welcome. Ken dragged up a garden chair, while Justin went and brought out another wine glass.

'Sorry to burst in,' said Kate. 'I got your note, Justin. What did you and Ken make of the movie?'

As Ken poured her a glass of Pinot Grigio, he said, '*United 93* is a masterly piece of film-making. The tension is conveyed to the audience as to the poor sods in the doomed plane. I'd say that to live through it is to understand the present day a little better.'

'It certainly has received good reviews everywhere. I don't know whether I could face it,' said Kate.

'One small detail that struck me,' said Justin, 'was that airlines still used metal knives and forks and spoons in those days. "In those days" – those days are now history. You only get plastic cutlery now.'

186

Marie said, 'But whatever is the point of making a movie of such a terrible disaster?'

Ken banged his fist on the garden table. 'You keep on asking that dopey question. The film marks an historic event, like the Bayeux Tapestry with Harold getting the arrow in his eye. After that day, after 9/11, our world was never going to be the same. Greengrass is aware of that. You glimpse the Twin Towers on fire from a distance, just for a moment, almost as if they are in quotation marks. This was the day of the birth of our present more dangerous age. Justin, I guess I'd better get us a gin and tonic, don't you reckon?'

'Great,' said Justin. 'That would be Real World stuff.'

He and Kate left together shortly. They had booked a table at the Café Noir for later. Ken and Marie could not join them. Some of Ken's many relations were due to arrive in an hour's time. As they walked along, Kate asked if she ought to see the film. Justin responded indifferently that it was up to her.

'You see, what I really feel is that any film that insults the Muslims should be banned.'

'This is a matter of history. These four Muslim fanatics killed a whole planeful of people, didn't they?'

'As far as I can see, it's not history. It's fiction dressed as real, but no one knows what went on in that plane.'

'Kate, it's an intelligent reconstruction. The central fact is that the Muslims got aboard that flight and in consequence everyone was killed.'

She made a moue of disgust. 'You say "The Muslims"? Only four of them, you know.'

He reminded her that the British police had just raided and searched a house, based on a piece of evidence that proved false. Some Muslims had been suspected of making a terror weapon of some sort, but nothing incriminating had been found. In response to this raid, a group of Muslims held a peaceful protest in London outside the House of Commons. The head of the police force had come and apologized to the gathering for the police error. The Prime Minister also spoke to them. The group dispersed, still dissatisfied. But supposing roles were reversed. Supposing a group of British Christians had protested outside a mosque in Tehran. They would have been killed. The mob would have cheered their deaths.

'You don't know that,' said Kate. 'You're just guessing. You are prejudiced. I'll get us some coffee to calm us down before we go any further.' She went briskly down the hall into her kitchen. Justin followed.

'I don't want any argument,' she said. 'You're prejudiced, I know.' She filled the kettle a careful half-full, so as not to waste water or energy.

'Kate, darling, I have two concerns here which I hope you can understand. The first is about the brutish side of human nature. Given fertile ground, that brute element breaks out and overwhelms us. You know what I'm talking about. Hitler's Germany, where a civilized country turned in short order into a fascist state, where cruelty was encouraged. The liberation of India from the Empire, which turned into carnage between Hindu and Muslim; the corruption of Russia under Lenin and Stalin.'

'If you're getting into religion, just remember Hitler was an atheist.'

'My second concern is about the tide of history. Maybe we are witnessing that old *Untergang des Abendlandes*. Because of our present folly, our self-indulgence – yes, and our brutishness with the unwarranted invasion of Iraq – all that, our beloved country may be overcome by a tide of historic process.'

'How you love drama!'

'How I hate cruelty!'

The kettle was boiling, a smart metal cordless kettle. She poured boiling water on the coffee grains of two cups, frowning as she did so.

'You're being old-fashioned, Justin – all this moralizing. Things are getting better. I keep thinking, your father was born in the nineteenth century.' Her words hurt as intended.

'So what difference does that make to the argument?' She took a bottle of milk from the fridge and poured milk sparingly into each mug while he struggled to find a better answer.

'The Aten Trust,' she said. 'That's one way in which we repay debts and fashion relationships between races and religions.'

He was annoyed to hear her Trust mentioned. 'Okay, you are doing astonishing work. You help all sorts of kids to better themselves. But it's a flimsy barrier against the tide of history.'

'I am returning to El Aiyat on Tuesday next,' she said, without looking at him. 'I was going to tell you.'

# 17

## A Funeral for Old Holderness

Justin was walking down Old High Street when a car went by. A small boy was hanging out of one of the rear windows.

'Old man!' he yelled out in derision.

'War hero!' Justin shouted back. 'You little squirt!' But the car was past. He shook his fist at it. That was the sort of thing he regarded as brutish. Minor brutishness. It could grow. He was feeling dark and nasty, feeling that the world was dark and nasty too. Possibly warfarin was having an adverse effect – although if warfarin was keeping him alive, then what could an adverse effect do? His legs were paining him and because his legs hurt his back also hurt. He forced his thoughts to other things. In the World Cup, brilliant Argentina had beaten Serbia and Montenegro six–nil. Justin supported the underdog, though not with much hope in this instance. Serbia was in any case in trouble. Montenegro had recently voted to separate from Serbia and seek its own destiny – meaning tourism, with the Montenegrin coastline as the chief attraction. Serbia possessed no coastline. Justin remembered the shock of driving from Croatia, crossing the Danube, and being confronted everywhere by forbidding Cyrillic. Nevertheless, the BBC made a half-hour programme on Serbia's little-known art treasures, their well-maintained Byzantine churches, dotted throughout that green land. But BBC governors canned the programme. Justin never discovered why. Serbia sheltered some villains accused of genocide and would not yield them up to the courts in The Hague. That might be an explanation: not a very good one.

Having crossed the main road, Justin walked down Latimer Road to the St Luke's Hospital – one of Headington's ever-increasing cluster of hospitals. This was a pleasantly quiet hospital, dedicated to foot and leg problems. He went straight to the toilet. The diuretic pills certainly worked, yet seemed hardly to reduce his weight. As he pissed, he contemplated compiling a guide to hospital toilets. He liked them. Many now operated a press-lever soap machine yielding a fragrant antiseptic soap. It looked much like semen but smelt better.

He saw Mr Cooke, another of the expert consultants he had recently encountered, an expert replete with whiskers and spectacles and a reassuring presence. Yes, his feet were very bad. His arches had collapsed. He must see another expert who would prescribe a tight-fitting stocking for a sort of mechanical support. It appeared he had eczema on his legs.

He re-entered the sunshine of the quiet road. Birds sang under the street lamps. He took all these matters in what had once been his stride. Stoicism had much to commend it. He wondered how he would manage when Kate was away. Of course, there was always Wendy. But he would be miserable without Kate. Dreams of the Greek island of Aegina and his favourite small hotel filtered back into his mind. Back home, he had a swift pee. The flower from the neglected yellow rose, in a vase on his mantelpiece, had withered and died. 'They don't last.'

He switched on the TV in time to see the Queen entering the Palace of Westminster for a service of thanksgiving. Justin felt no patience for the entire religious rigmarole, but he had a soft spot for the Queen. Astonishingly, she quoted Groucho Marx in her speech: 'You can achieve old age if you live long enough.' Something like that . . . Perhaps not sounding quite so funny, coming from cigar-free lips. After all, the Queen was not looking too bad, and she was Justin's age. Would that little bastard in the car yell out 'Old woman!' if he saw Her Majesty? Probably. Well, by the time the little bastard was seventeen, he would most likely be behind bars.

His feet were obstinately remaining painful. He was forced to admit to himself that he was feeling ropey. Slicing an orange in two, he squeezed the halves in a squeezer of antique design. How closely orange juice resembled urine. Only by tasting them could you tell the difference. He considered that really he had passed enough urine to last a lifetime.

As he kicked his shoes off and sipped the orange juice, he thought about his old mother. She had died twenty years ago. Sometimes he liked to pretend to himself that she was not dead, that perhaps he would meet her in Windmill Road, her stout figure – she admitted she was stout – coming towards him, wearing a light coat. How wonderful to see her again – his dear mother!

'Hello, Mum! Fancy seeing you! I'm bowled over. Where have you been all this time?'

'Hello, dear! My, how you've grown! I like the moustache.' She spoke in her usual cheery way, showing no surprise at their meeting.

'But where have you been, Mum? I've missed you so much, I can't tell you.'

'I took a house in Church Stretton. But then I moved to a flat in Yarmouth. I always liked Yarmouth, but I couldn't stand the cold east wind in winter. I've now got a cottage in Derbyshire, overlooking the lake. I meant to send you a card.'

'Golly, Mum, it's been twenty years. I quite thought you were dead.' She gave him her smile, which was not quite a beam, always with something of a question playing about her lips. He was so moved to see it and recognize it.

'I'm pretty spry for my age, though "I says it as shouldn't" . . .' He remembered her habit of quoting other people's slang. Tears of happiness shone in his eyes.

'My house is just down the street, Mum. I think you'll like the garden. Come and have a sit down and a coffee with me, and we'll talk about old times. How we used to laugh . . .'

'I can't, dear, really. I'm in a bit of a hurry. Some other time perhaps.'

He stood and watched her until she turned the corner. He was almost unable to bear the weight of his grief.

Justin pushed that rusty old wheelbarrow, his mind, on to more cheerful things. Tomorrow was the day for the funeral of Edwin Colin Holderness. He had better be there. He would have to look out a suit. And a black tie. First, though, a sit down. He slumped in his favourite armchair, picked up the *TLS* and began to read a review of a book called *Between Genius and Genocide*. He fell asleep somewhere in the second sentence . . . 'The Great Dream was a wild success, far beyond anyone's imagining' . . . 'He cried almost constantly, unlike his sister, and yet he flew over streets with great ease, and composed speeches that everyone applauded. All were persuaded to wear scarlet slippers.' He awoke, to search for those strange sentences. They did not exist. He had imagined them – yet they had been clear on an imaginary page.

\* \* \*

194

The funeral service for Edwin Colin Holderness was held in the church of Gloaming Magna, a church buried deep under layers of ivy, deep in the Somerset countryside. The afternoon sun shed a lemony light over the building; it resembled a cast-off from a Samuel Palmer painting. A bugger to get there, as Justin said. At least Kate drove him all the way. They sat in the rear pews, where woodworm had been at their pious work, generation after generation, amid the prayer books. The vicar, old and stooped, was the Reverend Roger Rossiter, dressed in the regulation white-and-black robes of his kind. His eyes, sandbagged round with puffy flesh, looked ever upward as if for inspiration or angels.

'You are all welcome to this humble seat of worship, this outhouse of God, to bid our dear friend and brother, Edwin Holderness, a final farewell.' As the vicar paused for piety's sake, Justin conceded that yes, there were farewells that were not final. But not in this case, one hoped.

'Edwin's visits to worship in our church were rare indeed, but one likes to think that we were always in his heart, and to know that we were a haven and a refuge here whenever needed.'

'Like a refuge from solicitors?' Justin whispered in Kate's ear. She hushed him with a gesture, smiling.

'Edwin was a generous man at heart, despite his many faults.' The gaze went up to the ancient beams overhead. 'He was one who liked to kick amongst the pricks. At one time, when our bells required to be re-hung, he sent me a cheque for fifty pounds, with an accompanying note saying that he considered himself a member of the congregation. We do indeed all value our members . . .' He paused because a ghost of a whisper of laughter had shivered through those assembled. '. . . although we were sorry when the cheque proved uncashable. We had to conclude that Edwin had financial problems. But how much more terrible than financial problems are spiritual problems!

'Supposing you were in a field near here and found yourself

195

being charged at by both a bull and a ram. Would you not run more rapidly from the bull, no matter how angry the ram might appear? You will all recall the parable Jesus tells about the butler who had only two coins to his name. In the road one day he met a poor beggar who also had only two coins to his name. They talked sympathetically, agreeing that a man who had four coins to his name would indeed be rich. So they decided to toss for it, and the loser would hand over his two coins to the other man.

'So they tossed for it and the butler won. But instead of handing over his two coins, the beggar struck the butler and took away his two coins. And as the butler lay there on the ground, watching the beggar making off with his wealth, he said to himself, "So there goes the one with the spiritual problems." How true that is, how very true, even today. The Chancellor may be with the man who has financial problems, but God is with those who suffer from spiritual problems.

'Our dear Edwin is beyond all that now, so may I remind you as we leave this place of rest that there is a collecting box by the door, needy like the butler, and God be with you.'

The organist started to play. The tune was 'Always Look on the Bright Side'. All the congregation joined in, singing heartily. After the burial, the reception was held only a mile away, in the mansion of the wealthy Holderness widow, a member of the congregation. Everyone was in a good mood. Witnessing the Holderness coffin go down into the earth had done nothing to quench that mood. Indeed, it gave the congregation a feeling of superiority, in that they, however decrepit they might be, were still above ground and looking forward to some champagne. Unlike poor old departed Edwin, already starting to smell a little high.

They had hardly joined the crowd about the bar when a man called Kate Standish's name. He was a senior member of the Aten Trust, and one of its more generous benefactors. They fell into rapt conversation; there was a question of whether helpers from the UK should or should not learn one hundred basic words of Arabic before going to Egypt. Justin drifted quietly away. At first, he was content to wander among the genial throng, exchanging a word occasionally with old acquaintances, catching fragments of others' conversation.

'L.E.G. Ames was England's best wicket-keeper ever. And, what's more, he hit a century against Australia. The only man to do it.'

'Didn't Len Hutton—'

'Hutton wasn't a wicket-keeper, old man!'

'They were starving in Malta during one stage of the war and under constant bombardment by the Luftwaffe. Some Maltese broke into underground cloisters in which the Ottomans had stored grain centuries earlier. It was still perfectly fine – kept perfectly – and they made bread with it.'

'Here's one about the Last Supper. Jesus catches Saint Matthew feeling up Mary Magdalen, and Jesus says, "You lucky blighter. Whenever I get my hand on it, it heals up . . ."'

'He barged into me in the pub. I spilt most of my beer. Of course, he apologized profusely. I said to him, "What do you do?" And he said, "I'm in logistics." "What the hell does that mean?" I asked him. "I'm a lorry-driver," he said.'

'I believe some French chappie coined the term "Industrial Revolution" in the – oh, the 1830s. All Toynbee did was to bring the phrase into circulation much later.'

'Billy Batskin? Silly old sod. He's overweight, overpaid and over the hill.'

'—But when you get cancer of the testicles, you know, they have your balls off.'

'Quite agree. I was always suspicious of her. She could remember her VAT number. Bet you never met anyone who could do that!'

Justin bumped into a French friend, Philippe Lafont, and asked him what he was doing in England. Philippe was as ever, elegant, clean-shaven, with small and nicely controlled mannerisms; he had aged considerably since they last met – although he was to prove to be as garrulous as ever.

'I am a representative of the EU Advisory Council in Brussels, as perhaps you will recall, but I am in England to observe the national mind, which I find – have always found – different from the French common mind. If I may use that phrase.'

Smiling, Justin said, 'I didn't know we had a common mind.'

'Oh yes, you have indeed, though it may be masked by some class differences. But you, my dear friend, are a sound representative of it. After all these years we have gone through, you still have a hangover from the days of Empire. That may be why you are so keen to ally yourselves with the USA and their new empire, as I see it. So a weary stoicism is cultivated – cultivated, I must say, with the herb of humour – a stoicism which largely precludes much interest in artistic endeavour. Hence the British madness for football, which is an enemy of art as I understand the term.'

Justin responded that there were elements in Philippe's analysis he was forced to accept. He then asked for Philippe's diagnosis of his own country's 'common mind'.

'Frankly, my dear friend, it is rather more severe than in the case for England. Under the surface, we are deeply divided. I can accuse your people of reliving constantly the Nazi war on television, but our historic heritage is more adverse. The first great *guerre mondiale* was fought out on French soil, while in the second *guerre mondiale* we were defeated and invaded by the enemy, Germany – now incidentally our great political friend. But scars remain, as we witness in the case of our President. Well – at least we breed intelligent villains. And we still have some philosophers, which you lack. But the common mind is defensive, greedy, self-absorbed.'

'And you have a large Muslim population.'

'As do you, although not so large, and you make a great

effort, as I perceive it, to draw them into society, which you will never succeed in doing. The Muslim, he does not easily unify. What is the saying you have about driving a horse into the water but it refuses to drink?' He made a small gesture and smiled at his own ignorance. Suddenly another thought occurred to him, so that he touched Justin's cuff, as if to detain him.

'The Jews are invaluable in Britain. They are guardians of what culture you have. You should appreciate them more.'

'No, no,' said Justin. 'That would be to mark them out. Let them be. Who, these days, knows or cares who is or is not a Jew?'

'Ah!' Another little gesture, and with a gentle guiding hand on the small of Justin's back, he led him to a quieter part of the hall. 'Perfectly correct. You know of course the example we have of the Spanish disaster, some centuries past. Of course, every country has its disasters. Indeed, some such as Russia, are in permanent disaster. But Spain—'

'I know what you are going to say, Philippe. The Spanish Inquisition—'

'Yes, but that is something of a joke in England, thanks to your Monty Python, whereas we in France take it seriously. Anyhow, the point is that the Spanish Inquisition in the late fifteenth century was responsible of the torture, killing—'

'Or else kicking out of the Jews, am I correct?'

'It was Torquemada, confessor to Queen Isobela, who—'

'And wasn't Torquemada himself a—'

'And so Spain went into decline for at least two centuries, because it had been the Jews alone who—'

'Yes, who actually understood how to manage the economy. Yes, why are you so interested, Philippe?'

'My grandfather on my father's side was an Hassidic, who fled from Poland to France in the early twentieth century.'

Justin patted Philippe's back. 'Congratulations on his survival. Let's go and have a drink, eh?'

'That is another item which mists your common mind. But yes, on this occasion, yes, *merci*!'

An hour later, Justin parted company with Philippe and was thinking of linking up with Kate and going home. He found the recently widowed Mrs Holderness seated in a rear room, where one wall was lined with shelves holding her collection of Sèvres china. Long glass doors overlooked the garden. The garden looked extremely formal and boring.

'I'm surprised to find you alone, Amy dear.' She seemed to be engaged in rubbing her nose, gently but persistently. Amy Bresson, as she had been in the old days, sprawled on a black leather sofa. She was known to claim that she was 'lost somewhere in the mid-seventies', as if in an enchanted forest. She was dressed on this occasion as she had always dressed, when she dressed at all, in black and white: tight black trousers, white starched blouse. For the occasion of her husband's funeral, she wore immense silver earrings, with what closely resembled a diamond necklace round her scraggy neck. One arm was resting on the top cushion, its delicate hand dangling over the rear of the sofa. She was being the sleek Brazilian jaguar of Eliot's poem. But no arboreal gloom showed in her smile for Justin.

'Hello, darling. I wondered if you'd show up. There was someone here. I can hear him talking . . . Or perhaps it's this tin thing I have.'

'Tinnitus?'

'I think he said his name was Tracklement . . . I saw you chatting with that charming Frenchman, but dared not interrupt. You looked so darned serious. I'm exhausted. I'll be glad when they all hop it.'

His legs ached. He seated himself gingerly by what was roughly speaking her waistline. 'Sorry about Edwin, darling. Gone but not yet forgotten . . .'

She sighed deeply. 'It was time for him to go. You know, he was falling apart. He spent his last months sorting out his stamp collection.'

'Really? I didn't know he collected stamps.'

'Don't sound so shocked. There's nothing rude about collecting stamps, is there? If only there was . . . He started the collection when he was a boy. It's not like filthy photos. There aren't any filthy stamps, I believe. Which reminds me. I expected Guy Fitzgerald to show up for the funeral. You know him, don't you? He lives near you. He's a second cousin.'

'Last time I saw Guy was in a bank. He'd just come out of a police station.'

'Good lord, which is worse? I could never stand his wife. Deirdre? We used to call her Dismal Deirdre. What's he done?'

'Nothing really. They let an Indian girl stay in their summer-house and she's done a disappearing act.'

'How was Guy involved?'

'It was nothing to do with Guy.'

'So why didn't he show up today, the sod?'

He was studying Amy's face. Amy wore rimless glasses these days. Her cheeks had sunk, giving her cheekbones additional prominence. Her complexion was poor, and there were wrinkles round her mouth. Justin calculated that she must be at least eighty-five, so she had lasted well, was still quite attractive in his eyes, although memory undoubtedly played its part.

Noting his scrutiny, she said, 'What was voluptuous is now bony. When I think of the old days – two gins and I was anybody's . . . How can I ride any more? I've sold off all my horses. Except for a pony that Beata rides occasionally. She looks after me.'

Beata was one of Amy's daughters. 'A thorough nuisance, actually . . .' Her thoughts wandered. 'How's that weird son of yours? David?'

'He's okay . . . Why are you alone here now, Amy? Why are

201

there not people round you, trying to console you, or whatever they do in these sorrowful circs?'

She made a sort of rotary movement with a thin left hand. 'I may have driven them off. I remember I talked about Alfred Munnings.'

'Alfred Munnings!?'

'No. No, we used to dance to his music. Whatever was his name? Before Victor Sylvester. They were too young to remember . . . I know it began with an M.' More silence, with some faint mutterings. She chuckled. 'Do you remember Lyons Corner Houses?' Then, 'I think I'm thinking of Henry Hall.'

'I seem to remember you had a place in Italy.'

'Oh, Edwin's shagpad . . .' For the first time she stirred herself to show a little emotion. 'How I hate Turin! I need some orange juice. Where are the bloody servants? Yes, we served the palazzo. I mean sold. We sold the palazzo. Not that I'm in any way broke. You know Edwin made a fortune from his dealings with Gasprom . . . Siberian gas – I ask you! Siberian gas . . .' The concept afforded her amusement still.

'I've got a cleaning woman – if I've still got her – who believes in the long-defunct god Baal.' He hoped she might laugh, but the remark was lost on Amy. He tried another tack. 'You're still at the Hall, then?'

'I'm too old to leave Gloaming.' Amy sighed and fell silent. Justin waited patiently. She said in a low voice, 'Gloaming Hall's still here: it's the old England that's gone.' Another silence, shorter this time. 'You can come and stay if you like. As long as you don't get up to anything. Fetch a servant, will you? – Be a dear! I need some orange juice. I've got to take my four o'clock pill. It's five already.'

He got to his feet. Looking down at her, he said with affection, 'You don't seem too upset that Edwin's gone, I'm glad to say.'

Amy waved a lackadaisical left hand. 'When you reach my age, you will find you don't get upset. It's bad for you. Some things die before others . . .'

As he was leaving the room to find a servant, he heard her saying, 'Besides he had become a bit of a nuisance. Honestly speaking.'

# 18

## *Preparing for the Tropics*

Morning light filtered through the curtains. On the flimsy fabric, fluttering leaves of trees imposed their shadow patterns. Distantly, church bells rang their traditional peal. 'Old Barney', 'Tristan 'Foredeck', 'Treble Threefold'. It was easy, lying in bed in a hypnoid state, to think up names for the various peals. The thing was standing close to the bed. It had a long animal face but stood upright, holding a spear. It wore tattered robes, once red, now faded. Seeing that Justin was looking, it curled back its lips to show its teeth in a wicked smile.

'Oh God, you don't really exist, do you?' said Justin in what he regretted was a mere whisper. At the mention of the name of God, it began to disappear, still standing, still smiling. The ordinary world reappeared. Justin blinked his eyes a good deal. The filtered sunlight illuminated a patch of carpet, across which a woodlouse slowly laboured. Birds sang under the street lamps. A fly buzzed intermittently, its single brain cell unable to distinguish the way out through solid glass. Justin roused and decided he was pretty well awake. Of course he felt awful. He was beginning to see things. He wondered if Scalli was working some kind of ghastly magic on him. He turned over under the duvet. On the pillow next to his, locks of dyed black hair curled like the pattern of an unfolding fern. Kate's face could not be seen, being buried between pillow and duvet. He looked at what was visible with love for all that was invisible. Of course, he could creep out of the room and get them both mugs of tea. But the bed creaked when he moved. He sat there, hesitating. His legs hurt. His bowels felt as if they had a brick in them. And he suspected an ingrowing toenail on his right big toe. And to be honest he was afraid. It could be – and in a way he hoped it could be – that he was suffering hallucinations.

He recollected that as he was coming back from Edwin's funeral, walking down the road, he found that blighter Hughes sitting on the old milestone that said 'Oxford 4 miles'.

'I was watchin' you,' said Hughes, as Justin was about to pass. 'All dressed up, like you owned the place.'

'I own this suit but not this place. Don't be so rude. I was showing a bit of fortitude – you have to when you get to my age.'

'Age don't make you dress up like that.'

'Oh, clear off!' He had had a bit too much to drink.

And Hughes had replied, 'I ain't going. I just bought this here milestone.' It was, in its way, fairly amusing.

Kate turned, half buried in the pillow. Her face was exposed, eyes closed. A sigh escaped her lips. How fine were her eyebrows, her eyelashes, how lovely the shape of her face. A hand surfaced from the depths and rubbed that face. Her eyes opened. She smiled at him as he sat there. 'Mmm,' she said. The eyes closed again. He kissed the warm hand. It withdrew.

'Kate,' he said, speaking quietly, almost hoping she would not hear what he said. 'Of all the women I have known, there has been none like you. There is a quality to you, compounded perhaps of contraries, of sorrow and mirth – all that you have been through – losing your brothers and all that – what you deeply understand and what you don't – you are adult, even sternly adult, with all sorts of judgements of behaviour which fly over my head, and yet the child is there too, showing itself in a proper amazement at dawn, dogs, daisies and – oh, Dutchmen. Disestablishmentarianism. You are amusing and easily amused. You have a conscience and a nice pair of tits. Over all, you are the most wonderful and complex person I ever knew. And what's more you seem to love me almost as much as I love you!' All this poured from him until he was chuckling.

She laughed too, and propped up her head with one elbow digging into the pillow. 'What brought that on? You're looking rather pale, aren't you?'

He sighed and pulled a face. 'Impotence, I suppose. Hangover certainly. Not indifference, no. But just the thought that these days it's such a labour to get it up. And although it's a joy to be in you . . . I don't know. Something has departed from me. Only to be expected, no doubt. Instead of a screw, all I can offer is a mug of tea. The position is less ridiculous. Perhaps the pleasure rather less momentary.'

She placed the warm scented hand on his cheek. 'The passage of time, darling . . . The galloping of the years. Comes to us all.'

'I accept that. If I think about it, I believe I really don't much mind. It's something Amy said yesterday – "When you reach my age, you don't get upset", or words to that effect. I mind for your sake, though.' He thought about it. 'Perhaps that's why people hate old people. Like robots, they don't have sex. And yet the subject itself still holds the same interest.'

'You were okay last week,' she said. 'Oh, sod it, I'll go down and get us some bloody tea. You stay where you are.' And in something like anger, she flung back her duvet and slid out of bed. She was wearing her sky-blue pyjamas, embroidered with swallows here and there. Justin wondered if it was by accident or design that one bird appeared about to fly up Kate's behind. The bumologist would have been interested.

'Another thing Amy said was, "What was voluptuous is now bony". Don't you find that comic?' But Kate did not hear. She had left the room. Justin climbed from his side of the bed, avoiding the spot where the threatening illusion had stood, went into the shower room and enjoyed a long pee. Looking down at his diminished sexual organ, he thought, *That's about all you're able to pass these days – urine. Remember semen, you little prick?* He then swallowed two of the diuretic pills he had been prescribed. He pronounced their names aloud, 'furosemide', and then, with a burst of apocopy, 'spironofuckinglactone'. He felt depressed. It was proving more difficult that he had expected to face his own decline.

'So this is what our relationship has come to,' Kate said. She put the mugs down so hard that tea slopped over on the table. Then she softened. 'Justin, you know I'm really sorry. I do love you but I have to go to El Aiyat.'

Downstairs, they found that Maude had already tackled half a round of toast and retired to bed again, leaving only a semi-devoured crust behind. They ate a little cold ham for breakfast – no eggs and bacon this time – followed by toast and marmalade. Kate turned on the television. A hundred English fans had been arrested in Stuttgart during the night. Some of them had been throwing chairs at passersby.

'Nothing like sport to bring nations together,' Kate commented. 'England play Ecuador tomorrow.'

'Don't say that! Eleven young English men play eleven young Ecuadorians tomorrow. I am just as much England as they are.'

'Oh, come on,' Kate said impatiently. 'What have you got against them?'

'Nothing. Only sorrow that, in the nature of things, they will find all too soon that what they now take for granted will have gone with the wind.'

When Kate had left, Justin walked round his garden with a pair of secateurs. The lovely kolkwitzia hedge was almost at the end of its flowering. Roses in bloom still covered the walls of his house. The syringa with its sweet scents was out. He felt dragged down by sorrow. To everything there was a season. It was not inappropriate that he could hardly achieve an orgasm. As the wise old pessimist of Ecclesiastes said, 'The almond tree shall flourish, and the grasshopper shall be a burden, and desire shall fail; because man goeth to his long home.' He accepted all that, had no quarrel with it. Indeed, there was even a faint sense of excitement that he was moving into unknown territory, the chilly tropospheres of old age. Only the thought that Kate was going back to Egypt saddened him.

Ken came over to have a chat, and they sat under the sun brolly in the courtyard, drinking a cool Pinot Grigio. Despite the heat, Ken wore a T-shirt with a pullover over the shirt. He was excited by a discovery apparently made by Adam Hart-Davis, an endearing and eccentric character who frequently appeared on TV to reveal new aspects of various matters. According to Ken, this time Hart-Davis had been looking into Stonehenge and the alignment of its stones. He found that the main lode stones did not – as had long been believed – point to the spot where the sun rose at dawn on the summer solstice. Instead, they indicated the spot where the sun sank at the winter solstice. Thousands of present-day people gathered at Stonehenge every year and had not, it seemed, noticed this remarkable discrepancy.

'If Hart-Davis is correct,' said Ken, 'it makes perfect sense. The people of that distant age would be concerned that the sun was going to dwindle and disappear for ever.'

'Profound anxiety, you might imagine.'

'Allied maybe with religious fear.'

'A punitive measure by whatever gods they obeyed? Or failed

209

to obey. And to survive the winters in those days must have been a challenge.'

Ken took a swig from his glass. 'I may have some details wrong. The annoying thing is that on TV you can't turn back two pages to re-read what he just said.'

'Still, if you have the equipment you could see the programme again on the BBC website.'

They discussed this Stonehenge discovery for some while. They found it striking that thousands of people celebrated Midsummer's Day at Stonehenge and were happy under the misapprehension. After all, not many people would turn up at sunset on the winter solstice. Not since electricity had been harnessed and houses basked in central heating. Not for generations. Not since Michael Faraday.

'Let's go and eat at the Café Noir this evening, to celebrate.'

Justin asked what exactly they should celebrate. Ken frowned at him. 'Why, a bit more truth seeping into the world! Are you okay? What's up?'

'I don't really feel much like celebrating. Kate is off to El Aiyat again.'

It was the first day of Wimbledon, and still the builders had not come back to finish the job on Clemenceau . . . The rain was pouring down. The weather forecasters were being plucky in an irritating way, saying that the covers were on the courts, and that there should be a chance of at least an hour's play in the afternoon. Tim Henman was reported to be in good form, despite earlier back problems. Justin was suffering from a touch of diarrhoea. He sat there on the toilet, wondering why he had never managed to know how to spell the wretched word. Typical of doctors to invent such a difficult word; why not simply say 'the shits'?

In the garden the pigeons were still condemning Walpole, not exactly in chorus. There was to be a G8 meeting somewhere or other, not that the pigeons cared. The politicians would, like the pigeons, discuss: again discuss, 'Make Poverty History' – the mere fatuity, the sheer hubris, of which slogan drove Justin crazy . . . If there were a God, he had ordained poverty, as he had ordained the shits . . . Baal was probably keen on the shits too. He was reading the newspaper to mitigate the tedium of his lower bowel, which spluttered like a child vomiting after eating too much chocolate. He noted that some old fool of a Muslim cleric had declared that the Indonesian earthquake was caused by people's immorality. What sort of a primitive mindset could such old shags have? What the old shag said was apparently much applauded by the crowd. It seemed this same old shag had been serving a stretch in prison for conspiracy, in a bomb outrage which killed 202 people. It evidently had not been a long enough stretch for him to have a rethink and gain a saner view of the world. With such old shags about, what hope for world peace?

Justin was not feeling well. In the night, he had had a nightmare about his father. In the dream, Charlie Haddock was working in a sort of wooden shed with animals all round him looking ugly and bad-tempered. Possibly they were a kind of zebra. Justin was frightened of them. Charlie would not look up at his son. He was working with a sharp tool.

'Father, I am glad to see you at last,' Justin seemed to be saying. Charlie looked up. He had enormous teeth, he was proud of his teeth. He had extracted them from one of the animals. The teeth made him resemble an animal. He claimed his son had done nothing with his life. Justin protested that he was trying to be a better son and more successful. Justin sat up in bed. He felt terrible, as though something inside him had been injured. What could the dream signify? His father's Christian name had been Allan, not Charlie; why was he Charlie in the dream? Was this the sort of nightmare men had shortly before dying? He certainly felt damp and cold as if near to death.

Eventually, when Kate had left, he took the morning ration of pills and made his way to the shops. His left knee was particularly painful, but he ignored it. He went to Abbey, which he remembered had once been called, much more sensibly, Abbey National, for a talk with the manager. Behind the counter stood a young Hindu woman with the most lovely eyes Justin had ever encountered. She asked him something. He was so stunned, he said, 'Your eyes are so beautiful!' She went off into peals of delighted laughter. He was alarmed he had said it, yet pleased that she was delighted. As she showed him into the manager's office, his sleeve brushed hers. After that, anything was an anti-climax, although the manager was pleasant. Justin felt happier for seeing this marvellous young woman; she acted like a consolation for the nightmare about his father.

He opened a small account with Abbey. He could have enjoyed slightly better interest rates if he had invested his money for three years, but there was the doubt about whether he would live that long. 'You look well enough,' said the manager kindly. 'Why not enjoy yourself? Go on one of these world cruises, on a luxury liner?'

'Good idea,' said Justin, thinking there were few things he would hate more than a world cruise. What sort of people would you meet on a luxury liner? And if you accidentally died on board, would they throw your corpse over the side?

By eleven o'clock, he drove the Toyota to Scabbard Lane, stopping outside Kate's house. He climbed out and rang her bell. 'Coming,' she called in that clear voice of hers, dividing it into two words. 'Carm-ing!'

Justin waited on her doorstep. Birds sang under the street lamps. At last she opened up. She was wearing a brown calf jacket with matching slacks and a floppy-brimmed brown felt hat. She was dragging a wheeled suitcase behind her. 'All ready for the tropics, I see.'

'As ready as I can be. There's another case in the hall.'

He went and collected it and stowed it in the back of the Toyota.

Impulsively, he clutched her arm. 'Oh Kate, I'll miss you so! When will you be back?'

'You'll be all right, Justin, I know. You have plenty of friends round here to go to.' They were heading for Heathrow down the M40 when he broke the silence between them by asking again when she would be back.

'Some of the children have contracted a form of flu. They think it's flu, or fever. The poor kids are so ill-nourished they are vulnerable to all kinds of diseases. Also, one of the section leaders has left unexpectedly. She's gone back to her village.'

'Is Len Overton there?'

She shot him a look, but he was staring sedulously ahead at the road. 'Of course.'

Heathrow, that great Mecca for transients, looked more like Cairo than ever. Justin thought that one terrorist bomb here would be devastating. Then indeed the peoples of the world would be united, as their blood flowed together like a tide. He kept such thoughts to himself. He realized he was terrified of almost everything. Now that he was less physically able, he found the jostling itself a cause for alarm.

Kate's plane was leaving at 2.35. She would travel business class. They drank a cup of coffee in the BA Business Pavilion. He felt miserable.

'You look tired,' Kate said. 'No point in waiting about, really. You go home and rest. You're not too well today. I'll be okay.'

'Are you sure?'

'Yes – and don't forget it's Dave's birthday next week.' He put an arm round her shoulders and they kissed goodbye. As he was turning to leave, she caught his arm. There were tears in her eyes. 'Look after your dear self.'

He watched her go through into Departures. On his way out of the building, he stopped at the W.H. Smith booth to buy a postcard for Dave. His son liked pictures of planes. Or so he told himself. Planes and penguins. Rain was beginning to blow in from Wimbledon. Once in his car, he sat with his face buried in his hands. A quarter of an hour passed until he felt in control of

213

himself, and the worst feelings of despair died. In compensation his bowels began to rumble again; he had better get home and hope there was plenty of toilet paper. He started up the engine and followed a line of traffic out of the airport and on to the road for Oxford. Farewell Kate! Kate, farewell!

# 19

## Another Visit to Eagles Rest

It was surprising how soon the syringa flowering was over. He thought how soon it was that everything went over; Kate's departure left him in a desert of dismay. Was there a plant called Dismay? He did a little lawn mowing, thinking all the time of Kate's wonderful spirit. To vary the misery, he sometimes dreamed of the delectable brown girl in Abbey. But he could not really think of trying to pick her up at his age.

The England team had beaten Ecuador. More drunken fans had been arrested in Germany. Wimbledon was functioning. The weather was fine, briefly. The builders had not turned up yet. The hollyhocks were growing tall. There was bindweed everywhere – such a greedy weed. The pigeons were at it again, strutting about like fat town councillors. Those sitting overhead in the trees were still vilifying the name of Walpole.

Blackfly were beginning to settle on the broad beans. The jasmine was in flower over the archway. The adolescent green apples were awaiting their first blush. Summer was passing, just as he felt his life – the valuable part of his life – was past.

He had come in to wash his hands under the kitchen tap and to drink a cup of coffee, when the doorbell rang. Opening the door, he found Scalli standing there, holding a limp dog in her arms. It was a dog of medium size, mainly white with brown patches. Its head lolled and its tongue hung out of its mouth. Its eyes were closed. Scalli hugged it to herself. 'Oh, Mr 'Addock, please to excuse me. I was so rude last time but please be excused of me. I am so sad. My doggie is hit by a car and I cannot carry him far. I have fear he might die. He is my dear love.'

'Yes, and my dear love has just cleared off to see her dear love . . . Come in, Scalli. Bring the dog into the kitchen. Let's see what the damage is. What's his name?'

'Is call Teddy, like an English dog. I love him so much, Mr 'Addock. I taught him to sit up and beg . . .' At the mention of the dog's name, she rested her head with her lank hair against the dog's coat. It opened its eyes momentarily. She carried the dog into the kitchen, spreading it carefully on the table. The dog had sustained a deep wound in its side from which blood was seeping. Justin put the kitchen towel over the wound to mop up the blood. He thought again of his nightmare. Blood again. Life blood – as if there were any other kind.

'Mmm, not good. We need a vet.'

'No, no, vet is too much money.'

'Nonsense, Scalli, I'll pay the vet's bill. Your pet is seriously injured. Broken ribs and so forth . . .'

She put her hands up to shield her eyes and cheeks. 'You see! I pray to mighty Baal for my poor daughter Skrita in Aleppo but

I not make a prayer for my dear Teddy. So happens this! He runs to a passing car and the car next hits him.'

He made a dismissive gesture and went for a saucer. 'Maybe Baal is a bit shaky on cars. Let's try giving Teddy some water.'

'I have not keep him on a – what is it? – like a string?'

'A lead.'

'Yes. A lead.' When the dog's head was lifted and the saucer put in place, it did attempt to lap once or twice, then no more. Justin searched in the telephone book for a vet, preferably one near at hand. He found one at Dunmore Road. They had no one they could send out. He asked what he should be doing to help the dog survive.

'Dogs so wounded generally die in the matter of an hour or two. From shock as much as anything.'

He turned frustrated to Scalli. 'You'd better try Baal. Vets aren't much help.'

But Baal was not much help either. Teddy lifted its head, kicked with its back legs and let its head fall. It gave a snuffle and died. Scalli was quiet. She fell back on a chair and bowed her head. Justin brought her some sherry, which she refused. He asked awkwardly if she would like him to bury the dog in his garden.

'No, he must bury in my garden. I go with poor Teddy in just a minute.' Her pallid face was distorted as she fought to hold back her tears. He patted her back rather helplessly.

She stood up and gathered the dog to her breast. 'I bring back your towel washed and dry in a day's time. Thank you for your much kindness. I am sorry I make the curse of Baal to you.'

'That's all right, Scalli, my dear.'

'I have no man, you know. Is difficult for me.'

He shut the door and stood by it. Feeling her loss, he felt like crying himself. And there was his loss too. He tried to suppress the thought. He went and had a pee. Sometimes there was a kind of weariness. Maybe there would come a time when it would simply not be worth going on. He sat in the garden under the sun umbrella, thinking in thoughtless way. One possibility was that he went in and watched Wimbledon on TV. Another that he stretch out on the bench and just snoozed in the warmth of the day.

His thoughts drifted to Scalli's dog. Had Scalli loved the animal too obsessively? She had taught it to beg. Maybe Teddy did not like begging. Maybe he did not like going out on a lead. The one time he had no lead, he ran into the traffic. Rather than submit to further slavery, he might have been committing suicide. Poor old dogs . . . One would never know. Everything was so random.

Almost as soon as he started to make notes on a piece of paper, regarding Chance, his thoughts wandered to his little black cat, Macaroon. He had loved Macaroon greatly. She died only a month after Janet had left for Carlisle. What an independent miss Macaroon had been. She did whatever pleased her. Yet she loved him. Of that he would swear. Of all the animals who suffered the misfortune of coming into contact with mankind, cats remained unique. Many animals had been forced to sign on to be slaves of some kind. The dog Teddy had been such a slave, together with the rest of his kind. Cats remained free to slouch about the place, looking elegant, purring if they felt like it, catching and torturing small mammals or birds, sunning themselves, cadging food, living a carefree hands-in-pockets existence. Good for them! He missed Kate. He missed Janet. He also missed Macaroon. And the curse of Baal? Had it been removed? It meant nothing, merely superstition, of course.

Setting these considerations aside, he returned to the question of chance. After a while, he went inside to his study and opened up the computer. A certain prickling sensation told him he was on to something important. He had experienced that sensation as a young man when he read a book entitled *The Worm Forgives the Plough*. It provided him with his first TV script, which had made his name. He worked on until the sun sank into the under-world and blue night gathered up her skirts to make her grand entry. These nights, there was never the saturating pitch-blackness of a winter's night. The Northern hemisphere was bowing towards the sun. Belief in Akhenaten, the sun god, must have been a reasonable assumption in its day.

Heatwave or not, Justin went to visit his son on the following day. When he arrived at the village on the outskirts of which Eagles Rest stood, he bought a can of Fanta Lemon from a glass-fronted machine and drank the liquid down. He felt slightly better as a result. A new pain on his left breast was bothering him. Better keep quiet about it. Justin was also going to keep quiet about Dave's birthday. He did not wish to remind his son that the year was passing. The sky was a pure blue, without cloud, without expression. Justin rang the bell on the mock-something door of Eagles Rest. He was admitted to its stale-smelling interior. Faint rock-and-roll music sounded, the music of inanity and despair, at least to Justin's mind. Gone were the days when Ella Fitzgerald, in a reasonable display of sorrow, sang 'Every time we say goodbye I die a little . . .' As he had died a little since Kate left for Egypt. He wondered why a little.

A woman with the complexion of a ghost, a fungus of hair hanging over her dead eyes, prowled the corridor. She was wrapped in the cerements of a dressing-gown. 'One two three,' she whispered to herself. 'One two three,' over and over. 'One two three.'

He found David outside, half-dressed, in a wheelchair, sitting in full sun. His bulging face was covered in sweat. Justin wheeled his son round the corner of the building into the shade. 'Poor Dave. Far too hot for you . . .' Dave was an inert lump. Exhaustion had closed his eyes. He could only gasp. 'Are you all right, old boy?'

'I um like porridge in the morting,' he replied. 'And teller-ibbon . . .'

'That's good.' Justin hurried into the room Dave shared with another man. He moistened a flannel under the cold tap and wiped Dave's face with it.

'Daddy,' Dave said, more brightly. 'Dear Daddy . . .' Dave was clutching something in his right fist. His father prised the chubby hand open. It held a postcard, folded in three lengthwise and then folded, with four turns, into a small square. Justin found it carried a picture of the new A380 Airbus and, on the other side, an affectionate message he had written to Dave. He had posted it a month ago.

Justin wrapped his arms about his son's neck and hugged him. He found himself crying compulsively. Great sobs burst from him. Love was so heartbreaking. Undeserved love in particular. When he managed to control himself, he wiped his eyes with a handkerchief. Tears still fell. He saw that Dave was smiling.

'Dear Daddy . . .'

'I love you so, Son. I'll always love you!'

He went to face Mrs Arrowsmith, to pay the bill and complain about David being left sitting in full sun. The way there was not easy. An extension had been tacked on to a less recent extension which had been added to an early nineteenth-century house. Each addition marked an accession to the wealth of the country with a corresponding reduction to the aesthetic sense of the past owners. Mrs Arrowsmith's room could therefore be said equally to be at the back or the front or possibly side of Eagles Rest. It was set in a corridor which never saw sunlight or the hope of it, but which nevertheless recalled a stylized version of nature in the wallpaper design of a man who believed in the virtues of the late Middle Ages, the late William Morris. The stale air of this corridor memorialized those bygone days. Mrs Arrowsmith sat at her desk, wearing a deep blue costume, to listen in grim silence to Justin's protestations. He saw that she too was ageing; she had taken on something of the faded complexion of the wallpaper outside her door . . . She looked, he thought, thinner than before, and was surprised to note that she had at least the beginnings of a goitre. Not a pretty woman . . .

She assumed a pair of tinted spectacles to listen more severely to his complaints. Then she spoke. 'There is a heatwave, in case you didn't notice, Mr Haddock. It causes problems here in Eagles Rest.' Her enunciation was less clear than it had been. 'It is not my fault that the Sun goes round the Earth. Such things are immu— well, they can't be changed. Shadows move. I can't be expected to see to everything. Besides which, my helper's gone sick. I'm not feeling too well myself, but you observe I don't complain.'

He contrived to speak quietly. 'Mrs Arrowsmith, it is the Earth that revolves round the Sun, not vice versa. You should know that simple fact – understood even by the ancient Greeks. You may have put my son in the shade initially, but you should have known that that would not long be the case. Why did you not think of that, even with your ignorance of astronomy?'

Mrs Arrowsmith rose to her feet, resting her knuckles on her desktop. 'I refuse to be called ignorant by such as you, Mr Haddock. What exactly the Sun does is none of my business. I'm here on Earth to do the best I can for my patients – no easy task. You just come here once a month and are always complaining. I don't want to see you here again. Do like the others do – stay away and pay by direct debit.' She sucked in her lips to show her displeasure.

'Mrs Arrowsmith, please! Dave could have died of a stroke, stuck for hours in the hot sun. Then you'd be in trouble.'

'Well he didn't die, did he? I'm running Eagles Rest, not you, Mr Haddock, thanks very much.' The tinted spectacles glinted with malice.

'Mrs Arrowsmith, I could report you to the health authorities.'

'Well then, you report away and see where it gets you!'

He said no more, afraid the woman would take her anger out on his son. Making his bedraggled way back to the bus stop, Justin acknowledged that Janet would have managed this affair so much better than he. Dearest Janet, what a hole she had left in his life . . . Together with regretting that he had foolishly forgotten to wear his straw hat, he thought seriously about religion and, in particular, his failure to be a good father. On reflection, he saw or thought he saw that here religion was totally superfluous. The genetic code alone held the promptings that made him a bastard. So religion was proved to be out of date. Nevertheless, he was tempted to pray for his son. It was an old if useless habit.

One of his favourite afternoon TV shows was *Cookery for the Obese*. A delectable blonde lady was cooking a chicken pie. He imagined the director saying, 'Yeah, terrific, Grace. But you just need to wear a lower-cut blouse and show a bit more boob. We want men to watch the show too.'

Certainly Grace was not obese. Justin imagined himself lying close to that lovely flat white tummy, full of her own chicken pie. Grace was herself so entirely edible. She was leaning over – well over – a plateful of her cooking as the show closed.

The Albertina rose was out, with its lusty brave blossoms. Justin went and looked in the patch where he had released the errant woodlouse. No sign of it. Of course these remarkable little creatures could travel, however somnolent they might seem. This particular creature was no doubt married by now and had nine hundred children. Dave would never marry, never have children. Would have very little of anything. Had no mother. Had a loving father – who, by his very nature, was negligent. Justin's spirits remained low. He thought, with attempted humour, that the curse of Baal was upon him. This was the day when the English eleven played – was it Portugal? – in the World Cup. Already English fans were gathering, shouting, waving flags in a small German city. What the inhabitants of Geisenkirchen were thinking remained unknown. But you could guess.

Another kind of warfare was being celebrated, or at least remembered, in France. It was ninety years since the Battle of the Somme. Justin knew that Allan, his father, had been there, one of the survivors, by a lucky chance. According to the BBC, fifty-seven thousand young Englishmen died on the first day of battle alone, mown down by enemy machine-gun fire. It was almost impossible to understand the figure. Fifty-seven thousand. And by the end of the battle, a million men had died. It was only by chance that some survived. Solemn remembrance was taking place today. So was Wimbledon. And Dave, sitting in the shade, knowing nothing about all of this.

First of all, Justin sought to decide what constituted Chance, and turned his attention to the grading of it. If he met the clever Mrs Broughton in the street, a lady who had published a book called *Sanity and the Lady*, and they exchanged a few words, that was plainly chance, but of no real importance. If he met Ken in the street, and they went for a coffee and agreed to see *United 93* again, that was more important, but affected the tone of their lives only marginally. If he was crossing the road and was knocked down by a passing car, as Teddy had been, that constituted an important chance. It might impede the flow of his life for a month or two, or for the rest of his life, say, if he lost a leg; or of course it might end his life. So this chance led inescapably to other chances. This, he decided, would be what he would define as Chance. The elephant in the room.

He had recently bought a book by Sir Anthony Kenny, with whom he had a slight acquaintance, entitled *What I Believe*. He found it enlightening and entertaining – not usually qualities he discovered in other philosophical books he attempted to study.

It was reassuring to read that 'Philosophy is not a matter of knowledge, it is a matter of understanding, that is to say, of organizing what is known.' This was precisely what Justin intended to do, for everyone knew about Chance – although not in any organized way. Similarly with religion with which, as Sir Anthony acknowledged, philosophy had often been involved. Indeed, thought Justin, nodding gently in agreement with his thought, novels too were another example of an attempt to organize what is known. He sat writing notes in the garden, in part listening to the birds. The birds were not carefree. Their calls were claims for territory or mates or, in the case of young birds as for young humans, for attention and food. Nothing in the world was idle – apart from cats, the little blighters, sitting about with their paws in their pockets. Macaroon was a perfect example. All her life, Macaroon had done nothing, except share his fish and chips with him and thus – purely accidentally – making his life several ounces happier! So he drew up a range of Chances. He was approaching something he could regard as a thesis. It needed no particular depth of thought to see this must include Chances from the past.

The example of Abraham came to mind. Abraham, the stupid old fruitcake, thought that God told him to offer up his son Isaac as a sacrifice. (*Did I read somewhere that something like 25 per cent of people hear voices in their heads?!*) Abraham was apparently happy to oblige. Luckily for the gullible Isaac, at the last moment, the very moment when Abraham was preparing to murder his son and had the knife raised, he spotted by chance a ram caught in a thicket. He killed that animal instead of his son. The account does not go on to report Isaac saying 'Bloody hell, I thought my number was up!' He would have liked to see an additional Biblical verse here: 'And the Lord God spake unto Abraham from a thunderstorm, saying unto him, "You fucked up!" . . .' *That's one thing about the Bible*, thought Justin in admiration, *it's generally not afraid to go into gory detail. How about, 'And Abraham was ninety years old and nine when he was circumcised in the flesh of his foreskin'?*

The rest of Justin's afternoon was spent indoors, citing various kinds of chance. The sunlight fell on his computer screen, so that he pulled the curtains over his window – curtains Janet had hung – to work in a pleasant twilight. Justin that evening attended a party given for Neighbourhood Watch. This branch of the Watch was run by his nice friend, Mrs Broughton. The neighbours gathered in Laura's beautiful garden off the Croft. Justin took a bottle round as a donation and was glad he did so, since drink seemed to be in short supply. Was he the only person who expected more than one glass? Here again he felt 'not competent about life'. While all these pleasant ordinary people appeared to know him, he could not remember any of their names. He remembered Mrs Broughton's name, though not her first name. He asked her how her book was selling. Immediately he had asked – as he was actually asking – he realized it was a crass question. He tried to cover his mistake by saying, 'I greatly enjoyed it.'

Mrs Broughton was a pleasant middle-class woman, smartly dressed, not flashy, tending towards the plump. She had a clear and carefully tended countenance. As if, having become cautious by habit, she suspected Justin of having failed to read her book, she asked him what exactly he had enjoyed about it. 'I'm not seeking praise. I am merely curious.'

'The main point you were making was that reason is to be valued among humanity, but that counts for nothing when encompassed within a largely hostile universe where causation is everything.' He was pleased he made the point so concisely.

'Full marks,' Mrs Broughton said, sucking in her cheeks with a smile, appeased enough to answer his first question. 'Of course it's not selling.'

'So you don't believe there's a God out there?'

She leant towards Justin. 'Hush, we are among churchgoers . . .'

One chap, a big man with a good supply of designer stubble – yes, Justin also vaguely knew and liked him. They talked together. The chap – was he Michael? – told Justin that the Anchor was going to be pulled down and a new building erected in its place.

'I know. What sort of building? Have you heard yet?'

'Another block of flats, I'd say at a guess,' said Michael.

'I hear a Kuwaiti consortium has bought the site.'

'Kuwaitis are good chaps,' said Michael, authoritatively.

Taking Mrs Broughton's – *yes, that's it! – Laura Broughton*

– taking her arm, Justin said, 'Do you feel like coming for a sip of something at the White Hart?'

She contemplated him from under her lashes before saying, with a smile, 'Well, just a sip, possibly.'

He caught a faint whiff of her perfume. Mmmm . . . When the party was over, they went through the well-worn rooms of the White Hart, that comfortable village pub, to the garden that lay behind. The garden was properly cared for, filled with a number of tables and benches. Most of the benches were already occupied. Justin and Laura found an unoccupied table and sat themselves down.

'Have you been to see *United 93*?' he asked.

'Yes, I thought it was excellent,' she said. A waiter came up, gave a slight bow, and asked them what they would like to drink. Justin jumped up and shook the man's hand. It was Akhram, of course. They exchanged a few friendly words until Akhram said he must not chat: he was in his disguise as a waiter. After some discussion between them, Laura and Justin settled for a bottle of Sancerre. Akhram accepted the order, bowed again and went off in the direction of the building.

Amid general chat, Justin told Laura he was trying to write a script about Chance. It had occurred to him that many foreigners in Headington – not to look further afield – had arrived here by chance. He felt that religion came into the picture and wondered what she thought about the matter.

'I have thought about it as a possible subject for a book, as it happens,' Laura said. 'It raises many problems. Some immigrants enrich our society – the folks at the Café Noir are good examples – while some hope to destroy utterly the rather nebulous "British way of life".'

'Nebulous? Hardly, Laura. I mean, here we sit, in a pub garden, within the sound of church bells, about to drink French wine. Isn't that the British way of life personified?'

She smiled. 'Yes, if you also include the subject we are discussing.

And, I hope, will discuss till over-population makes the oxygen run out.'

'And the freedom.'

'I hope you will take into consideration the way our religion – I mean the C of E – offers many people comfort and consolation.' She studied his face, half-smilingly. 'Reason seems a cold thing set beside comfort.'

Akhram returned with their Sancerre and poured a measure into their glasses.

'Tell you what,' said Laura. 'I'm having a tea party tomorrow. My friends would be interested in this subject. They're foreigners. Vivienne Adkins will be there. Do you know her?'

'She's my bank manager. Rather fierce.'

'Vivienne is a honey. Though perhaps not in the bank. She'll be bringing another friend, Claudia and her little girl. Claudia is or was Turkish, I believe. Do come, will you?!'

When all the tables in the pub garden had been taken Akhram raised his voice and asked if the customers would care to see his conjuring trick. A man sitting with two women at the next table heard this offer. 'Yes, show us your trick, Mohammed!'

Addressing Justin, he said, 'You want to see this!' Smiling and nodding, the waiter left. He returned in a minute with a plastic bottle full of coloured water and a small glass. Word had got round, and several people were showing an interest.

'Sorry to interrupt your pleasures, gentlemen and ladies,' said the waiter. 'This is my one small and only trick! Here you see I have a large bottle of water and a small glass to pour the water in. Don't be scare.' While speaking he slowly revolved, exhibiting his bottle. He stopped. He paused. Lifting the bottle high, he began pouring its contents into the small glass. He continued to pour. The small glass did not overflow. Finally, he had emptied all the coloured water into the small glass. It had not overflowed. The audience in the garden was baffled. A woman began to clap. Everyone was clapping. Akhram was bowing. A man threw him a fifty-pence piece. Everyone started to throw coins to the waiter's feet.

'Very baffling,' said Justin, wrinkling his brow. 'But are waiters supposed to do that?'

'I understand he does the same trick every night – but only once. I imagine he wishes to indicate that he has a personality beyond just being a waiter.'

The rest of the evening went well. Laura was humorous and seemed quite affectionate. She gave him a light and hasty kiss – nothing more than middle-class etiquette demanded – at her doorway and then disappeared. He heard the lock turn inside. Perhaps it might not be as bad without Kate as he had anticipated.

Justin got home and switched on the television before he went to bed. Maude was sleeping on the sofa. She woke. 'What's the time?' she asked, but left the room before Justin could answer. Justin was in time to watch some of the sports news. The English team had been beaten in the Cup by the Portuguese. The game had proved lack-lustre. Justin gave up on that, but then came the tennis at Wimbledon, where the brilliant Sharapova was on court, winning with flashing eyes and flashing limbs.

He missed Kate's company. He tried to make little of her absence, thinking instead of the horrid thing which had appeared that morning. No doubt an illusion, born of an overloaded brain. As he hoped to destroy gods with his Chance theory, an archaic part of his brain was probably struggling to preserve them . . . In the night, he dreamed he went to shop in a big store. He arrived ridiculously early, to find the store closed. But a man pushing a sort of bike appeared. Somehow, Justin knew in the dream that this was Mr Marks. He unlocked a back door with a huge key and let Justin into the store. All he wanted was a bottle of their well-flavoured apple-and-mango juice, but he could not find it anywhere. Waking early, when the day was still drowsy, he went downstairs, feeling in his bones that something was wrong. A strange object was lying on the hall carpet. He saw it as he made his slow way down the stairs step by step, and could not think what it was. When he stooped over it, he saw clearly enough. It was the whitened skull of a cow or possibly a horse, its large teeth showing in a marmoreal grin. He stood there, hands on hips to rest his back, at first puzzled and then becoming increasingly alarmed. Someone or something had been in his house overnight.

He limped round the ground floor of the house, checking the doors one by one, the front door, the side door, the back door, the doors from the living room into the courtyard. All doors were locked, all windows showed no sign of a break-in. Frightened, he went from room to room. He feared to find a stranger lurking, a skeletal thing with ghastly head and blazing eyes, but there was no one. With trembling hands, he made himself a mug of tea. He took the tea into his study, and sat down on the chaise longue. He was horrified to realize how deeply scared he was. The fright came on him like floodwater. The study was shadowy and dull. He had drawn the curtains over the window against the sun the previous afternoon.

Setting down his mug, he got tremblingly to his feet. He pulled the curtains back. He was looking at a gaping hole. The glass had been neatly cut from the window pane, creating an oval hole. A hole large enough for a man to climb through. He stopped breathing.

# 20
## *Haggard's* She

After a minute, Justin steadied himself against the window sill. He put a hand gingerly through the opening, to reassure himself that the glass really was gone. Terrible visions ran through his brain. He crept through all the rooms of the house, as he had already done, looking fearfully into each in turn, half-expecting to see someone there: someone not necessarily hiding, but perhaps sitting smoking a cigarette and reading a magazine as if they owned the place. Some twisted psychopathic personality . . . Perhaps they would turn suddenly and speak to him with assumed geniality before killing him. 'Hello, Justin, you surprised me. You're up early.' CLUNK.

He found no one. He sat down on the kitchen chair, wondering if his mind had not toppled over into a form of madness. At last, with shaking hand, he picked up his phone and dialled 999. He found difficulty in speaking. He cleared his throat. He apologized more than once. Within half an hour, a police officer arrived. He introduced himself as Sergeant Ebbes. Justin was still sitting in the kitchen chair. He sank back into it as he related the few events of his discovery.

'You say that nothing has been stolen, sir?'

'Nothing that I know of. It would be less sinister if they had stolen something.' He feared he might burst into tears.

'Very unpleasant, sir,' said the officer. 'Very unpleasant indeed. Of course you are badly shaken.' He examined the cow skull, photographed it, and made a note in an electronic notebook.

'Do you happen to know a Mr Guy Fitzgerald, sir?'

'Well, I do. But you don't imagine . . .' His voice petered out.

'I just asked, sir. You would not object, I trust, if I have a bit of a gander round the premises, sir?' Justin gave his assent. He remained sitting where he was. He listened to the officer tramping about. When the man returned, it was to say that Justin had a perfectly viable alarm system. He asked why it had not been used. Justin had to admit that he never bothered to set it.

'Many people make that mistake, sir, and then pay for it and bring us in unnecessarily. I'll just inspect outside, with your permission.'

The officer returned from the garden shortly. 'The oval of glass which the intruder removed is intact. It is propped against the house outside the window from which it was cut.' He spoke into his mobile phone, the burden of which was that a crime officer should come round to check for DNA on the glass.

Addressing Justin, he said, 'You need a glazier, sir. Do you know of one?' When Justin said he did not, the officer nodded and said he would take care of that detail. 'Although it's a weekend – that's a touch difficult, but you shall have the window restored before nightfall. Have you any close relations, sir, may I ask?'

'A son. My son David. But he's not well. That's all.' He added, 'As you can see, I'm a widower.'

'And no female acquaintances, sir?'

'No. Not really. A mother-in-law.'

The officer asked Justin's age. He nodded when told. He said that at Police HQ there was a lady officer who did counselling in such cases. He would see if she was free to come round of a Sunday and talk to Justin. Justin was grateful. The officer scratched his head and made a face as if he was sucking a prune.

'Meantime, sir, I'd get yourself a cup of coffee. It's a nasty experience at your age, sir, but you must comfort yourself that no harm came to you – or seems to have been intended.'

'A nasty experience at any age, I'd say.'

'Oh, quite, sir, quite. Very nasty. A bit spooky.'

Justin did not like to hear that, but he stood up and shook Sergeant Ebbes's hand before showing him to the door. He took the officer's advice and made himself some coffee. He swallowed two tablets of co-codamol. He sat in the chair to drink the coffee. He was still trembling, and slopped a little coffee on his trousers. But now the shock at the impudence of the intrusion and the fear of being burgled were wearing off. He began to feel anger rising in him. He thought he knew who had played this threatening trick on him: the name Jack Hughes came to mind.

A woman Justin estimated as being about fifty-five arrived at his door. She had dark dyed hair, a heavy woman with a reassuring presence. She introduced herself as Harriet. She said she liked to come and talk to people who had suffered a nasty shock.

'I've certainly had a nasty shock,' said Justin. They had hardly seated themselves on either side of the dining-room table before he began to pour out his story. Maude looked round the door. She did not come in. She did not speak. Harriet coaxed her into the room. She came and sat in an armchair, saying nothing. Harriet asked Justin a few questions in a concerned tone.

'Very upsetting for you at your age, Mr Haydock.'

'At any age, I'd think,' he replied, snappishly.

'Are you at all religious, may I ask?'

He surprised himself by his delay in responding. 'I was religious as a boy. But look, let me get you a cup of tea, Harriet. Sorry, I'm forgetting my manners.'

She followed him into the kitchen. 'Well, you have a snug little house here, and no mistake. Very nice. So are you saying you are not religious now?'

'I don't imagine it was Jesus Christ who broke in, if that's what you're asking.'

Harriet smiled in a way that indicated she did not find his remark funny. 'So that's a definite maybe . . .'

The kettle was boiling. 'I'm writing a thesis,' he told her, with exaggerated patience, supporting himself against the welsh dresser. 'Not exactly against religion, but showing that religion and belief in countless gods over the ages is in fact an attempt to ward off ill chance. And that chance prevails over almost everything.'

She nodded slowly, as if counting the nods and agreeing with herself to stop at Nod No. 12. 'It says in the Bible that God made man in his own image.'

'Oh, does it? Then clearly God is a bit of a scoundrel. He breaks into people's houses.'

'Well, sir, some would call that remark blasphemy.'

'I didn't mean to upset you.'

'It is just a bit silly, I'd say, to pretend that God doesn't exist. After all, the Church has been going for centuries.'

'Yes, well – the Church has a professional interest in the matter.'

She began to nod again, not exactly as if agreeing: more as if she was weighing up a neutral answer.

He poured hot water over the tea bags. 'I suppose you think I'm being silly.'

'Why should you suppose that?' His statement had troubled her. 'But why can't you have both religion and chance? Surely there's room for both in our universe. Millions and millions of people have worshipped various gods over the ages, haven't they? Are you saying they were all mistaken?'

He hesitated. 'We see things a bit more clearly today.'

She was annoyed. Flashing him a glance, she said, 'I don't know nothing about such things. That's not really my job.'

He looked her in the eye. 'Are you religious, Harriet, may I ask?'

'I'm a Baptist.' Spoken with some finality.

'I could send you a copy of my thesis when it's finished, if you're interested. I'm hoping it might make a TV programme.'

'Perhaps you're working too hard,' she said, sympathetically.

'Oh, I see. Milk? Sugar? You think I'm so overworked I went mad and cut the hole in my study window myself?'

'Just milk, thank you. How about a holiday? The Welsh hills are lovely at this time of year.'

'Or a world cruise?' he asked sarcastically.

'Yes, I'm sure that would be ever so nice for them as could afford it. You are of a somewhat nervous disposition, are you?' Harriet left trailing a scatter of platitudes. He realized he was going to offend many people. Most people?

When Harriet had gone, Justin returned to his favourite armchair and fell into a deep sleep. Later, a glazier came and repaired the window. A crime officer came and removed the skull and the extracted pane of glass to check for DNA or fingerprints. Justin went to sleep again.

Rather late in the afternoon, he remembered he had been invited to Laura Broughton's tea party. He hurriedly changed into a clean shirt and made his way unshaven to Laura's house. Laura was welcoming but somewhat surprised to see him.

'Sorry I'm so late.' He was introduced to her friends Dot Owen, Vivienne Adkins and Claudia Pine with her small daughter, Tricksy. Vivienne Adkins made no reference to her meeting with Justin at the bank. She was all smiles and talked a good deal about the tennis at Wimbledon. She had been with her husband to the opening day. Claudia was small and bony with short dark hair; she wore a skimpy summer dress and was being sweet to her daughter. She was in her late twenties, half Vivienne's age.

Claudia was holding forth and the women were listening intently. Justin was immediately bored. He longed for some male company. Even if they talked about Iraq. Over tea and sponge cake, served soon after Justin arrived, the ladies told something of their stories. Vivienne had married a Saudi man in London. All had gone well until they returned to Riyadh, and then she had found herself a captive in the house. Life for women was incredibly tedious. Two years later, her husband had gone on a business trip to London; after much insistence on her part, she had accompanied him. Once in the centre of London, she had fled. It had been painful. She liked her husband, who had pro-Western sympathies, and she had borne him a son. But she could never go back to Saudi and would never see her son again. Her voice faltered when she said those words. She got herself a good lawyer instead, and hired a bodyguard. She had been grateful when Dick, her present husband, had proposed to her.

Claudia told a different story. She had been born in Turkey, in Angora, of a wealthy but strict Muslim family. A lonely child, despite two brothers. Abruptly, she asked Justin, 'Why should we tell you these stressful things, Justin?'

'You probably know you have a sympathetic listener.'

'It is because we heard your lecture, where you spoke of the influence of restaurants on civilization. We admired your understanding. And we are keen to appreciate what constitutes civilization.'

'We all are,' Justin said. And they laughed, Claudia glanced at Vivienne and both ladies nodded and smiled, before Claudia resumed her account of her early life. She was a great reader, mainly of dull religious texts, but she taught herself English through items on television and suchlike. When she was still a child, but approaching an age when her parents would force a husband on her, the family all went to Istanbul for a holiday season. There in a bookshop, just by chance, she found a novel by Mr Rider Haggard – she pronounced his name reverently – called *She*. This, Claudia claimed, was the moment that changed her life. That an Englishman could dare to write a book bearing the title of a female, that this female was known as 'she-who-must-be-obeyed' . . . Claudia realized, as she put it, that there was another planet where girls were not a sort of sub-class, fit only to be the slaves of men, but were loved, respected and even feared . . . She needed to visit that planet. Daringly, she ran to the British Embassy. After much red tape and a small international crisis, Claudia – her new name – arrived in England, clutching her copy of *She*.

'It's terribly racist,' said Justin. 'Isn't it? I've never read it.'

'We were all racists then,' Claudia said.

'Have you ever regretted leaving your native country?'

'Oh, many a time . . . But the die was cast.'

Vivienne said there was always a division in their minds, even when they had found a place in English society. It was the lot of the exile. Her husband was an editor in a publishing house. He had recently given her a proof copy of a book entitled *Infidel*, by a Somali woman, Ayaan Hirsi Ali. It was the most unsparing, horrifying, truthful report of life in Islam she had ever read, and recommended it to one and all. Justin made a note of the title but was all the time preoccupied by the extraordinary chance which had changed Claudia's life. And the courage these women had shown.

The hours of another day wore away, and of another day and another week, and another lifetime.

Justin slept badly one night and was annoyed with himself for feeling nervous. Finally, he got up and crept about the house. It was five fifteen. He heard a quiet snore from Maude's room. Otherwise, the world was silent, absorbed in the process of dawn.

He felt nervous as he swallowed his morning diuretic pills. It terrified him to think that there was someone, anyone, about, who would play malicious tricks on him. He went cautiously into the garden. All things were beautiful. The air was so soft. The sun was as yet concealed by morning cloud. Everything was light and shadowless. He watered various plants while he was still in his pyjamas. He picked and ate a handful of wild strawberries. The little plants grew like weeds. He was thankful that the soil was so fertile in Headington. How difficult it must be to live in the infertile crescent of Mesopotamia. What had once been fertile had been over-cropped and the population had risen greatly. Many of the world's problems lay in over-population. Not all; the world's wickedness had always to be taken into account. The buddleia growing in an earthenware pot, where it had seeded itself, needed extra water. He gave it another canful, deluging it with enjoyment until the water flooded out of the bottom of the pot on to the slabs of Bath stone. He went indoors again reluctantly, ate a few cherries, and retired to bed with his Carlisle mug full of tea. How he loved these silent mornings.

He missed Kate. Come to that, he still missed Janet. To be alone was to be so vulnerable. Nasty things happened. Really nasty. Oh, Kate, how often did you say you loved me? I truly loved you.

Eight o'clock had passed when he woke again. There were hymns on the radio. Maria Sharapova would be resting her beautiful limbs. (Where Kate might be resting her limbs did not bear thinking of . . .) Sunday, the day of rest, first in July, and really hot. Now he understood a mild dream in which he wore two hats. The nightmare was another matter. Yes, it seemed to say, he was welcome to enter the large world of speculation about God and Chance, but should not expect to find anything new. This accorded with a passage in Kenny's book he liked, about combining 'unashamed pride in the loftiness of our goal with undeluded modesty about the poverty of our achievement . . .' The words would be fit for a tombstone – or an unfavourable review of a book. But then the nightmare. Of course it was just a nightmare; there could be, like life itself, no really firm interpretation. It was clear that someone had climbed into his house and built on a new room of vast dimension, where the body of his father lay, under a sheet he dared not remove. The irrational! How he hated it . . . One thing was clear: that Justin's father was of an earlier generation, tied to manual work of some kind or other. You might have said, upper working class. Son Justin did not think of himself as belonging to any particular class. At one time he had joked with friends, perhaps with Martin Sands, about the Meritocracy. They had decided they belonged to the Demeritocracy. They worked in television, an unstructured occupation which had not existed in his father's time. The same could be said of his lovers and friends who worked in new industries: the entire profile of England had changed over his lifetime. Was still changing. And he had hardly noticed it. Now the nature of television was itself changing.

He was eager to get on with the work he had set himself, his Chance theory. But first he must write his weekly note to his son Dave.

*Tell me if you are comfortable in bed. Is it a good bed? If not, I will buy you a new one. The pattern of your days does not conform to the pattern imposed on most of us. I trust you are free in your heart. Mrs Arrowsmith is perhaps not the best woman in the world. I hope she is not sharp with you. But as I am sure you know, she has her troubles too. Try to forgive her. Forgiveness is a good exercise – perhaps improved by being so difficult to achieve. But who is your old father to pass judgement? Most of the things I hoped to do in the week I have failed to do. And I have drunk too much wine. As always.*

*Your loving father.*

He signed off with a shaking hand. It would not do to tell his son about the break-in. An overwhelming sorrow passed through him as he sealed the envelope. Whatever he might do, it was nothing compared with the debt he owed his son. Wine? Wine? Did Dave even know what wine was? Well, he, Justin, was powerless to mend what had passed in bygone years, what sorrows. But some sorrows never passed. The thought occurred to him that perhaps it was sorrow rather than illness from which the really old suffered. Incurable sorrow.

He tried to put his grief aside. He set to work with a will.

He compiled a list of the major Chances, as far as he could distinguish them. Sharapova had won her match by skill and training; no doubt of that. Nevertheless, even there the little ferret of chance had been present. The ball occasionally arrived just on the line or just over. Surely that was an element of luck which the players sought to eliminate. Along with athleticism, they lived or died by it. 'Bad luck!' the crowd would cry. In other things too, Chance was acknowledged to rule. Skill, for instance, hardly entered into lotteries. It became necessary to classify chances, much as the strength of earthquakes was rated on the Richter scale, from one to ten. But it was so gloriously hot . . . His window glass had not been cut, no one had gained entry. There was no knowing why his hand trembled.

He was uncertain how exactly people jettisoned one god for another. He assumed that Vivienne and Claudia, leaving Islam, had not taken to the C of E. He had read in one of his encyclopaedias that when the ruler of Bulgaria was converted to Christianity, the entire nation had been forcibly converted. When Henry VIII decreed that England should be Protestant, everyone had to cease being Catholic; but that was more a change of gear than of god . . . It occurred to him he might quiz Scalli on that question. She might have practical knowledge. Scalli was renting a narrow house at the end of Cavendish Place. Her kitchen window looked out on Disappointment Street. Nasturtiums grew in a tub by her door. When Justin knocked on the door, there was a long wait before Scalli opened up. She peered round it, saying 'Oh, Mr 'Addock!' but not opening the door any wider. She let him in when asked.

'I have up the stairs a lodger,' she told him warningly. Justin stood there, uncertain how to proceed. He felt the painful lump in his left breast; he had heard that it was not only women who had cancer of the breast. He prodded it now, while circumspectly glancing round. The room was poorly furnished, most of the space being occupied by a table and an unmade bed. Photographs of two young girls stood on the mantelpiece.

'I wondered if you would allow me to buy you another dog, Scalli?'

'I don't want another one dog. Teddy was so much a nuisance.'

'But I thought you loved him.'

She shook her head. 'Too much a nuisance.'

'Might I sit down?'

'If you like it.' He pulled a hard-backed chair from the table and sat down on it. He said he hoped Scalli would come back and work for him.

She remained standing exactly where she was. She said she would be pleased to return. She needed the money to send to her daughter in Aleppo. He said that he wanted to ask her, without giving offence, something regarding the god Baal. He asked if he was correct in thinking that Baal was not quite as widely worshipped in these present days as he had been in the past. He wondered if she knew why this was. Scalli stood rigidly in her chosen place. After a pause, she replied. Her answer was brief. What she called the Muhammadan hordes had invaded her land. They had killed all the worshippers of Baal they could find. Scalli's family had managed to escape to Lebanon. While she was enlarging on some of the atrocities which took place – in which Baal had evidently not been very helpful – there came the sound of someone descending the stairs by a patent method of barging from side to side. The wooden door at the bottom of the stairs opened and into the lower room came Jack Hughes, wearing an old tattered shirt and jeans.

'Oh shit,' he said, by way of introduction. 'My bloody foot. I nearly done myself in.' He cast a sly glance at Justin and began to explain how the injury to his foot had happened while digging someone's garden. 'The awful things what happen . . .' He stomped about to display the effect of his wound, complaining meanwhile.

'What about your black preacher from Kinshasa?' Justin asked. The mere sight of Hughes made him nervous. 'Can't he do something for you?'

'Don't know any black preacher from Kinshasa,' Hughes muttered, still stomping about. In so doing, he accidentally pushed Scalli from her rigidly held position. This enabled Justin to see that she had been trying to conceal a small shelf above her bed. On the shelf stood his missing bodhisattva.

'All right, all right,' Justin said angrily to Hughes. 'I don't want to know about it. I want to know what my bodhisattva is doing here.'

'Please don't get angry, Mr 'Addock,' said Scalli, wringing her hands. 'I only bring it here to give a thorough clean and polish.' She treated him to a greasy smile in which a cringe was involved.

'No, you didn't. You're lying. You stole it.'

'I'm off if there's going to be a row,' said Hughes. 'I'm as innocent as the day is wrong.'

Justin turned and confronted him. 'I don't believe that either!'

'Please yourself!' With that, Hughes made off, slamming the front door behind him. Scalli took up the bodhisattva and offered it to Justin, saying he could have it back if he liked. He snatched it from her. He told her he could not trust her and did not wish to see her again.

'Mr Sir, I am so poor and you so rich. You pay me so little. I know you hate Baal.'

'Bugger Baal!' Her front door opened directly on to the street. As Justin went out, clutching the precious bodhisattva, he came across Hughes with his back pressed against the cottage wall. The man immediately fell in beside him, glancing at Justin with a hangdog look.

'You don't want my company, I can tell. I know I'm poorly dressed in this old shirt. I only want to be friendly. Be your friend. I got no friends. I don't ask you for no money, do I now?'

Justin sighed. 'You know I have good reason not to trust you.'

Hughes limped along by Justin, getting very close. 'You got a bad temper I see, but Scalli's only from Syria, poor old woman.'

He tried to get ahead of the man, but Hughes limped all the faster.

'What's more, this bloke as owns her house, he's a bastard too. Calls himself Captain. Me and her are them who never had much luck in life. What good's that thing to you?' He jerked his thumb towards the bodhisattva. 'It's a god and you don't believe in God, so I been told.'

'It is mine and it is not a god.'

'It looks like a god to me. But you'd know best, being educated.'

Justin said no more, again speeding up his pace. 'That window,' he said. 'I hate you, Hughes. I could have you locked up.'

'Huh!' – contemptuously – 'middle-class, arrogant, lock poor folk up . . .'

When Justin reached his front gate, Jack Hughes said, 'I got a job at Ruskin, doing the grounds. I should watch out for Scalli or she'll put a hex on you!' He continued down the road but, as Justin opened his gate, Hughes called to him. 'Here, Justin! You know if you want to be friendly, I'm always around. Not locked up.'

'Not as yet!' Justin went indoors, locked the door and immediately sank into an armchair, still clutching his bronze idol. His breast hurt. He marshalled his thoughts. He held no particular fixed role in society. He had worked among the similarly placed,

243

whether before or behind the cameras. Was this what the wretched Hughes had understood? It was possible he did wish to be a friend but had no way to go about it. He was permanently locked out of something of value. Getting into Justin's house, stealing nothing, doing Justin no harm – these were possibly his blundering attempts to show himself harmless, friendly.

Could this be the case, far-fetched though it sounded? Well, he could always act as if it were the case. A weight was lifted. He did not dislike or fear Hughes. Perhaps he could come to like this societal reject.

He felt very unwell, but considered himself obliged to go to a garden party, since he had accepted the invitation. Society was doing its stuff. He arrived at the garden at the same time as Annie Sloan, who had designed a door curtain for him. Many old friends were at the party, togged up smartly, and many new ones, including a young woman in a violet dress who looked as if she had stepped out of a movie of one of Jane Austen's novels. He met Richard Dawkins, who expressed approval of Justin's rather vague plans regarding the machinations of Chance. It was a relief to be among sensible normal Oxford people. He stayed only for an hour, after listening to what he considered an ill-informed argument concerning what had happened to Om Haldar; there had been no further news of her. So to be well-informed was not possible.

On his way home, Justin stopped at the Summertown Marks & Spencer to buy loads of cooling summer drinks, his favourites being orange juice and crushed raspberries, and pineapple, mango and passion fruit. Both drinks were delicious. He shared some of these juices later with Marie and Ken. There was again some speculation about what would happen to the old Anchor site. KIC was about to make a statement. They sat in the garden until shadows grew longer across the lawn and the frail moon rose in the sky. They talked, among other things, about the terrible carnage on the Somme, eighty years ago. Temperatures remained high throughout the night. That little moon sailed gently across the lake of the sky.

Fine weather continued the next day. Justin worried about his son. He went to the Manor Hospital, where he was examined once more. The orthopaedist decided that his problems consisted of three parts: his feet where his arches had fallen, his legs where there was oedema, and the stiffening of his backbone. Each of these complaints played against the others, but all could be dealt with. He was to have another pill and later to undertake spinal exercises at the hospital. He had another blood test, the test undertaken by a bright nurse from New Zealand, who joked with him. He found her adorable, even when she was sticking the syringe into his vein. Justin was reasonably cheerful about all this; at least he kept sorrow at bay. A sensible analysis had been made, and so amelioration was possible. He liked the nurse from New Zealand, but dared not attempt to kiss her.

When he returned to No. 29, he felt extremely tired. He stood in the hall, listening. All was silent. No sign of Maude. His mail had arrived. Although most of it was junk mail, there was nevertheless a cheque for £5,000 from ITV for something sold to Holland. The book on the British occupation of Indonesia had also arrived. It was a small book, expensively overpriced. A bench stood in a shady patch of garden. Justin took the book there to have a preliminary glance into it. The volume seemed to contain no description of the beauty of tumbledown Medan – no love for that little city. He woke with a start, to find it was one o'clock. A cat had roused him by jumping up on the bench. It was a large black cat and it jumped down to make its way with dignity across the courtyard, only once glancing back, in no hurry.

Justin had no knowledge of falling asleep. It was as if he had passed out. He had passed out. This had happened to him before.

Of course, there was the heart problem. The warfarin was helping. But passing out without warning was a relatively new phenomenon. Had the cat been secretly watching – waiting for him to fall unconscious? He considered that there might be a time when he would pass out in this way and simply not awaken again – would die, in other words. It would be a painless way of leaving this world. But who would tell Dave? How would they break the news to him? How would Dave feel? Tears burst from his eyes at that reflection. Once, he could have relied on his darling Kate for such matters. *Now I have got nobody's ear*, he told himself with a sorrowful smile.

He worked on the Chance question.

Perhaps because he had been thinking about death, he thought about his father, Allan Haddock, and the nightmare. One incident in his father's life had often formed a topic of conversation between him and Justin's mother. During the Great War, Allan – then Corporal Haddock – had been ordered to demolish a German mine discovered beside a small oil-storage plant. This was in the little town of Montdidier in Picardy. Allied forces had recently won the town back from the German Army. For obvious reasons, it was essential the oil-storage plant remained intact. Allan was down on his stomach, scraping damp dirt from the top of the mine. He knew the type of mine it was. With great care, he lifted up the object and delicately withdrew the fuse from below. He lay there for a moment, sweating, holding the bomb. A quiet pssstt was heard. He realized then that the bomb had been booby-trapped. It could have blown him to small pieces. But the fuse of the trap had become sodden by rain running off the refinery roof. It had exploded, or rather expired, harmlessly.

So Allan Haddock lived to fight on, and to marry Patricia. He had gone on to father the baby they christened Justin John. Justin's very existence was a bit of luck. Way off his improvised Richter scale. He thought he remembered his father saying he had prayed in those moments of life or death, there on his belly. He could well believe it. And no doubt many of the millions of Jews murdered in the Shoah had gone to their deaths with the name of Jehovah on their lips. No one had been there to respond. But the vicar, the Rev. Ted Hayse, still went about God's business as he saw it. He called on Justin, propping his rusty old bike close to Justin's front door. Despite the heat of the day, he was wearing his heavy woollen suit, his one concession to the season being a rosebud in his lapel. He entered No. 29 carrying a neatly folded newspaper. Justin apologized for the disorder of his living room, to which the vicar replied that all that concerned him was the disorder in men's minds.

'So you've come,' said Justin smilingly, 'to lecture me.'

'This is not just a social visit, I fear.' Ted plunged straight into a quotation from Adam Smith's *The Wealth of Nations*. '"In every improved and civilized society, this is the state into which the labouring poor must necessarily fall" – that is to say, into superficiality and stupidity – "and government must take pains to prevent it".'

'You've heard about my window?'

'It must have been alarming for you.'

'It was.'

'Justin, is it not just government that must attempt to eradicate stupidity and superficiality? That burden falls upon my shoulders too . . . Islam has become militant. Many Muslims enter Britain to better themselves. They do not all show humility, as we know. Many even demand Sharia law here. They are intolerant. I know you understand that our culture is based on Christian traditions – from which you benefit although you do not attend church. If we do not support those traditions, we are lost.'

'In no way are we ever going to vote for Sharia law!'

Ted merely nodded. 'You are neither stupid nor superficial. You do understand the situation. Bigotry may win against indifference.

This is not a time to speak out against our religion.' Ted was red in the face as he said this. His rosebud appeared to wilt. Embarrassment filled Justin too, since he understood that it cost Ted dear to utter this reproof.

He said with some humility, as if offering a new thing, 'Part of our traditions is the privilege of free speech. We must exercise it or – as with our sexual activity – we lose it.'

The vicar ignored this remark, asking instead if Justin imagined that people would be happier were religion to be abolished. Finding that he was looking rather nervously about, Justin said abruptly that he could not answer such a hypothetical question. He added, 'But people have to face the truth, even if it hurts.'

Ted contemplated the carpet before saying, in a more hostile tone than he had been using, 'Look, Justin, the hortatory mode does not suit me. Perhaps that's why I make such a bad priest, but you well know . . . well, you believe that you alone know this "truth", do you?'

'Not at all. Hundreds, thousands, of people live satisfactory lives without religion. They know that getting through life is like struggling through a dense fog with nothing at the end of it, but they face facts. They don't seek false comfort. Sorry, Ted. I merely try to articulate a point of view.'

It was a mark of Ted Hayse's discomfort that he took short paces back and forth, without looking at his renegade parishioner. 'Justin, I have concern for you. You are one of my parish; for that and for other things I value you. You do not want a mosque to be built here, on the old Anchor site. So I trust you will not speak out against Christianity. I beg you to understand that I ask this favour not only in my name – and am embarrassed to have to do so.'

With a sigh, he responded, 'I thank you for coming and speaking to me, Ted. But really I cannot set aside what I am doing. I believe it to be truth.'

'You mean – as against more traditional truths?' He smiled in a sickly way. 'I will say nothing more on this subject. But I shall pray that God will grant you a change of mind and heart.' On leaving, the vicar left his newspaper behind – clearly with deliberation. Justin unfolded it out of curiosity. It was the morning's copy of the *Oxford Observer*. Its main headline read: COUNCIL SUPPORTS PLAN FOR NEW HEADINGTON MOSQUE. A smaller headline below read KIC TO CONTRIBUTE AFTER STORMY MEETING.

# 21

## Quetzalcoatl & Co

Justin had to buy a few groceries from Somerfield's supermarket. This was the day, he was sure, he would visit the Greystoke Gallery, whether or not a mosque was going to be built at the end of the road. Shoppers went about their business as usual, unmoved by the news. A solitary young man in soiled jeans stood on the corner by Barclay's Bank, holding a banner which read: ACT NOW! KEEP MULLAHS HANDS OFF HEAD'TON! No possessive after 'mullahs', Justin noted.

He was returning to No. 29, aware that he was walking very slowly, going along the Croft. Fine trees overhung the quiet walk. To one branch, a grey squirrel was clinging. The animal appeared relaxed. Justin stopped and looked up at the squirrel. The squirrel stared back at him. There could be no doubt that this was a conscious creature. It was as if a rapport existed momentarily between human and animal. Then the squirrel decided there was nothing to be gained here. He turned, ran along the branch, tail following in faithful parabola, and swarmed right up into the leafy heights of the tree. Justin could never have climbed a tree more nimbly, even in his long-forgotten tree-climbing days. He thought as he made his way back to No. 29 that squirrels, those sharp-witted little mammals, had developed just as much consciousness as they needed for their successful existence. Intelligence, nimbleness, flight . . . Could the same be said for humans? Perhaps humans had ambition. It was ambition that troubled their lives. Was Sharapova not content to play tennis well, that she must stretch her beautiful limbs at Wimbledon to compete for fame and prizes? What did humans want, that made them so restless? Could the restlessness be connected with the active troposphere – an atmosphere blowing them towards intelligence? Or was there a greater opportunity to be restless than had been the case in previous generations? Could his inability to change, to see the world, have accounted for his father's bad temper? You could bet he had never been attended to by a New Zealand nurse! Nor had he ever gazed on a Hindu girl with such beautiful eyes . . .

Justin now read Chance in everything. Perhaps a chance remark, a push, early in life, directed him, Kate, Ken, Sharapova, into their future occupations. And Claudia with her copy of *She*. And the swine who cut his way through his window. Entering his kitchen, he half-expected to find the floor swarming with ants. Ants had been racing about there when he came down barefoot, early in the morning. Red ants, not only on the floor but on the draining board, along by a pipe near the refrigerator. Dozens and dozens of the hasty things.

The ants had staged an invasion last year and the year before, always at the same season. Their reconnaissance would be followed by the even more irritating flying ants. Justin had fought them off without much success. This was one life form he could not bear. Luckily, he had found in a cupboard an old machine of Janet's, a hand-held vacuum cleaner called, in those bygone days, a dustette. He had got it working again. The dustette ran off a self-charger and was ferociously effective, sucking up ants faster than any anteater. He also had a patent ant-killing powder called, appropriately enough, Ant-Kill, a powder which he spread to make sure that the ants realized to their dismay, directly they burst into his kitchen, that they were entering a pretty hostile environment. Many a human child, emerging, had made no less a discovery. These savage defences he had operated again earlier in the morning, almost before dawn. There were no further incursions. The floor was ant-free. 'Thank God for that,' he said aloud. Perhaps it was then – later, he was never sure – when he uttered that unthinking exclamation – that he made the connection between Chance and religion.

Justin worked on his new – he hardly dared call it a theory – his suspicion. He created a graph on his computer. At times, over a glass of wine, talking with Ken and Marie, he began to feel he had hit on a profound understanding of human nature. He wondered if the alleged accidental shooting of his sister had sharpened Ken's understanding of the workings of the brain. He had never liked to question Ken on the subject; nor had Ken ever volunteered a word on the subject. Yet he surely would not have forgotten such a terrible incident. Perhaps the entire incident had been merely malicious gossip. One thing Ken said interested Justin greatly.

'Take the case of the city of Sodom. Research shows it was destroyed by a stray meteorite – most likely heading in from the Oort cloud. The religious, the superstitious – and the smug, I guess – all claimed that God had done this because the inhabitants of Sodom were such a bad lot. Maybe they were a bad lot, like the inhabitants of most cities you could name. But this was just a cosmic accident. No judgement of any kind involved.'

Now Justin was investigating various websites for facts that would support or contradict his theory. Sociologists, astronomers, biochemists, biologists, geologists, clergy, philosophers, scholars of various hues.

'I believe you will find there is some disagreement about the mass extinction which terminated the Ordovician,' said a palae-ontologist with a creaky voice.

'Could be that religion is carried in the genes – in which case you got problems.' So said a woman's voice from a research centre in Chicago. But by and large no one on the net disputed his theory. Many applauded.

Brilliant tennis was being played at Wimbledon. Federer excelled himself. With the passing days, the blossoms of the hollyhock began their climb from base to top of their stalks. A particular dark red-black flower was his favourite; he had rescued the plant with its seeds from the roadside. Birds sang under the street lamps. A few rare butterflies mooned their ways from bush to bush to buddleia in irregular flight; those extra-clever butterflies who had learnt to fly in a straight line had long ago been eaten by birds, who understood predictability.

It was the day after a violent thunderstorm, when Sharapova was due to be defeated in the semi-finals. A phone call came from Kate in Egypt. Justin's heart became jelly.

'Where are you, Kate?' he asked. He heard his own voice clogged with a junket of hope and dread. 'You in El Aiyat?'

'As a matter of fact we happen to be in a restaurant in Cairo. It's rather noisy. How are you? Listen, Justin, darling, I don't know how to put this, so I will be brutally frank—'

'Kate, I don't want to hear—'

'I don't want to hurt you, but I have to be up front and tell you I am –' a second's hesitation – 'I'm head over heels with a colleague here. I have to be honest and admit—'

'You're what?'

She gave a high, 'Oh! You heard what I said.'

'Why not be honest and tell me his bloody name? It's this Overton fellow, isn't it?' He visualized the place in Cairo, the tatty over-rich furnishings, crowded tables, drinks, various obnoxious people guzzling the drinks, and that young lout by Kate's side, glass in hand, other hand on her waist, he fatuously grinning.

'Look, Justin, please don't get ratty. I'm just trying—'

'Ratty? Ratty? Of course I'm fucking ratty, whatever that means. I'm certainly upset. I thought we loved each other. I thought you—'

'I do love you, Justin, but this is different. Len is a special—'

'Oh yes, of course, it's Len. I should have remembered his first name. I've heard it often enough. So you're up there just to have it off with—'

'Please, please be reasonable, Justin. That's why I'm phoning you. It's late in the day here. Len and I—'

'Don't tell me! You two are shacked up in a hotel in Cairo while the kids in Aiyat can go to hell as far as you're concerned.'

'Little you care about those poor kids. Whereas Len and I have been there working hard all—'

'I don't want to hear any more. Can't you sodding well get the picture? I loved you, I trusted you—'

'Justin, dear, do please listen. I can't help it. It causes me grief to do this to you after all we've been through. I've known Len for over a year and we've always tried to conceal our emotions from each other. We've behaved—'

'I know! Let me guess! He's married, isn't he? Has a faithful wife and maybe children in somewhere like Walton-on-Thames?' He clamped his head between the palms of his hands. 'And now he's throwing it all up for a few quick—'

'You don't understand, Justin! Please! Please, it's not like that, not like whatever you were going to say. We've – oh, we've got so much in common—'

'I'm in perfect misery here, and you are trying to justify your affair with some other guy? What do you think—'

'Sorry, Justin! I sort of hoped that – I know you can't be expected . . . Goodbye!' And she had gone.

He thought that at the last he had heard a male voice prompting her to cut the connection. He was still standing there, nursing his mobile, when Ken arrived, panting and distraught. 'I suppose you've heard the news?' he said. 'The council are going to build a bloody mosque on the corner. A mosque! Maybe it's time to emigrate to Australia.'

'Of all the miseries in the world . . . If you think there's someone in the world, just someone, who believes you are special, who really loves you for all your faults . . . your pedantry . . . it's sort of a protection, a windbreak, against all the human wretchedness you know surges like a storm round everyone. The cold winds of the world . . .

'This is the very day, Seventh of July, the first anniversary of the suicide-bombings in London, when dozens of ordinary people going about their business were killed or injured by those filthy suicide-bombers . . . Prayers are being said – to what effect I don't know . . .

'But not just here. Israel. Palestine. The Ciftsgate next door is going over. Much of Africa. Incorrigible. Iraq, of course. Weeds springing up. North Korea. Now just launched its first feeble missiles. I don't know. The world is so awful. Everywhere, people fart-arsing about, greedy, avaricious. So much to be done. It was always awful. Maybe it's worse today. The population ever expanding – more mouths eating, eating, means less food to go round . . . Less water . . .

'The sorrow of it all. Sometimes I just feel like giving up. Why struggle when often enough you despise what you are struggling for? But Kate, my darling Kate Standish . . . to think . . . oh, hell . . .

'I always thought she really and truly . . . well, loved me . . .'
He played his CD of Gorecki's *Symphony of Sorrowful Songs*, with
the plangent voice of Susan Gritton calling at intervals. The Songs
chimed with his mood but did not heal it.

Justin tried to get on with his list. Was it chance or planning
that Kate had met Len Overton? Probably planning. But he
could not decide. Leave it out. Weeds grew. Days passed. He did
the washing. Maude slept on a rug in the garden. Scalli did not
attempt to come. The builders did not attempt to come. He had
thought bitterly and badly of Kate since her call from Cairo.
Now he felt differently. *Poor dear woman, she has to look after
herself. I'm far too old for her. Now if she's found a better prospect,
well . . . good luck to her! – Let's hope the little sod is decent to
her . . .*

A demonstration against the building of a mosque in Old
Headington had been held on the Barclay's Bank corner. Justin
did not attend. He heard that police had been called in. He understood that not many people had attended the demo.

'They probably thought that Old Headington citizens were a
lot of snobs who deserved all they got,' Ken said. His wife agreed.

'You notice the police are apparently doing nothing about Om
Haldar's disappearance. Isn't that racism? If it had been a white
girl who had suddenly disappeared, there'd be headlines in all the
papers.'

Working back through history, Justin stumbled on AD 1588 and
the attack of the Spanish Armada, consisting of 138 vessels, sailing
northwards to confound the English and turn them back into
Catholics. The English fleet consisted of 34 royal warships and a
considerable scatter of privately owned ships. Unseasonal weather
set in, driving the dispersed Spanish fleet northwards. Their ships
were forced round the north of Scotland and Ireland. Can we
doubt that the soldiers and sailors aboard prayed fervently to their

God? To the Virgin Mary? To the Pope? In the severe weather, something like thirty ships foundered. It was reckoned that some 11,000 Spaniards perished. The freak weather was largely responsible for saving England from invasion. This again was the operation of Chance on a considerable scale.

Pondering such things mitigated Justin's sense of desolation. Moreover, the desolation fuelled his research. He worked almost incessantly, without distractions. The milkman still called, leaving him his regular pint of milk. Birds sang under the street lamps. He forced himself occasionally to walk up to the supermarket for food. Otherwise, he took heart from the example of two ancient Greeks: the remarkable Eratosthenes, who by careful observation measured the circumference of the Earth with striking accuracy; and Hipparcus, the first astronomer who, by patient observation, established the latitude and longitude of many stars, and poured contempt on astrologers. Wonderful men, eager to comprehend the universe in which they found themselves. The accidental nature of the growth of the British Empire had long since been established.

A horse chestnut grew hip-high from a nut planted and forgotten by a squirrel. Two jackdaws quarrelled noisily in the little tree. The Headington roundabout was being steadily reconstructed, causing more traffic delays. A break from study came when Justin walked down Logic Lane to see his friends, Marie and Ken. They were ever welcoming, and plied him with wine and food and jolly talk about their plentiful relations. The subject of religion was of interest to them. Marie was French. She had come to England to exchange a restrictive Catholicism in her native village for atheism in England. She and Ken had recently visited the United States, looking up some of his relations. Passing through Kansas, they had stayed in a hotel where a convention of born-again Christians was being held. They were in an elevator with a large bony man wearing a T-shirt saying REPENT. He turned to Ken, a complete stranger, to ask, 'Have you found Jesus yet, my friend?'

Ken had the wit to look puzzled and ask, 'Jesus who?' Both Ken and Justin had a reputation for being cool customers. The Reverend Ted, meeting Justin on the previous day, apologized for his recent intrusion, and said that he regretted that Justin's sweetheart (as he put it) had gone. Justin had remarked with a drawl, 'Oh well, it was time I was getting a new one anyway.'

With Marie making an occasional witty interjection – and supplying them meanwhile with little delicacies – Ken and Justin discussed the state of play in the world. Not only the threat of a mosque on their doorstep. Ken had heard that British troops in Afghanistan were now permitted to grow beards, in order to mix in better with the bearded local population. Both men were dismayed that British troops were in action in Afghanistan again.

'Don't people learn from history?' Ken asked. 'You Brits waged two wars against Afghanistan in the nineteenth century and came away with bloody noses both times.'

'And I believe they tried again, oddly enough, after World War One,' said Marie, producing a plate full of strips of smoked salmon on fingers of brown bread. 'As if they had not had enough bloodshed. And of course another bloody nose resulted!'

'Then the Soviets had a go.'

'Did I read somewhere that the British and Americans funded bin Laden then, and supplied him with arms against the Ruskies?'

'Yes. Very murky waters . . .' said Ken. 'It defies belief.' He poured them more wine. They were drinking a Shiraz called Bin 555, from the Wyndham Estate in Australia. 'Happily, this wine isn't murky.'

'Happily it isn't water either.'

At another session, when the three of them were together, Justin sketched his planned Chance/religious theory, expecting Ken would be sympathetic. But Ken was not entirely sympathetic. He pointed to all the great art and music engendered by the Christian religion.

'But the geniuses, your Michelangelos and Bachs, would have found other outlets for their creativity. True, Ezekiel would not have been a great loss.'

Ken shook his head. 'Can you really see cathedrals built to atheism?'

Justin said, 'Wouldn't the money have been better spent on good drainage systems? That would have cut down on the plagues.'

'In Christendom, it was not the time for drainage systems. It was a time for lofty cathedrals to lift the spirits of the poor.'

'Food would have better served that end,' said Marie.

Pressing home his disadvantage, Ken added, 'I believe it was Voltaire who remarked that if God did not exist it would be necessary to invent him.'

'Two centuries later, he might think it better if we uninvented him.' Fortunately, Marie agreed with what Justin had said about Chance. 'Chance is like smoking – bad for you! Hence the well-known folk saying, Shit happens!'

Ken had advice for when Justin's thesis was completed. 'You must send a copy to the Bishop of Oxford,' he said. 'Then perhaps, if he believed you, he would air it on *Thought for Today*.'

'"I have learned to be truthful", said Marie, in the sepulchral voice she liked to think bishops used when conveying eternal truths, '"and to be frank the propositions of Mr Justin Haydock have turned me into a raving atheist, so up yours, the lot of you!"'

'Why doesn't the bishop protest against a mosque being planted here?'

'He's probably got shares in KIC.'

With such encouragement, Justin continued his work.

He was having a glass of wine with the Rev. Ted Hayse, who had come round to show there were no hard feelings between them. Justin felt like teasing him. 'You must be eager to see a mosque here – on the grounds that the more worshipping that's going on, the better.'

'My dear Justin,' spoken with feigned patience, 'I much prefer bums on seats to bums in air. Particularly female bums on seats.'

'Muslims don't let women into mosques, do they?'

'I am happily unaware of the foibles of their religion.'

Justin felt compelled to mention the animal-headed apparition; he had seen it in the garden on the previous day.

'You'd be surprised how many of my parishioners confess to seeing similar phantoms. Generally it signifies they are about to die.' Ted added, with a tender glance, 'I hope that's not the case with you. I would greatly miss your supply of Shiraz.'

'Forgive my saying so, Ted, but it is reason that stops me being religious – yet here is a phantom that defies reason, and which I have to concede exists.'

'Faith is greater than reason when it comes to belief in God. Human reason is a faulty thing, in my opinion. This unpleasant phantom you see exists only in your mind. Would you feel more or would you feel less comfortable if this creature had real existence?'

They were sitting companionably on the benches in the court-yard, under the sun umbrella. Justin showed some of his Chance notes to the vicar. The vicar took a pair of steel-rimmed spectacles from his breast pocket and studied them carefully. 'Very clever, Justin. But you know it is my duty not to agree with you.' He spoke in his usual calm agreeable way.

'Ted, can I ask you? Do you really, in your heart of hearts, believe in God and the Holy Trinity?'

Ted clasped his hands together. Then he looked up smiling into Justin's eyes. 'I believe in people. Perhaps that is one way an unworthy man comes to God.'

The majority of people all over the globe – those people in whom the vicar believed – lived difficult lives. In Justin's opinion, lives across which the winds of Chance blew. There was no possible protection from such winds. However, in whatever country you visited, you found there two items common to all: lotteries of one kind or another and temples of worship of one kind or another. Religion was needed, it seemed, to fight fickle fate. The one exception Justin could think of to this universal dual commitment was Albania in the days of the dictator Enver Hoxha. Hoxha had declared Albania an atheist state. After his death, the nation had gone in for a form of lottery, virtually ruining itself thereby. It was said that peasant farmers invested their little all for the illusory hope of bettering their lot – and lost the lot! Human desperation was such that those who entered lotteries frequently went also to places of worship.

He sat pondering this anomaly, wondering how to advance his argument – and indeed if his findings were verifiable. He fell asleep. Or rather – he had to face the fact – he passed out. One moment he was awake, alert; then, without warning, he was unconscious. When he roused, he took a moment to orient himself. This blank in his life, this absent slice of the cake of existence, puzzled him. He knew it had happened before, when he had ignored its implications. How simple it was to conclude that one day he might never awaken from such unconsciousness. Of course, it was an easy way to go, if disconcerting for onlookers. But he did not wish to go before his thesis was completed.

Next morning, after a grey dawn, the sun came blazing through. There had been a bomb outrage in Mumbai, crowded trains all but destroyed, with hundreds killed or injured. But Old Headington and Oxford remained safe for the present. The birds sang under the street lamps. Apples quietly ripened. A fly buzzed in the kitchen. Justin hated flies. Now he was old, their buzzing and the erratic course of their flight worried him. Here was the question: should he open the window to let the fly escape or would the open window only invite in more flies? He solved the question by leaving the window half-open. Getting himself a bowl of cereal, Justin noted that the floor was still blessedly ant-free. He poured some of Hartley's canned raspberries on the cornflakes, as if for a libation. He was due for another blood test, to check on the warfarin dosages. He swallowed his diuretic pills and then set out for the local hospital, the JR.

The grounds of the JR were pleasant, although patches of garden were neglected. He passed sick-looking people sitting on benches smoking. He restrained himself from telling them that breaking the habit might make them feel better. By the main doors of the hospital, various boxes of equipment were being unloaded from vans. The workers wore grey shirts and pullovers, despite the heat and the energies required of their trade. The wide reception chamber was always interesting. To enter there was almost to be magically transplanted to Cairo. Representatives of all races came and went. Some looked rational, some even cheerful, whereas others looked distraught – either on their own account or on behalf of some relation lingering in a ward on an upper floor. This was a great terminus; some of its temporary travellers alighting here were destined to continue on their journeys; others were heading for the buffers.

Justin made his way through the labyrinth of corridors to the Blood Test Centre. There worked the Anti-Coagulation Team, represented by pleasant nurses. Justin became unaffectedly cheerful and jokey, believing that most of the people having blood taken would be old and gloomy or silent and nervous. He was, he felt, none of these things – all things which must tend to depress the nurses. The nurse – not from New Zealand, unfortunately – who took Justin's blood spoke of a large solid sportsman she knew who had fainted away at the sight of the syringe. But syringes these days were modest little plastic things, delivering a mere bee sting, unlike the syringes of Justin's youth, which had been formidable chrome beasts, capable of removing a quart of blood as soon as look at you, or of giving you a monster clyster right up the anal orifice . . . Walking back through the hospital grounds, he was passing a nook where a bench stood amid a cluster of bamboo, when someone called his name. There sat Hughes, smoking the last inch of a cigarette, which he gripped inside his cupped hand.

'What's up with you, then, Jus?' he called.

Justin halted and contemplated the tumbledown man, as ever wearing his uniform of ill-fitting yellow jacket. 'I suppose you might say I am suffering from the human condition. Though I'm old enough to be well accustomed to it by now.'

'You trying to be clever!' That jeering note. 'You don't like talking to me. You think I'll do you a mischief.'

'More like wary than scared, I'd say. But inclined to be amiable. I don't know what you are going to do next, and I don't suppose you do. What are you up to today?'

Hughes took a last pull at the stub of his cigarette before throwing it down and grinding it underfoot, forcefully, as if it were a poisonous snake. 'You? What you doing?'

Well, why not say it? 'I am trying to formulate a plan to release mankind from its dependence on religion, as you from your cigarettes, so that we can live to create better conditions for ourselves.'

Hughes emitted a kind of laugh. 'You're a nutter. I don't mean ter be rude. A posh nutter – up agin us ordinary folk.'

'I wouldn't call you ordinary.'

Hughes stood up. He looked weary, his face smudged by inner conflict. 'Don't try and take the mickey out of me, Jus. That's my job. What's yours? To be posh?'

Justin showed some annoyance. 'What's this posh nonsense? We share the human condition – puzzlement, hatred, fear, squalor. Surely you can see that's the case?'

The other mumbled, 'Speak for yourself.' He sank back down on to the bench, elbows on knees, scruffy head between hands, in a position of deepest melancholy. 'I dunno what's the case. That's half the trouble.'

'Would it please you to know I feel the same about "the case"?'

Hughes looked up suddenly, grinning. 'You know half the time I dunno what you're talkin' about?'

Justin stood contemplating this unhappy figure. 'I don't much like leaving you like this. And you know we all have something to grieve about.'

'Oh, bugger off,' said Hughes. 'Leave me in peace.'

'But you're not in peace, Hughes. Can't you make an appointment to see someone in this hospital? They'd help you.'

He looked up suddenly with a distortion on his face like a smile, and shot out a hand. 'Shake my hand then, Jus!'

'What? You? How about my window?'

'Stuffy stinking house – not that I know anything about it.'

Anything to disconcert, Justin thought. He took the grimy outstretched hand and shook it. A chill of compassion, even of brotherhood, overcame him. Hughes' look never changed. But he said, 'No man ever done that for a while. May the Lord bless yer! Sorry if I buggered you about.'

Justin stood there scowling, contemplating Hughes, before recommencing his slow dragging walk back to No. 29. He felt slightly seedy, and promised himself a coffee when he got home. This coffee he took in its Carlisle mug, to sit outside in the courtyard under the sun umbrella and relax for five minutes.

Dreamily thinking of Kate, he sat, half-remorseful, half-spiteful. A movement caught his eye. A squirrel had entered the courtyard and was moving along by the edges of the low stone walls. Here weeds grew and, in particular, the wild strawberries, many now fruiting. The squirrel was picking the reddest of these tiny fruits and eating them. He then moved on to the next cluster, again picking the ripest berries. The squirrel ate sitting up, holding the strawberries to his mouth in his paws in a human manner. Justin dared not move in case he scared the creature and spoilt its enjoyment. When it considered it had had enough, it ran with its usual frisky movement, in the joy of action. Suddenly, it was on the bench, close to Justin. Startled, he made to brush it away. The animal was off. So was the Carlisle mug. Justin's unthinking gesture sent it flying. It shattered on the paving stones. As Justin stooped to pick up the fragments, he saw the shop where he and Janet had bought the mug – for no particular reason – and the dried-up little man who ran the shop had wrapped it in a page of the local paper. They had left the shop, chuckling just from happiness. He recalled her shining eyes, her cheeks, her lovely lips – lips he would never again kiss . . . he laid the pieces of the broken mug in front of him. So so sorry, my sweet wife . . .

Justin left the fragments of the broken mug on the bench and went inside. He set his fingers to the keyboard of his computer and wrote, hesitantly at first.

So Chance was uncomfortable to live with, both in practice and in prospect. What measures have human kind taken to deal with Chance?

As in Poe's story, 'The Masque of the Red Death', the prince and his companions sequestered themselves behind strong fortifications. Yet still the Red Death gained entry to the palace. Poe gives no explanation of how it entered. For mischance there is no explanation.

So, long ago, a form of protection was devised. No one can say how long ago it was that the concept of gods and goddesses was born. Concept? Mania, rather! Confronted by a volcanic eruption, a gigantic tidal wave or a forest fire, there must have been a tribal sense that something malign and with intention was victimizing them. They had sinned. Of course they had sinned, and so they paid the price.

He thought of the crazy Indonesian, who ascribed chthonic upheaval to the misbehaviour of the local citizenry. As if they were important enough to move mountains. As if Indonesia did not straddle a fault line . . .

Justin worked slowly. He had what he suspected was arthritis in his right hand. Also, the mere idea that there might be some callous creature high overhead causing volcanic eruptions and tsunamis greatly depressed him. Had this same creature put Len Overton in Kate's way, just to spite him? He admitted to himself that he was miserable without her, and misery brought out a superstitious streak which on reflection he believed most people possessed, passed on from generation to generation. Maybe the ghastly horse-faced apparition which occasionally confronted him was somehow generated by Kate's absence. Or was it, as Reverend Ted had suggested, a signal of his coming death?

The hospital phoned to say his INR number was now at 2. 'Great news,' he said, to encourage the person at the other end, who responded cheerfully by saying 'Well done,' before ringing off. But what had he done? And what exactly was his INR number? No doubt he would find out sooner or later.

And so this supposed malign force that sent lava down hillsides or despoiled crops or caused one's beloved child to die, acquired a personality, at first a malign personality. At best an overbearing personality.

Among the many violent gods of an earlier age was Quetzalcoatl, a violent creature of mixed nature, physically at once snake and bird, metaphysically heaven and earth, life and death. Quetzalcoatl presided over the Aztec state, where human sacrifice prevailed. Hundreds of captives were slaughtered every year, in order to renew the strength of this horrific god.

Quetzalcoatl was only one extreme example of the many gods representing the dark side of the human psyche. Spawned alongside them went countless malign or mischievous spirits of a lower hierarchy: hobgoblins, fairies, changelings, ghosts, ghouls, things that go bump in the night. And what of those so-called familiars

– demons, vampires, satyrs, succubi, incubi, banshees – all those terrible things spawned in the blindly constructed torrents of human thought, imagination turned murderously in on itself? He reflected that everything we strive to comprehend today entails looking back to the past, often to a smoky distant past. Or was that merely the fancy of an ageing man? Nowadays, these near- but non-human things had been updated. Assisted by Hollywood, many people now believed in the waking dead, in hostile aliens and in blank-faced robots. All these embodiments of fear and isolation survived in the minds of men and women. These inhuman things seemed to rush in and deflect Justin's mind from his main purpose. How terrible it was that humans should so readily plague themselves with these phantasms.

The front doorbell rang. He struggled into a vertical position and went to answer it. Captain Derek Dalsher, neat as paint, was standing on his doorstep.

'Good evening,' he said, with his usual punctilio. 'Do forgive my disturbing you.' He produced a clipboard. *Clipboard Man* thought Justin.

'We have among us, in our little society' – he nodded in complete agreement with his own phrase – 'a vagabond by the name of Hughes.'

'He's not a vagabond. He has a room locally – one of yours, as it happens – and works at Ruskin as a gardener.' Dalsher ignored this remark. With his free hand he delicately brushed it away.

'Master Hughes is causing discomfort and, I may say, anxiety amongst some of our older citizens hereabouts. I have taken it upon myself to gather signatures to have Hughes removed to a home, out of harm's way. I'm working together with Guy Fitzgerald. He's a friend of mine.

'Witnesses claim Hughes has been troubling you. I hope I can count on your signature, Mr Haydock?' He gave one of his carefully selected smiles.

'Sorry,' said Justin. 'Jack Hughes is a friend of mine.'

'Oh, but surely—'

Justin shut the door on his visitor. *What a rude bastard I am*, he thought.

He could not sleep that night. Just after 3 a.m., he heaved himself from his bed, preparing to go downstairs and make himself a cup of tea. He drew back the curtain of the window facing due east. A distant line of modest houses could be seen through the trees. A light shone in one of the bedroom windows; he always wondered about the occupant of that room. The moon was almost full. A grey light flooded the garden. He had rarely seen such brightness in the middle of a summer's night. In the distance, the church tower of St Andrew showed above the trees, only its glittering weather vane visible at this hour. All was absolutely still until a bat flitted by the window and flew in the direction of the church. Bats were rarely seen, and sight of this one was soon lost. *Poor solitary creature!* thought Justin to himself. Or was it the soul of Janet, his dead wife? He reproved himself for the foolish thought, entering consciousness unbidden. 'Oh wearisome condition of humanity – born under one law, to another bound . . .' He had forgotten how Fulke Greville's poem continued. An evil grey light seemed to devour all things in the mind as he stared motionlessly out through the glass. And Kate so far away . . . He had found Greville's poem in an anthology of Aldous Huxley's. Huxley had been a guiding light in Justin's youth. He regarded Aldous Huxley as a great man still. But there again ill chance had entered. Huxley died on the day John F. Kennedy was shot in Dallas. So Huxley had missed deserved and extensive obituaries, summing up a distinguished career, with its parabola from Eton College to the coast of California.

Later in the morning, he showered and powdered those parts most likely to become smelly. After a coffee and a banana, he was at work again. He had taken his diuretic pills, the effects of which interrupted his discourse every quarter of an hour. It was a good job that the penis was waterproof.

So all manner of gods and sods and goddesses had been invented to defend people from the indignities of Chance, as sticking plaster was invented to cover a cut. And why? One answer was that whereas there was no defence against Chance, no armour against fate, the gods could possibly be controlled, or persuaded to take one's side. Many were the ways in which propitiation could take place: burnt offerings, human sacrifices, hymns of obsequious praise, prayer, general whingeing mixed with nationalism, music, dance, bums in air or knees on ground. Prostration, circumcision, even castration. All to squeeze a little favouritism from whatever god was à la mode. Of course such ruses never worked. There was no compassion to be had: the babe died of whooping cough, the son became a liar and a thief, the husband ran off with the barmaid, the wife died of cancer. The car broke down, the harvest failed from lack of rain or from too much rain, the horse went lame, the swarms of locusts arrived. Your house burnt down, floods swept away your little all. Pray as you might, these things still happened. Shit happened. There was no one in to answer the call.

Of course, the idea of religion had been taken up by those who might have been regarded as the most enlightened, the rulers, the powerful. All claimed to hold authority by the grace of God. He, God himself, was on their side. He enhanced their enthronement. Queen Elizabeth the Second of England, by the Grace of God, was Defender of the Faith, with the faith presumed to be her defender.

Justin rushed to the loo again. As he emerged, Ken arrived for a chat.

'I'm frightening myself,' said Justin, grinning.

'Not to the extent of shitting yourself?'

'This was just a rehearsal, thanks.'

'A dry run . . .'

Ken helped Justin fix the leg-risers to Justin's favourite chair. They did indeed make getting up easier. But they looked hideous. Another step down the one-way ladder. Justin brought from the fridge two bottles of one of the summer's fruit juices, pineapple, mango and passion fruit, and filled two glasses. They went and sat in the garden under the sun shade.

'You must feel a bit stuck on your own,' said Ken. 'Come round and have a meal with us. Marie has got some steak from ASDA.' Of course Justin accepted the invitation. Ken was upset about what threatened to become the opening of a new war in the Middle East. He blamed Israel for over-reacting. Israel had been bombing Lebanon, killing children and innocent civilians, and also putting Beirut's international airport out of action. Whatever reasons Israel had for these attacks, the results could only be an increase in hatred on all sides. Hezbollah had fired one hundred rockets in return. Twenty towns and villages had been hit.

'The British bear some responsibility for all this,' said Justin.

'The Balfour Declaration, you mean? But the place was a desert until the Jews moved in.'

'How's the steak?' Marie asked.

'Still, it was a bit lavish of the British to pledge a slice of a foreign land to anyone, wasn't it?'

'The Israelis certainly set about irrigating and cultivating the land. Remember the time of the kibbutzim? Of course the Arabs want it back now that it's such a flourishing place.'

'Religion sharpens the conflict as much as does hunger.'

'How's the bloody steak?' Marie asked.

'Fine. Yes, but it's almost entirely a territorial struggle. It's just bad luck that Jesus Christ was born there.'

'Send the Archbishop of Canterbury out, make him convert both sides to the C of E. Then we might be getting somewhere.'

'That's the last steak you get out of me,' said Marie. The

271

discussion went on. They talked about the role America should play in the conflict. They graduated to a sound French wine.

'Well, the problems of the Middle East have been settled in Old Headington,' said Ken, as Justin finally rose to go an hour later. They agreed to meet at the Café Noir on the following evening.

'How old is the oldest skull ever dug up? Do you know?' Justin asked, as his friend saw him out.

'Don't forget the local meeting tomorrow night,' said Ken, patting his shoulder. 'I know you're a bit of a hermit. But' – lapsing into American English – 'you godda be there!'

Night had fallen, although it was not entirely dark. The planet rotated, bearing the world's denizens from light to dark or from dark to light. It made no special dispensation for Old Headington.

The site where the old Anchor had stood was now all but a flat concrete plain. Justin walked up the hill to St Andrews Road. The way was dotted by street lights, their illumination washing against old stone walls, where the old stone houses stood one beside the other, shoulder to shoulder against time. Then the road widened to make way for the little triangle of grass where roads divided. A fine sycamore grew on the triangle. By night, this junction resembled a stage set, particularly when rain had fallen and the roads gleamed. Then Old Headington was at its most beautiful.

Saying to himself that he was fortunate to have good friends, and was not at all lonely, Justin suddenly stopped. He steadied himself with one hand on the church wall to listen, thinking he was being followed.

'Janet?' he called questioningly. No reply came. Of course – she had gone to Carlisle to live. He leant against the stonework and covered his eyes, close to tears. 'You fool,' he whispered. He knew his wife was dead. In a flash of memory, he recalled sitting by her bed in the hospice, holding her hand. The hand was already growing chill. Love, fear and sorrow caked his mind, the desert that concluded a fine meal.

272

'I'll take a train up to Carlisle and see for myself,' he said now. 'I'll take Dave.' He realized he was posturing. He heaved himself into a vertical position and laboured on his way through the quiet street. Perhaps he was just a little drunk, and not insane.

# 22

## The Meeting at the Village Hall

It was back to the great work for Justin.

Palaeontologists have retrieved from the earth skulls of early humans, some dating back a million years. Through them we trace something of human development. That in itself is one of the great works of science.

As surprising is the fact that these trophies exist often intact in the ground for so long.

Evolution, that great artificer, concentrated on developing the strength of bone at the expense of what it was supposed to protect inside the skull. Ancient skulls so far rescued are bereft of skin and hair and brains. The brain developed in the darkness, left to shift for itself.

He paused before continuing:

> Evidence of the brain's slow development over the centuries is enshrined within the brains of our own generations. This is where the bogeymen live. This is where the gods and devils lurk. One in four people hear voices. Birds sing under the street lamps.
>
> Science – many sciences – have produced no evidence that any of these spectral figures exist in reality: reality, that weird place that goes on beyond the brain. Jesus came among us in human form. Did he also walk, eons earlier, in the form of a dinosaur, to teach such carnivores as Tyrannosaurus Rex not to eat its vegetarian brothers? Did he walk green-skinned among the Martians? There may have been some form of conscious entity we cannot imagine who gave the initial push that brought about the Big Bang. But if so, there has been no sign of him since. Only process. Left behind like a trail of urine . . .

The day was darkening when Justin looked up from his computer. He was startled to see, staring through the window, the phantom that haunted him, holding its spear, its pallid horse-face showing its yellow-toothed kind of mirth, as if its death, all death, was just an evil kind of humour. With a sudden accession of courage, Justin opened the back door and approached the creature. It was without movement, awaiting him, yet it had turned through forty-five degrees, so that it now faced him, still sick, still menacing in its very stillness. Justin took a deep breath and moved a few paces towards it. He was within two feet of it when the phantom faded and was gone. Triumph filled him. The thing was a phantasm of his mind. Of course there were no gods, no ghosts, no Baal . . . Only the bloody human condition. Age inevitably brought various kinds of deterioration. It could be that his primary visual cortex at the rear of the brain was impaired.

He returned indoors and poured himself a glass of wine. He raised the glass to himself. 'Bloody good!' he said aloud. It was clear to him and to many others of the educated all round the world that God in his various forms did not exist. So how was it that the religious and the religious maniacs still proliferated? Had they not heard of Charles Darwin, to name but a few?

There may be a genetic compulsion towards religion, yet to be diagnosed. Chance is neutral in this aspect, free of genes – if anything, possibly tending to keep people apart. But religion gathers people into crowds and congregations. True there are some hermits who seek religious sanctity in solitude, in deserts or on mountain sides. But they are exceptional.

Religion impels the construction of mosques and temples and chapels and cathedrals. There many of the pious press together, thus easing the tendency of diseases to propagate themselves and encouraging bacteria, which gain easier access to replication where the holy jostle. People are mere agents for illness, for the sly stilettos of any virus.

He thought this point he raised was particularly important, rewriting it several times until he arrived at,

Religious people are like shoals of fish. The closer they swim, the more easily they are caught in the nets of various illnesses.

Since humans do not find sickness and death particularly desirable, they would do well to avoid congregations. The person on the prayer mat by your side, the person in the pew next to you, could be your secret nemeses. When two or three are gathered together in God's name, infection gets lucky.

Faster than you planned for, you would discover that there was no heaven, no paradise, no virgins awaiting deflowering. No Resurrection, only corruption and the stinks of corruption.

Justin was fairly pleased with this speculation. On reflection, he became less pleased. He felt he had made a good case against religion in his first draft. No doubt it could be improved later. It was all very well to claim that religion had developed as a salve, a fortification, against Chance; but the strength of the case could be greatly improved if he could stress to grander effect the prevalence of Chance, and its devastations.

He glanced at his watch. Almost time for the meeting at the village hall. He then realized he had in his inner jacket pocket a letter from Kate. It had arrived by the morning post. So absorbed was he with his thoughts that even Kate's letter had been forgotten. He must be in a bad way!

With his letter knife, he slit open the envelope carrying an Egyptian postage stamp. As the page of thin air-mail paper was unfolded, it rustled with its brief message.

In her round hand, Kate had written

*My dear Justin,*

*I hope you are not too upset by my news of a new love. It seemed the most honest thing I could do, to tell you immediately. I did not want to be underhand. The truth is that Len and I work very hard here at El Aiyat. Not much time for romance!*

*The temperature is in the upper forties Centigrade. In other words it's B hot! The poor children need all our care. A little girl died yesterday – malnutrition and pneumonia – and so we are all very sad. Both a priest and Len said something to comfort us over her grave.*

*If you feel at all lonely, you could speak to kind Rev Ted in Old Headington – which at present seems so far away!*

*Love, Kate*

*P.S. – Also Len is about my age.*

What Justin found most melancholy was that P.S. No doubt Kate had added it to justify herself, but he detected, or thought he detected, an element of spite in it. He was too old to have a lover, she was saying. Well, truth is often spiteful. Belatedly, he realized how greatly Kate's love had buoyed him up. To face old age alone was a grim prospect. He realized what a rough sea surrounded him, with no prospect that the storm would abate. When he thought of his son Dave, whose entire life was spent in a kind of isolation, he reproached himself for his self-pity. When he died, his son would become even more isolated. It was a shame that Janet and he had not had a second son or a daughter, either of whom might provide company or help for Dave. But Janet had been too upset by Dave's handicaps to wish for a second child.

He went over to the village hall in a bad mood. The rows of chairs were almost full of locals. Ken raised a hand, smiling. He had saved a seat for Justin. Justin went and sat by Ken and Marie.

'Almost thought you had forgotten,' said Marie. 'Too busy changing the world!'

Terry Owen was busy carrying in more chairs from the store as people crowded in to the hall. Many of them Justin recognized, many he did not know. After a while, in marched no lesser person than Captain Derek Dalsher, bald head agleam with the importance of the role he was playing. Dalsher was escorting a smart sturdy man in a hairy brown suit; his own hair was rather sparse but, as if to compensate, he wore large horn-rimmed spectacles. Humbly following his master was a spotty youth with a crop of yellow hair, carrying a laptop under his arm. The duo settled themselves behind a table facing the audience, while the spotty youth, sideways on to the audience, set up his laptop. As the noise from the audience was dying, Dalsher cleared his throat and spoke.

'Good evening. My name is Captain Derek Dalsher. Many of you will know me. We are here this evening to discuss the utilization of the site of the former public house, the Anchor. And we have with us a brave representative of the County Council – under whose aegis the site and its development falls – Councillor Harry Bains-Jones.'

Some of the audience began politely to clap. Dalsher quelled it with a wave of his hand, and said, 'I need not remind you that we are a civilized community and therefore will not indulge in racist remarks.' A low rumble greeted this suggestion. A voice from the rear row of seats shouted, 'This is a racist matter!'

Terry Owen immediately stood up. 'There's no question of racism. It's a question of the maintenance of the unique character of the old village. I know that automobiles turn it into a kind of race track twice a day, at rush hours, but otherwise it is quiet and a refuge from the bustle of the town. Anything built on the Anchor site that causes additional disruption is to be deplored.'

A man two chairs away from Terry said, 'We must move with the times. We can't be stuck for ever in a sort of nineteenth-century time warp. How about a cinema with shops, or a luxury hotel? Let's hear what the councillor has up his sleeve.'

This gave Bains-Jones the chance to speak in his deep slow voice. 'I am here to listen to all your comments. You must understand that the Council has made no decisions as yet, contrary to what you may read in the press. We have various economic considerations before us, but I think I should warn you that, although you consider Old Headington unique, that is not the case. There are plenty of villages in Oxfordshire of the same antiquity and, if I may venture an opinion, we have here an anachronism that should be brought up to date, benefiting, for instance, from a road-widening scheme on which the County Council will shortly embark.'

There were cries of shame at this. Vera Owen, Terry's wife, was heard to shout, 'You're supposed to be doing away with cars! Are you doing away with old villages too?'

Above the din, Maurice's voice was heard. 'I understand that you plan to build a gambling casino on the old site.'

'Whatever gave you that idea?' asked Bains-Jones.

'I have it on good authority.' He added, 'I'm sure the vicar will back me on this.'

Thus called upon, Rev. Ted Hayse got to his feet. 'I confess I had not heard about a plan to build a casino. I'm a bit surprised. There are plenty of places in the London Road where you can place a bet if you so wish. I am concerned with the continuity of our dear country, its history and culture – for instance as represented by the church and possibly – though perhaps as a vicar I should not say this – by the homely little White Hart pub.

'As is well known, gambling leads many families into poverty and destitution. Though as much might be said of too great a reliance on beer. God is so much better for you.' His modest bearing and his modest speech drew laughter and sympathetic applause.

'We do not have plans for a casino,' said Bains-Jones. 'I have no idea where that idea came from. I can tell you now it has not entered into our considerations.'

Whereupon Laura Broughton stood up. 'But do you deny that there are plans to build a mosque on the old site? Why not be honest about that?'

Bains-Jones gave his slow answer. 'As I have said, we have no definite plans. We have made no definite decisions. However, we can see, in consultation with the construction companies, that the Anchor presents us with a splendid opportunity to incorporate Islamic styles of worship into our multi-national Headington.'

'Over my dead body!' came the voice from the back row. A great hubbub broke out. Many were standing up, haranguing their neighbours. There was much shouting and a great number of arms being waved.

'Religion again,' said Justin.

It prompted Ken to say, directing his words to the chair, 'Are you people culturally blind? A mosque in Old Headington? There are no Muslims here. How about a decent school, for instance?'

Justin spoke up, 'I have to contradict my friend in one respect. There are indeed people of Islam living peacefully amongst us. But they are here to escape from the lands of their birth – and so would presumably be the last people to welcome a mosque nearby.'

Ignoring Justin's statement, Bains-Jones said, 'Before we go any further, you should study the kind of mosque we have in mind. Mike, if you please.' At this request, the nervous young man pressed buttons on his laptop. On a wide screen behind the chair, a picture leapt into brilliant life. It showed a mosque faced with what appeared to be white marble. Its domed roof was in jade-green tiling, while a minaret loomed over it, also tiled in green.

'Observe its beauty and style, things which are sadly lacking—'

He was interrupted by a woman shouting, 'You mean we'd have to put up with a muezzin five times a day? The bloody church bells are bad enough!' Laughter and clapping broke out.

A retired architect called Hudson asked, 'And how much has this model already cost?' To which question, Bains-Jones replied that the KIC, the consortium which had purchased the site in question, had provided the model free of charge.

'It's a left-over,' Hudson responded contemptuously. 'I recognize it. It was designed for Baghdad, what's left of it, or Tehran or anywhere in the Arab world, but certainly not for Old Headington. It's a monstrous object.'

'Its beauty may not be apparent to you,' said Bains-Jones, in deepest tones. 'It is nevertheless a splendid example of Oriental architecture and would form a striking feature of Old Headington.'

Ken repeated his previous remark in slightly different form. 'Why not build a decent school with a playing field? There are children here but no Muslims.' In an aside, the councillor said to the computer nerd, 'Switch that bloody thing off. It only stirs up the animals.' He then resumed his calm authoritative manner to address the audience.

'There are no active Muslims nearby at present. I grant you that,' said Bains-Jones, apparently unperturbed by the general shindig in the hall, where many people were standing. 'But they will come if there is a mosque here for them.'

'You're offering that as a valid reason for building a mosque?'

'We need to welcome the Muslims into our community,' said the councillor firmly.

Again Laura Broughton was on her feet. 'You offer that as a sop to Muslims at our expense? It seems to me and to many others that many Muslims – such is their faith – do not wish to integrate. You must have seen the demonstration, televised last week, where a crowd of Muslims were parading round London with placards saying BEHEAD ANYONE WHO INSULTS ISLAM. Doesn't that tell you anything?'

'Yes, why weren't they arrested?' someone yelled.

'They're barbarians!' someone else said.

Laura's voice was hardly heard above the din as she pressed the case for those who had rejected Islam and sought sanctuary in England. She was sure they would be aghast at a magnet drawing in what she termed 'the fervent' nearby.

A thin clerical old man stood up. 'We are not a mob,' he said in a weak voice. 'Be quiet please, and let the voice of moderation be heard. I agree that those placards were disgusting, totally unfit for a civilized society. But those men know no other way of expressing themselves. They are victims of the brutal governments from which they have come. Brutal governments, yes, and – to my mind – primitive superstitious creeds. The next generation will learn better, so we hope. Most Muslims who come over here want only to live quiet lives. The madmen are few. Their misconduct is encouraged by our invasion – so far totally unsuccessful – of Iraq.

'I am not advocating the building of this mosque in our village. Indeed, I hold it as another example of the idiocy of the County Council, like the painting of double yellow lines all down the

Croft, where no car has ever parked. But I do suggest that the best example we can set is far from yelling at each other, but by being tolerant of those who appear in the present generation to be intolerant of us.'

'So are we supposed to tolerate those who blow us up with suicide bombs?' Terry Owen asked. 'Won't this mosque introduce that fanatical behaviour into our small community?'

'How many more years are we expected to be tolerant?' a woman asked.

'What's it matter? We're all as bad as each other!' This from Jack Hughes, who had been sitting on the floor on the fringes of the meeting. 'It's animals fighting for territory. Bloody history of the human race . . .' He now made off slowly and pushed his way through the outer doors into the night. His intervention caused a moment's hush, in which a middle-aged man, poorly dressed, rose and asked the councillor if he might speak. Given rather astonished permission, he spoke, looking from the audience from one side to the other.

'I am come from Saudi Arabia where I was born, and I speak here in the confidence that you will not kill or injure me for that fact. I live and work here, although I am only always a foreigner, an exile in your ranks. My name is Akhram Ali.'

Many of those present recognized him as the waiter who worked in the White Hart with his one conjuring trick.

The man went on, despite the odd cry of 'Siddown!'

'I wish to tell a brief story. The man who left here asked as he was going "What is the difference?" I tell you all, the difference between what was my country and this country of yours is as wide as the desert itself.

'I was an eye specialist in Riyadh, the capital city of Saudi Arabia. The country has many eye problems, because of a dusty environment. I prospered. My father was a strict Wahhabist – a stern form of Islam – and my brother followed him. Not so I. My life was made uncomfortable because of this quarrel. Nevertheless,

I married a woman and had a son and a girl by her. This daughter I greatly loved because she was so bright.

'One time, I fell ill with a form of diphtheria and thought I must die. In that case, my good kind wife and my daughter, both, would fall under the control of my stern father and my brother. They would have no freedom, such as it was, and would be undoubtedly ill-treated. They would become just house servants, to be beaten by the men whenever they wished.

'By good luck, I recovered my health. I feared for those two, mother and daughter, and immediately made plans to leave the country with them. I cannot tell about the difficulties but eventually, with the help from the British Embassy, we three all left Riyadh by aeroplane. Now I have a menial job here and my wife also, but my daughter goes to a good school. There she learns about the world and about freedom. I mean freedom of speech and freedom to live as a human being.

'This evening I marvel at what you all take for granted. You all speak freely without fear. Your councillor answers without anger, without threatening to kill you. Also . . .' Here he paused to breathe deeply before continuing. He spread his arms wide.

'Also, women speak equally with men. I cannot tell you how precious this is. Do not in any way – what's the word? – well, do not put this freedom in danger. Honour your women, think well of yourselves that such is the case.

'I see faults in England – above all the mistake of attacking Iraq – but I love your country very much. Do not let your tolerance allow villains and lethalists in, or you may lose anything. Do not permit to enter mullahs who preach hatred against you. Such men have no knowledge and live in the Stone Age. I ask God to bless you all and this night please vote against having a mosque to be builded here.'

He sat down. There was a moment of silence and then the clapping and cheering started.

Harry Bains-Jones rose to his feet.

'I don't see any need for a vote,' he said. 'You have all expressed your opinions forcefully enough. And I thank our Muslim friend for speaking up as he has done.'

He made for the door in stately fashion. Captain Derek Dalsher tailed after him, and after Dalsher went the youth, his laptop under his arm. Many of the audience followed Ken, Justin and co to the White Hart for a drink.

# 23

## *Every Existing Thing Has a Reason*

Flowers were few in Justin's garden. Janet had been the one for filling everywhere with flowers. For that reason, he paid particular attention to the self-sown hollyhocks which blossomed from the gravel by his side gate. One stem was small, as modest as a young girl, with pale flowers. Two others were yellow, others apricot. The proudest were the tall deep-red hollyhocks, the blossoms of which were climbing rapidly to their peaks. Justin sat on a seat in the courtyard to enjoy this chance display. The heatwave was operating at full strength – like Egypt, he thought. For his lunch he was eating a bacon-and-cheese puff bought from the Queen's Bakery. As he kept an eye on his flowers, so a robin kept her eye on his crumbs. Every now and then, he tossed a piece of flaky pastry to the bird. Still the builders had not returned.

He had lost heart over his thesis. He had been humbled by the courage of Akhram, the Saudi exile – of both his courage and his resourcefulness, not only in getting his womenfolk out of Saudi Arabia but, on a lesser scale, his dignity in facing an uproarious audience. Was he, Justin, prepared to go that far? Of course, there was no guarantee that a mosque would not be built. KIC was backed by immense wealth, and money speaks. It might whisper in the County Council's ear. Excuses could be made, reasons cooked up, and pockets lined. Not only was his, Justin's, reticence – his cowardice – to be faced. He spent a long while looking past the flowers into another world, that world where people suffered from a faith that impeded their humanity, or where starvation was never far away, or where permanent warfare was a way of life. He belaboured himself with the thought of how comfortable he was, he and the other inhabitants of Old Headington: yet for all their comfortable lives and fine propounded principles, British soldiers – Christians? – had been sent to war in Iraq, to face the slaughter there. He told himself it was not principle but the wish to continue to lead comfortable lives that had carried the motion not to permit a mosque locally. And yet, and yet . . . there were already mosques within a mile or two, in Marston and Cowley. It was extraordinary to think it worthwhile to build yet another mosque in a Christian country. Well, post-Christian country . . .

As for his theory, he had run out of clinching ideas. He saw how impossible it was to change the world, just as he had earlier scorned the message, 'Banish World Poverty!' He gave up. He must have a change. He would go to the Greystoke Gallery as he had long ago said he would. And tomorrow he would make himself useful and go to Eagles Rest to see his son. He took a bus into Oxford, trudging from the High to Gloucester Green where the gallery was situated. On the way, he tried to remember something about Hester Wilmot.

He remembered she was amusing, or someone was. And a group of them had driven down from the New Forest on to a beach near

Bournemouth one night, during a heatwave. Three men, four girls, had it been? It was so long ago. This must have been back in the fifties. The car headlights had shone across a supine sea. Waves hardly had the strength to break on the shore. The party all stripped off and ran naked, yelling, into the water. The sea was like warm gravy. God, but he had forgotten what it was to be young. Maybe he and she began to feel each other when they swam away from the others. Had that been Hester? It was so long ago.

Back on the beach, they made love in the warm sand. She was good at screwing if not particularly good at painting. Oh yes, and the odd girl who had no male partner had come and sat naked in the sand nearby to watch them at it. He had enjoyed that. Maybe it had not been Hester Wilmot at all. Another Hester? Bloody memory, always failing you just when you needed it . . . Before he could open the gallery door, it was opened for him from within. A man in a suit with a tie, oiled over-neat hair, long clean-shaven chin, greeted him.

'Good morning, sir, you have come to buy a few of our lovely paintings, I hope?' Unctuous smile.

Justin had trained himself not to dislike people on sight. 'I thought I might have a look round.'

'Good idea, sir, if I may say so. Are you a local?'

'A local what?'

He made a face and a slight cringe, saying sweetly, 'I wondered if you were from Oxford, sir, that was all.' Stretching the truth a bit, Justin replied that he was off to a Greek island shortly. Still the man was standing in Justin's way.

'How interesting, sir. Which island are you visiting?'

'Why do you ask?' His hands came a little way apart on the level of his hips, as he made a small bow.

'Just out of curiosity, sir.'

'That's a motive, not a reason.' Oh, blessed pedantry!

A female voice from the background called, 'Who is it, Norden?'

'The gentleman wants to look at your paintings.'

The voice rose an octave. 'I don't believe it! Show him in then, you fool!'

The exhibition room was not spacious. A large vase stood in a corner, stocked with lilies in full flower. Their scent filled the room. Air-conditioning was at work, which made the room even pleasanter.

Some oils had been taken off the walls and were standing propped on the floor. They were abstracts, rather in the manner of mid-career Kandinsky, mostly colourful, one or two in severe black and white with a small splash of colour. At first glance, he liked them.

'Who are you? Hello! Do I know you?' This from the invisible woman in a rear room.

'I'm not sure.'

'Oh, fuck!' Following the expletive, a woman dressed entirely in black emerged, rubbing her hands on a dirty towel. 'Sorry to swear. Just upset the remains of my coffee over a canvas.'

'Sorry about that. Are you packing up?'

'A bit, yes. Oxford's a lousy place in which to sell abstracts, and mine are overpriced. Come and have a coffee and talk to me. Preferably be amusing.'

'Is it convenient?'

'I wouldn't ask you if it wasn't, would I?'

At this retort, the suited man whinnied with laughter. The woman scowled at him. Justin said, as he followed her, 'Your problem could be that idiot on the door.'

'Christ, don't tell me. Bloody Norden comes with the territory. Do you want coffee or something stronger? It's only Nescafé.'

'That'll suit me. Sorry, do you think I could have a pee?'

'Go ahead. The loo's pretty sordid, I warn you. Down that way.'

When he returned, she stood with her back to him, waiting for the kettle to boil. She said, 'You don't look the type who buys pictures. What did you want, really – beside a pee, I mean?'

'You invited me.'

She turned round then. 'Sorry, what's your name?'

He told her, saying she had phoned to say they had gone out together forty years ago.

'Oh, shit, yes. So you're Justin Haddock. Of course. I remember the funny name. I was Hester Potts then – another funny name. So what do you think of the canvases?' The kettle boiled. She poured hot water over the contents of two mugs and pushed one of the cups to him, together with a half-empty milk bottle.

'I've only glanced. Reminded me of Kandinsky.'

With sudden fire, Hester said, 'Of course they reminded you of Kandinsky. Kandinsky rules the world of abstraction. Well, there's Victor Pasmore. But otherwise – it's Kandinsky who's the king, like Presley in pop music or Shakespeare in fucking drama. Kandinsky's the ultimate. We must follow in his shadow.' He ignored this outburst, being busy with the past. In particular with a warm night on a Bournemouth beach. Hester Potts? He involved himself with the cup of coffee. 'You don't know what I'm on about, do you? I'm sorry, I'm such a monomaniac. Since the late great Wilmot left me – well, I left him, I think it was – painting has filled my life. I'm too old to be a stripper.' She laughed without humour. 'Life's sodding difficult, wouldn't you say?'

'I'd agree with that.'

'Don't be weedy. Admit it's sodding difficult.'

'It does occasionally need a drop of fortitude.' He was both annoyed and amused by her manner. 'I can't drink this coffee without sugar, sorry. Can I have a proper look at your paintings?'

'Go ahead!' She reached out for his cup. Justin took a look at the canvases. One that particularly appealed to him was built from a series of black starburst-like patches with a bright red patch towards one corner of the painting – all on a white background. He asked her what she was charging.

'They're all around about five or six hundred pounds. You like that one? So do I. I call it "Serendipity". You can have it for three hundred. How's that?'

He was going to produce a credit card, but she said she wanted cash. He said he would be back and went to the nearest bank, where he withdrew the money from the cash slot. As he was handing Hester the money, he asked her why it was called Serendipity.

'I'll be honest with you. It was to be a plain black-and-white. That was what I intended. I dropped the red on it by accident. Pure chance, but the making of the picture. There's three hundred pounds' worth of advice right there: how to compose abstracts . . .'

'Hester, come and have dinner with me tonight, will you?'

Their dinner went well. Justin took Hester to the Café Noir. Good food, plenty of talk, plenty of laughter, plenty of wine. Mujeed always a genial presence.

As Justin kissed Hester goodbye afterwards, out on the pavement, he began, from old habit, to feel her breasts. She pushed his hand away. 'Hold on! I like you well enough but I don't want you getting up to anything.'

Walking home alone, he remembered that Amy, Edwin Holderness's widow, had used almost the same phrase, about 'not getting up to anything'. It must have been in common usage among women of that generation. A usage encouraged, of course, by men who were always eager to get up to something. He took his new acquisition to the framer's next day. Walking back to his house at his usual slow pace, he almost trod on a bumble bee. It was crawling over the pavement under a street light, every now and again giving a feeble flutter of its wings. He stopped and watched it. When it finally reached the gutter, the insect stopped and rested. Justin walked on. He had heard there was a disease that afflicted bumble bees. This seemed like proof of it.

There used to be a scientific witticism declaring that bumble bees could never fly because of their non-aerodynamic shape. Nevertheless, they must have been around for millions of years.

Perhaps from before the Jurassic period . . . It was then that the perfectly obvious idea struck him. Of course. Why had he not thought of it before? Rushing into the house, Justin began consulting first Google then his encyclopaedias. These encyclopaedias had kept him afloat during his professional years, a substitute for genuine knowledge. It was obvious – or it had become obvious through the labours of dedicated and patient scientists – that Earth's history over the five hundred million years or so of its existence had been punctuated by mass extinctions. The extinction ending the Cretaceous era was well-known. Sixty-five million years ago, a great variety of life forms had been wiped out. These included fish, plants and, of course, the famous dinosaurs. That extinction had evidently provided a chance for the things that were to become human beings to take the stage. A chance for zebras, too. But they had refused the stage and remained zebras. He could well imagine blackened skies and a decade-long winter. 'And darkness fell over the face of the Earth . . .'

There had been other extinctions too, evidence for which had been gradually uncovered. The extinction that ended the Triassic. The one before the Triassic period which ended the Permian. The one that ended the Devonian, together with all its flora, fish and invertebrates. And the extinction, the earliest known one, and possibly the most terrible, which wiped out the trilobites and many humble forms, when life had barely set its imprint on dry land. Everything died. So – five great extinctions, their effects showing up in sedimentary layers of rock and in various craters, for those with knowledge who searched diligently enough. As early as 1694, said Google, Sir Isaac Newton had wondered if the Caspian Sea had been formed by cometary impact. But all of these craters, these massive extinctions, had been forged by comets, asteroids or other cosmic debris, speeding out of nowhere, striking the globe by chance, so that layers of smoke and filth covered the sky and cut off the light of the sun. Chance! Here was the greatest proof of all: the most horrifying, the most undeniable: Chance governed everything. Chance that caused the mass extinctions. Chance that was indifferent. Chance that held sway over bumble bees, humanity, zebras, trilobites, bacteria. It governed the environment, the oceans, the land, and all living things. Justin was trembling with this belated insight as he went to his bookcase and took down Thomas Hardy's mighty drama, *The Dynasts*, from its shelf. He blew the dust from the top of the book. Hardy knew all along – or at least understood with a poet's intuition. It was there on the very first page of his work. The Shade of the Earth enquires hopefully regarding the workings of the Immanent Will. To which the Spirit of the Years replies: 'It works unconsciously, as heretofore, Eternal artistries of Circumstance, Whose patterns, wrought by wrapt aesthetic rote, Seem in themselves Its single listless aim, And not their consequence . . .'

Blind workings . . . chance . . . artistries of circumstance . . . He set to work on his thesis with renewed vigour. Yes, he thought, how wonderful to rid the world of every single ghost and god and Baal and banshee. He might call it 'Ban the Banshee'.

To whoever or whatever you prayed, Chance alone prevailed, grinding out its eternal artistries of Circumstance, indifferent to what followed . . . He walked about his garden, clutching the nape of his neck with his left hand, afraid the whole revelation, new to him, might escape. All about, the pseudo-acacias, the lofty pines, the daisies underfoot – all eternally momentary, momentarily eternal . . . He could not stop talking about it. Excitement irrigated old veins. He talked to Ken Milsome about it.

'Think of it – no more religion!'

To which Ken retorted, 'We live in easy conditions, so it's easy not to believe in God. But you pray when trouble comes.'

'Fat lot of good that does.'

Ken, smiling, shook his head. 'Okay, fine, you may have reason on your side. But that's not what religion is for. Religion is for comfort. Supposing you had accidentally killed someone you loved?' He paused, as if thinking over what he had just said, before diving as if for safety into metaphor. 'In bed, in a cold night, you switch on the electric blanket.'

'But, Ken, can't you see? No more cold nights! Pure daylight.'

'No more breast cancer?' Marie asked. They looked at her. She was making smoked salmon snacks for them. Laying down her knife, she confronted them.

'You go on about religion and atheism. I am sick of listening to you! Don't you realize that in another century all such arguments about God and evolution and the whole bloody cosmos may be swept away by some new understanding yet to be born?'

Ken went over and kissed her, at the same time grabbing the first salmon mouthful off the conveyor line. 'I'm sure you're right, my honeypie. But who can wait that long?'

The buddleia was in flower, each bloom composed of tiny florets. People were talking about conkers, and whether they would be scarce this year. The weather was cooler. Birds sang under the street lamps. Presumptuous blackberries were already putting on their gleamingest black. Justin's thesis was completed. He thought he would show it to Ramsay Cotterell first of all, to get his opinion. Turned into a screenplay it would make an excellent fifty-five-minute TV documentary. And then it should be easy to sell to a publisher as a book. Israel and Lebanon were at war. All sorts of people, from highest to lowest, were calling for the struggle to cease. Justin knew that the Katyusha rockets the Hezbollah were using were made in Iran. From Iran they were shipped across Syria and into Lebanon. With the connivance of the Lebanese government, the missiles were then carried down the Beqaa Valley to the south of Lebanon. There were 12,000 missiles, all aimed at Israel. What was Israel to do?

There came an unanticipated consolation for Justin. He was attempting to stick the pieces of the Carlisle mug together with a tube of UHU when he received a phone call from Eagles Rest. A strange and pleasant voice spoke.

'Oh, is it Mr Haydock? . . . Hello, sir, my name is Charlotte Francis. I'm a niece of Mrs Arrowsmith's. I'm sorry to have to tell you that my aunt has been taken rather unwell and is currently in a rest home in Banbury. She's receiving treatment. So I am taking over here just for a while until my aunt recovers.' He found her slight Northern accent appealing. Not to mention the news she gave him. 'That is, if she does recover, as we must hope she will.'

He felt so pleased. He strove to keep the pleasure out of his voice as he asked what was the matter with Mrs Arrowsmith.

'Well, sir, she has a rather rare disease called . . . Oh, what is it called? Yes, Thyrotoxicosis. It's rather nasty. Summat to do with the thyroid gland. Auntie's muscles have gone all weak. It's terrible to see her.'

'I can imagine . . . I'm sorry to hear it,' he said.

'I knew you would be, Mr Haydock. But please be assured we're looking after your son David. He's a proper dear.' After she had rung off, he sat by his mobile, scarcely able to contain tears of joy. This woman thought Dave was a dear . . . A proper dear . . .

He took the bus over to see Dave and Charlotte Francis. Charlotte was a woman of about forty, neat in appearance, rather plain, wearing a white apron, very business-like. Her husband Joe came in from the garden and shook Justin's hand. He had a rustic countenance and looked jolly.

'Good of you to come over,' he said. 'Some of 'em never bother.' ''Em' understood as standing for unspeakable relatives of their patients in Eagles Rest.

Charlotte offered Justin a coffee, whereupon Nurse Gillott wheeled Dave in to join them. Dave looked more alert than he had done for some months. Justin put an arm round him and kissed him.

'Is good, Daddy, goo,' said Dave, dribbling in his enthusiasm.

'Oh, he doesn't half like being kissed,' said Charlotte, with a laugh. 'He's as good as gold, sir. I always kiss him good night, don't I, David?' For answer, Dave began to sing in a clear voice and a Lancashire accent.

> 'On the boat express I ride.
> See us every day,
> Flashing by the countryside,
> Picking flowers on the way . . .'

Joe was embarrassed. 'I'm sorry, Mr Haydock, but I discovered your son knew an old George Formby song. So I was trying to teach him another. I hope you don't mind?'

'Not at all, Joe. George Formby has always been one of our favourites. I'm so glad you two are able to look after my son properly.' Charlotte evidently had less respect for George Formby than did her husband.

'On Sundays, we give the patients lots of nice church music, hymns and stuff. They all enjoy that. It's a bit of a comfort for them. It sort of lifts them, like.'

'Yes, it's a comfort,' Justin murmured. 'I quite see that.'

'Auntie was devoted, of course,' said Charlotte. 'But this illness has really got her down. They've taken blood samples and I don't know what all, but I'm afraid there's no cure in sight at the moment.'

'What exactly are the symptoms of this disease? What's it called again?'

'It's really scary,' she said, frowning. 'I don't know where she got it from. The name is Thryo— Thyrotoxicosis. It can finish you off if it's not properly treated.'

'Is it catching?' – said with a glance at Dave.

'No, it's not catching. You get trouble with your eyes. You can't sleep. You get all twitchy. You get hot when it's cold and cold when it's hot. It makes your life a misery.'

'Too bad, too bad,' Justin muttered. He smiled and nodded at his son. *Good for Thyrotoxicosis*, he thought.

Returning home, he found, as had happened before, that Scalli was sitting on his doorstep. Cheerful though he was after his visit to Eagles Rest, his heart sank at the sight of her. She wore a fluffy kind of mauve cardigan and an old faintly patterned skirt; her hair was lank and, as she rose to her feet, she looked frankly peculiar – all bones and angles. Still he was not moved.

'Oh, mister sir,' she said, wringing her hands. 'I am your penny tent.'

'Sorry but I'm tired. What on earth do you mean, "penny tent"?'

'I took a vantage of you. Now I am come to say goodbye.'

He left the garden gate open for her. 'All right, Scalli. Goodbye.'

The woman came near enough to touch his coat sleeve. 'Now I have to go away. I am turn out from my flat because I cannot pay rent. The owner from the flat is cruel man . . .'

Somehow, Justin experienced a change of mood. Anyone who had suffered from Dalsher had a claim on his sympathy. 'I'm sorry to hear it, Scalli. Dalsher is not a pleasant man. So where are you going?'

She showed some spirit as she replied, 'Where you think I can go? England is too much hard for me. I go back Aleppo to look at my daughters.'

'To look after them?'

'And in front also. They must be marry soon.' She raised a finger, pointing it to her eye and then to Justin. 'I see they get a man pretty quick.' He wished her good luck and made to go into the house, saying he was tired.

'Please,' Scalli said. 'You must be kind and give me money for my aeroplane from Stansted. Forgive my sins, please! I do weep for them.' He turned and looked at her, her abject demeanour, her soft brown eyes, the marks of age already on her brow. *Come on, Justin, you're not a hard-hearted bastard like*

*Dalsher. Give the poor woman some money!* He sighed. 'How much do you need, dear?'

Ken and Marie called to take Justin to Elden House. Justin confessed he had forgotten the appointment and asked if they were going to keep him there. It was not easy to tell whether or not he was joking.

'It's Eleanor's meeting,' said Marie. 'The brave old lady is holding a discussion – an open discussion – regarding the phantom mosque and what conclusions could be drawn from it. Everyone welcome.'

He asked who Eleanor was. 'But Justin, we took you to meet her. You liked her. Lady Eleanor Grimsdale – much married, now in her nineties. Still has all her marbles. You must remember her!'

'Oh yes,' said Justin. He could not remember. It had not been important. 'Sorry, I'm so busy, Marie.'

Ken said the meeting would be interesting. 'The discussion will be held in Elden House's back garden. Lady Eleanor will claim that the modern age began with the Holocaust, when families were broken up and killed. She says the breaking up of family life is a modern factor, part of the "Me syndrome". Hence the modern dilemma of so many disturbed children, so much hooliganism and drunkenness. She will admit her own faults. All her marriages. An over-concentration on self.'

Justin was rather vexed by all this and asked how Ken knew what Eleanor was going to say. He thought of Kate. He thought of Dave. 'I helped her write the speech,' Ken said. 'After she's had her say, we can all have a go. She figures that this concentration on self finds its counter-balance in the suicide-bomber, neglectful of self, hopeful of glory hereafter.'

'So it's a sermon?'

'No, no, Justin, dear boy. Or rather, it's the zeitgeist. We don't really care any more. That's why other beliefs are taking over. Our mosque symbolizes our indifference.'

'But we voted against it – pretty vehemently, didn't we?'

'Not from any inner conviction – that's what she claims was lost after the Holocaust. Just to protect our own self-centred lives. She sees England – Britain – as a big artificial comfort zone, doomed to fall. Come on, Justin. There's bound to be a big argument. It'll be fun.'

Justin sighed. 'Sorry, Marie, Ken. I don't feel like it. I'm too busy.'

'Please, Justin, darling!'

'I don't want to listen to these false diagnoses of the world's ills.'

Meanwhile, as the politicians talked, as everyone talked, the situation in the Middle East grew worse. Innocent men and women and babies were dying on both sides of the frontier. What were the Israelis to do, while Taliban rockets were being fired into their domain? Negotiation with Hezbollah seemed impossible. Israel did what other nations would have done in their place. They fought back. And the world's fear and misery increased. Justin added a sort of codicil to his great argument. Yes, this was a territorial struggle – but made more poisonous by strong religious differences. All religions must be smothered and ridiculed out of existence. People must face cold hard fact. After all, supposing everyone in the whole world got down and prayed together, that would not prevent the next huge cosmic chunk of rock from smashing into Earth, destroying all life, as had happened before. When might it happen again? Not this year, probably. Not this century, maybe. But certainly some century soon. Sure, the Americans were keeping watch, and would do what they could. But there was no knowing. Somewhere, distantly, out of the Oort cloud, a great random destroyer, much like a larger version of the one that had knocked out Sodom in past centuries, might already be on its way in towards the Sun. Depending on a number of factors, Earth might get in the way of its trajectory. Its speed would be colossal. Earth would burn. Blankets of black cloud would cover the land. Humanity would be wiped out – and with humanity, all its imaginary beings. Oh yes, the gods would also die. It would be a chance for the woodlice to evolve and take over. But he read that after the colossal impact finishing the Permian era, the ecology of the Earth, that whole struggle we call life, ceased. The Earth was a tomb that drifted dead in space for thirty million years. He had suffered from a pain in his left breast for some days and had been too preoccupied to do anything about it. The place hurt when he pressed it. The growth had been about the size of a pea. Already, it was the size of a broad bean. He would have to go and see Reid about it. He made an appointment with the surgery for the next day.

Ramsay phoned and gave the thumbs up on Justin's script outline. 'Great potential for a really startling programme. Large audience, DVDs. Fame. Awards.'

Ramsay came down by car. They had a whisky or two to celebrate. When Ramsay had left, Justin began to feel unwell.

'You drink too much. You're too old,' Maude told him. 'Muslims are sensible – they deny themselves alcohol.'

'That's up to them.'

'I don't want to have to look after you. As a matter of fact, I still miss that Muslim girl, her dignity, her calm. She was a real sweetie.'

'She's probably in Carlisle by now.'

'Carlisle? Why Carlisle?'

'It was only a joke,' Justin said. The sort of joke that did not make anyone laugh.

'I see you've broken your mug.'

Days were drawing in now. Night arrived earlier every evening. Summer was almost over. The dark hollyhock blossoms had reached the top of their mast. The squirrel had run out of wild strawberries.

Justin woke in the middle of the night. He got up and had a pee, feeling awful. It was after four in the morning. No sign of dawn as yet. Birds still sang under the street lamps. He shuffled slowly downstairs and made himself some tea in a yet unbroken mug. He sat huddled in his old kitchen chair, sipping the tea. He washed down a spironolactone tablet with the hot liquid. The world might be deserted except for himself. He put his feet up, to glance at yesterday's paper. He had been sleeping in the chair, still clutching his mug, when he awoke, to listen to a sound at his front door. He heaved himself up and made his way jerkily to see what was happening. The clank of milk bottles was easy to recognize. He unlocked and opened the door. The milkman was on the path by the gate, talking to Jack Hughes in dim dawn-light.

'Sorry, mate, I don't do free milk. I got a living to earn, so piss off, will you?' That was the milkman. He then drove away in his van.

Hughes called after him, 'You're in luck to have a proper living. In any case, no need to be rude.' As Justin was stooping to pick up his milk bottle, Hughes leant over the gate. He said in despondent tones, 'I s'pose you're on the milkman's side, Jus? Could you help me out with that bottle of milk?'

'Sorry, I need it.'

Hughes gave a mechanical laugh, as if there had been a joke. 'You got carpets on the floor and chairs and things to sit down on and lots of books. Couldn't you spare a lousy bottle of milk?'

'You broke into my house, you blighter!' Justin backed away and shut and locked the door against Hughes. When he phoned the police, a detective inspector answered.

'Yes, sir, we have checked over your window for the DNA. No, we didn't ring you, thinking it was not that important.'

'Well, it was important to me. Whose was the DNA?'

'Man, forty-five, sir, name of Jack Hughes. He's done two stretches since he was eighteen and was in a Mental Health Institute till last April. The specialist says he's quite harmless.'

'Harmless? He broke into my house!'

'So you say, sir, but he failed to steal anything.'

Justin felt himself getting heated. 'How about Damage to Property? Can't you get him for that? You know he needs proper treatment, poor fellow.'

'He's harmless, sir, as I said before. Locking him up would only make him worse than he is. Besides, the prisons are all full to the limit.'

'I shall report this, Inspector.'

'Very good, sir.'

Life was hard enough. Hard for Hughes, hard for the milkman, hard – for all he knew – for the police inspector too. Religion was the illusion he had always believed it to be. But after all . . . wasn't it a comfort for many, as Ken had said? For some, it might be the only comfort they had. Hymns were sung on Sundays to please Dave and the other occupants of Eagles Rest. How could he destroy that pathetic sliver of hope? He knew Kate would have asked, What's so important about your opinion? Who are you among so many? Justin was reading Tolstoy's mighty novel, *Resurrection*. By coincidence, that very day he reached page 374, where the prince asks himself, 'What if it should all turn out to be an empty vision?' Justin felt that Tolstoy's words were directed at him, like an arrow to the heart. And it was undeniable that he was rather superstitious, stubbornly though he tried to live by reason. Then again, there was Thomas Aquinas's argument, quoted by Anthony Kenny: 'Every existing thing has a reason for its existence, either in the necessity of its own nature, or in the causal efficacy of some other beings.' Not only living things but possibly beliefs too.

Religion might be the dry rot permeating the structure of human society. But the structure still stood, if precariously. In an uncomfortable world, religion acted as a kind of bizarre comfort zone. He was not going to be the one to remove it, in case the structure collapsed totally. He could not do it. Causal efficacy had to be considered. He had only to be free to believe what he knew to be true; it was, after all, something to have arrived at the truth. He was too old to turn the world upside down. If indeed the world took any notice of what he said. Perhaps it needed its scrap of comfort, as a child its teddy. He wondered guiltily if it was God who had made him change his mind. Justin found himself chewing over something Marie had said about all present-day questions becoming swept away in future . . .

Maybe he'd ring Ramsay Cotterell in the morning and call it all off. Maybe he would have another idea . . . Old Ram would not mind too much. First of all, he would have to go and see Dr Reid about the growth in his left breast.


At least, he thought, as he made his way to the chemist to buy some co-codamol, Old Headington was peaceful.

Even as the thought passed through his brain, the siren of an ambulance sounded. An ambulance came thundering by, to turn up Osler Road and into the grounds of the JR.

He got a bit further and saw a police car leaving the gardens of Righteous House. The pale, frightened face of Deirdre Fitzgerald looked out at him as the car passed. Justin stood struck by amazement. Standing under the portico of Righteous House, was Vera, the Fitzgeralds' maid, who had clearly been crying.

'Has there been an accident?' Justin asked.

The woman said in a choked voice, 'I reckon she has killed him. He looked like he was dying to me. Oh, it's so terrible. She nearly bashed his skull in with a rolling pin. And their cat's got loose and run off.'

'The woman hit her husband?' Justin asked. 'We can't be talking Guy and Deirdre?'

'He was asleep,' Vera said. 'She took advantage of him. Hit him several times. Bashed his head in. I heard the blows. I ran to see what was up.'

Vera told Justin the rest of the story. Mrs Deirdre had discovered some dirty photos in one of Guy's – the master's – jackets. She grabbed the rolling pin and attacked him straight off. She, Vera, had had to stop the missus and phone the police. Justin, puzzled, asked what exactly were the dirty photos. Were they of child abuse? The maid answered the question.

'I saw them, didn't I? They were all of a girl's – excuse me – genitals, but that's what they was. Ruined! Terrible!' She hid her eyes in her handkerchief. 'Honest, at first you couldn't recognize them. Female circ— what is it? – circumstition, someone said . . . They was all swollen. Awful. All stitched up. A really dreadful dreadful sight. The police took them away with them, of course.'

'Om Haldar!' exclaimed Justin. 'It has to be. Guy must have filmed her injuries.'

Vera's eyes glistened with tears. 'Poor girl'd been tortured, sir.'

Justin too was having a problem talking. 'It's not only cruel but based on a stupid antique psychology. This wretched stitching up of the genitals is supposed to kill sexual desire in the girls . . .' It hit him, the weight of misery people had to endure – not just Om Haldar and her like but the men too, the deprivation of colour and romance from their lives. He felt his head had struck a wall of misery, and suddenly to his shame he too was crying, as if at the self-inflicted sorrows of the entire human race. 'Guy is an anaesthetist. What was he planning to do with the photos?'

Vera spread her hands and to the sky. Justin found himself shaking. He wiped his eyes. He returned to No. 29 and poured himself a brandy. He phoned Ken and his wife, he phoned other friends. They came willingly to discuss this terrible thing, with some remorse and perhaps in some cases with a taint of prurient interest.

'It's terrible,' said one lady. 'And to think this happened in Old Headington . . .'

'No it didn't,' said her husband sharply. 'It probably happened in Baghdad.'

'And happens still, every day,' said Maude.

'It should not have been photographed,' Justin said.

'You know what I really think?' asked Ken. 'I was in New York, staying with my cousin in her apartment, when 9/11 broke. I'm always careful about what I say, living here, because you Brits are so damned moderate. Yeah, well, I surely admire moderation. But not in this case. Ever since 9/11 and the fall of the Twin Towers, I have hated the jihadists. Deeply hated them – and fear they will overcome us if we are merely moderate.

'Okay, we have or we had two Muslims living among us, here in the village. I certainly don't hate the poor girl, but she is a living reminder that it is not just the jihadists we must fear but those ordinary – ordinary! – people of the Koran we should also hate, because of their ordinary cruelty. Insensitivity. We know these disgusting strategies are undertaken without an anaesthetic. Doing this to this sweet fugitive girl. It's inhuman, without sense or reason.

'It's not goddamned moderate – that's why we should not be moderate to them – to anyone who is governed by these primitive and disgusting ancient rules.

'Well, I've had my say. My outburst. I want no arguments either.' Ken looked round angrily, but everyone hung their heads. Once they had left, Justin had painfully to reflect on his own diagnosis of the world's ills.

Justin was pottering in his garden, and wondering what useful role blackfly played in the grand scheme of things, when the front doorbell rang. *Could it be the builders at last?* he asked himself. When he opened the door, there stood Laura Broughton in her neat summer dress. He invited her in. The awning was out at the rear of the house, near the runner beans with the visiting blackfly. They sat comfortably together, sipping elder-flower cordial.

'There's a party for graduates at Wolfson College next week,' Laura said, 'given by their nice new female president. Oh, and others. I contributed a story to their magazine. *Romulus* – you've probably not heard of it. I wondered if you'd care to come as my partner . . .'

Justin hardly needed to think about accepting when his mobile rang, breaking into the process of not thinking about accepting. He raised his eyebrows by way of apology to Laura and said hello to the phone.

There was Ramsay, not at all as compliant as Justin had imagined, launching in on the attack straight away . . . 'You're mad, Justin, old boy! Why the hell should we scrap it? It will make a perfectly viable programme. Not a great one, admittedly, but interesting – at least with strong visuals, as we discussed. And a good narrator. It's bound to wind people up. I thought Percy Cook as narrator. Cook's decent enough looking and doesn't mind a bit of controversy.'

Listening, Justin could almost see Ramsay's eyebrows twitching. 'Of course I understand what you say, Ram. It's just that I've come to think that I was – not wrong exactly, but that there are factors in human life I failed to take into account.'

He gesticulated despair to Laura with his free hand. She was smiling, looking amused. 'Sorry, Ramsay, but I'm busy. Talking to a most delightful woman.' The remark cut no ice with Ramsay. He made a noise like a small explosion.

'Look, you're not writing an academic thesis, chum. It's only a lousy BBC space-filler – probably BBC 4 – an hour's worth of entertainment.'

Justin felt bad. 'I really don't know what goes on in people's minds. I mean – well, it's an important question, what lies behind our thought processes.'

'That's got nothing whatsoever to do with it. It's this worm forgiving the plough thing of yours cropping up again, isn't it? To be honest, I always thought that was a lot of hogwash. Do you imagine your notion is going to sweep religion away? The punters will either watch over a beer or they'll switch to Sky Sport.'

He let a thunderous silence gather. Justin put out a hand and clutched Laura's. Ramsay began again, on a more moderate tack.

'Look, old man, let's think about it. I've had to argue with the Director over this one. He says that with all this Muslim hoo-ha, it's no time to attack Christianity.'

Justin sighed. 'Ram, maybe at present we need the bastion of Christianity against something worse. What I mean is that perhaps we need religion as a function outside ourselves, in ways we do not yet understand. A wafer of comfort. Perhaps – well, perhaps I don't really understand other people's personal perspectives. I'm not sure I even grasp the workings of my own mind . . . You could call this my positive declaration of uncertainty.'

'Oh, for Christ's sake . . .' Ramsay exclaimed. He rang off.

Sighing again, Justin pocketed his phone. 'It's not important,' he told Laura. 'Wolfson takes precedence. Yes, I'd love to come with you, Laura.'

Justin was feeling very pleased with himself as, later, he laced up his shoes, preparing to go out.

He would have a talk with Dr Reid and see what he said. The thing in his chest was still paining him. It was not important, he told himself.